# Rising
# Stories

*A Novel*

# Rising Stories

## A Novel

# Don LePan

press forward

**Library and Archives Canada Cataloguing in Publication**

LePan, Don, 1954-, author
    Rising stories : a novel / Don LePan.

Includes index.
ISBN 978-0-9947474-0-2 (pbk.)

    I. Title.

PS8623.E63R57 2015      C813›.6     C2015-902559-1


Press Forward Publishing is an independent book publisher, incorporated in 2015: 408 Milton St., Nanaimo, Canada V9R 2L1

Editorial and publicity:
    pressforwardpublishing@gmail.com or
    don.lepan@broadviewpress.com

Press Forward books are distributed throughout North America by Broadview Press:

Canada:    Broadview Press, PO Box 1243,
            Peterborough ON, Canada K9J 7H5, Canada; or
            280 Perry St., Unit 5,
            Peterborough ON, Canada K9J 2J4

USA:       Broadview Press, 555 Riverwalk Parkway,
            Tonawanda NY, USA 14150

            Tel: (705) 743-8990
            Fax: (705) 743-8353
            email: customerservice@broadviewpress.com


Copy editing and interior design: Eileen Eckert
Cover design: Lisa Brawn


The interior of this book is printed on 100% post-consumer recycled paper.

# Rising Stories: A Novel

For Maureen

# One

*2006*

You didn't think of love as much, once you were married. That was what Carol had been thinking, on the last day when everything had still been all right, as she turned away from the children, turned her attention to the stove. The children would be all right if she wasn't watching them every second; they always were. Robin and chubby little Hope were so good together. She and Carl were lucky that way, it was a loving family all round. But no, love in the way the two of them had used to think of love, you didn't think of it as much anymore. No one did, not the lovemaking part of love, not once you were married and had kids. But when you did think of it, the feelings could be just as strong; just now Carol couldn't get Carl out of her head, couldn't stop thinking of him in that way, how hard he would get when she.... But of course you had to stop, you had to get on with what needed doing, you had to think of the soup boiling over and of back-to-school and of the laundry—yes, she had better get that second load in before she phoned to see if the plumber could come round about that leaky faucet. Should she phone? Maybe it was something Carl could fix after all. At any rate, that second load had to go in the washer. The kids would be all right left to themselves on the balcony for a few minutes. Yes, they were always all right; Hope could be a handful but never with Robin, it seemed.

Robin was getting older—it was strange, how a child could be so grown up so young. Of course they said seven was the age of reason, but how many other seven-year-olds were as responsible as Robin? As nice as Robin. Not many.

As smart as Robin? Carol found herself asking that too. Probably quite a few who were smarter, she had to answer herself. Not that Robin was slow, just that with some children you could see their minds going off in strange directions; who knew where their thoughts were going. But slow? No, definitely Robin was not a stupid child. Maybe even quite bright, just not in the ways you usually thought—it wasn't a brightness that would turn on when you pressed the usual switch, or that would light up the places you might have expected. Maybe they should have looked into some sort of special school for Robin; was it too late now?

As for Hope, she was as smart as anything—what a joy to hear her babble on. There might still be time for Hope, time to put her in for a special school—although, from everything people said, for any sort of really good school you had to have them on a waiting list almost before they were born. She would talk to Carl, yes, they would definitely have a talk. And Robin? Well, they would just have to hope that Ogden really was a decent school, hope that people were right that it was about as good as you'd be likely to find for a public school. So far it had all seemed fine; Ogden seemed fine, Robin seemed fine.

Robin had always been easy, right from before there had been a Robin. It was Hope who hadn't wanted to come out. Everyone always said the second one would be easier, would come faster, but little Hope hadn't been so little after all. And she had turned, she'd been a breech birth; you didn't want to think about what might have happened. How little Hope had screamed those first few months, screamed like she'd made her mother scream when she had come out into the world. No, not like Robin; Robin really had been easy.

Now the two of them could play for hours together, you wouldn't think it would be like that when they were almost five years apart. But Robin was so gentle with the little one, gentle but sometimes a little bumptious in the slaphappy way that an almost-two-year-old loves so much—in the way that Carol and Carl found it so hard to act themselves. It wasn't that Carol couldn't find it in herself to be playful; she reminded herself of how often people complimented her on her sense of humor. It was just that it was all so messy, playing with small children. And sloppy. And boring, truth be told. If something's funny the first time, it's funny the five hundredth time, that was how a two-year-old's mind worked—and it wasn't how Carol's mind worked. When did they stop being so messy and so boring? She knew the answer: when they stopped being so small. Maybe Hope would be like Robin, maybe in no time you'd be able to play Scrabble with her.

Except it hadn't been "in no time"—that was just the way it seemed afterwards. Had it happened when Robin turned four? No, five. Hope might be just as bright, maybe even smarter. But that still meant years (two more? three more?) before you could connect with her as a human. Sometimes it just seemed endless; there were times when Carol could hardly stop herself from screaming. What was the point of any of it? All the worry and the wailing and the boredom, and then they did become human, they did grow up, but what was it all for? They might make their mark on the world, she supposed, but what would that be? A tiny scratch was all it could ever be, and it would be a scratch on a pebble of soft stone that would be rounded into nothingness by sand and sea, perhaps they would have children themselves and then those would do the same, and on and on, but what was the point of any of it? *Live in the moment*, that was what people said, *enjoy your children while you have them, while you can, it won't last forever*, but what if it just wasn't very enjoyable, what if it sometimes seemed nothing but an endless grind? Sometimes it really was hard not to scream *No! Not one more game of pat-a-cake! Not now, not ever!*

That was what Robin had been playing with Hope just now. Just now and just before that, and just before that too—all day, it seemed like. Gentle, but a little bit loud; it would be better for them both to be out on the balcony, such a beautiful day, so bright out there, and the fresh air. Of course afterwards Carol had asked herself again and again just what had happened, she had tried to reconstruct every second of it. Robin had said *come on, Hope, let's go outside*, and outside they had gone. It hadn't been because of Carl she'd sent them outside—she hadn't even *sent* them, she might have *suggested* that maybe they would enjoy the fresh air. But that was a different thing. And whenever they were out there she would always keep an eye on them. Just like anyone would.

But then Carl *had* come home, it was an hour or more before the usual time, there'd been something in the Loop he'd had to do for work and then it hadn't been worth it to go back to the office; by the time he'd have gotten there, he would have had to just turn right around again and come home.

So there he was, and oh, what a joy it was to see him. When was it not a joy to see that smile, those shoulders, the light in those eyes? But when he got home like he usually did—at 6:30, at 7:00, at 7:30—the light could be a little dim. Dim? Hell, sometimes it was switched off completely.

But you had to be fair—maybe Carol wasn't always so chirpy herself a hundred per cent of the time, not with the kids and with working the shop at the Field three days a week; people always said how wonderful it must be to work at such a wonderful museum, when really it was just like any other shop, you rang in the dinosaur toys and the guidebooks and the souvenir mugs just like you would anyplace else, there were days when she could kick herself for having gotten out of publishing, had it really been that stressful? But still, life had its joys, and what a joy it was when Carl was like this—it was like Saturday coming when you didn't expect it. Carol's face lit up, *they're fine, they're on the balcony*, and her eyes met his and her lips met his and at once it was like it had been before Hope, before Robin; there was nothing between them, there was nothing but the two of them. His fingers traced the line of her dress and the line of her spine and then they pressed into each other. It had been so long, so long since it had been like this and then they were in the bedroom, you didn't have to think how to please each other when it was like this, or how to get your lover to please you, or how to—you just didn't have to think, it was all feeling, feeling of every kind, everywhere. Of course you couldn't cry out; it wasn't really just as it had been before Hope and before Robin. But close enough. Close enough to forget about—well, you can't describe what it's like.

א  א  א

It had only been a few minutes—maybe five or six minutes, Carol thought. Can any of us be responsible every minute of our lives? Maybe it had been eight minutes—ten minutes, absolute max. Carl swore it couldn't have been more than four or five minutes, *I'd better check on the kids*, he had said. *Oh, they'll be fine for another minute or two* was what Carol had thought, but she hadn't said that, thank God she hadn't said that. She'd said *of course, yes, we had better...* and it had been Carol who had gotten out of bed a little more quickly, had thrown on a shift and had made her way into the living room, "the living and dining area" the agent had called it, it wasn't as bright as the balcony but the light streamed in here too on a sunny day. On this day it had gone suddenly dark, Carol struggled for a moment to make out the shapes, she was still a little giddy, yes, the kids must be fine, there was Robin looking at—what was Robin looking at? It couldn't be Hope, where was Hope? And then another step and then Carol saw that Robin was not looking at Hope, that Hope was behind Robin and above Robin, that Hope was on the railing, was she singing? how could she? how could she climb the railing, how could she be singing up there? she was too small, too small, too little, too little, ...*baker's man, patty cake, patty cake, dough need your hans can do it my self*, Carol couldn't move, couldn't move.

Afterwards when she went over everything again and again, this was always where everything stopped. A part of her that

Carol hadn't been aware of at the time could hear Carl somewhere behind her, *is it all right, is it all right?* in the voice we all use when we sense that it is not all right, that something is terribly, horribly wrong. The sun must have been behind a cloud but now it burst over everything; if you had been looking out across the city you would have seen it glinting off the bright black of the Sears Tower, seen the bright rust of the insurance building start to glow. But Carol's eyes had not travelled across the city. When she went over it all later she would try to think of just where the little blue chair had been—a little sideways, a little askew. She would try again to see the knitting on the table, the newspaper on the couch, would try to see the things she had not noticed when she had stopped, when she had found for a moment that she could not move.

And then just as suddenly she *had* been able to move again, and she had surged across the room. She had been able to see Robin turn, could see that Robin saw, could hear the *No!* that came from Robin. They had closed the door to the balcony, Robin must have closed it, why had Robin closed it? She had told them a thousand times that door had to stay open if they were going to play out there, she had to be able to hear what they were doing and they had to be able to hear her too. And then a thought jerked open in Carol's mind, *had they heard? had they heard her and Carl?* Had they closed the door because of that? And now, and now, and no, the door wouldn't give, the door was jammed, no it had to give, she could see Hope's face through the glass, Hope's eyes, what was in them? what was there? finally she yanked the door free from the catch and started to pull it across and Robin was reaching out, she could hear Robin and see Robin reaching as the little one started to rock, *catch her, Robin, hold her, Robin, hold her, you have to catch her, you have to get hold of her!*

And then in a sliver of time you could tell it was all going to be all right, you could tell that everything could be brought under control. Carol could see that Robin was close enough to grab hold of Hope, that Hope would not fall, that Hope would not die, that life could be as it had been and that never again would she leave them alone and that never again would she and Carl, it would be all right, Robin's hand was there, Robin was in time, Robin's hand was at Hope's and Hope was taking the hand. And then just as suddenly the moment ended, Robin didn't, Robin couldn't, somehow Robin couldn't, small fingers jerked and fumbled together, and fumbled and jerked and Hope was teetering and nothing caught hold, nothing caught hold. She swayed for a moment, a shaft of light caught her for a moment, less than a moment. And then she was gone.

# PART 2

# Two

*2011*

It was pretty good, really, the poem that Robin had written. That was what Robin thought, anyway. *Curved* and *heard* only sort of went together, but all the questions were true; that was exactly what it had felt like and it sounded like what Robin had felt, and somehow that was like what falling felt like too. Robin and the poem made their way together south along the streets that went south from the place where the lake curved out, the narrow streets that curved towards the river. Robin savoured the poem a little, and now the sounds felt less like falling and more like a sort of success. Could a poem be a success all on its own, without anyone reading it? Anyone except you? A poem had to stand the test of time, Ms. McLenithan had said that (it was *Ms.* but she said you could pronounce it "Miss" if you wanted). And this poem had only just been written. Robin hadn't written it during English, when it was all right to work on a poem if you had extra time; it had been written during math—when you were supposed to do extra math if you'd finished what was assigned, and Robin hadn't finished what had been assigned, had hardly started. There was something down on paper for three of the eight questions—maybe enough that if Ms. McLenithan had walked by Robin could have pretended to be still working on it.

But Ms. McLenithan hadn't walked by, and now the poem was finished. Sort of finished. Maybe it still needed to be fixed up a bit more, polished. Maybe *blowed* would be better than *snowed*; could a snowflake snow? Why did people only use the word *it* before the word *snowed*? Could rain rain? Robin thought a snow-flake should be allowed to snow.

Robin was heading home while these thoughts were happening, and also dawdling a little bit. Home was on Erie Street, not far from where the rivers met, way up, way above the rivers, the 33rd floor of 300 West Erie, you could look south and see all the business buildings, a lot of them taller than 300 Erie, and so were a lot of the condo towers but you could see a lot of things from the 33rd floor if it was daytime and you were home from school, and you could look down too, and there were the honking cars and all the little people and all the little boats making their way along the river, but usually Robin didn't like to look right down. You could look a little bit out instead, across the water and up the river, or was it down the river, Robin was never sure, across all the bridges and in the distance Goose Island, that was a name Robin always liked. Sometimes it would be foggy and you couldn't see anything and the clouds would swirl low but not right down to the ground, you'd be right inside them and then out of them and then in them again, it was as if you couldn't know where you were, perhaps you weren't anywhere any longer, and that was a feeling you wanted to hang on to.

Today Robin didn't really have to be home before five, maybe even before six o'clock. Sometimes it could be good if you meandered a little before you got to where you were going, just like a story can meander a bit before it gets to the end, and if you're lucky the meandering can make it better. If your parents asked you, you could say there had been something extra, like when Robin had stayed late back in December to help Ms. McLenithan with the seasonal decorations, Christmas decorations they had been mostly, but no Santa Clauses and no Frosty the Snowman. Ms. McLenithan said that we were all of us too old to believe in Santa Claus, and when people who were too old to believe in Santa Claus used him for decoration it was cheap and tawdry. She said Frosty the Snowman was always cheap and tawdry, that was a word she used quite a lot, *tawdry*, also *chintzy*. So not those things, but shepherds and angels and wise men for Christmas and also some pictures that had nothing to do with the Christmas story but were about how Judah Maccabee led his rebel army and fought for freedom. Ms. McLenithan said it didn't matter how many Christians or Jews or white people or Hispanic people or African Americans there were in the class, none of that mattered for this school year or for any year, it didn't matter what color you were or what background or what religion, what mattered was that it was good to learn things, and Robin thought Ms. McLenithan was mostly right but maybe sometimes what she meant was that it *shouldn't* matter what color you were and all that. Maybe she was wrong to say it *didn't* matter because sometimes it seemed that it *did* matter, not in Ms. McLenithan's class, maybe, but outside. Was there a god who was slowly helping us to see what mattered and what didn't, and what should matter and what shouldn't? And to try to make it better? In the last little while Robin had started thinking about god and had decided not to be a believer, but it seemed right to believe what Ms. McLenithan said about people who did believe in a god. Who believed in different gods. There were lots of different people too, Miss McLenithan talked about how diverse the school was and how good that was. Robin was starting to notice that sometimes people would use that word—*diverse*—to mean there were lots of different colors of people, and sometimes they would use it to mean there were people from different cultures all round the world, and sometimes they would use it to mean that it was OK to be gay or straight, but sometimes people would say *What a diverse group!* when they were talking about a group of people who were all a lot like them. Every year it was declared that Ogden had *a diverse student body* and every year there were jokes about that. Robin sort of laughed with the others, but also thought about that word, *diverse*. A lot of people in the class talked about things that cost money and you could guess that nobody was really poor, there had been that nice girl with the curly hair and the sort-of-lopsided face who wasn't in the class anymore, Kathy Snyder said the curly-haired girl's mother and father hadn't been able to stay where they'd been, the rent had gone way up and now they couldn't afford it and they had to live on the South Side and Robin had thought *what's so bad about that? That's where the president lives, the South Side.* LeShonna. That had been her name. She had liked to paint pictures, not just when they were doing art but anytime. When Robin had said *I like to go the lake* she had said *I like to paint the lake,* and then neither of them had known what to say.

LeShonna had been gone a long time, weeks and weeks—months, even. It had been the end of fall, when everything started to get really cold. Now it was still cold but not so much. Soon it would really be spring, and in spring it was always better to take one of the long ways home. Sometimes Robin would even leave school a little early so as to have more time to take the long ways home; it seemed like a good thing when the day was especially lovely. Dawdling would often take Robin east, to the lake and to the Oak Street Beach. Which was actually north of Oak Street, it would be better if they called it the Elm Street Beach or the Cedar Street Beach, but they didn't. You could sit and look at all the tall buildings off to your right, always there was the looming dark of the Hancock—wider than everything, higher than everything, darker than everything—but sometimes it felt like a comfort to have all that darkness right there where you could see it *did that make any sense?* but it felt like nothing had to make sense when there was the sand and all the far away of water and sky, and up close there were the little waves and the people and the other animals, a lot of the people would go by with dogs. You could sit there for a long time and no one would bother you, and if the sun was out it would be quite warm, even when it was cold, and if sometimes you had been feeling a sort of hard knot somewhere inside you, maybe below where you breathed, maybe near where your heart was, you could forget that and it would be gone. It could be hard to know how long you had stayed there.

Sometimes Robin looked out at the water and started to daydream. Daydream about being one of hardly any people left at the end of the world, and about what Kathy Snyder would think about being all alone with Robin; daydream about Alexei Ramirez stealing home to win the World Series for the White Sox; daydream about writing a poem that would be read by everyone on the subway. Daydreams were so different from dreams, you could control them better—you couldn't really control a dream, no matter what you did. For years Robin hadn't dreamt at all. But back in the fall Robin had remembered in the morning a dream in which Kathy Snyder had...—anyway, it had been a dream. And then in January Robin had started to have dreams about how someone kills their sister, except near the end Robin would always become the someone—and know that it was about what had happened on the balcony. What made dreams happen? Nothing was different, really, there had been the day just after Christmas that would have been Hope's birthday when Carol had started to cry but that wasn't anything new, that happened every year and you just waited and then it stopped. What could make dreams stop?

Sometimes it was better to be looking out at the lake and at where it didn't end—for it was large enough that you couldn't see any end to it—than it was to be walking the rest of the way home. But after a long time Robin did start to think about going the rest of the way. The quickest way from the Oak Street Beach to 300 Erie was straight down Michigan to Erie and then west along Erie. But Michigan was where all the big shops were and where the crowds of tourists went, and it was where all the pickpockets went too, and a lot of other people who—well, all that was why Carol and Carl had said again and again that there were places a young person shouldn't be going, not unless it was with someone older or with a group of friends. For that matter, the Oak Street Beach was another one of those places. So Robin had told them again and again *I never go along Michigan on my way home*, and it hadn't been a lie, not really. There really wasn't any need to tell them how often Robin went to the Oak Street Beach alone, or that the most interesting way to walk home if you *had* been to the Oak Street Beach wasn't even along Michigan. They wouldn't understand anyway, that was pretty much certain. Parents didn't understand a lot of things—that was something Robin had come to realize the past year or so.

Michigan was bright and wide and cold; it was better when you left the beach to follow East Lakeshore as it curled around beside the rushing traffic on North Lakeshore, and then wander onto the streets that were narrow and warm, little Dewitt with its little trees and the tall buildings on either side, tall old buildings and tall new buildings that were pretending to be old, and there were flowers if it wasn't winter. Then you could cut through the little park by the tennis courts to Fairbanks, and then it was one way in the other direction; Robin liked the feeling of going in the other direction from the way everything else was going.

For a while it was the same after you turned onto Erie, one way in the other direction. There was always a lot of honking when you crossed Michigan but Erie was good, there was the old red and gray stone building with its high steps and its round columns and its flags, and another old building Robin liked at the corner of Wabash, red and squat with a round arch and trees in front. And then the traffic was in both directions and every-thing started to open up, the buildings were lower and there was more sky, and there were always people going in to one of the low buildings, the Kerryman Irish Bar, and you didn't see any-one leaving, not at 5:00 or 5:30. At Wells there was the low shiny steel of Ed's Diner with a red and yellow sign to let you know it was coming, *Good Food 200 Feet Ahead*, but you could smell a bit of it as you walked by and it didn't smell as if it had ever been good food. And then at North Franklin you went under the L and if a train was going past overhead you could watch the shadows shimmer across the street and for a half a minute the clacking din of it would be everywhere. And then you were there, you were at 300 Erie and who was to know you hadn't stayed late helping Ms. McLenithan and then walked straight home?

You could walk that way and always see things you knew, and Robin liked that, but you would always see something new too. *New* and *you* and *knew* and *too* could all be squeezed into rhyming with one another but you had to use a rhyme lever, *lever* rhymes with *fever*, not with *ever* like Ms. McLenithan said they said in England. Carol and Carl didn't like Robin rhyming all the time, *you sound like you're still a little kid*, Carl had said that one time. *And you're not; you're not a little kid any more, Robin.*

Levers were things Robin knew a lot about, that had been all they did in science class for quite a while. A shoehorn was a lever. Robin's granny had always used to use that word, *shoehorn*. As a doing word, a verb, *all the time I knew that family, they were shoehorned into that tiny apartment in Winnipeg*. Robin's granny was actually Robin's great-grandmother, but you didn't want to say *great-granny* all the time it was too clunky, so Robin had always called her Granny. Robin's mother had said that *really* she wasn't a great-granny or a granny or a mother at all, she had never had children, it was her husband's child from another marriage who had become her daughter, *Josephine* had been her name. It was Josie who would have become Robin's granny if Josie had lived but she had died giving birth to Carl, who was Robin's father. But it was easier just to think of Granny as Granny than to remember all that, especially if you were walking home and you could feel a little ache again from the hard knot inside you.

There! Off in the distance as you looked west—was it just off Michigan? That was Granny's building. Granny was the person who would appreciate most of all what Robin had written, excepting maybe Ms. McLenithan. When Robin had been little they would settle on Granny's big couch, all three of them, and Robin and Granny would take turns reading. Or if there were a lot of bigger words Granny would do it all by herself. Robin had spent more and more time with the sounds of words after Hope had died; sounds had a sort of kindness to them.

Robin would go up and show the poem to her now, *yes, that's what I'll do*, Robin thought, *I'll cut over to Michigan*, and in no time there Robin was in the middle of the bright lights and the crowds and a large woman pushing a stroller almost bumped into Robin and so did a man watching his cell phone and not where he was going but in a moment more Robin was past the buses and the honking taxis and through the revolving doors of Granny's building. There were a lot of stories about her building; people said it was still famous because of how tall it was and because of how it had been made, long ago. But people said that about a lot of buildings in Chicago, it was hard to keep track of them all and of how some of them had been the very tallest skyscrapers in the world, or the third tallest, or the fifth tallest. At different times, when they were new.

Robin's father said all that was all over now in Chicago, the Spire might have become the tallest but now that building would never happen, it would never be more than a dream, all the really tall buildings going up now would be in Chongqing and in Beijing, in Dubai and in Shanghai, and Robin's father seemed to think that was a sad thing even though he hadn't ever liked skyscrapers that much. Robin thought it was OK if other places were the very tallest now, and they were rhyming places, *qing* and *jing*, *bai* and *hai*.

Robin went right past the information desk; the bank of elevators for the upper floors was the one you wanted if you wanted to go up to Granny's—where Granny lived was the 86th floor. 86? Or was it 68? No, it was 86, Robin was sure of that.

Three of the elevators were busy—you could see the lights showing the floors, one was going 58, 59, 60 and another was blinking 64, 63, 62 and a third was on its way down from 50. The fourth elevator was standing open. Robin walked into that one and reached out to push the button for... . but there was no button for the 86th floor. Robin looked and looked and looked again and then felt a wave of embarrassment. You couldn't go to Granny's apartment, you couldn't ever go to Granny's apartment. Granny had been dead since the end of fourth grade, everybody knew that, and Robin knew it too, knew it through and through and through—what was wrong, what was wrong, how could you make a mistake like that?

Robin thought back. Granny's name had been Sandwell, Kathleen Sandwell she had been called and then K.P. Sandwell.

Women used to always lose their name and have to take the name of their husband; Robin wasn't sure what the name was that she had lost, but Sandwell had been her husband's name, and so it had been her name too. When Granny had died, Robin's father and mother had said that it was terrible how some parents made their children look one last time at the face of someone when the someone was dead. Granny had been going to have an open coffin. She hadn't cared herself, open or closed or cremated it made no difference, she'd said, but an open coffin was what her Arthur would have wanted. Mother and Father had said they couldn't see why that would matter more than trying to save the feelings of a living child. And then there had been a long pause, and Robin had known that everyone was thinking of Hope, Hope who had been Robin's sister and Mother's daughter and Father's daughter, and of how she had had a closed coffin. *Hope died in an accident.* That was the formula, *my sister died in an accident* were the words Robin had learned by heart until they had no feeling left in them, until there was nothing left of Hope anywhere in the words, until they were as empty as air. Robin had had to say those words or words like those words quite a lot; one thing everyone always thought of saying when they met you was "do you have any brothers or sisters?" Robin's mother and father had explained how natural that was, but it always made Robin's chest tighten when they asked it.

Robin's mother was called Carol and Robin's father was called Carl; they said Robin could call them by those names too, and sometimes Robin did that. Did it make them closer to Robin or farther away? Robin wasn't sure. Everybody always said they were closer to each other than just about anybody, there was only one letter between them, though Carol and Carl themselves said that a little less often as the years went by.

Carl had also often said how hard it must be for Robin, he knew how hard it must be. Robin didn't know about that; could you know about someone else's life when you were another person? Robin sometimes thought that maybe you couldn't know everything even about yourself. But now Robin was starting to wonder more often about what other people thought. Could you know about Kathy Snyder, about what she was thinking? Everyone always called her both names, because there were three Kathy's in the class, Kathy Curtis who was *Curty*, Kathy Scott who was *Kaths*, those were the other two, and everybody called Kathy Snyder *Kathy Snyder*. She didn't seem to mind that, but she was so quiet that it was hard to be sure. Robin often wanted to know what Kathy Snyder was thinking, what she was feeling, all you could see was the way she tilted her head and the way she held her pen, and you could hear her voice. Whenever Ms. McLenithan wanted an answer to a question straightaway without taking a lot of time while people gave wrong answers, that was mostly when Kathy Snyder would answer. She had a soft voice so sometimes Ms. McLenithan would ask her to repeat what she had said and she would be told to speak louder, and Robin liked that. But Robin wondered if Kathy Snyder minded that it was always the right answer that she gave; did she sometimes think of giving the wrong answer on purpose just so people wouldn't think she had her nose in the air? Most of all Robin wanted to kiss her, but probably you could never kiss a person if you couldn't tell what they were thinking and feeling and whether they would want to be kissed.

Robin's fingers were pressing on the console with all the lit up numbers, pressing on it from one side and then the other and then from the top and the bottom, pushing and pressing in different ways and then jabbing at *Door Close* once, twice, three times, not pressing but jabbing. And suddenly the whole display changed, the bottom number was not 50, it was not a 5 it was an 8, the 8 in 80, and the top number was not 79, it was 109. Everything else was just as it had been—and now, finally, the doors were closing.

"Here, hold that one moment! Can you hold the doors please?" You could hear rushing footsteps, and Robin's fingers started to stretch out to between where the doors were closing. But it was too late. And then when Robin turned back to the *Door Open* button and all the other buttons it was different somehow, somehow you couldn't see the buttons properly anymore, there was a strange shadow over them. Now there was no space between the doors. There was a soft sound and then there was nothing, no sound and no movement, just as there is nothing for a moment before any elevator starts to move. And then it did move; someone high above must have pressed the button to call an elevator up to somewhere, and then Robin remembered to press a number, to press 86, and there was no one else in the elevator and it was moving upwards, up, it seemed faster than an elevator should move, it was faster than the elevators in 300 Erie, wasn't it faster than the elevators ever used to go in Granny's skyscraper? Then there was an urgent slowing, and a gliding stop. Was this the floor where someone else had pushed a button? But the light said that this was the 86th floor. Maybe the floor where there was someone wanting to go down was the same floor where Robin had wanted to go. The doors opened as they always had, with no effort, soundlessly.

ঽ ঽ ঽ

No child would say what they were really feeling. Carol knew that, but sometimes she had to remind herself; for some reason she was reminding herself of it just now. But why? There was no child here. Robin was still at school, or coming home from school, and Carl was at work and....

Carol found herself staring out the window without any sense of what was there, her gaze travelling on out past the balcony, into air. How long had she been standing there? Did it matter? For months after the accident she had found that life kept stopping like this, she would force herself to keep busy through the day, but then as soon as there was a moment when she didn't have to be doing something everything would come back, and then it was as if living had stopped and suddenly the tears would be pouring from her eyes. At night it would be like that always, she would cry and cry night after night until there was no crying left in her, and then she would cry some more. That was how it had been for a long time after the accident, and even after it had started to get better these moments sometimes came to her, and living seemed to come to a stop.

But it would not be like that now; she would think of Robin, she was thinking of Robin.

When they were really young, of course, it was different; you could always tell what a very young child was feeling. Not at Robin's age. Not even when Robin had…. There was no way to know what Robin had felt, or what Robin was feeling now. All you could do was to…, was to…. And then it was all before Carol again, the horror of it, you could push that to one side but how could you push aside the pain, the loss, the aching, aching sharpness of it, on and on and on; why couldn't you make yourself think of other things? Of other people? Of your own other child? But you couldn't, you couldn't, why couldn't she make herself think of her other child? That one word *other* smashed hard into Carol's heart. Waves broke over her, waves that pounded her down, and again, and again; the undertow could rip you apart it was so strong and pull you out into deep water where there was nothing and for a moment that was what Carol wished for, for the current that would pull her away from land and from everything, would pull her down and away into a deep nothing that would be for always and then you would feel the end of pain but you wouldn't feel anything ending, there would be nothing, no feeling and no reason for feeling.

But whenever Carol would be pulled away like this it would never last. Some reason for feeling that she had once had would come back with the roll of the waves, and the waves would break again and there would be Hope, and Hope's shining face, and Hope rocking back and forth, and the loss the loss the loss and you couldn't stop it, you couldn't stop the rocking, rocking back and forth and calling out, calling her name, Carol kept rocking and crying as she heard the call that became no more than wailing, a wailing that fell away into the air, and in that wailing was the ache, the ache that would never end and all you could do was keep moaning and rocking until it was over but it would never be over she would keep on wailing and falling, never it would never be over, never never never never never, one day Robin would be older and maybe then Robin could understand that no one could..., that nothing could..., that it would never be..., that Carol couldn't....

ও ও ও

Robin peered about. There was no one wanting to go down; there was no one else there. Shouldn't it be gray? Hadn't the walls on Granny's floor been gray? Could it have been 68 after all? Everything was blue here, the blue of a thousand, thousand robins' eggs. Fourteen had been in the number of Granny's apartment—6814? No, 8614, 8-6-1-4. How could you be sure?

It would be all different now. There would be none of the things that there had been when it had been Granny's place, no painting with three old ladies and a teacup, no smell of rosemary. It would not be Granny there; it would be some different person. Now Robin was there, was right outside the door. This was the time for finding out.

Robin knocked three times, nervously and a little bit loud. There seemed to be a humming from some of the lights in the hall, a steady humming. Suddenly the door swung open and Robin looked quickly down. There had been no sound; all Robin could see was the same thick beige carpet that Granny had had. And then two deep blue shoes, and two very old legs.

"Robin! It has been a long time. I've been expecting you. I've thought for some time that you must be old enough to go visiting on your own. And that you *hadn't* visited; have you come to ask forgiveness?" She smiled brightly to show she was not serious; Robin looked confused. "Come in!" she added. "I can't say how pleased I am to see you. Look how you have grown, while I have become a wisp of a thing!"

But she was no older, she was no frailer, she was no different. She was as she had always been, tall and straight and elegant, not hunched and crinkled and strange like you always thought old people would be. In the strangest of ways, she was beautiful.

Robin said what you always said at first, what Carol and Carl had taught. "Are you well, Granny?"

"*As well as can be expected*—that is the approved way of answering for someone of my age. But what should one expect? I feel I've aged more in my ninety-first year than I did in all my previous ninety put together. Perhaps I should just say what is still a little bit true: yes, child, I am well."

Robin never knew how to respond to anything Granny said—but fortunately Granny would always say something else straightaway. There would never be an awkward space with no sound. Usually she would ask Robin something, and then Robin could say something about something Granny didn't know about, and then she would say more things, usually a lot more, and that was how they would have a conversation.

"Have you been singing much?"

"I'm not in the choir anymore, Granny."

"I somehow thought that had ended. No, what I meant was your other singing. Do you remember what I used to call it?" Robin looked down again. They were the sort of words that you used when you were talking about children.

"Yes, Granny," Robin answered very quietly. "You used to call them *mumbly hums*."

"I did. And now I see that I should call them *songs* instead." The child was really almost not a child any longer— K.P. could see that now. It was so hard to tell when to stop saying one thing to them and to start saying another. "Do you ever write down your songs?"

"Sometimes I do. Yes, sometimes. I haven't been singing much lately."

Robin thought for a fleeting second of the day before. Robin had started to make up a song—a song about Kathy Snyder. And now Robin thought that had been at just exactly the place on Fairbanks where Robin had thought today of Granny's building, and of seeing if she might be there. Kathy Snyder was taller than Robin was and would always finish first at the end of the term; no matter how hard Robin tried, Robin would be second. Kathy and Robin would sometimes smile when they passed each other in the hallway, hardly ever say anything, just smile. But Kathy didn't smile like some of the others did when you could see they were thinking of how they were smiling, it was the sort of smile that happened when a person's face just opened plainly.

"Does she smile that way at everyone?" Granny was asking. But Robin hadn't said anything, there hadn't been any words in the air, had there? They had just been words in the head, they had just been thoughts. What had Granny heard? Or was she able to know the words in your head?

Robin had seen how Kathy Snyder would smile at Ben Kwan, and at Virginia Buchan, and at Jane Britton, even at Jeffie Bertram. Did it mean anything special when she smiled at Robin? Robin looked at Granny, not meaning to say anything.

"It might," said Granny. "It very well might. Smiles can mean so many different things. But it's good to love someone who has a smile for everyone."

"Did you love that sort of person, Granny?" When you were Robin's age you didn't want any older person to ask you questions about love. Was it sometimes different in the other direction? Mostly, older people would always say *love's the most important thing in life* but would never talk about love in their own lives. Granny wasn't like other people, though. It was funny she had a name like Kathy Snyder's, they could both be Kathys but Granny was *Kathleen* and *Kathy Snyder* was from *Katherine*.

"Yes Robin, I loved that sort of person. Arthur was just that sort of person. Have I told you about Arthur?" She never said *my husband* or *your great grandfather* when she spoke of him, in the way other old people would have done.

"Only a little," Robin lied.

"Come out on the balcony for a moment. You know I don't go out as much as I should now that I am old, but I do love to look out at the skyscrapers, to go out on the verandah—". She stopped herself. "*Balcony. Balcony!* After all the years I have spent up here, why do I keep saying *verandah?*"

"Because it's old, granny. It's an old word."

"Tact, child, tact. Have your parents taught you nothing whatsoever about tact?"

"Are you sure you won't be cold, Granny?"

"It's the old that is the problem. Not the cold." She pulled a little awkwardly at the sliding door and then Robin was there, tugging at it beside her, and then they were in amongst the clouds, white and gray swirling past them and under them and over them, clouds broken in the near distance by the top floors of the AON building and by Water Tower Place, and then the old Tribune Tower and the Wrigley Building breaking through into open sky, and further on the Sears Tower, they had had a new name for it for years, but that was how K.P. still thought of it. She was not alone.

Below them shone patches of bright through the clouds, everything else dim or lost. Above them pure glow—the luminous blue of when the sun has died for the day.

"I wasn't sure if we would be able to see it tonight. Over there, you see?" K.P. pointed out past the Wrigley Building to a thin round tower, domed at the top. "It's the top of the old Jewelers' Building. Maybe you've never noticed that little domed tower on top. It doesn't reach as high as the Sears or the Hancock or some of the others, it's harder for it to get above the clouds."

"It's not alive, Granny. You make it sound as if it was alive."

"*Were*, child. As if it *were* alive. The subjunctive. Perhaps it is alive. I have thought of skyscrapers as living things ever since I first saw Chicago. But I never noticed the Jewelers' Building until one day when I was out walking with a young man named Paul." She stopped herself. "Why do I use the surname? He should be Kenneth, or Ken, just as he was then."

"Why would you call him Ken if his name was Paul, Granny?"

"Kenneth Paul. Paul was his last name; it's one of those things that can be both first and last. We were walking along the river and we looked up, and all of a sudden we were curious. The next thing we knew we had found our way up to the—oh, what floor would it be? The floor where the tower begins. From there to the top you have to take a separate elevator—a little round elevator."

"And it travels up to little round rooms?"

"Exactly! It travels up to little round rooms, little round offices. In fact some of them are quite large and quite lovely. Or so I know now. That afternoon we never found out, Kenneth and me. We stepped inside the elevator and we pulled the heavy gate closed and then we pulled the elevator door closed—in those days you would sometimes have to do quite a bit of pulling and pushing before an elevator was ready to go. But this one wouldn't go. We pushed the button for the top floor; nothing happened. We pushed it again; again, nothing. Then we pushed the buttons for all the other floors—perhaps there were six in all to the top of the round tower. We waited and we waited and we were just on the point of trying to pull back the door and the gate when suddenly there was a clanking sound and a crunching sound and a little jolt. And then up we went. One floor, two floors, two and a half floors—then the clanking sound again, the little jolt again, and the clanking sound once more. That was all."

"You were stopped between the floors."

"Stopped. Stuck. Nothing we could do seemed to make any difference. We pressed all the buttons for all the floors, again and again. Nothing. And then we pressed the alarm—there was no intercom in those days, just a button that said *press in case of emergency*, and you pressed and you hoped it rang somewhere, that whoever was supposed to hear it would hear it, that they wouldn't be on a break, that they wouldn't be taking a nap, that they wouldn't be gone for the day. We both kept looking at our watches. It had already been after 5:00 when we had had our crazy notion, the crazy thought of trying to come up here; neither of us wanted to think that there might not be anyone around now, anyone there to hear an alarm after hours." Robin held Granny's hand a little tighter in the chill wind. The top of the Wrigley building had been hidden while she was speaking, but now it burst forth again, its own strange white, and behind it the four turrets and the central tower of the Jewelers' Building.

"So what happened?"

"We waited for a long time, and we worried for a long time. And then we stopped worrying. I don't know how else to put it.

What was the worst that could happen to us? We would be stuck there all night, and we would be found in the morning. Both of us had to push ourselves to remember that a lot worse things can happen to people. But we did remember that, and we began to talk of other things, things that we had never spoken of. Things that people tend not to talk about when they are out walking together, things that some people hardly talk about at all, ever. We talked of how empty much of life is, and we talked about death and about how nothing comes after it except for other people—other people and other animals, and the earth and the sky and the stars. And we started to talk of the poor..." She stopped for a moment, and somehow Robin felt a little anxious about what she might say. "They don't call them the poor now, do they? We spoke of how many people were poor, were struggling, this was '38, so many people had been without steady work for three years, five years, ten years even, and the rest of us would say *it's tough times, everyone's struggling*, you'd say those things when you had a job so you wouldn't feel you should give away any of the little you had.

"That's what I think now; it wasn't what I thought then. And it wasn't what Kenneth thought, either. He fancied himself to be some sort of socialist but I remember him arguing that art mattered more than anything, art was the only thing that would last. Why would he have been *arguing*? I agreed with him! I agreed with him completely. But that was the sort of passion he had. For quite a time he was really heated. Then time went on and the air in that strange round place became cooler. We talked about darkness, and again we talked about death. He started to speak of how worthless he sometimes felt. And then suddenly we were kissing in a way we never had before, and then somehow we were on the floor of the elevator together and he was—well, I don't need to tell you exactly what he was doing. But I think if the elevator hadn't suddenly started to move a minute or two later, the two of us would have been... I will use the words people use now. Making love. The words didn't mean then what they mean now. Back then *mak-*

*ing love* meant saying romantic things to each other. Courting. Whereas nowadays...."

"You don't have to say what it means nowadays, Granny. Everybody knows that..."

"I thought you might know something of what it meant." K.P. did not smile. "Back then, children your age would not have known. A lot who *weren't* children didn't know much about it either. You weren't supposed to know about that sort of thing unless you were married. Of course a lot of unmarried people *did* that sort of thing sometimes, but most people thought it was shameful, sinful. And whenever..."

"Will you tell me about skyscrapers, Granny?" K.P looked hard at the child, but Robin persisted. "You know about sky-scrapers, don't you Granny?"

"I know a good deal about skyscrapers, Robin. You must be remembering that I..." She let the thought trail off. "Am I telling you too much, child? About other things?"

"No, Granny. Just not enough about skyscrapers." There was a silence. "You could tell me a story about skyscrapers. You used to..."

"I could tell you a hundred stories about skyscrapers." She looked hard at Robin again. "They are taller and straighter than love. But less down to earth." K.P waited for a smile that did not come. The child liked words; why did K.P.'s little *bon mot* not amuse? "All right. I will tell you more. They are always about money, but sometimes a sort of magic creeps in. Shall I start I start with a story that has some of the...?"

"Magic. Yes, Granny. I would like that."

Once more K.P. looked sharply at Robin. "Maybe I should begin with a story about a skyscraper and a child. A child your age or thereabouts. Was he twelve, thirteen? Maybe a trifle younger. It is like a fairy tale—perhaps when one is thinking of telling a thousand stories one should always begin with a fairy tale. Tall buildings have their fairy tales. As much as castles, as much as little cabins tucked away in the middle of the back-woods..."

"You are going to tell me a fairy tale about a skyscraper?"

"I am going to tell you the tale of Wilbur Foshay and the Foshay Tower. Once upon a time when Wilbur was little, his father took him to visit his nation's capital. They visited all the sites, and for Wilbur the most exciting of all was the Washington Monument; it had taken them almost a hundred years to finish it, and now it was finally done. A strange obelisk, a squared-off tower going high into the sky, a tower with nothing to do with George Washington except that it had his name attached to it. Young Wilbur, as the story goes, was greatly impressed, and he said to his father, 'when I grow up I will be a business-man and build a tower of business as large and wonderful as the Washington Monument.'"

"And did he do that, Granny?"

"After a fashion, yes. Yes he did. He founded the W.B. Foshay Company—in fact I believe he founded two or three companies called the Foshay Company. They were utility companies—they made power. This was in Minneapolis, not in Chicago or New York, and so the W.B. Foshay Company never became as famous as the Woolworth Company or the Wrigley Company. But it did very well—or at least so it seemed. When Wilbur was starting to build his third company he commissioned an architect to build just the building he had thought of when he was a boy. As much like the Washington Monument as a business building could be. But it was not to be all business; Wilbur planned to live on the 27th and 28th floors himself. He had luxurious apartments built there, with a fireplace and a large library and walls of marble brought all the way from Italy.

"When the Foshay Tower was finished they said it was the tallest building west of the Mississippi. They were wrong about that; the building that was *really* the tallest west of the Mississippi was still the Smith Tower in Seattle, just as it had been since— since 1914, I think. But of course no one could google back then; I wouldn't be surprised if *tallest building west of the Mississippi* was a phrase used to describe half a dozen towers in places like Oklahoma City and Kansas City.

"At any rate, the Foshay was by some distance the tallest in Minneapolis. Nowadays when you stand on the observation deck—I say 'nowadays', but in fact I do not know, it has been years since I was in Minneapolis. I have heard they have made the Foshay Tower into some sort of fancy hotel. I do not even know if they have kept the observation deck. But this is a fairy tale, and we can pretend. Nowadays, if you stand at the top of the Foshay and look out, everywhere you look there are towers that rise high above you, gleaming glass towers from the 1980s and 1990s and 2000s. It has been a long time since the Foshay was the tallest or the most impressive. But for its beauty, and its oddity—it is still a wonderful thing to behold."

"And Wilbur? What happened to Wilbur?"

"He did not have a fairy tale ending. It was 1929 when the tower opened. There were cheering crowds and a big brass band, but Wilbur was in trouble. He was behind on all sorts of debt payments, and by year's end he was broke. He lost the tower, the company, everything, and he was dead within a year. So it is a story of triumph, but it is a sad story too."

"Next time, will you tell me a story about Chicago?" The clouds had all cleared. It was cold, and the darkness had come in all around. The lights of the city twinkled all around them and below them. If you looked up you could see the bright stars.

"I will, child, I will. But let us go in now."

"I brought a poem to show you, Granny."

"Lovely! We'll make a hot drink and you can show me your poem. Then you should be getting along home, shouldn't you? There's not much light left. Poem and home…"

"Is it always this high, Granny? Up here I mean. Has your balcony always been this high? Have you always lived on this story?"

"That's an odd question. I have lived here a long time. And it has always been high. It has always been very high. Let us go in before we both freeze." She let go of Robin's hand, and back in they went. There was still the picture of three ladies standing in front of another picture, in front of *Washington*

*Crossing the Delaware*, just where it always had been, and one of them held a teacup, just as she always had done. The ragged rug that hung from the wall was just as it had always been too—the rug that Granny always said had got that way from her cat scratching away at it when she, Granny, had been very small. And the heavy sideboard was where it had always been, and so were the cases and the strange sculptures from South America, and the candelabra, and so was the little collection of seashells, all in a circle on the little side table. Robin remembered the little curly ones, and the scallop, and the one that was called a sand dollar.

"I remember when you used to play with those when you were very little. They're lovely, aren't they."

"I can't remember that, Granny. But yes. Lovely," Robin agreed. Robin looked at them again. Grownups didn't keep seashells. Not most of them. Not usually.

"You know they're nothing special—they're just shells like you can find the world over. Would you like to have one of them? To put it in your pocket right now?"

"I would like that very much."

"But you had better not take the sand dollar; that one is too delicate for a pocket, I think." So Robin took one of the shiny oyster shells, and put it very carefully in a pocket and then said thank you.

Granny did not make any tea or hot chocolate for herself. Just as Robin remembered her always doing in the evenings, she poured herself a glass of a clear liquid. Robin saw now that it came from a large green bottle that Granny had on the counter—that part Robin did not remember. "Finest Dry Gin" was written on the bottle.

"Don't you need to mix that with something, Granny?" Robin had seen what Kathy Scott's mother's friend Rita did with gin, how she poured a little measuring glass of it into a big glass—sometimes two little measuring glasses went into the big glass—and then added tonic water. Granny had poured quite a lot of the liquid, the Finest Dry Gin, straight into the tumbler.

"Ice is all you need with this, child." She sipped at the drink quickly, quietly, and when she put it down Robin could see the level of the liquid was a half-inch lower. "That's the mark of a truly good gin. You wouldn't want to do this with Gilbey's." It was not easy for Robin to know what to say.

"The hot chocolate is good, Granny." Robin felt suddenly warm, and very happy.

"So you want to know more about skyscrapers. Are there other things you would like to know more about?"

"About how you became grown up, Granny. And about—" Robin paused. How could you say it?

"About love?"

"Maybe there are lots of things that I could ask you, that you could tell me."

"I think maybe three is enough. I will tell you tales of sky-scrapers, not all of them very tall. And of humans, growing up. And of love. But for now—you will be late getting home. Should you phone your parents?"

"I'll just go now, Granny. I don't carry a phone. Not usually. And that thing you have with the…"

"The dial, Robin."

"…with the dial isn't…. I don't know how…"

"I thought everyone below the age of fifty carried one of those nowadays. Those prison phones. *Cell*, I mean, *cell*…."

"Not everyone, Granny. Kathy Snyder—she's in my class at school—she says people who use cellphones all the time never really have conversations. And she's right, that's what I think; I think she's right. There's a whole group of us now who won't use our cellphones. Lara and Luke and Jai and—anyway, we can't make our parents not buy them for us, but we can—…"

"Well, I won't make you use the old rotary in the other room, either. But you should go, child. Really."

There was no one in the hallway when they said goodbye, no one with Robin on the elevator going down, and no one in the lobby—not even the concierge. The street was half lost; fog was still everywhere. Soft colors glowed through the gray—streetlights, and the red and green of traffic lights, and lights that said OPEN in bright flashing neon and lights that said CLOSED in plain neon, and the lights of trucks, and of buses and taxis—a city on a great lake in late winter, at the beginning of evening.

# Three

"Where have you been, Robin?" Carl tried to keep the sharpness out of his voice; both he and Carol had been starting to get a little worried.

"I stayed late. I wanted to finish a poem." It wasn't a lie; Robin had stayed late. And they didn't press it any further. Kathy Snyder said her parents would sometimes ask her almost exactly the same question three or four times over, as if they were trying to trip her up. Carol and Carl weren't like that, but they had other...

"It's almost dinner time. Can you set the table? Don't forget the napkins this time."

"Why do we need napkins, anyway? Do we need to cut down trees for that?"

"We always buy the recycled brand; you know that, Robin."

"Always?" Kathy Snyder had talked about how some recycled papers still weren't good; you had to look for 100% recycled, and there were other things you should look for too. "Anyway, even with recycled it's not perfect. I was reading that..."

"I don't mind if we use napkins as conversation pieces over dinner. Just so long as I can have one in my lap as well. *Do* get on with it, Robin; we'll eat in a moment."

Carl was paying attention to the food; he looked appreciatively at what was coming out of the oven. "Lovely," he said, and he and Carol smiled at each other the way they did when it had been a long time since they'd had an argument. Robin saw that, and thought of how Joey Burgess had said he could tell just from how his parents talked to each other at the dinner table how long it had been since they made love. Except that Joey hadn't used those words, *made love,* and the way he had used the word he did use made it sound like something no one would want to do, ever. No one you'd ever want to know.

Now the food was on the table. And the napkins.

"None for me, please. I can just have the potatoes and greens."

"But this has no meat in it, Robin, just eggs and cheese and...."

"But I keep telling you. I'm not eating animals any more. Non-human animals. Not meat, not eggs, not milk, not cheese..."

"I know that's what you said last week, but then you had that piece of cake and I thought...."

"That was different." Robin paused. "No, it wasn't really different. I guess I knew there were eggs in there. I just wanted there not to be. I shouldn't have eaten any."

"Well, I don't know what's going to happen if you really decide not to.... Even eggs?"

"Eggs are maybe the worst; I've told you that. The way they treat the birds when they..."

"Not at dinner, Robin. Not at dinner. And if you think you're going to shame your mother and me into changing our ways, you're going to be disappointed. A child can't dictate what the whole family has for dinner. It's just not..."

"It's not like it's earth shattering if your kid goes vegan. You don't need to..."

"I'm going to change the subject," Carol stepped in. "Earth shattering. Did you hear what they're saying about earthquakes?" Carl certainly had heard what they were saying; it had been all over that week's news. First there had been a leading seismologist who had said there was a twenty per cent chance of an earthquake in Chicago within the next five years, maybe an earthquake as severe as the earthquake in San Francisco and in Oakland that had happened before Robin had been born, the one where the bridge over the bay had collapsed and people had died. A lot of people. But then other seismologists had said no, that wasn't something you should expect to happen in Chicago any more frequently than once every 500 or 1,000 years. Carl and Carol bounced the idea back and forth.

"It's not like there haven't been earthquakes here before; it's just that people don't think of the midwest as a place where earthquakes happen."

"Exactly. Robin, you won't remember the little earthquake in 2002, but your father and I do. There was one in 1968 too— the year when *everything* was in a state of upheaval. That's a little before my time."

"And apparently there was one back in 1895 that made them worry that those early skyscrapers would collapse. And before that there were even bigger ones."

"That's what this guy says could happen again. A really big one. Seven on the Richter scale, maybe higher."

"You never know; *could happen* leaves a lot of room. But it's interesting what happened way back. A whole series of them, quakes ripping right through the mid-west, Chicago right the way down to Indiana, to…"

"I heard about it on the radio. To Missouri, even…." Were they competing, Robin wondered? Competing over who could agree with the other one the most? Why did they have to be like this? "That fault…" Mother was saying. "Named after some town on the Missouri that was at the center of those really bad quakes in 1811, 1812, when hundreds died, maybe thousands, it could be that…"

"New Madrid. It was New Madrid. Maybe tens of thousands. I'm sure no one really knows; I can't imagine they kept good records back then."

Robin had to break in. "It can't be really dangerous. How could it be? There's nothing like, like…"

"Like a San Andreas fault right here in Illinois? No, there isn't." Carl pursed his lips and Carol started to talk about how easily people forget about tragedy, and also about how you never can tell what will happen, or protect against everything, but then again how unlikely it is that anything out of the ordinary will actually occur. Robin fidgeted. "I suppose in the end it always depends on where you are, and on how it's been built, the building that you're in. It must always depend on that, don't you think? I'm sure they'll be having second thoughts now about trying to design anything that goes any higher than what's there already. Maybe they'll be looking at a lot of the skyscrapers we have now, too."

"Sure they will," Carl agreed. "Be calling in the engineers to have a second look."

"As a precautionary measure."

"As a precautionary measure. Exactly." There was a pause, and that made it Robin's turn.

"The building that Gran—," Robin stopped short, and then began again. "What about here? What about right here? This is a skyscraper."

"I'll go ahead and say the obvious; we wouldn't want to be inside it if it fell down."

"Maybe we should raise this at the next meeting of the association, Carl; you never know."

"I wouldn't think it's worth getting too worked up about, dear. I'm sure our chances of getting killed crossing the street are far higher." Robin had noticed how this happened. Carl and Carol would be talking back and forth as if they were two halves of the same brain, and then suddenly one of them would start to invent a difference where there really hadn't been one.

"I wasn't getting 'worked up' about it, Carl. All I was saying is that maybe we should do what we can to make sure nothing happens. I don't know about the rest of you, but I don't want anyone killed in this family." There was a long pause; her stricken face said *anyone else, I mean*, but there were no words spoken. She had told herself a thousand times not to say anything that might remind them of Hope. But there were so many topics that could take a turn; a word could slip out, a few words. It would always be a little different when the memory came back. Suddenly there was chubby little Hope, balanced on the railing, tipping forward a little bit and then somehow catching herself, holding herself, laughing, then tipping back the other way, straight against the sky and then a little lean backwards, a little lean, and then Robin's hand reaching out towards her, and then horror filling Hope's little face, her eyes wide, her left arm flailing free, her right hand pulling at the railing until everything ripped away, all of her, and then a voice that was not like her voice, echoing downwards, on and on, you wanted to stop your thoughts, you wanted her to keep falling through the air forever.

"Not to suggest that anyone else does, that anyone else wants..." Carol let herself trail away. She was making it worse, she could see that.

"Is it all right if I clear the table now, and then do my homework?"

"Of course, Robin," said Carol and Carl, almost at the same time. And Robin cleared the plates and started to do the math that was due in the morning. But the questions started to get all tangled up, and after a while Robin put them to one side. Ms. McLenithan had said they would be starting a debating team the next month, and Robin spent a little time daydreaming about being on the team and about saying all the right things in front of everybody. And then Robin started to work on a new poem, a poem about snow and mist and the night.

Later Robin fell asleep to thoughts of Kathy Snyder's kiss, and of Kathy Snyder's touch, just there, and then just there, and then lightly, just there.

ॐ  ॐ  ॐ

LeShonna Jones sometimes took off from school early too. It was a different school now, Emmett Till it was called, named after a boy who had been only a little older than her when he died, that was what LeShonna's teacher's had said and LeShonna had looked it up as well. The boy had lived in Chicago with his mother but when he died they were visiting his uncle in Money—not no uncle who'd gotten rich, an uncle who lived in a little town in the Mississippi Delta which was called that, Money was the town's real name. What everything was called was confusing on account of the Mississippi Delta wasn't where the Mississippi split up to join the sea, it was where the Yazoo started to be part of the Mississippi at flood time, and that was a long ways upriver from the Mississippi River Delta and from New Orleans and all that.

Anyways, Emmett had gone to the Money grocery store and meat market and had gotten friendly with a woman at the till. It was funny, she had a name like *buy*—*Bryant*, that was it, Carolyn Bryant—and his name was Till and the till was where the trouble started except he didn't do nothing, just started talking to the woman, being friendly and such. But the woman was married and the woman was white and when the woman's husband, he was called Bryant too, when he heard that a young black boy had gotten fresh with his wife—that was what he called it, *fresh*—he came after Emmett. Mr. Bryant and a friend, they both came after him, and they took out both of Emmett's eyes before they killed him and dumped him in the river. And they even admitted it, but no jury would convict them, send them to jail, like, and that was a time that made people think and wish white folks would stop doing horrible things to black folks for no reason. It made some people do more than think and wish, too, they got real mad and started fighting for change. And that was why they had named the school after him, Emmett Till. This was a long time ago in the nineteen-fifties.

Everybody always talked about how the South Side was poorer than the North Side and a lot of people said it wasn't safe but LeShonna thought that wasn't fair, wasn't true, you could walk anywhere anytime. Once she had walked almost to the president's house, that was almost twenty blocks north and they were the long, long blocks you get in a lot of Chicago but mostly she walked south or east. East was towards the lake, those were long blocks too and it took forever to reach the lake you had to go past all the vacant lots, *some people say there's nothing down here but there's lots of lots*, her mama would say, and there were a lot of trees too, and a lot of old brick buildings with the stuck-out windows on every floor, *bay windows*, that was what they were called, and then Marquette Street would go under the railway tracks, the clackety boom clackety boom was so loud from underneath, and then it was still a lot of blocks to Jackson Park, and even then you had to walk a ways to get to the water, if you went all the way to the water where Marquette curved round by the Children's Hospital it was so lovely with all the open air and the green and the water and the shore curving into far away where you could see the skyscrapers dark gray against the light gray and the light blue, so far away and so lovely, but it was so many blocks to get to where you could see that, usually LeShonna didn't get that far. She had to go as far as Ellis anyway, where they lived now was on Ellis Avenue near Marquette, and some people said that the pairs of sneakers that had been thrown over the telephone wires were a sign that you could buy drugs at the nearest house but LeShonna didn't think that was true. There were three young men who lived there but they seemed all right. One of them worked construction and the others said they were going to college and LeShonna believed them and she'd only even seen them drunk once, she'd never had no trouble no how, not anything she couldn't handle. Her mother always said there was a lot of ways things was not safe in the world, but you weren't going to get killed by no stranger, not hardly ever. Sure, there might be a few times that'd happen to someone, and sure, that was terrible, but for every time like that there were probably ten thousand times when someone'd get killed or hurt bad by someone they thought'd loved them. Wives, their husbands'd beat them up, sometimes kill them. Foster kids, their foster parents'd beat them up, sometimes kill them. Or the other kids would beat them up, kids who didn't get enough food, or food that was any good for them. And then they'd get fat and die of diabetes before they were fifty, Miss Murphy at school talked about how there wasn't no nourishment in what people ate, there was just a lot of chemicals. Everybody was eating chicken nuggets and burgers and fries and cokes, and nobody eating no collard greens and such, not like they used to. Like *we* used to, Miss Murphy'd say; we should be proud of our heritage.

Or the police. Unless you were in with a gang or something you had a lot more to fear from the police than you did from thieves or muggers or murderers. Way back in the 1970s all that used to be a lot worse than it was now, that was what LeShonna's mother and father said. But the police were still plenty bad now. Everyone knew what they liked to stop people for. Driving while black. Walking while black. Sitting on a park bench while black. There wasn't nothing you could do to stop it, except maybe now it was getting a little better than it had been in the other century, people said maybe it didn't hurt that we had a black president, sort-of black. People said maybe it was making other people think twice about what it meant to be black. To be black in *America*. Being black wasn't the same everywhere, that was something Miss Murphy talked a lot about. Being black in Ghana and being black in Australia and being black in Chicago was all different things, same as it was different to be a white Russian and a white New Yorker, it was culture that made things what they was, not how people was colored. Miss Murphy talked about all that a lot more than Miss McLenithan had done. Miss McLenithan had sort of suggested that nowadays it never mattered what color you were, that race was becoming like something from long ago. That was how it *should* be, anyway, Miss McLenithan had said, and now we had a president who was black and mostly it didn't matter anymore what color you were, and LeShonna sometimes wished it was really like that. But it wasn't, it just wasn't. Not really, not yet, maybe not for always; how could you know? Miss McLenithan had a good heart, you could see that, and she had said a lot of true things. Not just about math—everyone said what was true when it was math; LeShonna thought Miss McLenithan had been true about a lot of things. But not color. Maybe Ms. McLenithan just didn't know about that.

When LeShonna went home it wasn't to no skyscraper, four stories was all there was, and theirs was the back part of the fourth story. You didn't need a lot of space for three people, that's what

LeShonna's dad always said, LeShonna would have had an older brother except he'd been stillborn, just one time her mama had talked about that, and at first LeShonna hadn't understood, she'd thought *still born* was like *born again* and still living. When it got hot LeShonna would have liked fewer stories than that. Or else more—if you had more than four stories then the building owners had to put in an elevator. When you had to carry groceries or even just your schoolbooks up to the fourth floor and it was one of those really hot days it wasn't no picnic, that's what her father said, *it ain't no picnic and it ain't no fun.* Miss Murphy said it was good for people to walk upstairs instead of taking the elevator, it stopped them from getting fat and dying, *obese* was what she said, but she couldn't have meant it was good to have no elevator when it was like this. One time LeShonna's mama had boughten a new chesterfield and LeShonna's daddy had had to carry one end and LeShonna and her mama had had to carry the other end, all the way up those stairs, four stories was a long ways.

א   א   א

You might have thought that after what had happened Carol and Carl would never be able to get over the guilt, perhaps would never manage to make love again. But never is a long time, and life is complicated. First, when Hope was not long gone, Carol had asked *what's the point of it all? What's the point of anything?* again and again, asking in the sort of way that is only anguish and emptiness and pain. And always the anguish had been laced with guilt, guilt for what she had been doing with Carl, guilt for not having been with Robin and with Hope, guilt for having thought even for a moment of her life as pointless and empty back then, back when it had been so full, when she had still had two children playing on a balcony in the sun.

A few months later she still felt that anguish, she still felt that guilt. But now she would sometimes also feel desire—the sort of raw need that can block out everything else, at least for a while. Carl felt it sometimes too, and sometimes they felt it together, and sometimes they would satisfy it together. But of course it wasn't wholly satisfying afterwards, not in the old way, not when all the thoughts would come crowding back in. And after a while what came afterwards made them shy away once again from taking physical pleasure with each other—even of thinking of physical pleasure with each other. They could manage a sort-of love, but for years they couldn't manage what the world calls making love.

Did that mean they stopped feeling desire? No. Not either of them. But desire became a creature of their imaginations, their private thoughts—and something they hid from each other. That stage lasted two years, maybe more. Then Carol decided it was time to make an effort. The ache and the pain and the anguish of losing Hope became less sharp year by year, but she and Carl were not coming any closer to each other. She insisted they talk about it, she insisted they try to be closer, and Carl agreed that yes, that was what they should do. And they both went together to someone who told them that it was all right for them to let imagination into the bedroom. They both had more than enough to feel guilty about without feeling guilty about their desires having come unmoored from each others' bodies, and coupled instead to their imaginings. She told them they could say anything, think of anything, that it would be all right.

Miraculously, it seemed that she was right. Maybe part of it was simply that enough years had gone by, but Carol began to be able to feel desire almost with no strings attached—desire in the present, desire in the imagined time-out-of-time, desire everywhere, shooting through her, through and through and through again. She could suddenly see that, so long as at some level it was still true that she and Carl loved each other, fulfilling desire need have nothing to do with the great arc of their lives, the arc that contained Hope and Robin as well as the two of them. She could let herself imagine anything, and so could Carl, and that was all right, and that would be all right.

And something similar happened to Carl, and for a while it was indeed all right. They started to be less self-conscious about the whole thing, and sometimes afterward there was hardly any anguish. It felt as if some sort of healing might be possible after all.

But that was only for a few months, maybe a year. Then suddenly it wasn't working. For Carl. Nothing was working at all. Carol would start imagining something that would please her or that would please Carl, *I'm going to keep touching you ever so slowly just like this, no, no, you have to stay still, you're going to be teased until…* , the sorts of imaginings that for those few months had given pleasure to both of them. And Carl said that they gave him pleasure still. But you could tell that wasn't entirely true; you could see that wasn't entirely true. They talked about it. A little infrequently, a little reluctantly, perhaps, on Carl's part, but they did talk about it. They just couldn't get it to change. Couldn't make themselves change. That was how Carl put it. Whenever he came to the point of feeling desire, there was almost nothing to show for it. Even when Carol was—well, when you could see her desire—it wasn't the same for Carl. He didn't know what to do or to think, but, after those few months they had had, a year or whatever it was, he felt sure that this time it had nothing to do with the guilt or the anguish of Hope having left them.

To speak of Carol and Carl trying to grope their way back to physical love is only to scratch the surface. What was it like for them to try to grope their way forward in the rest of life? Was it even harder for them to work out how to deal with Robin's loss than it was for them to work out how to deal with their own? Perhaps so. Fairly quickly Carl came to accept that there would have to be some emotional distance between the two of them and Robin. You had to expect that, really. Was there blame and hurt and pain inside everyone? Of course there was. And guilt? Of course there was. For a long time the pain felt like it would never go—the sort of searing pain that can tear through a person like a rip blade on a circular saw tears through plywood. And then somehow the person becomes fresh plywood again, day after day after day, until the blade finally dulls. It wasn't until the blade had become dull that Carl could think again, that he could think about the long term, about what they could do that might make it easier, for all of them but for Robin especially. You had to think of the child's feelings; after what had happened it didn't seem right to expect Robin to feel close to them in the way that other children felt close to their parents. He was pretty sure Carol felt the same.

It would never be easy, but there were things they could do that would make it worse, and things they could do that might not make it worse. Carl and Carol learned to speak to each other about shame and guilt and blame, and the deep hate they would always have for themselves. They learned early on that they would try not to build habits of hating each other for what they had done. It came naturally to them both not to hate each other—it was lucky, that. But they learned instead to hate themselves together for what they had done, as if they had been a single being all the while. Doing that did not get rid of the guilt or the anguish. But it left a little space for loving the other person as a separate person, an individual. And a little space left for loving yourself. No. For not hating yourself.

It was a way of coping, Carl would think to himself. But it began to feel natural to let something of a hard edge come into his voice—into their voices—when they were calling Robin, telling Robin to do something, telling Robin what needed to be done, telling Robin what hadn't been done, telling Robin what would have to be done better. That wasn't getting any easier as Robin grew older. Carl knew that as humans grow up they reach a stage where one moment they're like children, younger than their real age, and the next they're like the most cantankerous of adults. These days it seemed that Robin would either be childish or else would be continually scrounging around for ways to be difficult. That was what it seemed like to Carl. No cell phones, no meat and eggs—what would be next, no clothing?

And school—was Robin really keeping up at school? It seemed Robin never had much homework to do this year. Shouldn't there be a little more each year? Shouldn't Robin have to—well, it was hard to know exactly what Robin should have to do. Maybe they should have a talk with this Ms. McLenithan.

Carl didn't make a habit of prying into what went on at school, and neither did Carol, but they had talked about this just the other day—how Robin seemed to have even less interest than ever before in math, and how there seemed to be so little homework this year. And then Carl felt a little twinge. Perhaps he and Carol hadn't done enough themselves. Hadn't cared enough about whether Robin was interested in this or that thing at school. Maybe they had held too much of the past in their minds and their hearts, and not enough of the present.

Of course what had happened to Hope hadn't been Robin's fault. Really it hadn't. But at some level it didn't matter how true that was. Robin had been there. Robin had been closest to what had happened, and hadn't been able to stop it from happening. They mustn't find themselves learning to resent the one child they had left. They mustn't, they couldn't. But sometimes Carl started to feel that they had been doing exactly that. Of course they loved Robin too. But the love kept being left behind, kept having the door closed in its face when it tried to tag along.

৯ ৯ ৯

"We have to move, Carol," Carl had said a couple of months after they had lost Hope. "We can't stay way up here. We never go out on that balcony now, any of us. And we never will. And it's not just that. I don't imagine you can even stand to look out the window. That view…"

"No. No, Carl. Sometimes I feel that being in this place is what keeps her close to me. Yes, it rips me apart to look out that window. But I don't want to lose that pain. I don't want to lose what I feel about her, I don't want to get over it, I don't want to cover it up." She paused for a moment. "Of course part of me does. But I don't want to let that part win."

"I suppose the people who believe their loved ones are waiting for them somewhere could…"

"Who believe in a god? And in a heaven? Yes. But I'm not going to will myself to believe what we both know isn't true."

"We don't *know* it. What we know is that we can't know."

"Like we can't *know* that leprechauns aren't dancing on the Navy Pier and mermaids aren't swimming up the Chicago River. Sure. We're just talking probabilities."

"I'm not going to start in about mermaids. Or gods. The question is do we stay here or do we move?"

"Carl, we can't move. It's the money, too. We can't not think of that. If we moved we'd want a nice big ground-level apartment in a graystone house, one of those lovely…"

"We used to talk about how we would…. Yes. And one day we will. One day…"

"But for now? We're one and a half salaries. No. You're a salary—and not a great one. I'm wages. We're a book publishing salary plus half a wage. Even if I went back into publishing full-time that wouldn't be nearly enough; we can barely afford this little condo. If we wanted to live on the ground we'd have to live in some nasty place miles inland and spend half our lives commuting."

In the end, then, they stayed where they were. They learned, as humans do, to accustom themselves to places where tragic things have happened, where loved ones have died. And in the end they learned to talk of tall buildings without mentioning Hope, without even thinking of her, not in any conscious way. They became more or less able to speak of skyscrapers as they had years before, before they had had children, before they had decided to try living in a high rise "for a little while," "until we can save for something better."

Robin had never said anything about any of it, not back then. But now skyscrapers were something Robin cared about, they hardly knew why. Their child kept on about them, asking odd questions, reciting odd facts.

"In Shanghai they're going to build something even taller than the Burj Khalifa."

"Why on earth would anyone want to?" asked Carl.

"Don't you think it's cool?"

"I think Paris is cool," was Carl's response. "Nothing higher than five stories. Everything on a human scale. Just like Jane Jacobs…"

"So why do we live here?" Robin asked. "In a skyscraper."

"The way they've made Chicago, this is what we can afford if we want to live anywhere close. Close to work, close to where things are happening."

"You and Mom hardly ever go out except for work. How do you *know* what's happening?"

"Things change when you get a little older and have children, Robin," put in Carol. "You get used to not knowing as much."

"How should they have made Chicago, then?"

"More carefully," said Carl. "No, seriously, more like Paris. With a lot of low buildings close together. Everything on a human scale."

"Why can't we be human right here? Right here on the 33rd floor? A five-story building is more than five times the height of a human. That's not on a human scale either."

"It's a lot closer to it, Robin. Do the math. More importantly, do your math *homework*!" Carl couldn't help bringing that in. Sometimes it can be important to care about your children in ways they don't like.

"All right, all right. But fifty stories up is a lot closer to the sky. And you can see so much more."

"People never do, Robin," said Carl, more gently. "Look out there. How many people do you see checking out the view from their balcony? Nobody. Balconies are there because people like the *idea* of themselves sitting out in the open. Above it all. Looking down on other people. It's hubris. Smugness. Pride."

"You don't have to look down. You can look out. And up."

"But look at how skyscrapers began," Carl persisted. "They were like a god substitute. Cathedrals of commerce. Built by rich businessmen who read about the camel and the needle and half suspected there wasn't any heaven anyway. So how were they going to be remembered? Something big and tall—and permanent. No one thought the Singer Building would ever be torn down. Plus, in the here-and-now they wanted to show how superior they were and how superior their companies were, wanted to show the world who could…"

"Stick his the highest?"

"Robin!" Carol exclaimed sharply.

"But it doesn't have to be that way, does it?" Now it was the child who wouldn't let go. "You can want to be high up for other reasons," Robin insisted, and kept on insisting in what seemed to Carl and to Carol to be less and less coherent ways, and perhaps they truly weren't coherent, for all the while Robin was also thinking about the strange elevator, and about trying to ride it once more, about the door closing and then the rushing feeling as it went up, up, and on up, all the way to the 86th story.

# Four

*2011, 1938*

It was with real relief that K.P. sat down again after the child had left. Children take such energy! If you were as old as K.P. was, you really had to sit down and let yourself relax for a time afterwards. Sit down with whatever might be left in your glass— perhaps top it up a little before you... while you...

K.P. had another sip of the colorless liquid. Yes, it was good to be on her own. And yet the stories; she hardly wanted to admit to herself how much she enjoyed telling the stories. She found herself imagining Robin's presence, imagining stories she could tell. Would tell. The Jewelers' Building, for example, and how beautifully.... But there would always be a sadness about the Jewelers' Building. The grand idea for having parking inside the building had gone all wrong, the grand idea for everything had gone all wrong. And the story of Frederick Dinkelberg, the architect—that was the greatest sadness. What happened to Dinkelberg after the Jewelers' was done.

For some little while after the Jewelers' Building opened, he had prospered. But then came 1929. Dinkelberg had invested all his savings and more in the market. Like so many, he had bought on margin, borrowing to buy shares that everyone agreed could only rise in value—shares in utility companies, companies just like the ones Foshay controlled. Dinkelberg lost it all: his savings, his home in leafy Evanston, everything. No, not quite everything. He and his wife Emily survived together, and it seems that whatever love there was between them managed to survive as well. But they were living on relief, renting a small apartment, when Dinkelberg started to go senile. Not just any sort of senile—the sort that years later everyone started to call *Alzheimer's*. He was losing his mind in the way he had seen his mother lose hers, seen her waste away to a babbling husk, listless and vacant, spoonfed and cooed to like a baby. Frederick could imagine how it would end for him, and what it would be like for Emily. So he arranged things with her, arranged for a quiet death before what had happened to his mother happened to him. There were no histrionics; Frederick was not the sort to jump off the Brooklyn Bridge. He wrote a warm little message about his love for Emily and her love for him and how rare and wonderful that love had been. It was a letter for her eyes only. She was not to show it to anyone unless she was accused of anything to do with his death; it finally came to light only long after she had died. Wonderful as their sort of love had been, Frederick wrote, and good as they had been to each other, he and Emily had come to agree that it was almost as important to try to be good to the whole world, to people on the street, to animals in the woods or on the farm, to strangers in Bechuanaland. That was what people should learn as they grew up—that, and also learn that you had to imagine before you could learn to love. To imagine others as well as yourself. This was all in the note, and she agreed to hide it away once he was gone, and not to try to stop him from doing what he said he was going to do. And then he lay down and Emily helped to make him comfortable, and he took far too many sleeping pills. Emily held his hand as he died quietly, *it was his heart*, she told everyone afterwards, *he's always had a bad heart*, and that wasn't true, Frederick had always had a good heart, but everyone nodded because that was what one did, and the American Institute of Architects chipped in to pay for his funeral; it was an act of kindness, Frederick and Emily had been so poor.

But then after the funeral Liberty National informed Emily that Frederick had taken out a policy on both their lives, had she known nothing of this? Evidently not; tears came to her eyes when they told her. It was not an especially large policy but the amount was large enough that Emily would not need to worry about money now.

Emily had stayed in the tiny apartment, though—it was so much trouble to move, really. And every month she had given a good deal of what Liberty National gave her to the hospitals in Francistown and Serowe in far-off Bechuanaland, and to the Provident Hospital right there in Chicago, she knew Frederick would have approved.

K.P. had a large sip. She could remember Emily's own funeral. In '44? Or had it been '45?

How different Frederick Dinkelberg had been from Kenneth Paul! K.P. thought once more of that night in the Jewelers', and of how it had all gone wrong with Kenneth. She would tell Robin. She would tell Robin some of it. You could forget yourself in the stories of others—in the lives of others. And her young self had been another person in another world.

৵ ৵ ৵

K.P.'s mind wandered back further into the past. 1938. Kathleen Schuyler she had been, and Winnipeg had been the whole world. She could still feel what it had been like to be six. And then eight. And then ten. She could hear it, she could smell it, the shuffle and the smell of the horses pulling their wagon loads of milk, of lumber, of barrels of beer, and then in the evenings the smell of beer on her father's breath. The heat and the mosquitoes in July, wave after wave of them, and the months of white, the dry crunch underfoot of the packed snow, the white clouds puffed out of the churning black engines that pulled the long, clacking trains, the crisp white of the linen on the tablecloths when they went out for a special dinner of a Sunday at the Marlborough, her daddy kept calling it the Olympia but everybody knew it was the Marlborough now, the Marlborough Hotel, all nine stories of it.

One time Kathleen had gone to an even more special meal at the Marlborough, *a fun raiser* she had heard them call it, for years afterwards she would sometimes puzzle over that phrase. They had held it in the ballroom and that was on the eighth floor and you could see everything, you could see the railway station, you could see the Grain Exchange, you could see Portage and Main, everything.

By the time Kathleen was fifteen, sixteen, Winnipeg had become smaller. Now it was 1938, and the city was smaller still. Her friends had begun to make plans. One was to go to the new university, another had applied for a job at the Grain Exchange, a third was being pushed by her parents to go to secretarial school. Kathleen wanted to go to art school, but there were hardly any art schools anywhere, not in Winnipeg especially. Her parents wouldn't pay for something like that—*we can help you if you want to do something with your life*, they had said—but her Aunt Ella had died and had left her two thousand dollars, not in trust for her when she got older, but for right now. You could live for a year on that, easy. Two years, maybe even three if you were careful and if you got some work along the way.

In the Canada of those days, young people who felt the world they were living in was too small would light out for Montreal. Or Toronto—but Toronto was stuffy, the people who moved there were not the real adventurers. Montreal was the real place for adventure. New York? No, no—these were *Canadians*. To think of going to New York would have been—it would have been to think too highly of oneself. Just about no one except Kathleen thought of going to Chicago—though you could read that it was the fifth largest city in the world, and everybody in Winnipeg used to report that people who visited would say it was like a little Chicago. That was because of the way the skyscrapers looked. The Childs building, the Grain Exchange, Bankers Row. Chicago Style.

The day Kathleen turned nineteen she took all the money her Aunt Ella had left her and in the middle of the night she packed two suitcases. She would leave ever so quietly before the sun had a chance to rise, but it was so hard to know what to take and what to leave. Why did she feel she had to take her little box of paints? They were child's paints, really; she would buy real things when she was there, when she had arrived in Chicago.

She worried and worried about what to say in the note to her mother and father, for they had been everything to her when she had been little. And she loved them, she was sure she loved them both, her mother had always wanted what was best for her even if it meant working and worrying more, and her father too, except that he was hardly ever home, it seemed.

It was a kind note but she signed it *with love, always*, as if she might not ever come back.

She wanted a larger life, and when you were nineteen they couldn't refuse to sell you a train ticket. She would take the train to St. Paul—not the Winnipeg Limited with its sleeping cars and its club car, it would be important to spend what money she had carefully. Instead she took the daytime run of the Northern Pacific, and then in St. Paul it was dusk and everything was confusion and shouting and the hissing of steam but a man showed her where to change to the Empire Builder, the fast train from Seattle, she could ride it overnight, you could adjust the back of your seat to make it more comfortable, it was as fine a train as you'd find anywhere, the man said, and that was how she came to Chicago. She was dozing as they came into the city but then suddenly everyone was moving and a nice woman helped her with her bags and then she was in the Great Hall, you could hardly see how high it was. This was the Union Station everyone who had ever been to Chicago always talked about, whether they came from Winnipeg or from anywhere they would talk about it; they always said how much larger and grander it was than the Union Station in Winnipeg where Kathleen had been only yesterday, and now it was a new life.

But where would she go from here? There were too many people to ask anyone about anything, and all of them were moving. Outside it was morning but there was fog everywhere, swirling, you couldn't tell where anything was. She followed a street called Canal and then Canal came to Lake but there was no lake there was a river, oh, there were two rivers, she had to stop, her arms were aching from the weight of the suitcases and Kathleen just stood in a vacant lot leading down to the river beside a drawbridge, and she looked across the river, and the fog began to lift and suddenly there it all was. All the world, wide and tall. The buildings kept rising higher and higher, and they were everywhere, and everywhere was moving, all the tall shapes shifting in and out of the gray, the swirling clouds and fog. Kathleen's arms and legs were stiff but her heart leapt up, she could hardly think as she fumbled for the little child's paint box in the old suitcase from the Eaton's department store. Suddenly it felt as if all life was in these buildings, was in this sky; her thoughts scattered and soared as she started madly to sketch. A light rain started to fall and to wet the paper more than she ever would have thought of doing on her own. And gray on gray, blue on gray flowed into one another, the colors soft and bright and deep. All life was there, and death was there too. Kathleen had just arrived, she had not even found a place to sleep, but it was morning, it was Chicago, it was a new world.

By nightfall she had found some hostel—it was the other way from the railway station, she'd had to retrace her steps with those heavy bags. And then almost at once she fell in with a group of artists; it had nothing to do with whatever had happened to her with that little box of paints by the river, it was the purest chance, really. The only soul she knew in Chicago was a cousin of a classmate in Winnipeg; Kathleen had confided in the classmate and the classmate had pressed the address into her hand—*here*, she said, *you must look up Anneke*. And so on her second day in Chicago Kathleen looked up Anneke, and Anneke knew someone who knew someone who was looking for a roommate, and on her second night in Chicago Kathleen was sharing with Anneke's friend's friend Maya, living in a tiny flat on Elm Street in a not-so-fashionable part of the Near North Side. That was what they called the larger neighborhood but there were a lot of little neighborhoods within it, there was a wide strip near the lake that people called the Gold Coast, a rich man called Potter Palmer had built his fancy Palmer House hotel downtown and then built a mansion for a home on the Near North Side, and after that they had begun to call that part of the Near North Side the Gold Coast and it became only for rich people and their many servants, but then there was Smokey Hollow with the warehouses and the factories by the river and the canal, and there was Little Sicily and there was Old Town and there were houses that had once been grand and now were rooming houses and there was row housing worse than anything in Winnipeg and there was a funny-looking tower they called the Water Tower, and the area round there was called Towertown and Anneke had said you could find a lot of artists there, from there right on over to Washington Square, and west of there you'd find Irish and Italians and people from Africa except they weren't from Africa that was where their great-great grandparents had lived before they had been taken away and made to work as slaves, Kathleen had learned all about American history in school, and a little bit of it was her history too.

Anneke didn't have much time for the bohemian crowd and neither did Maya, but Anneke's brother Pieter didn't have time for anything else; he was one of the artists who spent a lot of time around the Water Tower or in Washington Square. Pieter introduced Kathleen to Giorgio and to Giorgio's lover and to their ever-changing group of friends. It seemed that all of them were artists, and of course Kathleen became swept up in it all. Giorgio and Claude had rented a vast space in an abandoned warehouse off Kingsbury near the North Branch Canal—at least "rented" was what they said, though Kathleen once heard that there never was any rent money changing hands, the place was just abandoned and Giorgio and Claude had started using it. It was hard to know what was true. "Our studio" is what they called it but it was just one big empty floor, really, and it was six stories up, you had to walk up twelve long flights of stairs to reach it; *Higher Ground*, that was the other thing they called it, Kenneth especially, though Pieter and a couple of others thought they should call it *Common Ground* instead. Thought they should emphasize what they all had in common, not that anyone was higher than anyone else. But you could see how Jacob would look at Pieter when he said something like that, as if he thought Pieter were naïve, as if he thought there'd always be some folks thinking they were higher than other folks.

At one point there must have been a couple of dozen of them sharing that space. Some needed space just to show they were artists, to be able to say they had a studio. But eight or ten regulars would be there every day, dawn to dusk and often much later than that, it didn't matter if it were baking hot or freezing cold—weekdays, weekends, it didn't matter. Some of them more or less lived there. Everyone pretended that nobody lived there, of course, because nobody was allowed to; if you brought a mattress it had to be for something else besides sleeping—so models wouldn't get sore elbows or knees, or so you could rest for half an hour in the afternoons. Officially, no one ever stayed overnight.

There were Pieter and Giorgio and Alice and Claude. And Garrison and Grant, who often seemed to have nowhere else to live. Giorgio was called the soft G; he was from an Italian family, of course, but he had no mother and his working-class father who lived only a few blocks away would never speak to him because of the art and also because of Giorgio's lover, Patrick, who would never say much but would stretch in graceful ways and would model for anyone, even if they couldn't pay anything. And Judith, and Judith's lover Leslie—that was more a boy's name then. But Judith.... No, there is no reason to tell you about their private lives.

And Aaron and Jacob, who were fast friends though there was a lot that was different about them. Aaron's family had moved to Brooklyn only a few years before. From Germany—they had gotten out just in time. But none of Aaron's friends had gotten out; it was hard for him to talk of them. As soon as Aaron had finished high school he had taken a train to Chicago. So Kathleen and Aaron had something in common, even though Winnipeg was so different from Brooklyn. Or Berlin. Aaron said you wouldn't want anywhere to be like Berlin—not now, not in 1938. And Aaron said that one day soon he might take another train all the way to the coast and later that year he did, right after it was in the news about Kiristallnacht, and years later Kathleen heard he was still drifting about, somewhere down near San Diego.

Jacob had come north to St. Louis from Barbados when he was a child. His parents still said they didn't feel real comfortable in Chicago 'cause they *hadn't* just arrived from Alabama or Mississippi or Louisiana and they didn't talk like they had ever come from any of those places, they were from a place more like England, really. But Jacob said he was comfortable anywhere and he had started to make paintings that told stories, stories of sharecropper families leaving Alabama and Mississippi and Louisiana and coming to the north, to Chicago especially. It was Jacob who would sometimes say on a Saturday, "Come on, let's go South today" and they would take the L down to 47th Street and stroll the shops and buy their socks and underwear cheap at the South Side Department Store and maybe take in an American Giants game or maybe go to the Savoy Ballroom where the music never stopped; just as one band would take a break another band would come on, you could see Earl Hines or Louis Armstrong or Duke Ellington and Kathleen couldn't see why it was all right for anyone to go to Schorling's Park on 39th (now it's Pershing, but back then it was still 39th) to see the Giants play or to go to the Savoy to see Earl Hines play but with a lot of the places on the North Side it was as if there was a sign that said *whites only*. The law said anyone could go anywhere but that wasn't what it was really like. You could tell what it was really like underneath without anyone having to tell you about the race riot back in '19. Some black men had been swimming at the 29th Street beach that white folk said was for whites only, and a white man had started throwing rocks at the black men and he had killed one of them, hit him right in the head and killed him. And when the police came they arrested one of the black men for causing a disturbance. That had been not even twenty years earlier, *not a lot has changed* you could hear people say, you could hear people say that all the time. Even in the poor parts of the near North Side, where there were lots of people of any color you could think of, there were a lot of places where it felt like there was a sign saying *whites only*,

It didn't feel like Winnipeg. Just about everyone in Winnipeg except maybe Kathleen had been pinky white or browny white and Kathleen had been told when she had been little about her father's father and her father's mother being different colors but mainly Kathleen had always thought of everyone as not having a color, really, just as she had always thought of vanilla as not being a flavor, really. It was just plain, it was neutral, though of course you knew if you thought about it that sometimes what they called vanilla was pretty close to white and other times it was more like beige. And now when she thought of it she could see that the *actual* color of vanilla could be dark as anything, like vanilla extract. Maybe what she had really been assuming was that everyone would always treat her the same as anyone else, which was to say treat her as if she were white.

Here in Chicago Kathleen found that a lot of the time it was still like that, a lot of white people would treat her as if she were just like them, but sometimes people would look at her long and hard and you could tell they were asking *what sort of white is that?*, or *what sort of colored is that?* and sometimes they would treat her as *not-quite-colored-but-not-quite-white*. "You sure you're 'lowed to be in here?" a woman once said to her in a Ladies Room that was one of the places that felt as if there were a *whites only* sign. And in different parts of town people would sometimes treat her as *not-exactly-black-but-black-enough-to-be-in-the-neighborhood*. "You're so white you could almost pass," a woman said to her once when they were watching the American Giants play the Kansas City Monarchs. All she could think of to say was "I'm from Winnipeg," and the woman had looked at her strangely.

They had gone to the Kansas City game specially, not only because Kansas City were the best—Jacob and Pieter would talk about how the '38 Monarchs had Hilton Smith and his curveball and Willard Brown and his big bat and his speed, right through the order they were good, so good that Satchel Paige couldn't even make the team until late in the year—but also because Gwendolyn was from Kansas City, Gwendolyn who lived on the South Side but who would come round to the studio sometimes to see Jacob and to see the others as well. She had a wide smile and everyone loved her except that Kenneth would laugh at her behind her back for making up poems that rhymed, and for believing in God. When Gwendolyn had mentioned one time that she had written some poems, it was Kenneth who had asked her to read some of them and she had begun "I think it must be lonely to be God."

Just about everyone who hung around Higher Ground was the sort who would never shy away from thinking strong thoughts, or from saying them, telling a person to his face that he didn't know nothing—that was the way Jacob or Giorgio might have put it. But then Gwendolyn would say *anything*, and that two wrongs didn't make a right. She was a schoolteacher's daughter and grammar mattered to her in a way that it never did to Kathleen back then. But Gwendolyn cared about other sorts of right and wrong too; she told Kathleen what it was like to go to a school where only one color of person was allowed. And she told Kathleen what it was like to live in Bronzeville, as they were calling it now, and how Gwendolyn's parents were trying to buy a place there, it was the sort of neighborhood they thought they could afford and they liked all the life in it, *it feels like a tall time*, her father would say when her parents were about to step out of a Saturday night. But the government had drawn red lines on a map around the areas they said would be undesirable for the banks to be lending in, and Bronzeville was one of them. It just happened that all the areas where black folk lived were among the areas that had red lines around them, and in practice you couldn't live anywhere else if you weren't white. Gwendolyn told Kathleen about that too, how all the housing in the white areas would be sold with a covenant attached saying that the buyer couldn't sell to anyone who wasn't white.

"Not to no Jews, neither," put in Aaron.

"*Any*," said Kenneth, just as Gwendolyn was about the say the same thing. "*Any* Jews."

Gwendolyn thought Kenneth wanted to be right before anyone else, and more right than anyone, but that was something she didn't say. Kathleen told herself that she didn't know what to think about Kenneth. And then she started to think of him as a special category. How could she *not* be attracted to him? Years later she would let her voice take on an ironic cast and say he was everything young girls from Winnipeg (or Omaha, or Bloomington) thought an artist should be. He was temperamental. His hair was dark and unkempt. He was unsmiling, even a little surly. His clothes were often dirty (but he did not smell). And he painted with real flair. Badly, but with real flair. He was moody, he was often depressed. He was thin, almost wispy. When he was there he was intensely there—but you could never tell if he would be there or not. You might not see him for days at a time and then he would be there working twenty-four hours straight, never saying a word, not even to Kathleen, making dark colors, squaring things off, making paintings.

Was it inevitable after that afternoon in the Jewelers' Building that they would go to bed together? No. Nothing about love or about desire is inevitable. They were drawn to each other; for a while that was all. He would look at her and hum the Chick Webb tune that was everywhere, *I betcha a nickel—I bet you I win, I betcha a nickel that you will give in*, and she would look as if she didn't know what to think, but that she didn't mind it, didn't mind it at all. And they started to draw each other; they would take turns trying to make each other's angular faces perfect in the angled light. It was a south light, and sudden shafts of it kept coming and going with the clouds and the wind.

They took turns less often when it came to talking. Kenneth would sound off about art or jazz or baseball or politics, and Kathleen would feel the warmth of it and not mind having her words crowded out. For Kenneth, she quickly lost her name; he wouldn't call her *Kathleen*, as she said she wanted, and as everyone else did; to him she quickly became *Kip*. It was unlike any word she knew, and she soon decided she liked it. Where had it come from? He wouldn't say. But he told her once that she reminded him of the boy in the Kipling novel—*Kim*, *Kip*, perhaps that was it. She found herself sometimes rolling it about on her lips, on the edges of her lips, and sometimes she would breathe *Kenneth* and *Kip* to herself, just lightly, the words never touching more than her lips.

"People say knowledge is power, Kip, but that's not true. Imagination is power. Knowledge looks to the past; imagination looks to the future. Imagination takes hold of the future. You have to have imagination if you're going to soar above everything and anyone—anyone now, anyone who has ever gone before." She loved it when he talked like that, filled with passion and a little crazy.

She smiled.

Kenneth saw that Kip was looking at him a little oddly, as if she were amused, as if she didn't believe what he was saying. Perhaps she didn't fully understand. "All the great artists have understood what I'm saying. From Michelangelo to Picasso—all of them. And the great writers too. Shakespeare, Milton, Nietzsche—they understood. Pound, Eliot…"

"George Eliot?" She smiled at him, innocently. He couldn't help raising his eyebrows. Did she truly not know about T.S. Eliot? Did she think this was some sort of joke? He felt not for her hand but for her wrist, and his fingers wrapped around her. She felt him turning her; maybe she shouldn't have said that about Eliot. She checked herself; she was bemused but she loved it when he warmed to a topic like this. And somehow it made her warm to him, even if she didn't agree with what he said, even if she didn't agree with any of it, even if she knew it was all wrong. If you had passion, did it matter if you were wrong about something? Could it be wrong, if you gave yourself to what you believed? If you gave yourself to art? Did it matter how ideas might get twisted up, how love might get twisted up, one strand twisted again and again into others, like a rope, all the strands imagined, imagining, art, power, and.... And he would twist a little again, until they faced each other. She had to look into his eyes; it was as if anything could happen. But this was the middle of the day, and everyone was about, Giorgio, Pieter, Gwendolyn. Nothing could happen.

He would quiver as he spoke. "Ashcan School!" he would rail. "I can't stand it when people go on about the Ashcan School as if it were anything important. Those painters had nothing to say. Nothing. And if one time by some freak chance they found something to say, they said it badly." On the topic of American realism in the first 38 years of the twentieth century Kenneth could go on for hours. Often he did just that. John Steuart Curry? *Cartoons; his paintings are nothing but cartoons.* Thomas Hart Benton? *What the people in his paintings do is a grotesque parody of motion.* Grant Wood? *He's a pansy; you can see it in everything he does.*

"What does it matter who he goes to bed with, Kenneth; you don't mind when Giorgio and Patrick..."

"No one's claiming Giorgio is one of the greatest American painters of the century. Are they?"

"What about John Sloan, then? John Sloan is someone who..."

"That's who Norman Rockwell would be if Rockwell were pretending to be a socialist."

"But you think there's something important in socialism. I know you do. All of us do," she added. Kenneth shook his head. "Change is too important to be in the hands of someone like that. Real change. Real change means real change in art, too. We need to show something real—but we can't be ceding all abstraction to the fascists. You can't just copy, and you can't make everything cartoonish. You have to *do* something to it. Paintings can't just be bad photographs."

But what, specifically, would Kenneth do to the world? That was where he fell silent. He would tell Kathleen that everything he was showing her now—everything he was doing now, everything he had done so far in his life—was just preparation for the great work to come. It was too early to speak of it; she would see. *It's not a lot—I tear up anything I don't see greatness in. True greatness.*

What he showed her now were a few small pictures. Rectangles, squared-off heads, squared-off trees, squared-off blocks of color that might have been buildings. "It's not cubism," he said strenuously. "It's building a foundation for something that will go far beyond that."

How can you know about a person? How could Kathleen know what he might or might not be able to paint? Might or might not be able to build? All she could see and hear and feel was a person who needed help more than he knew, who needed love more than he knew. Who did not know he needed either.

He almost always had a flask in his pocket, and he was almost never completely sober. He would pull out the thin square of tin, twist off the top, gulp down a pull or two of whatever was inside, and then the flask would be back in his pocket; no more than two or three seconds would have elapsed. He was not trying to be blatant, but he was not trying to hide anything, either. Sometimes he seemed to have no more awareness of what he had just done than a person has of having scratched himself, once the itch has gone.

"What is it?" Kathleen would ask.

"What?"

"What you drink?

"Drink. That's what it is. Drink." Once he let her sip it—he almost *made* her sip it—and still she was not sure what it was, though she felt how it burned.

It changed him less than you might think. Even in the late evening he could keep his mind engaged, his consonants almost crisp. It was the emotions that he couldn't control. His lust—could you call that an emotion? And his anger.

"They'll have to like it," he would sometimes say of a painting he was working on. "I'll make them like it." But he could never make them like it *enough*—and that made him fiercer, hungrier, emptier. Kathleen told herself she could help. Help make him less angry, help make him sober, help make him happier, gentler, more whole. Better. And the thought of helping him, of taming him, filled her with excitement. She found herself shivering as he spoke.

He liked it when he saw her do that. He wanted to feel her shiver. And to put her straight about art, about life. About him. She wasn't like some women—like *most* women, when you came to think about it. Kathleen was capable of learning. She could *listen*—truly listen.

And she could paint. You had to admit it, she could paint. Not the way a great painter can paint, but in a way that required real cleverness—a way that could appeal to a lot of people. What if a serious artist were to paint the way she painted—even if he were to do it only for a brief while, as a sideline to his real work, even if he were to paint only a few works in something like that style? Letting the fruit and the flowers bleed like that, just enough to make them seem soft, to make them ripe.... You could do that to the sky as well—Kenneth could see how you might do that to the sky. It might make a lot of people sit up and take notice. Some of those might be people who would never see the truth, who could never appreciate real art. But mightn't there also be a few who would have their attention captured by the cleverness, by the lively dross, and would then look a little deeper? Who would then, at long last, see the strength in his more serious work, be ready to appreciate his truly great work, just at the moment when he would be ready to create it.

See the strength in the more serious work of a real painter, is what he meant. *Any* real painter.

Why should the two of them not share? Why should he not have her?

Talking was an investment, Kenneth often thought. It took time that he could have invested elsewhere. Doing great things.

Making great things. But talk was what a woman wanted. Oh sure, talking could be interesting to a man as well; talking to Kip interested Kenneth, he admitted that readily enough. But with a woman it was more than interest; talk was what they lived for, more or less. And if you talked to a woman hour after hour, if you made that sort of investment, it was fair to think of getting some sort of return. Kenneth wanted that sort of return. He wanted Kip.

# Five

2011

It was two weeks before Robin tried calling on Granny again. Of course there were a lot of things to keep you busy, with school and everything. Or that *should* have been keeping you busy. It had used to be that Robin would always do the assigned homework. All the math, even, though the math was mostly stupid and boring. Would always do all the extra things too—and the extra things had always felt special, you could choose your own topic to write about and it would be specially yours. It had been like that right from the start, before Hope had been born, even, long before Robin had started at Ogden. But this year was different. It sometimes just didn't feel like any of it was worth it. Like any of it mattered.

Sometimes it could be hard to make the hard knot inside you go away. This year it had been harder. And Robin had been starting to have the dream again, the same dream, the dream about somebody killing their little sister. It had happened this past Sunday night, and again on Tuesday night; it felt like it would keep happening.

Was the time with Granny on the 86th floor one of those things that could keep happening? Or could it happen only once? Robin wanted to find out, but was also scared of finding out. Scared of what was strange, maybe. Scared of anything to do with—no, Robin was not afraid of death. But could it all have been imagined? Could Robin have just been daydreaming? Granny had given Robin that seashell, and Robin had put it away in a pocket, and it was still there now, you could feel it right here...— no, it wasn't there. Robin must have taken it out and must have put it beside the bed; was that it? No, not there either... Well maybe it was on the dresser, or it had fallen in behind something. It had to be *somewhere*.

Nothing seemed quite clear—about Kathy Snyder, about Granny, about anything.

And it was getting harder to talk to Ms. McLenithan. That was partly because Robin wasn't doing all the homework any more, of course. They had had a talk about that the week before last. Ms. McLenithan had said she understood that sometimes it could be hard to do things, even when you knew they had to be done. And Robin had nodded and said all the things you felt should be said at a time like that, all the things you *wanted* to say and that you really *meant*, too. But somehow even after that Robin hadn't been doing a lot of what had been assigned; there had been three math assignments since then, or maybe four. How many had Robin handed in? Two?

But it wasn't just about the homework. It was also that Robin had made another of those stupid mistakes. It had been after school; Robin had volunteered to stay to help with the big History project. At first there had been six or seven of them but by 5 o'clock everyone else had left and it had been just Robin and Ms. McLenithan, and Ms. McLenithan had said that maybe Robin shouldn't be part of a big group thing like this History project if Robin couldn't find time to do the regular work, and Robin hadn't answered and Ms. McLenithan had said, "Anyway, you should probably head off now too, it's starting to get late," and Robin had said, "that's all right, Mother, I'm happy to stay and help out a bit more if there's more to do." Ms. McLenithan had pretended not to notice, she had just said *no, there's no need to stay*, but she must have noticed—did she even look a little annoyed?—and ever since then Robin had felt a little odd in class, a little out of place.

*It will be all right*—that was what people always kept telling themselves when they made mistakes, and Robin kept repeating it too. It wasn't as if there had been anything behind it. Just a silly slip was all.

Robin thought of Carol and Carl and then of Granny, and began to walk a little bit more quickly. Sometimes when you had decided you knew where you were going there wasn't any sense in dawdling. But not *too* quickly, you didn't want to be walking too quickly when you passed the concierge and the security guard. So Robin just kept up a brisk pace, eyes front, across the wide lobby and right past them both and round the corner to the elevators.

This time it was busier. Robin had to pretend to be studying the directory while one elevator headed upwards filled with people. And then a second, a third. Then, just a moment later, a fourth elevator opened and emptied. A quick glance around; now there was no one. In Robin went. Fingers quickly pressed the edges of the console, anxiously feeling for... —for what? Robin did not know what had happened the first time. What did you have to do to make the elevator go to all the floors above the 80th floor? And then somehow Robin must have found it, touched it. The buttons showed 80-109, and there it was, 86, and then quickly *Door Close*, and then up and up, gathering speed, higher and higher. It was just as it had been the first time—the doors opening and the empty hall on the 86th floor. And just as she had been the first time, Granny was there to open the door.

"Come in, Robin. I somehow thought you might drop by today. And I hoped you would," she added, with a small smile. She started forward as if to hug the child but then thought better of it; she held a tumbler of the clear liquid in one hand.

"Are you well, Granny?"

"Today I feel like an amputee. I feel a dull ache everywhere, and there are parts of me that seem completely missing; even those seem to ache."

Robin didn't want to talk about how you could still ache in parts that were missing. "I had a kink in my leg from Tuesday, but it went away," was what Robin finally said. They walked together to the balcony, and stood again above the floating world.

"Is that clouds out there, or fog? I suppose it amounts to the same thing."

"It *is* the same thing, Granny. Fog is just clouds on the ground."

"Or clouds without shape." K.P. paused for a moment. When Robin had been truly a child, K.P. would have started now to play. She could hear herself: "Let's call them *flouds*, we are lost in the *flouds*," she would have said, and she could still hear the delighted squeal that would have come from the little one. K.P. tried to imagine the polite little smile she would get now if she tried the same sort of play—it would be like the *mumbly hums*. And yet Robin *did* like words, and the sounds of words. It was so hard to know other people's minds.

Life as a diplomat's wife hadn't helped. All those years away from Chicago, the times in New York, London, Ottawa, all those years with Arthur. People always thought diplomatic training helped make you more sensitive to others—not in the least. It dinned in politeness, but politeness as a matter of form, not as a matter of feeling. You and all the people you were paid to meet—everyone trained to hide their feelings under layer upon layer of formality. She had changed, that much was sure. She had learned to talk differently, to move differently, in so many ways to become a different person, a diplomatic wife. She stopped herself. Diplomatic *spouse*, you had to say now, diplomatic *spouse*; there had been Albright and then there had been Rice and now there was Clinton. It was a new world.

"*Diplomatic wives*, Granny?"

Had she said that out loud? Surely not. She couldn't understand how...—No matter. Pretend, pretend, that was the thing. "Why yes. Arthur was a diplomat, you know, so that made me a diplomat's wife. *The diplomatic wives*, that's what we called ourselves. And even the wives received a diplomat's training, or a good deal of it, at any rate. It made me into a different person, I often think, being the wife of....—did you know that Arthur was an ambassador? No, why should you have known? I can tell you about it, if you like."

"You were telling me last time about Kenneth Paul. You could tell me more about that. About when you first came to Chicago. From Canada."

"Perhaps I will tell you more of the story of Kenneth Paul in a moment. It is also part of my story, of course. You know I'm a Canadian still, don't you? A Canadian to this day."

"And an American too. Carl told me that."

K.P. paused for a few moments, and the level of the clear liquid in the large tumbler went down quite a lot. "Carl. Yes. My grandson, your father. Children need to be told about where they have come from." Again she paused; this time the clear liquid was untouched. "But you should take everything I say with a grain of salt. Everyone my age thinks everyone else has taken the wrong approach to bringing up their own children. It means nothing in the end."

"So you don't think Mother and Father did a good job bringing me up? Bringing up Hope and me?"

"I do, Robin, I do. For the most part. For the most part I think they have done…"—K.P. let it trail off. But we all have to bring ourselves up a good deal, don't we? I can remember when I was a child. So many years have gone by. Perhaps… It's so hard to know… I remember hearing that…"

K.P. started to tell a little story of Winnipeg, and that led to another little story, and another.

All old people talk like this sometimes; Robin knew this. What you had to do was just wait and let them go on. But you could think of different things while that was happening. Robin thought of how Kathy Snyder had walked by with sort of a half-smile on her face as she had been leaving science class. Half? It was hard to be sure with fractions.

And then Robin looked about on Granny's balcony, and thought of other balconies and of how it was not always so easy to be out on a balcony, how sometimes people were afraid to look down, afraid to be out on a balcony at all, and thought of little

Hope, and of how Robin should never have said *let's go out on the balcony*. It hadn't been just that once, either. When Carol and Carl had been busy in the kitchen or doing what they did on Saturday mornings, when they would go back into the bedroom after breakfast and close the door and Robin and Hope had been allowed to watch TV, instead they had sometimes liked to go out on the balcony and watch the world. Robin had taught Hope how to make paper airplanes and watch them fly off into anywhere. But then Robin had made up stories about how it wasn't just anywhere, and they had made planes fly to New York, to Moscow and to Moose Jaw, to Shanghai and to Goodbye, *let's fly to Goodbye*, had Hope said that? Almost anywhere but not to wherever Granny was talking about, how long had she been talking?

"Granny, do you think there is a god?"

"What I think, Robin, is that we need to learn on our own how to be good. We mustn't be scared into someone else's good by believing in some extraterrestrial being."

"Jesus wasn't an extraterrestrial. Mohammed wasn't an extraterrestrial."

"But nor were they gods."

There was a long silence.

"Have you heard what else they are saying about the skyscrapers?"

"Who is saying? Do you want me to tell you more? I will tell you about the skyscrapers in Brazil."

"In Chicago, Granny. What they are saying about the skyscrapers in Chicago. That they could fall. My mom and dad were, like, there could be an earthquake."

"You mean your father and mother *said* there could be an earthquake. But they are wrong: Robin, earthquakes are what happen in California." She paused and considered. "Almost anything can always happen almost anywhere. I grant you that. There are so many things that could always happen. I will tell you a story of the skyscrapers in Brazil."

"*Brazil*? But Granny, if…"

"Soon after Arthur and I arrived in Rio de Janeiro there was a report about an engineering professor who had inspected a ten-story office building. Fissures had been reported—cracks running right through from one story to another. The tenants were moving out *en masse*. The engineer had been called, I suspect, not so much to assess the risks honestly as to reassure everyone that all was well. He duly pronounced exactly that, after some hours of poking about. I want to believe that he believed it, that he wanted everyone to be happy. That he had not simply been paid off, that he was not…"

"And what happened, Granny?"

"A great many people had moved out already. One family was moving out even as the professor was looking around. But there were five families who had stayed on after he had left, after he had inspected the place and declared it safe, completely safe. Six hours later it collapsed. The whole thing fell in on itself, collapsed into rubble and dust."

"And the families? Were the people…?"

"Yes. All dead. Twenty-one people, twenty-two, no one was quite sure, it seemed. And it was not the only case like that. In the first few months Arthur and I were in Brazil there must have been five or six other skyscrapers collapse. I remember a newspaper predicting at least twenty more in Rio alone.

"The strange thing was how people reacted to all this. There was so little outrage. Of course there was talk of toughening up the building code—and a good deal of talk of toughening up on the enforcement side of things. Was any of it more than talk? I don't remember. But I remember that there seemed to be no outrage, no righteous anger, as we would call it. I remember at some diplomatic gathering speaking to a lawyer about this. He could see my dismay.

"'Why do you expect a beautiful thing to last?' he asked, speaking of that skyscraper. 'Do you ask a flower to live forever?' He spoke gently, but he shocked me to the bone. I did not yet know Brazil. I did not yet know their…"

"Granny, do you know if *this* skyscraper could fall?" Robin looked round at the walls of the apartment.

"This is the United States of America. Unless people fly planes into them, skyscrapers do not fall. Even during an earthquake. Even in California. Though California is surely different in…"

"It has faults, Granny."

"Even in the mid-west we have our faults, Robin."

"That's what I'm saying, Granny. There is a fault that…"

"But our faults are less obvious than those of California. And Brazil—we were speaking of Brazil…."

"*You* were speaking of Brazil, Granny."

"You were keeping your end up perfectly well. The listening end."

All right, Granny. I will listen. Brazil. And now you will tell me what their…"

"Carelessness. That is their fault. If there is any danger they…"

"*You* won't be careless, will you, Granny? If there are warnings, you will leave, won't you, Granny? You won't be like those families? Staying when it isn't safe?"

"It will always be safe here, child. And even if some disaster did happen—at my age it's best to take my chances. One cannot live forever, child. But none of this is going to happen. Really, it is not."

"But if it did, Granny? If it did, please say you'd leave if it happened. I will come and get you."

"If it matters so much to you."

"Thank you, Granny." There was silence for a moment. "You were going to tell me more about…"

"My painting. So I was." K.P. paused for a moment. None of this would be what the child expected to hear. But children have to learn that nothing in life is likely to be as you expect. "The thing I can't understand—the thing I can hardly forgive myself for—is how long I worked, with so little purpose."

"On your paintings? You painted the sky, Granny. And you painted all the tall buildings scraping it. That's a purpose. You said you did. And that's why…"

"I said I did it *once*. That one large picture. The one that won the prize. The picture that broke all the rules."

"What rules, Granny? And what prize?"

"The rules of balance and proportion, to start with. In those days you were still told that a picture should have certain proportions. *A painting should be balanced like a work of art—not like a set of scales*—I can still hear my art teacher at school saying that. You weren't to put the horizon exactly half way up a picture—and you weren't supposed to put strong vertical lines exactly halfway across; you shouldn't break a picture in two, we were told. But this one large picture had its strongest lines swirling upward, dead center, right smack in the middle of the painting."

"You broke it in two."

"I broke the painting in two, and I broke other rules too. Nothing was straight—that was going against a sort of rule as well. If you painted cities in the 1930s you were supposed to use hard lines. Hard and straight. I didn't want any of that."

"What was it a picture *of*, Granny?"

"I did it from that first sketch I had made by the river; it was a picture of the clouds and the fog and the skyscrapers. I didn't know what I would do when I worked it up into a large piece, how I would…. I just felt in my bones that I would be breaking the rules. And I didn't want anyone watching me. So I waited until everyone had gone before I began; it must have been very late. I had two bright lamps; I could work all night if I wanted. I pencilled in places for a few of the towers, but nothing more than lightly. And then I began to work with a wash, a huge wash. I drowned the whole vast sheet, crumpled it under the tap until it was sopping. And then I let great gobs of color spin across all the wet of it, spin and sink and swirl into sky and water. I splashed on more water, more paint; there were feverish bursts as I threw paint about in the half light. The buildings took shape. I took shape and lost it, and found it again in new ways. I threw everything onto the paper, and the water somehow worked with me, the colors made themselves into..." She stopped for a moment. "In the end I didn't know what had happened. I felt as if it had been something I had no control over. I think I must have felt that losing control was something I wanted, deep down. But that was not what you were supposed to do. Not if you painted in watercolors. And definitely not if you wore a skirt."

"You could have worn pants, Granny."

"*Slacks*, Robin. In those days women wore slacks. And no, you could not wear slacks all the time and still—it would take too long to explain everything. All that matters is to know that I lost my nerve. One great picture, and I started to live in fear. I began to paint still-life. Tried to fill oranges with some sort of energy. Grapes."

"To make them move?"

K.P. glanced sideways at Robin; surely the child was not trying to make fun of her.

"I never *actually* made them move. That at least would have been something different. Not-so-still life of bouncing grape. Study of rolling orange, unstill. There might have been different prizes to be won for that sort of thing."

"You haven't told me how your picture won a prize, Granny."

"I am getting there, child. I am getting there. We tell stories differently, you and I. Sometimes it takes me a long time to get going. To get to the point. Points." K.P. reached for her drink, and thought for a moment without speaking. "I was not going to tell you this, but I think perhaps you are old enough to be told things."

"Is it about love, Granny? And making love? It's about Kenneth and you, isn't it?"

"And about the picture. Yes." She began to tell Robin more of what had happened in 1938.

ॐ ॐ ॐ

"I decided that I wouldn't be able to afford to make art my whole life. That Aunt Ella's two thousand dollars would be gone too soon. And also, I suppose, that I didn't want to be spending all my time with artists. After—what was it? one week? two weeks?—I got a job. I told myself any job would do, but any job has to be *some* job, and jobs were so very, very hard to get in 1938. Even bad jobs: I was very lucky. I got to wait tables and wash up at the St. Regis lunch counter. Corner of Grand and State. People would always be joking about that, *it ain't grand and it ain't stately*, they'd say, a *Jap lunch*, people would call it, we used some awful expressions back then. It wasn't even Japanese folk who went there, it was Filipinos, they were new to Chicago and no one knew what they were, who they were. They'd point at the menu, you couldn't understand them, but it didn't really matter. I couldn't understand the other waitresses either, they were all from the back of beyond, most of them from a little town that had been called *Miner's City* but then someone had changed its name to *War*, it was somewhere in the mountains of West Virginia. It was a strange way those women had with words—strange to me, at any rate. But they'd all been around the St Regis a while; it was always the new girl who'd have to help the boy in the back with the washing up, and the new girl was me, so…"

"You and Kenneth, Granny. You were going to…"

"I *am* going to. I am getting there. Kenneth. I can still hear the radio playing that Ella Fitzgerald tune. I used to sing along, under my breath. *He's just a gem in the rough, but when I polish him up…*"

It wasn't clear where the song fit in with everything else, but Robin knew that old people's minds sometimes worked like that. Robin kept listening. Granny kept going.

"The St. Regis didn't do dinners, so I would be done at four, and after work I'd go to the studio. I'd hardly ever go straight back to that little apartment, some nights I didn't get back there until ten, eleven at night. But even by 4:30, 5:00, when I'd get to the studio, things would often be starting to thin out. People would be heading home, people would be drifting off to the park or they'd be going for a beer. Some nights it was only Kenneth and me. And if he saw it was only the two of us you could be sure he would make a pass at me. That was what we said then, *made a pass*, as if the man were passing close to you and no more than that. No more."

# Six

*1938*

The first night they had tried to make love was like any other night. Kenneth and Kathleen were both at the studio late and they had started talking. He started to say a few things; she made it plain that nothing was going to happen. That was what women did in 1938. And they moved on to other things. Serious things. Art, mostly. Kenneth talked, mostly. Kathleen listened. She told herself that she liked the strong lines in his work. And she told herself that, if anyone was going to like her own work, it would be Kenneth. She told herself she would stay quiet and let him say whatever he…. And yet the next moment—

He stopped sounding off about the colors Sheeler used. "You know I need you, don't you?"

"I know you *have* needs, Kenneth. We all do. But we can satisfy our needs ourselves if we can't get others to satisfy them." She could hardly believe she had said that. Oddly, she remembered her mother had said the same thing to her—but which of the possible meanings had been meant? Which of them did she mean now? Why did she find it exciting to spar with this man?

"No. I really do need you. Or…" he thought about it seriously, "I need someone *like* you. Someone with less ambition than I have. But with strength. Someone who can…"

"And what do I get out of the bargain? Or what would someone *like* me get?"

It was obvious that the question had not occurred to him; it was several moments before he thought of an answer. He would have to try to be faster on the uptake, he knew that. "You get something from me when we talk. You know you do." Kathleen blushed. "And you could get something more if we did more than talk. But neither of us can find out how much. Not if all we do is talk," he finally added.

He was so awkward, so clumsy. He didn't have any idea of what to do with his large hands. But that was part of what Kathleen liked about him—everything that he didn't know how to do. Could she teach him? Teach him about how to hold someone else, how to care for someone else? Things she only half guessed at herself? She could be learning at the same time. Could anyone teach anyone else any of that? Yes! Kathleen wanted so much to think yes. How could you not think yes?

She got up in a moment to make herself a cup of tea, and as she passed him she let the fingers of her left hand trail against him for a moment. And then he said something, nothing, she could hardly make out the words. She turned, and their lips were breathing into each other, and then they were kissing, they were once more as they had been in the Jewelers' Building, *how could you say no to everything?* and this time they did not stop, it almost seemed as if he would not let it stop even if she had wanted it to, but she did not want it to stop, this was something that had never happened in Winnipeg, it was a time of the month when it would be all right, oh, she knew there was always some risk but she had left Winnipeg, this was not the Childs Building, she was living life, and life had risk to it. And surprise. And joy. And love; was this love? In a moment he would be part of her and she would....

But no, he was not part of her, it was not happening, not yet, and he was groping at himself and then pushing against her but he was not inside her, something had gone wrong, *it's all right*, she whispered to him, *everything's going to be all right*, she had no idea if that were true but that was what one said, wasn't it? She said it again and again and then after a while he stopped trying, *you're tired*, she said, *and you've had a lot to drink, it doesn't matter, another time*, she would be good to him, she would be good for him, she would help it to happen, tonight was not what she had thought would happen but you could never know, to be here and to be feeling these things, it was a new world, this was living life. And next time it would be different.

ও ও ও

The next morning Kathleen found herself thinking of her parents for some reason. And wanting to write to them. Even to ring them up, but no, long distance was too expensive, and besides, that would give them a chance to pump her about what had been happening and to pressure her to come back. She would not be coming back, she knew that in the deepest part of herself, but sometimes you had to think of where you had come from as well as where you were going. And you had to think of their feelings too. How much would her mother have been worrying? Kathleen couldn't leave it at *with love always*, she could see that now. She would have to follow up with them, let them know what had become of her. For now she would not tell them where she was; if her mother got one whiff of *Chicago* or of *art studio* or (especially) of *working at a lunch counter*, she would surely be on the next train, determined to find her, to bring her home, to ruin everything.

But Kathleen had to tell them she was OK, *am I OK?* she sometimes asked herself, and always she knew *yes* was the answer. *For a while I was in St. Paul*, she found herself writing, after she had written *Dear Mum and Dad* and the other things you always began with. It was not a lie; she had been there, she had changed trains in St. Paul, and *for a while* could be any length of time, really. *I've been working a little bit and earning some money and also painting, I don't mean houses I mean paintings, you remember how I used to love doing watercolors and I still do, I think it might be what I will do with my life, especially painting cities. One day I took the train to Chicago and when I arrived I painted all the buildings downtown in swirling colors, not all of them of course but a lot of them, there's one called the Mather Building that has a tower so thin and tall you wouldn't believe it. I put that in the middle, all wet with clouds and I made it so you can feel the wind and it made me swirl as well, I don't know that I've ever felt anything like it. And now I've made the little sketch I did that day into a large picture, still a water-color but much larger, and I think I'll keep painting, I've got space in a sort-of studio here and I think for a while I'll keep...*, no, she wouldn't say anything about Higher Ground or about what she might do, they would figure out that she was living in Chicago, she crossed out that last bit and started a new paragraph, *I've been through a few places and now I'm off again. I don't want you worrying and I'm not even sure myself where I'll settle*, that was all true too, *off again* could be to anywhere, even across town. She wasn't lying, not in any of it, really, *but when I'm settled I'll write again and you can come and visit maybe, and of course some day I'll come back and visit you too.* "Visit," it was important that she add "and visit," not leave it at "I'll come back." And then she wrote a little bit about them, *I hope so much that you are both well and that everything is going well in Winnipeg, and I hope work is going well, Daddy, and Mum, that it's not too cold and you mustn't worry, really Mum*, and then she thought of writing *I miss you* but was it true? Kathleen wasn't sure it was true and so she didn't write that, because you should be honest and you shouldn't lie. She wrote *Your loving daughter*, it was true that she loved them, and she signed her name and sealed the envelope and borrowed a stamp from Pieter except she made it two stamps so it would be enough to get over the border to Canada. And then she put it in one of the post boxes except they didn't call them that here, they were called *mail boxes* in Chicago, and she guessed that was what they were called all over the United States of America.

Would she leave Chicago one day? Would she try New York? It seemed that everyone who painted said they were planning to go to New York. But Kathleen thought no, it was too early to think of anything like that. Quickly she put the letter in the box and rushed off, she would be late for the St. Regis, she would have to go back to the flat to get her uniform, yes she would have to hurry.

ঽ ঽ ঽ

"Why did you tell me about the letter, Granny? It doesn't seem as important as the rest of it."

"But so often we can't tell what is important, can we? Not until much later, and sometimes not even then."

"All the other things sound important, Granny. Can you tell me more about them?"

"Next time, child, next time. It is late now, and I think I had better ask you to leave. People say it is rude to do that, but I do not think what they say applies to anyone who is as old as I am. Is there anything else today that we should..." She paused. "Your poem!" Do you have it with you? Come, we will read your poem together."

"I forgot it, Granny. I must have left it at home." Robin felt for the wad of paper with the poem on it. Why would you say you had forgotten to bring something, when in fact you had it in your pocket all along? "There are lots of other things I'd like to talk about, Granny. But I don't have to tell you about them now. Or even next time. And you don't have to read..."

"The poem? But of course I do. You will bring it next time. Next time we will read your poem and you will do all the talking. I will listen. If you do want to ask anything, you know I will try to answer. Next time."

And that is what they decided to do. They said goodbye, and Robin went home, and K.P. went back to thinking. Not of Robin, and still less of Kenneth or the others at the Higher Ground. She thought of love, and of the air in Rio. And of the sun glinting off the beach and off the skyscrapers at the end of the day, and the air still holding so much heat that a thought is barely born before it melts.

א   א   א

Some days LeShonna thought it was hotter in South Chicago than it had been on the Near North Side. Of course they had air conditioning but it didn't always work so well, maybe it was that there was more of a breeze on the North Side, did that make sense? Sometimes she missed Ogden. She had liked Miss McLenithan and she had liked Billy Martin and she had liked Naomi Ladja and Torii Fielder and she had sort of liked Robin Smith and Kathy Snyder too. But had they liked her? She hadn't thought to write down no numbers for any of them and then her cell phone had stopped working in the rain and the phone had had all the numbers inside it and her mama and her daddy said they couldn't afford another one, not just now. But one day when she hadn't come back to school after lunch and she was out walking she had found herself thinking of all them. She had thought maybe she would walk over to the skyway or all the way to the Dan Ryan and paint a picture of the trucks flashing by on the toll road with their heavy whoosh. It was a strange thing to paint but she didn't feel like trying to get to the lake today, it felt as if that would be a foreign place somehow, wasn't that weird? She had thought all that, but then instead she found herself walking north and a little sideways too until she was at Garfield, at the Red Line station, and from there it was only a dozen stops or so to Chicago Avenue, Chicago was the nearest station to Ogden, she would be able to walk from there, probably there would still be a bunch of them hanging around after school, in fact school would have just gotten out by the time she arrived, LeShonna was thinking.

But it was so busy on the Red Line, and so slow, and then when she got off at the Chicago stop she got confused somehow and started going east to beyond Wabash and she had to turn around, it should have been five blocks from the train station to Ogden and she must have walked a dozen or more. Finally there it was, Ogden School, just as she remembered it. There were still a few kids at the playground and some of them—that wasn't Naomi, and that wasn't Robin, was it? No, there was no one. No one. No one she knew.

Someone she didn't know saw her and called to her, a boy who must be in one of the lower grades and he asked her what she was doing and she said nothing but then she finally told him she'd come back to see if she could find some of her old friends, and the boy told her that it had all ended early today. There was some teachers' meeting and they had cancelled the last class. So that was that, maybe she would try again but then again maybe she wouldn't think to or wouldn't have time, her mama and daddy always said that was how life was, everything moves on, it happens to everyone.

ℵ ℵ ℵ

Next time turned out to be soon, and Robin arrived early; something had been cancelled at school—K.P. wasn't quite sure what, sometimes it was hard to tell from the way Robin expressed things. It was strange that the child seemed to want to hear about her past. Strange to have a young person interested in something so dusty, so long-ago. Not all of it was easy to tell; could she manage to tell all of it? She would try, that was all she could do.

ℵ ℵ ℵ

*1938*

Kenneth had views on everything, not just on art. "Dizzy Dean!" he exclaimed when it was on the news that the great pitcher had been traded to the Cubs. He and Kathleen had started sometimes to listen to the radio when they were at the studio together; often there would be talk of the White Sox or the Cubs, and often the games would be broadcast. "There's nothing left in his fastball any more. Nothing! Wrigley is the stupidest owner in all of baseball." Then, when Dean went 7 and 1 for the Cubs during the stretch and it started to look as if they might win the pennant: "They should have picked up Dean before they did—we'd have had the pennant wrapped up by now and be able to rest up for the Series." And then, when Dean lost Game 2 of the World Series, pitching bravely with a tired arm, finally giving up a two-run homer in the eighth to lose the game 2-1, "Hartnett should've taken him out in the seventh. Any fool could tell he was getting tired. But Hartnett's not any fool. He's the supreme fool, the fool of fools." The flask had been coming out more and more often as the innings went by, and Kenneth's voice had become louder and louder, sometimes almost drowning out the radio. Now the game was over; he turned the knob hard until it clicked off. Kathleen let the silence settle for a few moments. Then she said, "Kenneth, I want to show you something." He turned toward her, his mind still on Hartnett's stupidity. He could see in his mind the free-flowing little sketch of flowers she had been working on.

"My picture," she said. "My one true picture."

"The flower one? The latest flower one?" She shook her head and smiled.

"It's not flowers, it's not fruit, it's not pretty people."

"Not crocuses? Maybe you should be like Clarice Cliff, Kip. She's very successful, you know. Half a dozen assistants she has, helping her paint those crocuses onto those little jugs. Five days a week, fifty-two weeks a year. Very successful. Very rich, I should think."

Where did his sneer come from? Where did it end? He must know she thought as little of Clarice Cliff as he did. "Chicago. This is of Chicago, Kenneth. It's a painting I did not long ago. No one else has seen it. I don't know why I want to show it to you." But she did show it to him; she pulled it out from behind a stack of other work.

Kenneth was very quiet; it was as if something were strangling his voice, Kathleen thought.

He could hardly believe it. There was so much of it—so much life it took his breath away. And then immediately he thought of her. How could someone who...? For one moment, for one painting at least, this girl had somehow pulled it off. Had gotten lucky, perhaps.

"It's different from the others," Kenneth finally said.

"Different from anything I've done. There's a competition, the..."

"New Horizons."

Of course he would know; it was brand new, everyone had been talking of it. Funds had been raised through the Art

Institute to support a new prize for 'the most accomplished individual work by an artist under the age of 40.' Everyone said it was wonderful to have such a prize. But prizes always made things more difficult.

২ ২ ২

Kathleen had fallen in love with the Art Institute early on. In love most of all with the great Caillebotte at the top of the stairs. But also with the Monets, and the vast Vuillard hillside, and with a little series of lithographs that had only recently gone on display. *Some Aspects of Paris Life: Houses in the Courtyard* and *Narrow Street Viewed from Above*, and *Street at Evening in the Rain*. Bonnard. Kathleen liked to say the name quietly to herself. **Bonne-are.** In Winnipeg she had heard Miss Smithers at school say it *Bonne-**ard***, with a hard *d* to rhyme with *lard*, as if none of it were French. It had been like that a lot in Winnipeg, even though there were all those French people in St. Boniface. *They keep to themselves*, that's what everyone had said about them. And now other phrases came back to her, and she realized that she had already heard the same sorts of words in Chicago: *they don't cause any harm, really, most of them, but they're not the sort you'd want to have over for dinner, are they? I suppose they don't know any better, poor souls.* Or, with less charity, *they're no good, those people: they'd better be damn sure they keep to themselves.* But no one had ever looked at her in Winnipeg as if they weren't sure whether she were French or English—not the way some people looked at her now, not quite sure if she were white or colored.

She had not asked any of the others yet whether they thought of her as white or colored. They were artists, they wouldn't care. But she hadn't told the others anything of her thoughts of entering the competition, either. Or of her love of the Impressionists, of any of that. Artists did care about some things; Monet and Bonnard and Caillebotte were not in fashion with these people, and these were the people she ran with. These were the people she liked.

Did it matter if you liked Manet and Monet, or Stella and Sheeler? Or if you were open to liking all sorts of things—old things and new things, clean lines and dirty lines, sky colors and sea colors and gutter colors?

She would not have a chance, perhaps, but she would enter. And she would not say anything of it to anyone—except that now, somehow, she was telling Kenneth. She lifted the painting and began to return it to its place behind the others.

"You're not going to put it in for that competition?"

"Why shouldn't I?" But he didn't answer. Was something wrong?

"What are you calling it?"

"At first I didn't know what to call it. It was a newsreel I saw that gave me the name. Maybe you've seen it? All about the skyscrapers and new buildings in the city. *Rising Stories, Chicago*. So that's what I'm calling it."

Kenneth suddenly wanted her to think he liked her other work better than he liked this, and not the other way round. He made as if to help her put away the painting. "Very different," he said once more. "It's not like the flowers and the fruit. The things you've been showing me." Again there was a moment's silence. Finally he shook his head slightly and repeated, "yes, indeed, Kathleen. Very different from the others." She could tell his tone had shifted. And it wasn't just his tone.

"You just called me *Kathleen*. Not *Kip*. You haven't done that for I don't know how long."

"Maybe it's not just the painting that's different. Maybe you're a little different too."

"Or maybe we've always been what we are."

She would give it just one more try with him, perhaps. One? Or maybe two, or three? For a moment she wondered if it had been a mistake to show him the painting. But you couldn't go through life second guessing; there'd be no point.

৯ ৯ ৯

The next time was no different, and the next time after that. Kathleen was beginning to think that you can't always help someone—that sometimes people have their own problems and they need to sort them out on their own. Maybe this would be the last time that she would let him—that she would let herself.... It wasn't just her, and how inadequate and frustrated and mixed up it all made her feel. It was him as well; if she wasn't right for him, then that was no good for either of them.

৯ ৯ ৯

It was still dark, it was the middle of the night. But she could hear something. Kathleen turned over. It was nothing; she would go to sleep again in a minute. She reached out, her fingers would brush against Kenneth again. They had come back together to Kenneth's flat, she was in Kenneth's bed now, if you touched someone it meant... no, he was not there. And then she heard it again, a muffled sound, and then something almost like a gasp. It was coming from the next room, the little room that was everything except a bedroom in that little flat. Ever so quietly she got out of bed and tiptoed to the bedroom door. He was sitting faced away from her, looking towards the fireplace that wasn't a fireplace, it was meant to be decorative, you could just make out the shape of it in the darkness, but he wasn't seeing it, he was hunched over. He was crying. There were sounds shuffling in and out of his mouth, and then the sounds became stronger and louder until his whole body was shaking with sobs, *why can't I?*, *why can't I?*, and Kathleen was filled with guilt. Surely she could have done more to help him, to make it happen, but the sobbed words kept coming and now she could hear that it was not about what she had thought, it had nothing to do with what they had or hadn't done together. *Why can't I paint like that, why can't there be something there?* The words were in his breathing, they kept coming on and on like thoughts, they would catch at the air and then more would come out, *why can't I do it, I just can't do it, there's nothing there, there's nothing there, and then a girl like that, she gets off the train and some goddam miracle happens and she can paint something that….* And then, again and again and again, *there's nothing there, there's nothing there, there's nothing there.* He kept rocking back and forth, *there's nothing, there's nothing there, there's nothing there.*

Her face was stricken but he would not be able to see, no one would be able to see. Kenneth had not turned, he had not seen her, no one had seen her. She tiptoed back to bed.

Was it fifteen minutes? Twenty? Finally she could hear the door close, feel the bed creak beside her, feel the weight of him shifting the mattress. She kept her breathing steady for the longest time, and then one of them must have fallen asleep.

৯ ৯ ৯

Another two days had passed. Neither of them had spoken about that night, about any of those nights. Again he stood watching her paint. He started to say how good she was with detail. With the ornamentation on a cornice. With petals.

"What about with skyscrapers?" Suddenly she found herself challenging him. "You saw that painting. But you didn't say if you liked it." It was evening; there was no one else about. She pulled the vast sheet of watercolor paper forward again from behind the stack, pulled it roughly forward.

"I'm going to enter it," she said, a little defiantly. "Enter it in New Horizons."

He had known what she meant by *enter it*. "It's the day after tomorrow. The deadline." Was he planning to enter any of his own work?

"I know. Friday. I know I'm going to submit it but I don't know about the name."

"*Rising Stories.* You said that was…"

"I don't know about my *own* name. It's so different, this painting. No one has seen it; you are the only one. If you did not know me, would you think a woman could paint like this? Would you think a woman could paint at all? Look at what painters are named. Charles. John. Joseph. Henri. Pablo. Not a Kathleen among them, is there?" She could see Kenneth recoil a little. "So I'm not putting it in under my own name. I'm going to call myself something else." She waited for some response, but he said nothing. "Pace, I'm going to call myself. P.K. Pace." Still he said nothing. "So what do you think of it? What do you really think of the painting?" she persisted.

He backed away a little. "Well," he hedged, "what you do with skyscrapers is nothing like what Stella does with them. Or O'Keeffe, if you want to think of a woman. Even what Marin does with them. Or anyone else I can think of." He looked at the great swirl of the painting once more, and pointed out two of the towers, then another. "Do you think you might be a little bit off track with those?"

A little edge came into Kathleen's voice. "A little bit off track? Or do you think they might be a little bit original?"

"Original doesn't always mean good, Kip. And it doesn't always lead anywhere. Sometimes it's just a blind alley."

"And you think this is a blind alley?"

"I didn't say that. I'm not going to say that. What I said is, it's hard to tell. And what I also said was, you do detail well. Really well. Look at the petals in those flowers you do."

Kathleen could hardly contain herself. "Petals!" She was close to spitting it out. He didn't answer. He had nothing to give her. Then his fingers found her wrist and tightened round it. He pulled her towards him, pulled until her lips were against his. But she was able to break away.

"I know what you *really* think of it. I know what you think of that painting."

He let go of her. Something drained from his face. "I don't know what you mean. I was just telling you what…"

"But I heard what you really think of it. I heard you the other night, Kenneth. I heard you crying, I heard you talking to yourself. I heard what you said."

"You shouldn't have listened to that. You shouldn't have heard." His face tightened, reddened. "I wasn't myself."

"Are we ever the selves we want others to think we are, Kenneth? You lied to me. And I was wanting to help you, I was trying to…"

"Maybe you weren't trying hard enough. Maybe it's time you tried a little harder." Now his fingers had found her wrist again, both wrists. "Maybe you'd better try again right now. You think you're better than…"

"All I think is that you had better let go of me. Now."

ରୁ ରୁ ରୁ

*2011*

"I'm not proud of any of what happened," was how K.P. put it to Robin. "And a lot of what happened I'm not telling you."

"Ms. McLenithan says we all do things we're not proud of. She says…"

"I'm not sure that your Ms. McLenithan.… " But K.P. did not finish the thought; she was still in 1938. "I remember the hoarse voice, the scratchiness of it. And the hard pulling. And a good deal else I will not tell you." She paused a moment.

"Things I did that a woman was not supposed to do. In bed as in painting, we were not supposed to be 'forward,' as they called it. If you were forward, it would make a man think less of you—and think it would it be all right to…"

"You don't have to tell me that part, Granny."

It was as if K.P. had not heard the child. "But people never thought about whether or not a man would be able to do all those things. And how tangled or angry he might get if he couldn't, if he were ashamed of…" She let herself trail off again. "Of course people also still thought it was unnatural for a woman to have needs. I remember what Kenneth said to me one day outside the studio—we were sitting in the sun on a couple of old canvas chairs, taking a break. It could be like silk, his voice; did I tell you that? *A woman never needs to paint. Not like a man does.* That sort of talk never offended us, not in those days. I just let him go on. *A man has to make something that will outlive him, put his name on something that will outlive him. A mountain, a company, a painting, a plaque, an entry in the encyclopaedia. Perhaps it doesn't much matter what the plaques or the pages say. James Jones, President, University College, 1925-1930; Frank Myers, Founder of Myers Industries; Charles Sheeler, Inventor of Precisionism.* I'm half making this up, of course—I don't remember who all the Joneses were. But the gist of it has stayed in my head; I'd heard a lot of the same things before. It was the way just about every man thought back in the 1920s and '30s, even into the '50s. *A man has to put his name on something that will outlive him.* 'And a woman?' I asked him finally.

"'A woman has no need for anything to outlive her—anything except that which she creates. As a force of nature. That's what woman is. A force of nature. Why are there no great women artists? It's simple—a woman artist is also a woman.' There was more along the same lines; he went on and on until finally I just got up and walked away, mid-sentence. I went back upstairs. Back to work."

"Mother says sometimes girls aren't as ambitious as boys."

"And sometimes they're not, Robin. But sometimes they are. Sometimes we are just as ambitious. And people can be ambitious in so many different ways. It doesn't have to be so as to make a name for themselves, or so as to make money. It can be for the thing in itself. Or it can be so as to make a better world. There are so many ways…"

"What about you, Granny? What did you want?"

"I was not one of the pure ones, Robin. I know a part of me wanted to be remembered in that name-on-plaque way. And why? I never asked myself why. Was I willing into existence something large to be remembered so that other things could be forgotten? So that I could forget I had abandoned my parents? So that I could forget all the things I should have done, and had not done?"

"And vice versa?"

"Yes. And vice versa. When I was your age we all went to church, and every Sunday we would all say this together: *We have left undone those things which we ought to have done; And we have done those things which we ought not to have done; And there is no health in us.* It was called a General Confession but years later I could still feel as if it were just me. If I could make one great work, might that make up for the other things? Was that why I wanted to do something that would make me famous? I cannot be proud of any of that.

"But I didn't *just* want to make something famous, and be remembered for that, and have everything else forgotten. I wanted to see the world in a way that thrilled me, a way that felt new. And even then I think I knew I would come to nothing if I couldn't forget about myself, forget about making a name or winning prizes. If I couldn't lose myself in the paint, the buildings, the fog, the sky. But I lacked courage. It seemed to take courage enough just to be among all those boys, all those men, and to try to be like them. I don't think I could have come right out and said to them, 'those hard, straight lines do nothing for me. I need to make a world where the concrete and the steel are wet and alive, where the sky is wet and alive, where the two can bleed into each other.' It was a strong way of seeing things, but they would not have seen it like that, Giorgio and Grant, even Pieter perhaps, not if they knew it was a woman's work. They would have said what I once heard Kenneth say: *soft lines are what you can expect from a woman.*" There was a long pause and she looked out at the low clouds. This time Robin did not say anything, and finally K.P. spoke again. "But that wasn't what he said to me that last night," she finally added. "The night he wouldn't let go of me."

ও ও ও

1938

What had he done? What had he done? She had run from him as if he were some monster. He had only—he hadn't done anything, that was the thing. Once again, he hadn't done anything. Not in the end. And he'd told her exactly that, he'd told her that twice, three times, as she was walking away: "I didn't do anything." But she'd acted as if—well, as if he'd been trying to kill her. "Would you say you hadn't done anything if you tried to shoot at someone, shoot to kill, and your gun misfired? It's intent, Kenneth, it's intent. You tried to rape me." But that was what she had wanted, what she had said she wanted, to *help* him to do it, to do it to her. How could it be rape? If he'd managed it, she wouldn't have…. There was no way she would have been complaining. That was the way the world worked, he guessed he had known that; people would end up complaining at you no matter what. But it ate away at him, he couldn't help it. To get to that point, to be holding her there, to have her just where he could—well, wasn't it what she had wanted all the other times? Oh, he had been forceful—what man isn't a bit forceful sometimes? But she had to have expected that. Anyone should understand that much.

And then suddenly a wave of shame swept through him. Shame at how he had somehow offended her, shame at how he had embarrassed himself. Shame at what she knew about him, about what he had done, and most of all, about what he hadn't been able to do. The withering look on her face as she had scampered off, pulling angrily at her stockings and her skirt. The disgust that had been in her eyes, the contempt—could he bear to see anything like that again?

He was outside now, he must have been outside for some time. Grand and State. There was that restaurant where she worked. All closed now, all dark. Already he had walked—how many blocks was he from the studio? How far was he from anywhere? Why would he want to go anywhere now? It was all a twisted dream, lies and deceptions, he was going nowhere. There had been rain, but now it had eased into little more than a mist. It had barely taken the edge off the heat. It wasn't supposed to be hot in October. It wasn't supposed to be a lot of things.

He thought again of Kip's paintings—of that one painting, of that one great painting. He forced himself to complete the thought, to acknowledge it, almost to say it out loud. How little time she had put into it, into working at it! No, it was better not to think. But what if you couldn't stop yourself from thinking of a thing? What if everything he had been waiting for, everything he had been wanting with every ounce of his being—what if none of that would ever arrive? Would never arrive for him, but would arrive for someone else? Not someone else far away in New York or London or Paris. Someone else right here in Chicago, some nobody who was barely arrived from Winnipeg. Winnipeg! It might as well be Joliet, or Palatine, or Walla Walla, Washington. What if he would never feel what he had always imagined would one day come to him? That fierce burning of greatness he had dreamed of, that heat, that flash of lightning which would take something from within him and sear it for all time onto canvas. As it tore through him he would be filled with a desire to express through his brushes and his fingers something so powerful, so profound, that the world could not help but take notice. What if he would never feel that? What if none of that were ever to happen? What if all he would ever feel would be the desire for that desire, and never the thing itself?

You could be eaten away by something like that. If you began to know that you would never find within yourself anything so powerful as what some woman had found in a few brush strokes—no, no, he was not to think of it. There was nothing he could do. Nothing could be done to pay her back for the way she had… There was no question she had treated him badly.

It had to be nothing more than a fluke, that she had been able to paint that one large piece. A girl like that. No proper background, no training to speak of. If anyone deserved to have the sort of success a picture like that might bring, it was Kenneth. It would be a funny thing if…—no, there was no way something like that could be made to happen. No way you could know that a painting, however great it might be, would make your name, truly make it, make it so that you were more than well-known. *Fame* was not too strong a word. And then more fame, the sort of fame that brought retrospectives, that made women smile at you in that special way, it didn't matter if you were no longer young. No, there was no way you could be sure that a great picture would ever do that, even a dozen great pictures, even two dozen. The only way you could be sure of getting fame was to die young. Kenneth snorted to himself. But it was half true. Masaccio. Giorgione. Géricault. Boccioni. Modigliani. He snorted again. Modigliani. One great painting had been all he had done; he had just gone and done it again, and again, and again. And perhaps it hadn't been all that great in the first place. As great as *Rising Stories*? Once more he closed off a thought in his mind. If you died young, people paid attention. People would always think of you in a special way, would ache with a sense of lost potential. They would think of the work you might have done, the work you could now never do. And they would be sad they could never know you, never hear your voice, never touch you. Sad almost *because* they could never know you, never hear you, never touch you. What if there were one painting they could always think of when they thought of your name? One painting that would live within them, live with the thought of your name, of your face....

That was the only way it could possibly happen. There were no guarantees; it might not happen anyway. But if it did not happen that way, it would not happen at all. He could see all that now, he could see it clearly. There had been something lacking in him—no, luck had been working against him. Whatever: fame would not happen for him, he would never reach the top. Never. And there wasn't anything you could do about it, really. Not unless. Not unless. Not unless...

Kenneth walked and walked, over to the canal and on past the deep shadows of the Merchandise Mart and the warehouses, past the bridges and then past the bridges again, past all the bridges. And a wild idea took shape.

# Seven

Among the most interesting of all the many images of sky-scrapers in Chicago is a 1933 Illinois Central poster. A smiling young woman in a bright orange hat leans over a stone para-pet at the top of a skyscraper. Her gaily patterned scarf flutters in the breeze as she looks out at the sky. The skyscraper must be somewhere just north of the Wrigley Building—if you look for it you can just see the tip of the Wrigley near the bottom of the picture. From there the view below her spreads out to the south: the Tribune Tower, the Jewelers' Building, the Mather Building. You can spot the old Reliance Building and a few others too. Beyond and to the left the vast, orderly green of Grant Park recedes into the distance; beyond that everything slopes into horizon; you have to imagine the place that would become the grounds for the 1933 World's Fair—you have to imagine the whole South Side. To the left again the wide water, the lake dotted with tiny sailboats, diagonals stretched to the horizon on that side. Overlaying the painting at the bottom are the words 1933 WORLD'S FAIR CHICAGO LAKE FRONT / ASK AGENT FOR FREE BOOK. And below that ILLINOIS CENTRAL—THE ROAD OF TRAVEL LUXURY. In red and white and black across the sky: CHICAGO—VACATION CITY. The poster is all light, color, joy— the dreamed joy of the Depression years.

What is easy to miss is the vantage point—just north of the Wrigley Building, but also far, far above it. The parapet over which the woman leans is at the top of a building that must be two or three times the height of any of the skyscrapers below her—the skyscrapers that were at that time the tallest in the city. This was more than thirty years before the Hancock Building, the Sears Building, and the Amoco Building remade the skyline in the early seventies. The perch she looks out from must be far higher than any of those. A skyscraper of the mind so perfect that it never occurs to us it might not be real.

৺ ৺ ৺

"Were you hurt, Granny? Did he hurt you?" K.P. looked down. The child was holding her hand.

"You know how you can hurt inside even when you haven't fallen, and no one's hit you, no one's touched you, but it hurts? Sometimes you have been hurt like that, I'm sure."

"Sometimes everyone gets hurt like that, Granny. Sometimes I...—anyway, I know." Robin had not let go of her hand. She would say just a little more—that would be enough.

"Of course I never wanted to talk to him again, never wanted to see him again." She paused. "I had to steel myself to come in to Higher Ground, that first morning after that awful night. I dreaded seeing him, dreaded what he might say. But I had to. I had to make out that application, for one thing. I had told him I was going to enter *Rising Stories* for the prize, and damned if I would go back on myself now.

"I did not imagine there was much chance of winning, but I had to try. And it was a chance that turned out to have been worth taking. There was one prize for works on canvas, another for works on paper; it was the 'works on paper' category that I won. Of course it was a long time before I found out. A couple of months, I think, I think. It was..."

"How much was the prize, Granny? Were you rich after that?"

"There are few prizes that make people rich, child; even with the prize money I would still have been pretty poor."

"What do you mean, *even with it*? You did get the money, didn't you?"

"Not a penny of it; not a cent. How can I explain this? I told you, didn't I, that I had decided not to submit the painting under my own name?"

"Yes. And I don't understand, Granny. Who were you pretending to be? Why couldn't you have been yourself?"

"It was just a name; it wasn't anyone I was trying to be. P.K. Pace. It had come to me quickly; I think I thought *space* and somehow I thought *peace* at the same time and out came *pace*, and I thought I would reverse my initials and that would be one little change more. I could have called myself anything, really, so long as it wasn't a woman's name. So long as no one could say *We can set that one aside. Woman's work.* We women were not supposed to win things like that, not then. That was made clear-as-day once the winners had been decided. I can remember it all, right from when the letter arrived. I can see the look on their faces."

"On whose faces, Granny?"

"The others at the Higher Ground—at the studio. It was Jimmy who called out when the letter arrived. 'Anybody know a P.K. Pace? No Pace here, is there?' 'I think it's for me!' I piped up. I could hardly contain my excitement—of course I knew it was from the Art Institute; there was nowhere else I had used that name.

"'But it doesn't say it's for you,' Jimmy said. My heart was in my mouth. 'It's a long story; look, don't make me explain until I've read the letter, all right?' I suppose I wasn't thinking clearly. *Maybe I've won!*, my heart pitter-pattered.

"If I had tried to explain everything before opening the letter, they would have had more reason to believe me later. I could have described *Rising Stories*; I could have named it. No one had seen it, that was the thing. No one knew it existed—no one except Kenneth. When the others had seen me working I had been painting those still lifes. Or sometimes they might have seen me painting very different sorts of city paintings—in the daytime with everyone around I tried a few that were all hard lines, a little like what Stella and Sheeler were doing. And like a lot of others were doing too; I had taken to heart what Kenneth had said about not straying too far from the pack. I had been afraid no one would want what I wanted to..."

"But the judges wanted it," Robin broke in; "the judges liked it. They *must* have liked it. You said it won. What did they say about your painting?"

"They called it arresting. They called it bold. They said it suggested new possibilities for abstraction through the curve rather than the cube, they...—oh, I can't remember half of what they said." She paused; more came back to her. "They mentioned El Greco. They mentioned John Marin. But this was not a derivative work, they said; no, they were sure of that. It struck out in an entirely new direction, struck an entirely new chord." K.P. smiled, and then went quiet.

"What do you think they would have said if you hadn't lied, Granny? If you had sent it to them as a painting by K.P. Sandwell..."

"It wasn't Sandwell then. That was what I became when I married Arthur. I was a Schuyler. And it wasn't K.P., either; I was always Kathleen then—or Kip. It was only after all this that I started to call myself K.P."

"If you had sent it in as a painting by Kathleen, then. By Kathleen Schuyler."

"Oh, I can well imagine that. *The softness derives from Marin, the grandeur from El Greco—and the mixture is not a happy one. Schuyler has so distorted the urban landscape as to compromise not only its verticality but also its integrity. To the extent that this work does take artistic tradition in a new direction, it is not a fortunate experiment—as is the case so frequently with women artists, we regret to say, when they endeavor to be original.* That's what they would have said, almost word for word; I am sure of it.

"But they *didn't* say any of that. And they couldn't change round when they found out it had been painted by a woman, could they? They had to still say it was good. That it was whatever you said. Arrested."

"*Arresting*, child. Arresting. No, they could hardly reverse course on the matter of whether or not the painting was any good. What they *could* do was resist any suggestion that the painting might have been by a woman. When I wrote to tell them that P.K. Pace was me, Kathleen Schuyler, they hemmed and hawed and said that they would need to verify things. That there were questions relating to confirmation of identity that would need to be cleared up whenever a pseudonym had been used. That it all might take some time."

"Couldn't the others help? The ones at Higher Ground? They wanted you to win, didn't they?"

"They no more than half believed me themselves, that was the thing. I remember the tone in Giorgio's voice after he finally saw that letter from the judges: *well, the world is filled with surprises*. That was the sort of remark they all made—and how could I blame them? I hadn't had the courage to show the painting to anyone—anyone other than Kenneth, that is. *But Kenneth can tell them*, I thought. *Kenneth can set them straight.* I had a telephone number for the rooming house where he had been staying. I had to screw myself up to call him; it's not easy when someone has treated you as badly as Kenneth had treated me to call them up out of the blue and ask a favor. And I couldn't do it in private; in those days nobody who was young had a private phone—nobody who wasn't really rich, I mean. So I had to call Kenneth from a payphone. I remember it was a booth just off Illinois. That was about the quietest place I could find anywhere near, but it was hardly quiet. Big trucks were going by constantly; every time one went by you would just have to leave your words hanging until it had passed.

"Of course it was the landlady who answered. *No*, she didn't think he was in but *yes*, she could check. And then, after only a minute, *no*, there was no response to a knock on his door, and *yes*, she had knocked more than once, and called out as well. *I'm starting to wonder about that young man*, she went on. *It's been weeks since I've seen him. Weeks and weeks. I don't know why a person would keep a room if he didn't intend to use it. But perhaps he's not planning to keep it much longer; the rent's due day after tomorrow; we'll see if he pays up.* I asked her, if she did see him, to ask him to be in touch with me, and I said that it was important. But I had no reason to expect he would. That was that, I thought; there would be no one to tell the others at Higher Ground what had happened. No one to say to the judges, and to the whole world, *yes, Kathleen painted that picture, Kathleen Schuyler. She showed it to me in the studio.*

All that would have been made to seem trivial, I suppose, by the news of what had happened to Kenneth. Except that there *was* no news. It wasn't until I finally met with the judges that I finally found out what had happened.

"What did happen, Granny?"

"The judges for the prize called me in to see them all together—this must have been almost two weeks after they had sent me the letter, and more than ten days after they would have received a letter back from me, doing my best to explain. I had hardly spoken to anyone else in the meantime—and hardly anyone had spoken to me.

"The meeting was held in a large room in the Art Institute offices. Judge Little chaired the committee; he is the one I remember best. Someone must have thought it would be cute to have a real judge as one of the judges of an art competition. For years Judge Little had cultivated a reputation for being a connoisseur—a connoisseur of the daring, the modern, the new, not merely of Eakins and Sargent and Homer. I'm sorry, Robin, you won't know those names, will you? They painted people in rowing races, and people swimming, and tall rich women standing in front of rich backgrounds, and boys and men sailing. They had all been something in their day, but by the 1930s no one thought any of them were daring or modern or new any longer. They were…"

"They were dead, weren't they?"

"Well there was that, yes. No longer new or daring—dead. At any rate, Judge Little fancied himself as knowing a good deal about all of them, but also a good deal about Sheeler and Demuth and Stella. The men who had taken the hard, straight lines of the modern city into their imaginations and turned them out again a little more colorful, a little harder, a little straighter. He had a Stella in his dining room, I am told."

"But you haven't told me what he said, Granny. Why he wouldn't let you win the prize."

"Let me play the judges for you." She looked round for her drink and could not see it anywhere. It did not matter. "I will play Judge Little. *I have to say, Miss Schuyler, that this is most ir-regular. The only evidence you seem able to produce to support your claim is a sketch that might well have been done after the fact, after you had seen someone else's completed painting...*

"'But who else could have...' I started to interrupt. He would have none of that.

"*We will get to that in a moment, young lady; you will let me finish. It is not only a question of the lack of evidence. It is also our considered judgement that the sort of boldness one finds in this paint-ing, the striking vitality of it, is distinctly unladylike in character. To put it bluntly, Miss Schuyler, this is simply not the sort of work we would expect...* I remember how he let that sentence drift off. *There is a dramatic freedom to it, an almost undisciplined force of a sort that—well, none of us could conclude that the claim of a young woman to have painted such a... we felt the claim to be lacking in....* He paused. *We felt it to be lacking, Miss Schuyler. We felt it to be lacking.*

"'And I have explained, your honor,...'

"*You have explained nothing, I am afraid. And you will not help your case by calling me 'your honor'; we are not in a courtroom here. 'Judge Little' is quite sufficient.*

"'I *have* explained, Judge Little. I have explained that I sub-mitted the work under a pseudonym because I know that in *some* artistic circles the work of women artists is not taken very se-riously. But leave that to one side; surely the facts must count for something. The fact is that the work was submitted with an address as well as a name, and that your notice was sent to that address—and that it reached me. Surely occupying the correct address must count for something.'

"*No need to be strident, young lady; I must ask you to keep your tone civil.*

"'I ask a civil question: how likely is it that someone else would have painted the picture, submitted it with a false ad-dress—and that that false address would have just happened to belong to me? Surely it is reasonable to ask that question! And I do ask it. Civilly.' My voice was trembling with rage. I could see a corner of Judge Little's mouth turn upward; he knew he held all the cards. But he stayed silent; the next voice belonged to Mrs. Vinall—second of the three judges.

"*Miss Schuyler, we can all see how determined you are not to be shown up in this matter.* Hers was a softer firmness. *But as to what is likely and unlikely—well, I do not think you have covered all the possibilities. We made inquiries early on about this address of yours. You are not the only one occupying this… space, are you?*

"'I have never pretended that I was. It is shared studio space—shared by more than a dozen of us.'

"*And of these dozen or so who share the studio, are there any who can attest that you are the one who painted* Rising Stories? *Any who saw you paint it? Saw you paint* any *of it?* The more she went on the harder she stressed the incriminating syllables.

"No one saw me actually applying paint to paper, no. And only one other person saw the picture itself before I submitted it; we have had a falling out, I'm afraid, and are not in communication. I tried to contact him, and left a message asking that he be in touch. I've had no response." I had no wish to mention his name. To say it even once.

"*So there is no one?*

"'I can produce no witnesses to attest that I painted the picture, no. I have explained all that.'

"*I should say rather that you have* spoken of *all that. I fear you have* explained *very little.'* Mrs. Vinall paused before administering the coup de grace. *Is it not true that when the painting was submitted there were others at this … studio, others who are now no longer associated with it?*

"'I have never pretended otherwise.'

"*And who are these people who are no longer sharing the space? Would you be kind enough to name them for us?* I tried to collect myself as best I could.

"'Philip Wellner has moved out of the city, I believe, I heard to St. Louis. Kenneth Paul is another who is no longer in the studio. And there was also with us for a short time a painter by the name of Griese. Samuel Griese—he did not like to hear his last name spoken. I have no idea who he was or why he left or where he went.'

"*This Kenneth Paul...*, the woman began again. Her voice seemed to clang shut behind me. *I will remind you that you are obliged to tell us everything you may know of this person, and of what may have become of him.* A chill went over me. I could not tell her everything. Even to you I have not told everything, Robin. To these judges I thought I would say as little as I could, and I would lie if I had to. But I would have to give them the gist.

"'He stopped coming to the studio some time in early October. One morning all his things were gone. That was that; he must have cleared out in the middle of the night. I believe he may be still in the city, but I have no definite knowledge.' I paused for a moment. 'He is the one I tried to reach on the telephone ten days or so ago. The one who could tell you that I painted *Rising Stories*,' I felt I had to add. 'His landlady said she hadn't seen him in many weeks. I'm sorry that I...'

"*You know nothing of what has happened to him? You are absolutely sure of that? I should caution you, Miss Schuyler, that we have received new information in the past week. Information that may shed a clearer light on this very strange situation.* It was Judge Little again. 'I am quite sure. Nothing,' I answered. My body clenched.

"*You had no idea he was missing.*"

"'None whatsoever.'

"*Then you know nothing of the circumstances of his death?*

"'His death.' I could hardly breathe the words." Even now K.P. was having difficulty, telling it all to Robin.

"You don't have to go on, Granny. I don't have to know how it ends."

"Everyone needs to know how things end, child. But perhaps I will stop for a moment. Perhaps that is enough for now. You will find out soon enough, I imagine."

ৰ ৰ ৰ

Kenneth had tried to think through the timing of everything. The deadline was tomorrow; he would need to be gone by then. It would need to happen in the morning. And he would need to leave something behind—something that would make them pay attention when they discovered it, when they discovered who he was, who he had been. He would not make that easy for them. He would carry nothing on his person— his wallet, anything with his name on it. He would give nothing away, he would make them work for it. He would leave everything behind, in the rooming house. It might be weeks before they broke into his flat and went through his things. That's when they would find it—the note. Oh yes, he would most certainly leave a note. He took another pull on the flask. He would need to clear his things out of Higher Ground. Could he fit everything in a cab? He would try. And then home, if you could call that rooming house a home. He would leave everything in that one room. And he would not think of Kip. It was time to think of himself.

He found a cab and told the driver where to go, and then to stay and to wait. And then he clambered up to Higher Ground and pulled together what he had there; it didn't amount to much, in the end. His pictures had been so small, and he had kept so few of them. He could fit everything into a couple of boxes. The cabbie had started honking by the time he came down again, sweating with his load; the two of them had words. But the cabbie still took Kenneth's money—*they always do, don't they?*, Kenneth thought—and dropped him and his two large boxes at the rooming house. Kenneth let himself in silently, struggled up to his room, fumbled for the key. The place smelled of damp and heat and sweat. And always there was the smell of cooked cabbage from down the hall. He dropped the boxes carelessly in a corner, and pulled the flask from his pocket. He had to refill it from the large bottle in the cupboard. He downed one shot quickly, then another, before he refilled the flask. And then he found paper—writing paper—and silently went about his last business, the words spreading over the pages like butter in the night heat. Another pull, and then another; the thoughts were gathered, marshalled. Keep it neat, he told himself, everything neat, everything legible. All that was important. Within the hour it was done. Sleep? He had no need of sleep. Time enough for that—all the time in the world for that.

Was he afraid of death? Of course. That was built in, wasn't it? Into any animal, into all of us. But the finest part of being human was being able to conquer fear. To find within yourself whatever strength it took. Cowards were never able to do that, perhaps not even able to dream of doing it. They lived their little lives, they had their little loves and their little children, and their little bit of money if they were lucky, and they felt themselves lucky for having these small things. What need had he for any of that?

Now he was on the street again, he was walking. There was no more rain, though a sheen was left on the pavement. To the east the sky was lightening; the traffic was beginning to pick up. It would still be an hour or two before the buildings in the Loop began to fill. The commotion and the noise would help him do what he needed to; what was one man in all that? Time enough for them to figure out afterwards what he had been, who he had been. Now the flask was empty. Drowning would be slow; you could gag, you could choke, water entering your lungs, trying to scream, flailing against the water, there was no dignity to it. A gun? He had never fired one in his life. Carbon monoxide? He had no car; he knew no one who owned a car. This was Chicago, this was the city of towers and of wind and of sky, of high ambitions, of high places; that was the way you should choose.

He had always been afraid of heights. Not in that strange love-hate way so many feel, afraid not that they might fall but that they might give in to the endless attraction they feel for the edge, for going over the edge. Kenneth's was real fear, fear that had to be willed under control, muscles tightening in the gut, fighting down panic. The sort of fear that needed to be risen above. That needed to be conquered.

The Board of Trade, that was the tallest. But you couldn't get past the lobby without a pass; he would never manage it. The Mather. It had been the tallest in the late '20s, when Kenneth had been still in his teens. So thin, so beautiful. And the windows were double-hung, you could see that from the sidewalk. Even now, so early in the day, he could see half a dozen of them open. There were two women by that window on the third floor, turned away, deep in talk. Far up a man in suspenders was looking straight out; he was holding something, was he dictating? It would be the easiest thing in the world to find some office on the 30th floor, or the 35th, to distract whoever might be at their desk, to stride to the sash, to throw it open, to pull yourself out and onto the ledge, to look up one last time at the hot, gray sky that held no heaven. There would be no time for fear, he would have to jump clear of where the building was stepped-in—was that at the twentieth floor? Yes, yes, he could do it, he could do it, he would do it, he was doing it, it would be in all the papers, *a man in his late twenties, as yet unidentified, took his own life today in...* Before his eyes were the faces when they heard, distraught at what he had done, appalled, thinking what they might have done for him that would have..., yes, yes, it would be...

Did you have an appointment? No? *Well, I suppose Mr. Carson or Miss Shipley might be able to help you. Would you wait here a moment?* And then in a flash he could be there, he was there, pulling himself upright on the sill, fingers pressed to the sash, to the pane, and before him the broad, wide air, the space of it, the depth of it. The air stretched out the thin morning light, stretched out all the space below, stretched out time—a thousand thoughts flew by in a moment. Could there be a better place and time for an ending? A better time to stop time than here and now? When everything around you is air, when the cares of the world have shrunk to tiny specks far below? What did it matter if people had screwed you around, day after day, year after year? What did it matter if most of your paintings weren't any good, and if nobody but you liked the few that were? What difference did it make if some stupid girl could bring more life to one painting than you could put in a dozen? None of it amounts to anything more than luck. Talent is luck, money is luck, love is luck. Money and luck, they make the world go round. Why go back to depending on any of that? What would it matter if you took that elevator back down and spent another twenty or thirty or fifty years slapping paint onto a flat surface, or scraping it off again when nothing worked? Some people lived for the sake of little brats who would mewl and giggle and groan, tugging at your pant legs, pressing themselves against you with lumps of pudding or spaghetti stuck around their mouths, staining your life, needing and needing, and then being grown and gone and someone else's, what would it matter if you spent all those years doing that? What would it matter if you spent twenty or thirty or fifty years making money, or trying to make money; or twenty or thirty or fifty years making love that wasn't love? In the end it made no difference. If you didn't have the brats someone else would; if you didn't paint the pictures someone else would; if you didn't make the money someone else would, and the world would go on. Now the air was here and clean and blue, and you could know that the end could be here and clean and... one foot, another, *don't think, don't think, feel, feel, feel*; just *feel*, and then everything would be air, the long, long rush of it. But panic jerked at him suddenly, filled him, held him. He could not think; he felt only an aching tightness in his gut.

*No*, you had to will it to happen, you could hold on only so long, and Kenneth thought of the long note on the clarinet in "Chant in the Night," Sidney Bechet could find it and hold it like nobody else, find it and hold it until it seemed like it was forever but even for him it had to end, no one could hold it forever, now, now, now was the moment, now. Will it to happen, *now*, and then it was done, he had pushed off into air and there would be an end to all thought there would be nothing but feeling nothing but the wind and the air, he had no feeling in his hands, no, he couldn't be doing this, what had come over him? and then fear filled him like lead, *what had he done? what had he done? what had he done?*

# Eight

Each time, Robin would start to look forward to going to Granny's again within a day or two of having said goodbye. But thinking ahead, getting on to the elevator, finding that strange floor—there would always be a little fear mixed in with the looking forward. Was it really Granny? Would she stay Granny? For how long? Robin didn't want to find her not the same, or find her gone. And Robin wanted to know what had happened to Kenneth, but also didn't want to know.

Also, Robin had other things to look forward to, now that Ms. McLenithan had gone ahead and helped the class start a debating club. There had been a little frown on Ms. McLenithan's face when Robin had volunteered, and she had looked hard at Robin. She didn't mention the homework or anything else, she just went quiet for a moment like she was thinking, and then she said, "All right," and so that made it Jeff and Robin and Kathy Snyder on one of the teams, and the first topic was *should factory farming be banned?*

They were supposed to work as a team right through, and the first evening they had worked on it everything had been great, Jeff hadn't shown up and mostly it had been Robin and Kathy Snyder talking about animals, non-human animals, Kathy Snyder had a light little voice and she said they should always call them that, *non-human animals*, to remind people that people were animals too, that all of us are animals, and Robin felt a deep shiver at the thought of what Kathy Snyder might be if she wasn't dressed all perfectly, at the thought of how her voice would change, and her words, and how she—but then Robin had to stop and save those thoughts for late at night when no one could guess they were there.

It wasn't easy at home. Of course Robin had to mention being chosen for the debating team, and say who else was on the team and what the first topic was, even knowing that might make

Carol and Carl a little uncomfortable and, sure enough, Carol had asked if Ms. McLenithan was trying to turn the whole class into little vegetarians or vegans, except Carol's voice didn't turn up at the end which made what she said sound more like a statement than a question. And Carl asked if every teacher nowadays thought she had to change the world, and that didn't sound like a question either, but then he did start to ask questions, "And who's this Kathy Snyder? You've mentioned her before, haven't you?" And Robin blushed, you couldn't help doing that sometimes, and Carol said, "Whoever is on the team, I know you're going to do well," and asked how they were going to treat the topic and said *isn't it an interesting topic?*, it was almost as if she had changed right around, *perhaps it's a bit controversial but it certainly is interesting*, and then everything was better and Robin didn't have to worry anymore about them getting really irritated about the animals, or about them guessing what Robin was thinking about Kathy Snyder.

Except Robin couldn't resist telling them something about some of the ideas for the debate, how a little calf has life in it, a little piglet has life in it, just as much life as a little human baby, so that both Carol and Carl were provoked, *why do you have to add that bit about human babies?* they both asked. And why couldn't Robin put this sort of energy into the regular subjects? It would be great if Robin could work just as hard at the things that *weren't* extra-curricular, those were the most important things, after all.

"Is it more important to pass math than to try to make there be less cruelty to animals?" Where had those words come from? Robin was flushed; sometimes you could say things that sounded angry when you didn't think you were angry.

"It's important that you pass math. Full stop."

"Who says? Who makes the rules? What does it matter if I pass math? There's no god who says people have to get their math in every grade of school."

"There's no god at all, Robin. God is dead, and has been for a long time. Math is important, that's all. You won't get anywhere if you don't—" he broke off, oddly. "God has been gone for a long while," he finished.

"It's all right, Carl. Robin doesn't believe in God. But as to who does make the rules? It's not…"

"It's simple. We do. We all do. We make our own rules. Except for children: parents have to make them for children. Believe me, I don't want to be a rule maker. Neither does your mother. We're…" he trailed off.

"Free spirits," Carol put in, a little uncertainly. There was a long pause.

"All that was a long time ago," said Carl.

"Maybe it was. Maybe it was. But we still don't *want* to be rule makers. We don't want to play god. We just want to do what's good for you, Robin, and what's good for everyone else too."

"But what if they're different?"

"Different?"

"What if what's good for me isn't good for you? What if it's good for how *you* think things should be that I pass math but it's not actually good for *me*? What if…?"

"It's possible that's the way it is, Robin. But we have to act as if it isn't. Carol and I do. We have to ask you to try."

"When did God die?"

"In the sixties. The nineteen-sixties. You could google it; *Time* magazine had a cover story."

"There's no need to be flip, Carl," said Carol, but she couldn't stop herself from smiling. "The thing is, Robin, you can't die if you've never existed." It wouldn't hurt to have a real conversation with the child about being and non-being, about existence. "So if …"

"I know that, Mum. I really know that. It's just that…," and Robin paused.

"It's just what?" asked Carl, leaning a little forward.

"Nothing. Nothing."

ৰ ৰ ৰ

God hadn't been something Robin had thought of much, really. Hardly ever. *Something?* Maybe you had to say some*one*. But then last September Kathy Snyder had told Robin about how she had used to believe, about having signed her bible where it said you could sign your life over, *I pledge my life to Jesus Christ,* etc. etc. and then you had to date it. And about what she had thought after she had done that, what she had worked out in her head and how special it had seemed at first. But when you signed your life over to Jesus Christ you were supposed to pray every day and read a part of the bible. And, when you did that, it was hard not to wonder about all the stoning of people and all the killing of lambs, and at the center of everything was someone being tortured to death and other people eating his flesh and drinking his blood to remember him, it had started to seem a little weird. A lot weird, in fact. And then a little while after that Kathy Snyder had seen a movie about what had happened in 1994, *Hotel Rwanda* it was called, she wasn't supposed to watch anything that was marked "14+" unless her parents had said it was all right but they were out and she went ahead and watched it except that sometimes she had to look away, like when the car was bumping along the road and you thought it was running over potholes but it was people's bodies. And three weeks after that she had crossed out in her bible where she had signed her life over to Jesus Christ but she used pencil when she crossed it out, just in case. Probably there was no god, that was what Kathy Snyder thought now, almost certainly there wasn't. No god who was good could have let something like that happen to all those people. So either there was a really bad god, or there was no god at all, and Kathy Snyder believed there was no god at all.

Of course Robin knew some people in their class who did believe, who believed in a Christian god or a Jewish or a Muslim god, was there a Buddhist? And Kathy Snyder talked about Hinduism and how you weren't supposed to eat meat if you were a Hindu, it should be if you were a *human*, Kathy Snyder thought. But most people Kathy and Robin knew just never thought about all that, any more than they seemed to think about believing, about whether there was a god and a heaven, or nothing. Carol and Carl said some people who didn't believe still thought it was good to believe so they went to their church or their mosque or their synagogue and acted as if they believed. Which sounded better than *pretended to believe*. But you shouldn't just pretend, should you? Any more than you should just make things up. Should you?

ঽ ঽ ঽ

It wasn't just that Robin didn't put in as *much* effort into regular schoolwork as into debating over the next few weeks; a lot of the time Robin didn't seem to put *any* effort into regular schoolwork. Of course Ms. McLenithan had seen this sort of thing before with other students. And sometimes it wasn't that big of a problem. Some kids are bright enough that they can sail right through grade school and junior high and even high school without ever having to apply themselves. They can let their minds wander most of the time and still take in enough when they do pay attention that they'll get good marks, sometimes very good marks indeed. But Robin had never been that sort of child, Ms. McLenithan was quite sure of that. Especially in math; Robin really had to do the work in order to keep up. And that had always been what had Robin had done, reliably. Until this past fall, Robin had been an A student all along. But then things had started to slip, and slip, and since January—almost nothing. Should she contact the parents now?

But it had been Carol and Carl who had gotten in touch with Ms. McLenithan first, right after they had received a report card for their Robin that was filled with Cs and Ds, even a couple of Fs. They had to think part of the problem might be Ms. McLenithan. Maybe most of the problem. From the very beginning of the year Robin had gone on and on about all the things Ms. McLenithan was teaching them about poetry and art. But what about science? What about math?

"I can't interest Robin in any of those subjects, I'm afraid," she began. "Even some things in English…," she trailed off. "And when Robin isn't interested, Robin doesn't do the work. Not this year, anyway. Not any more. Even sometimes when Robin *does* seem to have some interest, things aren't getting done"

"Like what? What precisely?" Carl always thought it was important to be specific.

"Like that big project they did on South America last month. They had to think up a topic and make a presentation and write the whole thing up to be handed in. It could be pictures as well as words, but there had to be at least 1,200 words."

"And what did Robin hand in?" Carol had never heard of Robin having been given this assignment.

"Nothing. It was the same with the science project, and with the short story they were supposed to write. You didn't know about any of this? When I heard you wanted to meet with me, I assumed..."

"That we knew."

"I don't want to pry, Mr. and Mrs...."

"Carol and Carl. Please."

"Carol and Carl. But I do feel I should ask. Has Robin ever talked to you about having trouble doing assignments? About somehow not being able to finish the work?"

"No. I mean, not much. Hardly at all." Carol paused, and then thought that there could be no point in hiding the extent of their ignorance. "Not ever."

"And we do sometimes ask directly," Carl insisted. "We both do. *Have you finished your homework?*, we ask. All that sort of thing. Robin always says *yes*, or *yes, it's almost done.*"

"I have to think Robin sometimes believes just that. I know we can all fool ourselves sometimes as to how much we've already accomplished, how much is really left to do. That goes right through life. And when you're that age—well, maybe it's surprising there aren't more like Robin."

"But there aren't." Carl was blunt. "I'm sure you don't have many students who just don't hand in the work."

"Some. But it's a fair point. I don't remember running into a student quite like Robin. Someone who is so obviously bright, a real thinker. And with such a wonderful imagination. Perhaps too good an imagination—perhaps that makes it more difficult to…"

"Tell the truth?"

"Fair enough. Robin has not been entirely truthful."

"Are you being entirely truthful, Ms. McLenithan? We can take the full truth."

Christine—for that was her name, Christine McLenithan—couldn't help but start to blush. How could you keep your feelings out of it? Out of any of it? Out of life? She would have to answer as directly as she could.

"I am being as truthful as I can, Mr., Mr….. As I can, Carl. While trying as well to be diplomatic." She thought with longing of a long gin and tonic when the night's interviews were over. "Diplomacy is not always easy." She paused. "And perhaps Robin has been as truthful as Robin could be. At this time of Robin's life. Certainly Robin has not been truthful about these assignments. That picture can't be painted any other way. But this is only about schoolwork, Carl. It is only about one thing, about one part of Robin's life. I truly believe that on the whole Robin tries to be true…—excuse me, to be truthful. To be honest."

"I had a grandmother who used to say that nothing is only about one thing, Ms. McLenithan."

"Christine."

"Christine." For a brief moment there was a standoff.

"I suspect your grandmother was right," said Ms. McLenithan finally. "But I'll say again, Carl: I can tell that Robin's a good child, a good person. Whatever the two of you have done as parents, you've clearly done an awful lot right; I hope you don't mind my saying that." When had any parent ever minded anyone saying that? "A good child with a very good mind. And a child who's *capable* of working very hard. You look at how hard Robin has been working on this debating…"

"So you don't think we should say no to that?" Carol broke in. "Insist that Robin…"

"I don't. Certainly not for the moment, no. I don't think that sort of punishment is likely to be productive. It might well be counter-productive. Maybe it's something you could look at if things don't improve. Suggest that if…"

"As a threat, you mean."

"As an indication that at some point there will have to be consequences if things don't change."

"Life is about what you have to do, not just what you want to do. I've always believed that," Carl insisted. He looked down at the floor. "And if…"

"There's something about Robin that goes beyond *want to* or *have to*. But what that something might be, I have no idea. You are the parents; I can well imagine that the two of you…"

"What are the chances that Robin could fail?" Carl pressed forward on his chair.

"Fail the entire year? It's becoming a real question." Ms. McLenithan nodded, and then shook her head. "I know a lot of schools will just bump kids along to the next grade even if they have failing grades. And a lot of teachers feel that…"

"Social promotion," Carol broke in.

"That's what they call it, yes. But at Ogden we don't like to do that. People may think it won't matter a whole lot at this stage. But sooner or later it's *going* to matter. And we like to see kids straightened out sooner, not later. So I hope we can work together on this. I'd like to suggest to you that…"

"Yes. Absolutely," Carol jumped in. "From now on we'll keep a very close eye on Robin. A close eye on what homework Robin's doing, a close eye on where Robin goes after school, a close eye…"

"Robin has to learn." A firmer note had crept into Carl's voice. "You can spin any number of fantasies about skyscrapers or poems or what to do to make the world better, but this is real. Robin has to understand that. Where you live is real. Having to live with your parents is real. What you have to do for school is real. You have to come to terms with all of that." There was an awkward pause for a moment.

"I have to say that it's good to see parents who care." Christine almost always said this near the end of an interview. She paused, and then she added, "thank you, Carol; thank you, Carl. Robin will be all right in the end. I feel that."

"God knows what we'll do if you're wrong," Carl put in. But in the parking lot Carol reminded him that God didn't know anything because he was dead and it had all been in *Time Magazine*, like he'd said, so they were on their own.

ॐ ॐ ॐ

LeShonna didn't know why some folks thought there wasn't no God. Why would anyone think that? Think that there was no one to look out for you, protect you. How could it be worth living in a world like that? Knowing that there was a god and also that He was on her side always made LeShonna feel better at night, when sometimes the bad things would come crowding in. Her daddy said God was more something we thought of to help us, and not someone who was actually there. But what was wrong with having someone to help us? Nothing was wrong with that, and why couldn't He be someone who was *actually* there as well? That wasn't wrong neither.

LeShonna's mother said He was there all the time, looking down on us from somewhere way up, somewhere above the clouds. One time LeShonna had asked her mama *How high is He, really? Is He sometimes in the middle of the clouds? Is He always above them?* And her mama had said that He was everywhere, and that it wasn't our place to ask such things. When they had had their class trip up the Willis Tower they had been looking out from above the clouds; LeShonna hadn't seen nothing, and she had looked very, very carefully.

That didn't mean nothing, though; her mother had said when she'd told her about the Willis Tower, "He's not really a *he*, anyways. He's more of a presence. You can *feel* Him if you're a believer, if you believe strongly enough, but maybe you'll never see Him. Not see Him looking like a real person, you know?"

*Why couldn't He be a She, then?*, LeShonna had asked but that had made her mother a little fussed. He just couldn't, He just wasn't, and that was all there was to it.

৯ ৯ ৯

Sometimes the hard knot seemed to get a little closer to where the heart was. Sometimes it wouldn't go away even if you were almost asleep or almost lost in word sounds, bird sounds. You could be afraid you might have the dream again, you could be afraid of other things. Robin had written another poem, a poem about birds and the terrible things human animals did to birds before they killed them and ate them, not birds that they shot and made fall from the sky but ones they bred so that the birds could never fly and had to live in cages, suffering all through their little lives. Would it be good to show Granny both poems right away? It was an afternoon when there was no debating and there was no need to be home for hours. And there were things Robin wanted to ask Granny; how could you know how long Granny would be there to talk to?

Lines of sun shimmered off the lake, and on the pathway by the Oak Street Beach there was a child, maybe seven years old, maybe eight, holding the hand of a littler child, and the littler child was saying *fly away, fly away*, was it to a ladybug or a butterfly? It didn't seem to take any time at all to walk down Dewitt and Fairbanks, and, when Granny opened the door to Robin the very first thing Robin said was, "I have the poem, Granny, and another poem too, but I don't want to talk about those now, there's something important," and of course Granny said yes and that they could go out on the balcony. "You like it there, don't you Robin?"

"Sometimes. I used to never want to go out on balconies. Now I don't mind. But that's what I want to talk to you about. What happened on the balcony."

"It is still with you, isn't it, Robin? It will always be with you; she will always be with you."

"I have a dream, Granny, and in the dream someone kills their sister and I don't recognize who it is but then I can see that the person is me, and it's horrible, and then I wake up."

"Child, you mustn't think…"

"Granny, I haven't told you everything. It really *was* because of what I did that…"

"It was because of what *many* people did." K.P. was not giving any ground. But Robin didn't seem to believe her, hardly seemed to hear her, kept going on about all of it, told her about how Robin and Hope had gone out on the balcony not just that time but many times, about how they had played, about how Hope could sometimes be a little irritating but that was what you had to expect from really little kids. And how on this day Robin had shown Hope about paper airplanes, and how Robin had reached out for Hope just as Hope had been off balance, and maybe jostled—it was so hard to be sure…

"Of course you feel guilty. And is that a bad thing?"

"I don't know, Granny. It was a bad thing that I did."

"There are so many things we could all feel guilty about, Robin. *Should* feel guilty about; guilt can be a great force for good in the world. You can find a lot of people nowadays who will say we should never feel guilty, that guilt is bad for us, that we should have no time for it, that there should be an end to guilt. Full stop. I think that is all foolishness. That is like saying the wind should stop blowing, the waves should stop short of the shore. We can never end it. And we should not try. Guilt can make us try to do extraordinary things. Cure malaria. Build great libraries. Build churches that soar with their beauty. What is bad is when you let your guilt turn all inwards. Turn and twist itself like hot wire inside you. Then it can burn through your roots. It can destroy you. But you can turn some of that heat outwards. You can turn it towards making beautiful things, towards making a better world."

"Why can't I learn things anymore, Granny? Why can't I study and learn?"

"Perhaps you *are* learning things. But perhaps at the moment they are not so much school things. Perhaps you are learning about yourself, perhaps you are learning how to think about other people. I am just guessing."

"What if a person can't imagine doing much good in the world?"

"Then you must imagine better. Imagine other people first. Imagine how they think and feel. The good will come. You can make the good come. You can learn how to desire, learn how to love, learn how to care in a way that is not just thinking about yourself. Learn how to protect the parts of you that are able to care. These are not things I have ever learned perfectly myself. Many people never learn them at all."

"Never learn to think of other people?"

"Oh, they think of others insofar as it affects them; everyone does that. People act nicely to other people, because that way others will be more likely to act nicely to them. Or they act out of some sense of duty, as they have been trained to do. But to truly feel for others *as* others? It may be the hardest thing to learn. And there is no one way to learn it. It can begin with desire, it can begin with guilt. It can also begin with doing. Sometimes if you push yourself to act in some sort of do-gooding way, even if you don't feel any strong connection with whoever you are trying to do good for, it can become habit and the habit can turn into something you feel—you start to care truly and deeply for other people. But there must be some…"

"What is it that makes *you* feel guilty, Granny?"

Children almost always ask too many questions. But usually you could evade them; it was not that difficult, really. "Sometimes I think I have forgotten all that," said K.P., as if she were trying to answer the child. "Sometimes I think I never knew. I will tell you one day if I can."

"Maybe you could tell me a story, Granny. One of your skyscraper stories."

"Tonight I have something better. A newsreel about skyscrapers. We can sit together and I can save my voice."

"What is a newsreel, Granny?" She told Robin of how things had been long ago, of how short films had been played before long films when people went to the movies, and of how some of the short films were cartoons and some were newsreels. And K.P. talked about some of the films she remembered. By the time she had finished, the light in the sky was going, and there were streaks of mauve and of crimson trailing out past Grant Park, past Lincoln Park, and in the other direction all the way to Milwaukee, all the way to forever.

They went in and made popcorn together, and Robin helped Granny with the buttons on the machine, *I don't use them so often anymore*, Granny kept saying, it was a video, not a DVD or a Blu-ray or anything modern, and Granny said the video had been made from old reels of films, and then she described all of that, big heavy reels in their metal cases.

Then they turned down the lights, and the pictures sputtered and coughed and made a clickety-clickety-clickety sound, and then it all flickered into life, first a shot from below a building with a tower that was like a pencil it was so thin, the old building near the Jewelers' Building that Robin didn't know the name of—except in the picture it didn't look old. The things that were old were the moving pictures themselves, but they showed the pencil-like tower almost new, with a sort of shine coming off its tall white sides. Then the camera swung so that you could see on the other side of the river. It swept slowly across the face of the Wrigley Building and then it showed the walkway that joined the two towers of the Wrigley Building, and then it went shooting up to the cupola on top. Then quickly to the Tribune Building and then back across the river, all of this happening jumpy and fast. And then huge block letters spraying onto the screen, RISING STORIES, and underneath in smaller letters *Ever Higher for America's Second City*. A voice jumped out from somewhere under the letters, a deep, man's voice.

This is the city where the skyscraper was born. Chicago, Illinois. The city that Carl Sandburg wrote about: "hog butcher to the world, tool maker, stacker of wheat, player with railroads and freight handler to the nation." As anyone who's been here can tell you, there's a lot more to Chicago than that. Back in 1890 they built the first skyscraper here—or so folks say, you could probably argue till doomsday about exactly what was or wasn't a skyscraper back in those times, was it the Wainwright in St. Louis or the Monadnock right here in Chicago? There's no arguing when it comes to the Mather Building—

Here the picture skittered up to the top of the pencil-like tower—

you can feel it scraping a bit of blue off of the sky as those big clouds off Lake Michigan roll by. And this…

The camera found one of the turrets on the corners of the Jewelers' Building and then went up, on up to the very top—

this is the tallest building west of New York. The Jewelers' Building they call it, and it's a beauty. For a long while they weren't allowed to go this high in the Second City. Back in 1899 when skyscrapers were still a new thing, the city fathers took it into their heads that the city would look better if it were more wide than tall. Four hundred fcct, they said, that would be the limit for skyscrapers. Maybe they thought that's what the number one city of the *spreading* mid-west should be—a city spread wide.

The camera jumped to a picture of a broad open field—a wheat field, perhaps—and then to trucks unloading cattle at the stockyards.

But that's not what they think any longer. In 1920 the city got rid of that law, and now Chicago can be every bit as tall as anything in New York!

At that, the camera was in amongst the towers again, the camera man must have been on a boat in the river, the Chicago River, and the pictures went all around, tall buildings in every direction, the busy river below, scudding clouds above.

"We can have it all here in Chicago," I heard the mayor say. "We'll go tall—we'll have a brawling, sprawling tall." Makes you think of Carl Sandburg, doesn't it? And there's more to come. There's the story of the Tribune building, of the contest to try to build the world's most beautiful skyscraper.

The camera settled on some of the baubles near the top of the Tribune Tower, and then it climbed on up to the decorations at the very top.

And there's the story of the Board of Trade Building—45 stories it's going to be, when it's finished next year. Yes, there are a lot of stories like this in Chicago... rising stories!

And then the music swelled a little louder and the camera left the boat on the river and was somewhere high up, zooming in on one story of a skyscraper, you couldn't tell which one, then the next story, then the next, and then quickly zooming past story after story and on past the building's needle and on into sky and then vanishing in a swirl and a spiral, a black hole, and then big block letters again, THE END.

"Did you like that, child? I know it's old fashioned but I've always thought that however much..."

"Granny. You said that the next time we talked it should be all about me talking. Not about you."

"Yes, Robin. That was just what we were doing before the movie..."

"But I don't want that, Granny. I want you to tell me things. I want you to tell me how you know so much about skyscrapers. I want you to tell me more about why you like skyscrapers. And maybe more about how you were an artist. More about that prize."

"Talking about prizes sounds like boasting, doesn't it?"

"It sounds like you did well, Granny. It's good to feel proud of what you've done; everybody knows that. Ms. McLenithan..."

"That's what they teach nowadays, isn't it? When was it exactly that pride stopped being a sin? 1949? 1950?"

"How old are you, Granny?"

"It's rude to ask that. But I can tell you that I must have been twenty when all this happened about the prize." She looked closely at Robin. "Can you imagine what an old thing like me might have been when I was twenty? Or when I was your age, in Winnipeg? When I was your age I used to think old people were creatures who came into being fully formed. I think in some theoretical way I must have accepted they could have once had a previous existence. But only in the way I could accept that a butterfly once could have been a caterpillar, that a frog once could have been a tadpole. Not in the same way I knew about myself and how I had changed. That I had once been six, eight, ten." She paused a moment. "My train of thought. I have lost it. How old did I…. Where was I?"

"Winnipeg, Granny. You were in Winnipeg somehow." Now she would ramble on. Maybe it was better not to hear right now what had happened to Kenneth Paul. "Winnipeg; of course! You mustn't let me get off track like that." And she told Robin all about the skyscrapers of Winnipeg—the Childs Building in particular, and how it had been Chicago School.

"What's 'Chicago School', Granny?"

"Come. We can look at it now." Again they went out on the balcony. But they couldn't really look at it, not from K.P.'s. They couldn't see the Reliance Building, or the Brooks Building; they couldn't see Carson, Pirie, Scott; they couldn't even really see the Gage Buildings. They looked and they looked, and their eyes kept coming back to the white of the Wrigley Building. You could see the top of it gleaming and twinkling with light, the tower all lit with bright white light on bright white stone. You could see the layers of it, the angles, the windows in the tower, the old clock, the narrowing to the needle. Suddenly K.P. had forgotten what she had been going to tell the child about Chicago School.

"Anyone who lives in Chicago should learn about the Wrigley Building, child." So she told Robin a little about it, a little about Wrigley himself and a little—a very little—about Charles Beersman of Graham, Something, and Something (who could remember all the names?), the man who had designed the building all those years ago. And then they stood silently and looked out together at the light shining up on that tower, and at what was left of the light of the world as it went past them, went west, the glow moving on and on and always, on to where it was already tomorrow.

# PART 3

# Nine

At the monthly meeting of their association, Carol and Carl had gone ahead and raised the question of how well their building would withstand an earthquake. *You know the way things work*, Carol had said, *there'll be someone who'll say they'll try to talk to someone who knows someone who might know something about it.* Harry Phelps had been the head of the association for as long as anyone could remember, and Harry said that he thought the whole thing had been raised maybe ten years before, and that they had been told then that it was only in the south of the city that there was any chance of earthquake damage, the south and maybe also the southwest suburbs. For some reason the level of hazard was a little higher there. But for anywhere near the center of the city or to the north it was all right, you didn't have to meet any seismic code, nothing like that was required.

"But maybe it *should* be required, Harry," George Dorsey had interrupted. "That's what we should be looking into. Not just *do we meet code?*, but are we actually *safe?*"

There was a lot of to-ing and fro-ing about that, but as George Dorsey himself eventually pointed out, neither he nor Harry nor any of the rest of them was even remotely qualified to "look into" anything at all when it came to seismology. That was when Harry had said that for sure he would try to talk to somebody who might know something about it—and invited others to do the same. Harry being Harry, no one figured anything would happen quickly. But with Harry you knew that *eventually* he would indeed talk to someone, or to someone who might know someone who might know something, and you knew that he would report back. For sure.

ॐ ॐ ॐ

*Another day*, Granny had said. But how many other days could be left to spend with her? That was more important than any need to finish a geography assignment or a math exercise. Robin had promised not to be home late, but maybe you could stop for just a little while on the way home, and that wouldn't count as making you late. To see if she was still there. And she *was* there, but she had forgotten again about the picture that had won a prize and the pictures that had been lost, and she had forgotten once again about Robin's poem—or was it poems? Instead she told the child about the Chrysler Building and about 40 Wall Street in 1929—the wondrous struggle to be the highest in the world, a struggle she dimly remembered from when she had been ten years old herself, or was it eleven? How at the last minute the builders of the Chrysler had tricked their rivals by hoisting the beautiful spire from where it had been hidden inside the tower. How the spire had made the Chrysler the world's tallest building, just a few feet higher than 40 Wall Street. Did it matter that the Chrysler held the title for only a few months before the Empire State Building went yet higher? No more than it has mattered for all the others who have been world's tallest for just a short time—Taipei 101, the World Trade Center, the Singer Building, all the way back to the Milwaukee City Hall, the Philadelphia City Hall.

"Why does it matter at all, being the tallest, Granny? I don't think it should make a difference."

"I am sure you are right. Like so many things, it shouldn't make a difference. And yet somehow it used to. Used to for me. I have hardly any sense after all these years of the person who used to be fascinated by these things. And yet the person was me."

Other days came, and K.P. told Robin of the Reliance Building and the Monadnock Building and the Board of Trade, and all the great buildings of Chicago as it had started to grow up. And she told Robin more about her years in Rio, and in New York, and in a cold place on a river, a capital city, had it been Notawa? And more about Robin's father and when he had been little.

It was after K.P. had told one of those stories that Robin ventured timidly, "I still have that poem, Granny," and K.P. been about to reply *oh dear* and *now it's a little late, it's really time for you to be going* but she had stopped herself. Why had she kept forgetting the poem? Surely she could think a little less frequently of herself and of her past, a little more frequently of the child, and of the future.

"Of course!" she said, and was surprised to find that she meant it. "You must finally show me your poem." Robin's heart gave a little leap. A paper many times folded and a little bit crumpled appeared from a pocket where it had been waiting for a long time.

"It started out silly, Granny. You know, just putting sounds together. Until they sound together."

"I do know, Robin."

"But then it was as if real thoughts were coming into the sounds. I didn't want them too, especially, but they did. And after a while the thoughts and the sounds seemed to be all mixed in together."

"It should be read out loud. Shall I read it? Or will you read it to me?"

"I would like it better if you read it, Granny." And that is what K.P. did. She looked it over quickly, her eyes skipping for a moment down to the last stanza, and then she began to read out loud, from the beginning.

What if water never flowed?
What if snowflakes never snowed?
What if lightning carried words?
What if horses moved in herds
At night.

What if nobody had phones?
What if salmon had no bones?
What if fires made no smoke?
What if nothing ever broke
In two.

What if every line was curved?
What if every sound was heard?
What if planets never moved?
What if nothing could be proved
At all.

What if nothing wasn't there?
What if everything was air?
What if birds were all that flew?
What if now were never new,
Or true.

What if all lost things were found?
What if stars were all around?
If a railing were a wall
If a child could never fall
Fall, fall.

Neither of them said anything for a moment. Then Robin: "At first I wrote *in pieces*. Then I made it *in two* so it would be like all the other last lines. Two syllables."

"Yes. Two syllables. At first iambs and then the last stanza ending on a spondee. Two strong stresses. Weight."

"Mr. Humphrey, he was my teacher last year and he was, like, a poem is all about pictures. When I try to make a poem it's always about sounds. And then thoughts. I hardly ever get pictures."

K.P. looked closely at her great-grandchild. "When you wrote that last stanza, Robin—when you put a child into your poem—did you...?"

"I don't want to talk about that part of it, Granny." And Robin had told her more about Kathy Snyder, and the debating team, and about how Robin's mother and father had said maybe Robin was spending too much time with the debating, and not enough time on mathematics and science, not enough time on history. Robin didn't say anything about the big argument they'd had. Was it an argument if you didn't argue back? Carol and Carl had talked about how they had talked to Ms. McLenithan, how everything had to change. Robin would have to tell the truth about what had been assigned at school. And Robin would *have* to do what had been assigned, or else do the year over again. Robin didn't tell any of that to Granny. But Granny asked about the debating and Robin told her about *Resolved that food banks should be abolished,* all the arguments on both sides. That was on Monday.

When Tuesday came K.P. told Robin about when she had lived in New York and how she didn't think New York moved any faster than Chicago, it was just more compressed. And how you shouldn't have to choose between New York and Chicago, a lot of people always seemed to feel that if you praised one city you had to put down the other, why couldn't you love them both? and LA too, and Pittsburgh and Sydney and Chongqing, for that matter, "Chicago on the Yangtze" except that now it was larger than Chicago, far larger. And they talked of the new tower going up in New York that would soon be higher than the Empire State was, higher than the World Trade Center had been, but not as high as Burj Dubai. And how lovely it would look, and how maybe it was just as well they had decided not to call it the Freedom Tower.

And Robin told K.P. about how Kathy Snyder had been saying that people who debated important things shouldn't just be talking about the things they debated. They should be doing something about them too: they should be volunteering at food banks or shelters for homeless people or picketing some of the restaurants and food companies that treated non-human animals the worst. Robin agreed with Kathy Snyder, but Robin's mother and father thought finishing school and finishing university was what mattered; before you should think of helping others you should think of those things that would help yourself. What did K.P. think?

K.P. thought all those things were important but that maybe helping other people was the most important thing, and that there should always be time for that. She told Robin how she had worked with poor people in Rio and tried to help them read but she had not done enough, for long stretches of life she had done nothing whatever to make the world a better place. She talked about something someone was supposed to have said: "the best way to find yourself is lose yourself in the service of others."

"Someone called Gandhi is supposed to have said that. You know about Gandhi, I suppose, Robin?"

"Mahatma Gandhi. Yes, Granny. It means 'with a high soul.' I learned it from…"

"Your Ms. McLenithan, I suppose."

"You guessed." Was it surprise in the child's voice, or the beginnings of irony? No, there was no irony. "Change through peace, and also being disobedient. That's when…"

"Yes, Robin, yes it is. But I shall tell you the interesting thing about this quotation—this thing Gandhi is supposed to have said about finding yourself and losing yourself. There is no record of *anyone* having said it before the end of the twentieth century. Certainly no record of Gandhi saying it."

"So it's not real? The person who said it isn't real?"

"Is it real or isn't it? I suppose that's the question. It exists, certainly. What can we imagine happened? Someone somewhere said something like it at some social gathering and someone else said *that sounds like something Gandhi would have said* and then someone else a couple of days later repeated it to some friends as something she had heard, and said she thought she'd heard someone say Gandhi had been the first one to say it, and before you know it a dozen people are saying to a dozen more, *I think it was Gandhi who said,* ... and that's that."

"So it doesn't really matter where things come from? If they're true?

"Why would it matter, child, if they are true? But is this true? Is it true that the best way to find yourself is to lose yourself trying to do things for others? Perhaps it is half true, or perhaps even a little more than half. They say it makes you happier—happier than you would be otherwise, if you are helping others at least as much as yourself. Though surely that can't be the best reason for doing good."

"You should serve others for their sake, not for your own? Is that right, Granny?"

"I think it is, Robin, yes." She smiled a little wanly. "You would be well advised to do as I say, not as I have done."

"What about your paintings, Granny? Doesn't it make the world better when you make something beautiful?" And then they remembered that, weeks before, K.P. had been going to finish telling Robin the story about the picture that had won a prize. And about the pictures that had been lost: they were pictures with no names on them, she had said.

"Do you know, child, that sometimes you can be in the middle of a story and you know how it has to end but maybe you don't want it to end as you know it really did—or as you're sure it's going to? So you leave it for a while. You talk about other things. You do other things. Everyday things, mostly—things that feel as if they don't have an ending, you'll just keep repeating them, day after day, forever. Or you tell little stories about things that feel as if they won't ever have an ending. As if they will be there forever. You know it's not true, but..."

"Like skyscrapers?"

"Like skyscrapers. I remember what I told you: everyone has to know how it ends." But it was late; they decided that on Wednesday K.P. would have time to tell Robin the rest of the story. On Wednesday, for sure.

৯ ৯ ৯

And Wednesday came, and now it had been four days since Robin had last had the dream about Hope. The hard little knot near the heart had come back, but it did not ache quite so much. Wednesday was sports day so everyone got out early but Robin knew that Carol and Carl didn't know about sports day. So if Granny was home and it was all right with her, Robin could stay there for hours. And Granny *was* there, and very happy to see Robin. She said that before she started in on a long story she wanted to ask about Robin's debating, and about life at home. Robin told her how Kathy Snyder was having all the ideas now and when Jeff Bertram did have an idea she sometimes sort of ignored him; even Robin sometimes felt now a little as if Kathy Snyder wasn't always in the right. And K.P. talked a little bit about how Arthur hadn't always been in the right either but that they had sorted it out, mostly, and Robin said that at home Carl and Carol had started arguing, they kept arguing about politics. Carl always thought the President should be doing more, and Carol always thought that he was doing as much as he could, that you shouldn't blame someone who was doing so much more than anyone else had been able to do, not for a long, long time, at least. Carl had muttered something about needing to get done the things you were supposed to get done, and he had looked at Robin hard, he must have meant Robin to think about getting homework done. But it wasn't necessary to tell Granny all of that—especially just when Granny was finally going to finish the story of the pictures.

Of course they went out to the balcony. There were clouds massed above Pullman and Hammond and Gary, and on towards Michigan City. Robin looked away from K.P. for a moment and out across the flat calm of the lake, the wide horizon. From up here it almost always looked flat; it was only up close that you could see the steady waves, the swell. But then suddenly it was shivering, unsteady, not just the lake but everything, the two of them were shivering, the balcony, the whole building—

"Wait, Granny. Do you feel it?"

"Feel what, child? I am a little unsteady tonight."

"It's not you, Granny. It's everything. It must be..."

"No, Robin, it is not an earthquake. You and I have been through all that before. We do not have earthquakes here in Chicago." She paused. The shivering went on. From the kitchen came the sound of glasses jostling together on the shelf. "A tremor. At most a tremor."

"We should go inside, Granny. We should..." Robin was about to say *get under the table*, but you couldn't tell your great grandmother to do something like that. "We should get under a doorway. Under the lintel." K.P. looked at the child with real surprise, and said nothing. "That's the top of the door, Granny. It's where..."

"I *know* what a lintel is, Robin. The wonder is that you do. I rather think..."

"I looked it up, Granny. When I was researching earthquakes. It's where they say you should..."

"Yes. In case everything collapses. I remember about earthquakes, child. When Arthur and I were..." K.P.'s thoughts drifted off for a moment. "I will humor you, child. We will stand together in the doorway. Below the lintel."

"Thank you, Granny. It's just in case the..."

"But I assure you, nothing will collapse. Nothing will fall. Nothing will..." The sound of breaking glass came from the kitchen. "Those glasses mean nothing to me," K.P. went on. "They are silly with their long stems. They *were* silly. They were a gift from your father the year that Arthur and I..."

"It's stopped, Granny. It's over."

"Why, so it has. Did I not tell you it was nothing?"

"Will you tell me the rest of the story now, Granny?"

"Perhaps it is not yet time for that, child. Perhaps there must be other stories first."

They went back out on the balcony again, and K.P. started to tell Robin about the Hancock Building and the Sears Tower. It was still Wednesday.

# Ten

Harry Phelps *had* been in touch with someone. With Nico Mora, to be precise. Nico was going to come and have a look at the building—maybe the next day, maybe the next week, but Nico would be coming. Nico was always being pushed and pulled in every direction to do this, to do that, to do the other. But Nico would come and Nico was good; Nico would know if there were any danger. Harry was quite sure of it, Nico had said so himself, sight unseen. *Not that you can tell a lot from what's visible*, Nico had said. But he would come and have a look, and he would poke and pry into things as he felt was necessary.

Nico had said one interesting thing before he was even able to come round, Harry reported: Chicago hadn't kept up with the International Building Code. Especially not when it came to seismic regulations. *You won't see many skyscrapers in Chicago that are built to withstand a 7.5 or an 8.0,* Nico had said. Not that anything of that magnitude was likely to happen; everybody knew that, and Nico had wanted to emphasize it himself. *Once in a thousand years*, he'd said, *no more than once in a thousand years*. But things that happen no more than once in a thousand years do happen. And if something like that did come along, Nico wouldn't wager a lot of money on the skyscrapers of Chicago. Not any of them. Those were his thoughts, Nico had said; he'd be round soon to have a look. It was still Wednesday.

ॐ ॐ ॐ

"Carol, it just can't keep going on like this. I phoned Ms. McLenithan today. Did you know Robin's missed another deadline?"

"No. No, I didn't know any of that."

"And this afternoon: where *is* Robin?"

"Well, let's be fair, dear. It's only 5:30. If there were anything after school…"

"They had a Sports Day, Carol. School was over at noon. Robin never went, never showed up at the sports. I told you, I phoned Ms. McLenithan. She says she kept an eye out for Robin, and Robin was never there."

"Oh dear. Oh dear. What are we going to...?"

"We're going to have to sit the child down and—this has to be the end of it! No more going anywhere after school. No more anything until Robin has finished every single assignment, until Robin has..."

"And the debating? No debating?"

"I don't see how we can let the child..."

"A lot of people would just shut down if they weren't allowed to do the things they love."

"A lot of people aren't Robin. Do you really think if we cut out the debating that Robin would refuse to...? Robin's not *like* that."

"I don't know. I don't know what Robin's like. Not any more. I doubt if either of us does." Carl gave her a look, but then he stopped himself, and he found himself nodding.

"Yes. Maybe we haven't known for a long, long time. All those years when Robin was so quiet, so polite, so perfect. But so sad. What was happening inside? I said that I understood; I tried to offer reassurance. But I don't think I ever really asked what was going on in that head."

"And Robin never told."

ও ও ও

Robin hadn't meant to tell Granny *everything* about school. Hadn't meant to tell her everything about not finishing the assignments, about not even starting many of them. Or about not quite telling the truth.

Telling her everything had happened as they had been looking out at the city. That was Thursday. And K.P. had listened very carefully—the listening seemed to happen more slowly than Robin's talking.

"But it's not like you were saying the other day; I'm not learning about *anything*. Not about me, not about other people, not about anything."

It was hard to know what to say to a small person who was distraught, but after a time K.P had told Robin that it would be all right. "I know you will find a way to get done in life the things you have to do. I do not know *how* you will find a way, or where, or when. But you will, child. Your mother and father are anxious that all of it happen right now. And perhaps it will. But I think it will not hurt you if it takes a little longer. And I think it will not hurt you if you spend a little while longer with an old woman. It will not hurt to do that before you finish all your assignments."

"But there are so many, Granny. So many I haven't even started, so many that..."

"The more you have to do, the less helpful it is to think of how much of it there is. Now calm yourself and take a deep breath." Robin took a deep breath, beside where the knot had been tightening. The two of them looked out together over the city. It was a little foggy but only a little; they could see beyond the Wrigley Building and the Marina City towers to the vast gray of the Merchandise Mart. When you were this high up and everything below was so far away, it was easy to forget about history projects and math assignments. The knot loosened a little. K.P. talked about how fresh it had all looked back in 1938, and she pointed to the place beyond the Merchandise Mart where the old warehouse with their studio had been—where 'Higher Ground' had been. And then they looked to the left, out over the long green of Grant Park, and she asked if Robin knew how history had been made there.

"Everybody knows that, Granny. It's where the President gave his speech the night he was elected. Carl and Carol took us, it was a school day the next day but they said such a thing would happen only once in a lifetime and I could stay up late. And when I couldn't see, Father lifted me up and set me on his shoulders, I was too old for that and he said it would probably be the last time in our lives I would sit on his shoulders. It felt silly, really, for somebody older like me to be way up there. But I *could* see! I could see all the heads and the hats, on and on and on, and far away I could see the President's head and I could hear every word, *yes, we can,* and I remember that he said his Grandmother was watching, even though she wasn't there, she had died. I don't know why I remember that. And it was dark, but light at the same time."

"Yes, Robin. It was dark, but it was light at the same time." She paused for a moment and they looked out again. "It was a special day, and it is a special place. They made that park out of rubble. Rubble from the Chicago fire. 1880. You could call it visionary, I suppose. But visionary by accident—and by money."

"How by money, Granny?"

"The real estate on the west side of Michigan Avenue had been sold with a guarantee that there would never be any buildings blocking access to the lakefront for the millionaires who were buying up the properties—yes, once upon a time there were rich people's houses along Michigan opposite the park, not that long row of hotels and office buildings." K.P. paused again. "Maybe they had good intentions, maybe not—it's hard for us to know. But they made something good here. The Art Institute, the green space for everyone. And space for the new things—the Gehry, the Kapoor..."

"The Kapoor, Granny?"

"The sculpture, Robin, the Anish Kapoor sculpture. 'Cloud Gate,' it is called. The clouds come down to it and shine back from the metal. They say everything shines back from the rounded metal. But I hardly know it. You know I don't get out much; I haven't gotten out much for some time. I must try to get out to see 'Cloud Gate.' Really see it, sit beside it. And see how other people see it too."

"The Bean," said Robin. "That's what it's called, Granny. It's 'The Bean.'"

"There are formal names, child, and also informal ones." She smiled. "But where did I begin? You will remember."

"You talked about the park being where history had been made. About the President on election night."

"Ah, but that was not the history I meant. I asked if you knew history had been made there."

"Before the President?"

"Another President, child. Another time. Forty years earlier. It's hard to know how to begin to tell you about all that. But I suppose I had better try." And K.P. told Robin about one of America's wars, a war in another time, against a small, far-off land, and about what had happened in Chicago, in Grant Park, forty years earlier, *hell no, we won't go*, the crowds had chanted, and there had been the police with their batons, their tear gas— telling about it had taken a long time. But then K.P. had come back to the President that Robin knew, and the speech he had given when Robin had been on Carl's shoulders, Daddy's shoulders they had been then.

"It is one of his finest speeches, one of the great uplifting speeches that anyone anywhere has ever given. So much of what he says should inspire us, even now. And yet, and yet—I am an old woman, I am a crank. I am too old for uplift. There is something in those words that rings hollow. I choose my words carefully, for once—not false, but hollow."

"*Yes, we can?* Is that hollow, Granny? I think we really can. I think we really can make the world a better place."

"And so do I, child, most days. Most days I believe that. But even on the days I can't bring myself to believe that, even on the days when I cannot find any hope within me, I think we should try. And I believe the president would think that too. Would think we should try. *Let us summon a new spirit of service and responsibility, where each of us resolves to pitch in and work harder and look after not only themselves, but each other.* That is one of the things he tells us. And he asks us to join in the work of building and rebuilding—*block by block, brick by brick, callused hand by callused hand.* Personally I do not see the need for calluses. Not in all circumstances. But I take his point: it all takes work. What I don't see is why any of that should be conditional on our having some rose-colored view of the future, or of ourselves. Of ourselves as Americans, as Canadians, as Russians—as human beings. Trying to build a better future and a better world shouldn't require believing that that we are good, that we can always succeed if we try, that we can be perfected. That *anything* can be made perfect. We are imperfect creatures and we will always be imperfect creatures, and what we build will always be imperfect, and it will never be for all time.

"Yet we must not take that as reason for doing nothing. For not trying. Too often the people who accept that humans will never be perfect, even that goodness does not come naturally to us, decide they can do little more than accept the world as it is. With all its appalling inequities, with all its appalling cruelties. Too often they tell each other, if they are god-believers, *wait for another life, wait for heaven.* Or, if they are not god-believers, *there is no point, there is nothing to be done.*

"All that is laziness. I say it is laziness, Robin. There is never a good reason for not trying to do good. For not trying to make ourselves better, for not trying to make the world a better place." She paused, but she could not stop herself.

"But nor should we assume we will succeed. We should not assume that; we should not expect that. Sometimes, for some of us, it will be too much even to hope. Yes, even that. What the president calls our *unyielding hope*–sometimes we will lose hope. And that is not something we should be ashamed of, or something we should be blamed for."

"But Granny. What if…" Robin's voice was small.

"I must try to be clear. No one will say any of this in speeches. No doubt that is as it should be; this is not the stuff of speeches. But sometimes hope is too much to hold on to. Sometimes chance will take hope away, and sometimes despair will be necessary. Often, of course, it may be harmful, even paralyzing. But sometimes despair is necessary to the human condition. *Bellowing humans call out in vain to an empty sky*; sometimes we must be like that. Sometimes we must let go of hope if we are to grow, if we are to understand the world as it is, if we are…."

Finally she let her words drift off into nothingness. K.P was looking out into the dark and empty sky. She did not see Robin—it was dark, and the child was a little to one side. She did not see Robin begin to quiver, and begin to cry. She began again to talk, she talked on and on. "I don't say that hope is not sometimes something good within us. It is often something good within us. Hope, and hope's first cousin, optimism. Of course they can do good. But are they *inherently* good? Is there anything inherently good in hope, as there is something inherently good in kindness, or in freedom, or in fairness? Is there anything virtuous in the *unyielding hope* the president speaks of? I do not think so. Hope, optimism—the good in these things is only instrumental. Hope is at most an instrumental good, it is…."

"Instrumental, Granny?" The words came through quiet tears, but K.P. did not notice, could not notice. Not right then, not as she was so feelingly in the midst of what she was in the midst of. "If we find those things within us, hope and optimism, they may help us feel better, and then we may be better able to do good in the world, for ourselves and also for others. So the hope and the optimism become instruments to help us build those good things."

"Instruments? For building? Like shovels? Like wheelbarrows? Are those instruments?" Again and again came the small questions from the soft voice. "Or do you mean pianos? Or scalpels?" It was not only tears on Robin's cheeks; the wind was starting to come up, and something like rain was being blown into all the balconies from the open sky.

"Yes, I suppose like those. Instruments, tools—they are much the same, I think."

"People who use instruments aren't like the people who use tools, Granny. Pianists use instruments. And doctors. Diggers use tools."

"I suppose you are right, child. I don't know that…"

"And you haven't said about despair. Not really. Is it instrumental? Can it be instrumental?"

"Instrumental, child?"

"Instrumental. Granny. An instrumental bad."

"Perhaps it can be that, child. Perhaps it can be that." She looked at Robin hard. "Sometimes you know less than you think—have I told you that? But sometimes, perhaps, you know more." She looked out again at the dark air, and reached for her glass. "All I say, Robin, is that the feelings and the deeds may not go together as we think. Sometimes we may hope and believe and do nothing good, nothing to make the world a better place. And sometimes we may do good things without hope, do them when we are in despair, do them when we have let go of hope. We must be able to let go, to think and feel and imagine all that the human animal is capable of thinking and feeling and imagining. We must be able to see our fellow creatures plainly, and to see ourselves plainly. Which is not always a pretty thing to see, which is not always a sight to inspire optimism, to inspire hope. We must not be made to feel lacking if we cannot hold on to hope, if we cannot…"

K.P. broke off. Had the child begun to cry? Yes, now she could see. The child was crying silently but very hard, and at first K.P. did not know why and then it came to her, it clutched at her throat, the thought of Robin holding on to Hope, trying to hold on to Hope, reaching for Hope, and then all that way away, again and again for Robin over all the years, and tears began to come into K.P.'s eyes too, and she reached out awkwardly to put an arm around the child's shoulders.

"Hope. Hope. I am so sorry, Robin. Robin. I should have…" There was nothing else she could find to say. "I am so sorry." No, she could not make any of it better. She remembered how Carl and Carol had wanted an old name for their new child, a name with character, and how they had thought of *Faith* and of *Charity* as well as of *Hope*, names that had been everywhere a hundred years before but that no one thought of now. And now the name could do nothing except make memory more painful. Yet K.P. could not bring herself to wish that the child had been *Ashley* or *Sarah* or *Kaitlyn*. *Hope* had seemed just right.

K.P. could see now that Robin was shaking, was rocking back and forth and shaking.

"I keep dreaming her, Granny. She keeps coming into my dreams. Hope. Now it's just one dream, really. Over and over. In the dream we are playing together. We send our paper airplanes out into the air, and they flutter away."

"You told me of this not long ago, child. You don't have to..." But it was as if Robin had not heard her.

"... Hope never peers over, never sees them lose height and fall, but it is all right; when they fall they never really crash, they swoop and flutter and skim along the pavement and they are always all right. She is playing a game, at first a game with me, then just a game in her own head. I say to her *let's go in now, Hope* and I reach out. *You're not going to touch me, not going to touch me,* she says, and then it is a constant stream of words, *not going to touch me, Robin's not, Robin snot, snot, snot, my nosey's going to blow, my nosey's going to blow, Robin use hanky, Mommy use hanky, Hope no hanky, Hope no hanky, nope, nope,* and then in the dream I turn away and look for Mother, and she isn't anywhere and then I turn back and Hope is on the railing, she is on the railing, rocking, and saying *Hope high, high Hope, Hope high, high high Hope, no one more higher than Hope, more higher than Hope—no no no, Robin, no no no, mussen grab, mussen grab, nope, Robin, me put my armies in my sleevies, you can't reach me, no no no, Robin, mussen grab, nope, mussen push,* and then there is a space in the dream, and then I see her turning away from me, looking over, looking at air, *not go to make me, not not not.* And then I can see her looking back over her shoulder, and then calling again, all different, *Robin, Robin, Mommy, Mommy, Mommy, please! Mommy,* she's teetering, teetering, and then she is gone, and the dream is over. I wake up. And I know the dream is true, that it is all what I have remembered, that I have not saved her, that I have let her die, that I have let my sister die."

"Dreams are not the truth, Robin. Memory is not the truth. The truth moves on. If you must think back to that moment, you should know what your mother has told me. And your mother does not lie," said K.P. with feeling, lying and knowing that it was a lie. "You know that, don't you?"

"Yes Granny. I do."

"Your mother says she *knows* you could not have saved Hope. She says no one could have saved her."

"She said that? Really?"

"Really. She says she saw Hope pushing you away, and she saw you reach out again towards Hope just as Hope was already beginning to fall from the railing. And she says she saw Hope pushing, and then—I'm sorry, Robin, perhaps we should not be doing this. Perhaps I—I *am* sorry!" Tears had started to stream down Robin's cheeks again, and they would not stop. K.P. put her arms around the child, but Robin was rocking back and forth, back and forth, and could not feel her touch.

"She won't come back, Granny. She won't ever come back. And she's not been put back together somewhere in some baby heaven. She's just gone." There were choking gasps in Robin's crying now; if you brought your knees up to your chest and held them tightly, people said sometimes it could help, and that was what Robin did now. K.P. stayed close for a minute more, then two minutes, then three minutes. "Will everything of you go when you die? I don't mean just you, Granny. I mean the *you* that is *everyone*. For me it feels like there is some part inside that's not connected to my body—does my brain make me feel that? It feels like that part will somehow keep going even if the rest of me all disappears."

"Then perhaps it is the same for Hope. If you say *some baby heaven* it sounds foolish as a thing to believe in. But if you say *another world*—suddenly it seems possible that such a thing might exist, doesn't it?"

"I don't know, I don't know, I don't know. We shouldn't have been playing on the balcony. I shouldn't have let her go out there, I shouldn't have stopped paying attention to her, even for a moment, I shouldn't have…"

"No, you shouldn't have been playing on the balcony. And your mother and father shouldn't have taken their eyes off a toddler, not even for a few minutes." They had gone over this ground together; the child kept coming back to it. K.P. would have to say something a little different, try something a little different. "These are very, very small *shouldn'ts*. In every life there are thousands of these tiny *shouldn'ts*, tens of thousands. Has there ever been a small child that played only just where it was supposed to, only just when it was supposed to, only just how it was supposed to? Has there ever been a parent who did not become distracted and let their small child out of their sight for a moment or two, a minute or two? Or three? And with most of us, every one of those hundreds or thousands of times, nothing bad happens. What happened to Hope and to you and to your mother and father was bad luck. Horribly, horribly bad luck. But you should no more be blamed for that than any other child should be blamed when they play for a few minutes where they are not supposed to. Your mother and your father should not be blamed any more than should all the mothers and fathers who think of themselves for just a few minutes, and for those few minutes forget about their children."

On Robin's cheeks the tears had become salt, caked on. *I love you, Granny* were the words that came from Robin's mouth—though these were not words Robin had thought of saying. There were no words to say, there was only the ache that sometimes you couldn't make go away. Most of the time you could make it go away but then it would come back, and when it came back nothing that you said or that anyone said to you could help, you couldn't think of the sky, or of what was happening in the world, or of the sounds of words and of how they went together, or even of Kathy Snyder and how she smiled. Nothing would stay, nothing mattered.

"You know how you said that sometimes you can be in the middle of a story and you know how it has to end but maybe you don't want it to end like that?"

"Of course I do, Robin."

"But you can also be in stories that have ended but you can't get out of them. You can try and try but you can't put yourself in another story."

"Perhaps then it has to be another person's story you put yourself in."

"You'll tell me how that story of yours ends, won't you? Tell me now?"

"That was a death where there was more than enough blame to go round. More than enough. Sometimes if we know how terrible other people have been, it can make our own lives and our own selves seem better."

"All right, Granny. Go ahead and tell me now."

"They kept asking me if I knew how Kenneth had died. I will take you back to what they said, how all of it happened.

ৰ ৰ ৰ

*1938, 2011*

*"His death, Miss Schuyler. Last week. His death. Surely you do not mean to tell us that you had no knowledge of…*

"'None. I know nothing.' And then I went on. 'He was a strange man. In brief flashes it seemed as if there could be something wonderful there. But then he would be horrid. Horrid. I am afraid I never understood him.'" I looked at them hard. 'What happened? Can you tell me how he died?'

"They did not answer me question directly, not at first. Then Mrs. Vinall turned her gaze on me, and began to speak. *Yes, we know how he died. We do know how he died, Miss Schuyler. He took his own life. Are you sure there was no talk of any of this in your…. your 'Higher Ground'?*

"'Suicide.' I could hardly say the word. 'He had to have it all, or none of it. How did he…?' But I think already I somehow knew. He was afraid of heights, he said he had always been afraid of heights. It came to me that he would have seen death, and choosing death, as a way of conquering fear. He loved conquest, but he was not cut out to be a conqueror. I did not say any of that to the judges. I waited.

"*Do it, Miss Schuyler? How did he do it? He jumped from a tall building, Miss Schuyler. The Mather Building, as it happens. A window on the 23rd floor.*"

But K.P. was suddenly aware that Robin had stopped listening. That Robin was looking at nothing, far away.

"It isn't just bad people who think of killing themselves, Granny. Who think that..."

"No, Robin. No, it isn't."

"And it isn't bad to think that, is it? Not if you don't do it? Ms. McLenithan says there is a church that says it's a terrible sin to..."

"One of the churches, yes. They say it's a sin to lose hope. To give up. To try to kill yourself. And that if you do that they will have to bury you in a place where..."

She broke off. Robin had gotten up and was running, running quickly to the door and spinning and jerking at the handle to make it fly open and then running again, quickly down the hall, not to the elevator but to the stairs, and somehow Robin was going up the stairs, not down, taking the stairs two at a time so that the stories passed quickly. Ninety, ninety-one, ... ninety five, ninety-six, ... one hundred and four, one hundred and five, ... Robin could hear a thumping now. One hundred and six, one hundred and seven. You could hear your feet echo, as if the stairwell were a hollow place. One hundred and eight, one hundred and nine, and then no more floors, just two more flights to the top, would there be a way out?

The door said *Open in case of emergency only*. This was no emergency but Robin wanted to be out, out in the open, out in the air above everything. If you pushed hard on the metal door it would open, surely it would open. And it did: it swung outward and no alarm sounded and there was nothing but a light, deep blue. Light was in everything and Robin skipped across the gravel, wide and open, to where it was only air, and a breeze pressed the skipping figure forward, a steady breeze of fresh, endless blue. And then from right at the edge Robin looked over, burrowing flat in the gravel of the roof, eyes taking in the full world far below, the world of gray and silver and green and brown, of metal and of asphalt, of human stench, of glitter and rags and greed and love, the world of endings and of endless beginnings, all the clatter and ache of it lost in the squared-off air far below, so far, far below.

Robin went to all four sides of the roof, one by one, digging down in the gravel each time and looking out into the distance, to where the L stops at Wrigley Field, to where the planes glide one after another down to O'Hare, and to Midway, to all the sky-scrapers that Granny loved best and that maybe now Robin loved too, the Jewelers' and the Mather and the Sears and all of them, and beyond them the trains running south, to Soldier Field, to Comiskey, Robin's father said you should always call it that, *Comiskey*, not the new name, and to the Ferris wheel at Navy Pier, and on into the deeper blue that stretched away towards the sky, towards nothing. This was the world from a hundred and ten stories, the world from the roof of the world, and Robin forgot about Granny and about Hope and about everything, in the way that it is possible to forget everything when you have reached an empty and endless and wondrous place.

You could feel how the urge might come to someone. Not an urge to conquer fear or to conquer anything—not for Robin, anyway. But all that space pulling at you, pulling you towards it, into it. Pulling you to forget yourself, to forget everything. You could just let yourself go and there would be all that endless air. Everything vivid, everything endless and now. Past and future rushing past in the air, in all the great air. It wasn't that you *wanted* to jump. All of your wants and all of your fears had been sucked away, were no longer a part of you. All that remained was space, drawing you into it, drawing each breath closer, until the air you breathed in and breathed out was at one with the wind.

Robin inched away, forcing the space to be itself again. How many people had felt like this when they were in a high place, in such a very high place? How many had felt this need to be at one with the wind, with the sky, with the air that the wind and the sky were made of? Carl had said that most years something like a couple of dozen people would jump to their deaths in the city. *Jump to their deaths*; Robin forced the words to take shape. Not *would let themselves go into the air*; not *would forget about every-*

*thing, and the wind would take them.* What were the percentages? What were the odds? Twenty-four or twenty-five out of five million was 1/1,000 of a half of 1%. Was that right? Should you count the ones who never went near a high place from one year to the next? Say half the population was like that. Twenty-five a year would be one in.... It took a moment to work something like that out. And what about earthquakes? They always talked about earthquakes happening once every so many years. But that wasn't what the odds meant; Robin had been looking into all that a bit. When people talked about a *once in a thousand years* earthquake, that was the sort of thing that *might* happen once every thousand years—but it might just as easily wait two thousand years to happen again. Or it might happen again ten years later. Or five. Or two. It was all a matter of averages, and of chance. The New Madrid earthquakes of 1810 and 1812—those had been almost two hundred years ago. Robin took a couple of minutes to do a little bit more mental arithmetic. Then a couple of minutes more. The light grew fainter, and then fainter still.

Suddenly the wind had begun to gust more strongly. Much more strongly. Robin knelt and then stood and then staggered, staggered back in the face of the wind, and suddenly fear gripped Robin's small heart tight. If you leaned forward into the wind it was a little better.

No. Robin staggered again. One step forward, two, sideways, *lean farther, farther*, another step, two quick steps blown sideways. With one strong gust Robin would be lifted away, away. *Keep low, low, yes, right down*, Robin said the words out loud but the words were silent in the wind, *flat, down flat, kneel, crawl, that was better, better*, Robin could feel the wild air slackening a little but still it was whipping round everywhere. *Slowly. Slowly forward.* Soon there would be shelter, the square box that covered the top of the elevator shaft and the stairs was just ahead, soon Robin would be.... *The door.* Only now did Robin think of the door. What if it were one of those doors that clicked shut behind you and locked? That would be it; you could never open it again. How long would it be before anyone thought to come? Never.

They would never think—not for days, weeks even. It might as well be never. No one knew where Robin was. No one. Not even Granny would have any idea that Robin was here. If there was a Granny. Why would she ever even start to think that her grand-child might have come here?

Now Robin was almost to the door. Two steps, sideways forward, sideways forward, the wind pushed sideways once more, and that was all. Robin was in the lee, pressed against the wall, protected from the wind, in a place that would be safe. It was the door that meant death, not the wind. No handle, nothing to pull. No opening, not even a keyhole. Why would they build it like this? Robin tried to fit one little finger between the door and its frame. Maybe the door had not closed, not completely, maybe you could.... Robin worked away at it, pushed and pulled, wiggling fingers into the crack between door and frame. Nothing, no movement.

And then suddenly Robin heard it—heard it clearly. A little sound, a firm click. The click of a sprung latch that had not quite caught finally sinking in, catching—and firmly, finally clicking closed. No, no, no, it couldn't, it mustn't be. If Robin had only thought of trying with the penknife—the door could have been pulled out gently, easily.... No, no, no, this couldn't happen. But Robin knew through and through that it could happen, that it had happened. That the door had not been locked before, but that now it *was* locked, that one little finger must have pushed a little for a second instead of pulling, pushed ever so little, but enough. And now it was locked.

Robin slumped back down to the gravel. A time like this was a time to empty your mind and listen to the whistling air. Robin brought both knees together and wrapped both arms around them, and held on tight. Held on for a minute, two, three. Then into Robin's emptied mind came the thought that it had been a good little life, and that maybe that was all right. You shouldn't think of only the bad, you should think of the good things, of the bright things, and maybe a helicopter might see you, or maybe workers might come in the morning to fix something on the roof. Or window cleaners, to swing their beams and ropes out over the roof's edge. Maybe anything might happen. But Robin knew what a very little *might* it was. *Please, please let it happen before very long.*

Some time went by with the wind, and then suddenly it was cold, and the dark started to fill the air all around, and tears started to come down Robin's cheeks again and they kept falling, more and more of them, until Robin's whole face was wet, and still they did not stop. Robin rocked back and forth, knees up to chin, crying for mother and for father and for Hope and for K.P. who was Granny, *Granny, make it that you are real, make it that you know where I am*—maybe somehow she would be able to think, think of....

*Click. Click-thunk.* And then it was open. The door was open, and she was there. Somehow she had thought, somehow she had known.

"Robin? Are you there?"

Robin hugged her so very tightly and then cried more than ever, rivers down both cheeks as Robin and K.P. hugged each other, *thank you, thank you Granny, thank you ever so always.* And Robin was safe.

অ অ অ

"It was after September 11 that they told us." Granny had always said *September 11*, never *9/11*; it was all very well to have a convenient short form for something, but she didn't see little numbers as being properly respectful in a case like that. "I do acknowledge," she would say, "that mine is very much the view of a minority."

"They told you what?"

"They told us that if anything went wrong in the building, such that you thought it might be best to try to escape by going up rather than down, the north staircase was the one to use. When I looked down the hall and saw you running towards the door that leads to the north staircase, the thought somehow came into my mind that you might go up rather than down. But whether you'd gone down or up, I didn't want to run after you. A person should be given time to be on their own if they want to be on their own. And besides, I'm not much for running after people any more. But after a time—how long was it? Half an hour, an hour?—I thought I had better just be sure. And so I followed you. Or at least I followed where my instincts told me you might have gone."

She paused for a moment or two, as if resting. "It is a long way up!" She managed somehow to sigh and to laugh at the same time. "But here you are, and that makes me very, very happy." The tears were gone now; they hugged each other for a few moments longer.

"What can I do, Granny?"

"Do? What do you mean, child?"

"Do for you, I mean?"

"Just try to make the world a better place. That's all." She paused. "No, I am wrong. There is one thing." It was always good to give children something to do—especially as they got older. "You could help me find out what happened to my pictures. Have I asked you that before?"

The first question was the only one that needed answering. "I will, Granny. I know I can. We can do that together." For a moment they stood together, and walked slowly together back down the stairs to the 86th floor. There they hugged once more before Robin got on the elevator. It was still Wednesday.

Wednesday, and almost dinner time, and being on time for dinner time was something that mattered. Especially now that Carol and Carl were so upset about Robin and school; it seemed to matter to both of them a great deal. Did it matter to Robin? Not like life or death, or earthquakes, or debating on a team with Kathy Snyder. But yes, it did matter. Perhaps a little more than before.

# Eleven

Carol and Carl might be more worried about Robin than they had been in years, but they were starting to be less worried about each other, and whatever it was that held them together. Oh sure they argued—who didn't? But they felt as if they were on more solid ground than they'd been since—well, than they'd been on for a long, long time.

A lot of it had to do with Carl. How long had it been that things hadn't worked so well for him? It had gone on quite a while. It hadn't mattered if it was 10 at night or 10 in the morning, it hadn't mattered if he was relaxed or if he'd been stressed at work, it hadn't mattered if he was a little tipsy or dead sober. Nothing had worked for him. He had still tried to give Carol pleasure and they had both been grateful for that. But what had gone wrong with him?

They had tried talking about it, and now Carl could say with confidence that talk made no difference. The talk always led back to Hope. And of course the memory of her was precious, and he could still feel the pain of her not being there. But he *had* been able to put all that to one side for those months when he and Carol...—way off to one side. Why had it been so different the past year?

For months and months and on into years Carl thought the problem he had with Carol must be psychological. Must have to do with a pain he hadn't yet acknowledged, a pain that would have to be brought to the surface if the thing were going to be solved. But who needed to bring more pain to the surface? And who could afford a psychiatrist? Even a psychologist could cost a small fortune, and Carl's plan from work wouldn't cover any of it.

It was when Carol was out for coffee with her old friend Sandra that the penny dropped. Sandra and her Guy—*my guy Guy*, she would always say—had never tried to hide the fact that a lot of the force that held them together was physical. That was the way it had been when they met, and that was still the way it was. Except that it wasn't. Or it hadn't been, according to Sandra. *It's his valves*, she confided to Carol that Sunday. *And I don't mean the ones in his heart.* It was broad daylight; Carol looked around her to be sure no one at the nearby tables could hear.

"His valves?"

"His valves. It's all tubes and valves, when you come down to it. Even a lot of the brain part is tubes and valves."

"And?"

"What do you mean *and?* So we got him a pill, of course. We got him a lot of pills. And now he's his old self again. The valves work again, everything works again. Life is good."

"It's that simple? Sandra, you can't pretend that something as complex as—that it can all be reduced to tubes and valves, and pills for the tubes and the valves. It's a matter of *feelings*, it's a matter of…. Of feelings," she repeated with an oddly uncertain vehemence.

"I can feel him a lot better when his valves are working. And I don't see it as reducing anything. It's adding. It's making things possible that weren't before."

"But it's not *natural*, Sandra. You know it's not natural."

"It's not natural to get an artificial hip if your natural one gives out. It's not natural to get a heart bypass. It's not natural to take a pill for anything, for christsake. But if something goes wrong with your body and there's a way to fix it, you fix it, right? You try to fix it."

"So you think it's his body?"

"I *know* it's his body. I don't say that's always the problem with everyone. Plenty of times I'm sure it's in the head, it's something psychological. But not with Guy. There's never been any problem since—." She broke off. She had noticed something in Carol's expression. "What about you, Carol? What's happening with you and Carl?" Carol looked down, looked away. "You might as well say," Sandra prompted. And Carol did.

It was the next weekend that Carol made a special mango drink for Carl. He said it tasted a little funny but he liked it; she pressed him to have a second. And not long afterward she touched him in one of the ways that had used to lead to—well, Carl didn't need any reminding of where it used to lead. And he tensed; she should know he couldn't do this; it wasn't going to be now the way it had been for all those years, or again for those few months. But then he felt something stirring, rising, and the feeling grew stronger, and soon, very soon he was finding it hard to remember why he couldn't do this, or that he couldn't do this, and then they were doing this, and this, and this, almost as if it were something they had just blissfully discovered how to do.

When Carol told Carl that she had been given some pills by a friend and that the mango drink had been special, Carl guessed at once that the friend must be Sandra, and they had a good laugh about that. They had a good laugh about a few other things too. Sometimes humans find that, through some accident, a drug has been found that can help.

# Twelve

*2011*

A thousand thousand pieces of light swam across the little ripples in the water. It was so glittery, and so calm. You didn't have to think of the geography assignment or the math homework or any of the troubles of the world. Robin knew that the troubles of the world were more important than your own troubles, and it could make you a better person somehow to think of them. But as soon as you tried to think of other people's troubles, your own troubles could so easily find a way to start crowding in again; was there some trick you could learn to keep them away if you wanted to?

If you looked at the shimmer on top of the water you could sometimes make trouble disappear while a little bit of time passed—all the trouble, your own and everyone else's too.

It was Thursday. Carol and Carl had had a long talk with Robin Wednesday night. At lunch time Robin had talked with Ms. McLenithan about feeling sick. Robin *had* felt sick, right then at least. *Then you had better go home*, Ms. McLenithan had said, and then she had said it one more time with a little bit of emphasis, *home*.

Robin didn't head *directly* home; Robin headed for the Oak Bay Beach. For Robin it had so often been a good place to stop. To think of things, and sometimes to daydream. So often the light had shimmered across the ripples in the water, and Robin had felt warm everywhere.

But it suddenly felt cold today as Robin walked onto the sand; you could feel the wind gusting off the lake. The brightness on the water and on the sand and the brightness dancing in the leaves of the trees behind the café had gone. It was still early afternoon, but if you looked up you could see a dark bank of high cloud moving in from the west. Robin could feel the knot just below where you breathed, and then a shaking. It was like the shivering on the balcony the day before with Granny—not a violent shaking, just everything shaking enough to make you uncomfortable, maybe a little bit fearful. This time it was only Robin shaking, though. It was suddenly so cold. There was a sweater in Robin's bag, and Robin put it on. But the shivering didn't stop, wouldn't stop.

How did you know what the chances were? What chance was there that a real earthquake would happen—not a tremor but a real earthquake. That tall buildings could break up and fall? That someone like Granny would still be there after all that, would still be real? Robin started to move, started walking and then walking faster and faster. The clouds were closer, darker; would it start to rain before you could get to Granny's? Now Robin was half running, Chestnut Street, Pearson Street, Superior Street— no, it would not rain, Granny's building was already in sight and already it was warmer. It would be all right.

ৰ ৰ ৰ

When someone in the building trades says they'll *try to get to it, maybe tomorrow or the next day, maybe next week,* how often does it turn out to be tomorrow? It did this time. Nico Mora had been getting a lot of calls since that seismologist had started all the loose talk on the television and in all the papers. Now everyone wanted to be sure. Everyone's insurance company wanted to be sure. And so Nico had three dozen places he was going to try to get to in the next week or two. But it only made sense to begin where there might be the greatest risk. Those towers near the river that they'd thrown up quickly in the 1960s and 1970s—had anybody ever looked at them, really looked at them? Looked at the concrete, checked out the steel? Done any sort of seismic analysis? When all this had started up about earthquakes and everyone wanted someone to tell them *their* building was safe— well, you knew a lot of engineers would start with the buildings they knew were safest. You could collect top dollar for those, and it didn't take a moment's thought to sign off on them. Oh, you'd still put in all the usual riders and disclaimers, of course: *nothing in this document should be taken as an assurance that no earthquake damage will occur,* and then, always near the end, *structural assessments as to the probability of catastrophic occurrences and as to the probable extent of damage in the event of said occurrences can never be more than estimates; this report is submitted on condition that those preparing it are exempt from any and all claims of liability in the event of said occurrences.* All the boilerplate had to be in there. But an engineer would know there was no real risk, not with any of those shiny new buildings—and most engineers Nico knew would be in no hurry to take a look at the buildings that hadn't been new for a very long time, at buildings that really *might* collapse if there were a real earthquake. Liability or no liability, they didn't have much interest in trying to figure out the risks. Trying to figure out where things might actually go wrong.

Nico was the other way. The older buildings were the ones that interested him. The shiny new ones—well, anyone could put together the boilerplate and sign off on those, they'd had the proper testing before they were built, almost all of them. You couldn't sign off so easily on these old towers from the '60s. That tall tower on West Erie, for example—now that was an interesting one, one that Nico thought might actually not be so safe if…. Well, you didn't want to think, but Nico thought it would be a good one to put right near the top of the list. Besides, it was Harry Phelps who had asked him, and Harry had done Nico a favor or two over the years; Nico didn't forget things like that. He had pushed a couple of other things aside so he could spend Thursday at 300 West Erie.

ও ও ও

> Will we be like sky?
> Will we be like air?
> What will we be
> When everything stills—
> And where?

Those were the words that Robin had thought up in the elevator, and Granny had been there and everything had been just as it had been before, and soon they were together as usual on the balcony. Granny talked of how things had changed in the 1970s. Of how a great space had started to open up between rich and poor, as had happened in the 1890s, as had happened in the 1920s. And of how great new towers had grown up into that space—the towers of the '70s, the Hancock and the Amoco and the Sears. Of how Fazhur Khan had come to Chicago from what had become Bangladesh—"it was the poorer half of Pakistan," Granny said. "Came to Chicago and went to work for Skidmore, Owens, and Merrill. And he had discovered a way of constructing skyscrapers that they called tubular, making it so the load of a very tall building could be shared among all the pieces of steel. Making it more resistant to hurricanes and to earthquakes and to goodness knows what, and also to make it…"

"Is *this* building like that, Granny? Is it built that way?"

"I believe it is. Yes. I'm sure it is. Why do you…? Oh. You worry about earthquakes—it comes back to me now. It is easy to worry too much about that. Everyone is always predicting earthshattering occurrences that never happen; that is one of the foundational truths of America. Yes, I am sure that this tower is built according to the principles of tubular design. Now, where was I?" And she told the rest of that story and then all about the Amoco Building too, how it had been the second tallest building in the city and how the marble had begun to fall from its walls, fall from a great height. And she had been about to pick up the thread in the story about her pictures, but then she felt hungry, surely it must be dinner time, she thought, she had lost track of how late…. And she had nothing to feed the child, her cupboards were bare. "You must go home, Robin. And perhaps I will put my feet up. I think… But do come tomorrow and we…"

"Granny, I think I'm going to have to start coming here a little bit less."

"You have been spending a lot of time here, child. I had thought…" But in fact K.P. hadn't thought, she hadn't thought at all about any of that. "Do your parents…? Does Ms. McLenithan…?"

"They think I should be spending more time on schoolwork, Granny. And Ms. McLenithan thinks that…, that maybe I might be held back at the end of the year. Not be able to pass, that in math especially…"

"Then surely, Robin, you should be…"

"I should be spending more time on debating too, Granny. We have one on art next week, *Should the taxpayer pay for art in public places*, Kathy Snyder says the wording is set up so that the *No* side will win, but we have the *Yes* side and she says if we talk about art that people really like, like the Bean…"

"Cloud Gate," said K.P. with a gentle smile.

"Like 'Cloud Gate' that a lot of people say is very beautiful, Kathy Snyder says if we remind them of that then we have a chance. But we have to practice quite a bit more before next week, next Tuesday."

"I imagine that Kathy Snyder is right about the Kapoor." She paused. "What do your Mother and Father think about the

Bean? And do they think you should be spending more time with Kathy Snyder?"

"Mostly they think that when Kathy Snyder and I *do* get together we should be working on homework. But that's what we do already. They don't know that Kathy Snyder and me...." Robin stopped. "Granny, could we try soon to get your pictures back?"

"Yes. Yes, we will do that soon. One never knows. Long ago I lost all hope of ever seeing them again. Did I tell you that?"

"Yes, Granny. I think you told me that. But sometimes I don't remember too well. Sometimes I get distracted."

"So we must not get our hopes up too much now. But soon it will come to an end."

Everything would always come to an end. K.P. looked out once more towards the Sears Tower, that black and beautifully soaring monument to pride and to greed and to wild expectations, black steel and glass against the black sky. From this distance it looked still in the dark air, but the winds were up and off Lake Michigan; in a high wind she knew it could sway up to six feet back and forth. It would always be one of the world's most beautiful buildings, she thought. But she knew too that *always* was never true.

"When all that began, Granny—the rich getting richer and the poor getting poorer, and they started building their towers— was that at the same time as what happened in the park that you said was like America dying?"

"Just about the same time, Robin. Just about."

"I have to go now, Granny."

"I know you do, child."

"I love you, Granny."

"I love you too, Robin. I will finish the story of the pictures the next time you come, and then..."

"And then we will find them."

"Perhaps so. And then the story will be over."

৯ ৯ ৯

LeShonna thought quite a lot about rich and poor and how most kids at her school were poor or sort-of poor but a few were pretty rich, and of course there wasn't hardly nobody on the North Side who wasn't pretty rich, it seemed. LeShonna didn't like being told what to wear but she was starting to think it would be all right to go to one of the high schools where everyone had to wear, like, the same thing. Her mother said *nobody knows if you live in a mansion or a shack if everybody's wearing a uniform.* LeShonna knew her mama was exaggerating as usual, people could tell, the rich people would find ways to mention casual-like where they'd been on their holiday and that they'd gotten $200 tickets to the Bulls or the Bears game, and the poor people wouldn't say nothing about no holiday or no Bulls game and you knew what that meant. But still, LeShonna thought her mama was right, it would be one less way to show off, one less way you could look down on other people, if all the clothes at school were the same. And Miss Murphy said Hansberry Prep was supposed to, like, really teach you stuff, what LeShonna hated was when people didn't care about that. LeShonna was looking ahead now, she hardly ever thought about Ogden and Miss McLenithan and Naomi and Torii and Robin and them. If she went to Hansberry maybe she'd go to UIC after or maybe to art college, the College of the Art Institute, that was supposed to be the best and maybe you shouldn't expect the best but LeShonna thought *why not go for it?*, hope for it, work for it, what was the harm in that? Math was the only thing you didn't have to have good marks in for art college but LeShonna liked math just as much as art or English, there was something magical about it, look at the nine-times table and how neat it all was, 9-0 was the reverse of 0-9 and 8-1 was the reverse of 1-8 and 7-2 was the reverse of 2-7, and so on right the way through; and each of the pairs added up to 9, 7 and 2 was 9 and 6 and 3 was 9 and so on; and on the left and the right side all the numbers were in order, up on the left and down on the right, all the way through, God showed Himself in the wonder of that, just as much as he did in the shine of the sun on the water of the Great

Lakes, and the great blue sky, and the Willis Tower and all the other tall towers that human beings had built but they couldn't have done that without God's help.

Whenever LeShonna did well in a math test (and LeShonna did well on all the math tests, it seemed), Miss Murphy would always say how remarkable it was that someone who liked painting so much could also like math so much but LeShonna didn't think it was surprising, Leonardo had been really good at math and he had been, like, the best painter ever in the history of the world. No, not *like* the best painter, Miss Murphy said LeShonna had to try to stop writing *like* like that, she could talk however she wanted with her friends but in writing it mattered more that you got everything correct. Leonardo had been the best painter ever in the history of the world. Right?

ক ক ক

Robin could not go to see K.P. on the Friday, or on the Saturday, or on the Sunday. There were long, serious talks with Carol and with Carl, and times when Robin was forced to catch up on schoolwork. Except that most of it was sitting at a desk pretending to catch up on schoolwork. No, not pretending. But sometimes only, like, half trying.

On Monday Robin took sick again in the middle of the day. Schoolwork was important, but so was learning more about Granny and her life. And there would be more time for schoolwork in Robin's own life than there would be time with Granny; somehow Robin knew that.

Robin went again to the Oak Street Beach, and for a time looked out at the water and the sky, and then went on down Dewitt and Fairbanks, and up to the 86th floor. "Now you can tell me about the pictures, Granny, and the prize."

"The prize. Yes. It seems a long time ago that I was going to tell you about all that."

"It was last Thursday, Granny. Now it's Monday; it's time to tell me what happened. And you have to tell me how I can help you find your pictures."

"It is all so distant now—and yet it meant so much to me that one year. Ambition, anguish, anger—I don't know if…, I don't know how I…"

"The pictures, Granny. Just tell me about…"

"Yes." There was a long pause. Robin succeeded in staying silent.

"At the Art Institute," K.P. said finally, "do you know the Caillebotte?"

"What is a Kai Bot, Granny?"

"Something made by Gustave Caillebotte, child. A painter. When you go up the grand staircase of the Art Institute, a Caillebotte is the first thing you will see. It fills a wall; it must be twenty feet across. A Paris street scene: a couple walking, cobble streets, the lines of buildings, a bit of sky. And right in the middle a black lamppost, breaking the whole composition in two."

"And breaking the rules."

"Exactly—and breaking the rules. I remember how I flushed when I saw it. Someone else had gone before me, someone else had broken that rule. Not that I imagined that the Art Institute would be in favor in 1938 of anyone breaking that particular rule. Praise is always lavished on those who have broken the rules in other eras. How many want the same done in their own time, in their own backyard?"

"Not many?"

"No, Robin. Not many. I will tell you what Judge Little said in the end."

"Will you pretend to be everyone, Granny?"

"If you like. I will pretend to be everyone."

ॐ ॐ ॐ

Judge Little picked up the thread. *In itself, Miss Schuyler, taking one's life by jumping from a tall building has become unremarkable in the present age. No doubt there are dozens every year somewhere in America. Even in Chicago there are more than a few; people conspire to keep most of them quiet. But so far as your own situ-*

ation is concerned, Miss Schuyler, surely this death is remarkable. Someone who had the same studio address that you have given us. Someone who decided to leave the world from the upper stories of the Mather Building—that is one of the buildings featured in this Rising Stories, is it not, Miss Schuyler?* Judge Little did not wait for an answer. *Someone whose ability as a painter of dark and brooding works of art is more established, shall we say, than your own, Miss Schuyler.*

"'Kenneth didn't paint watercolors. I know he never...'

*"But how can you know any such thing, Miss Schuyler? Think of what you have told us of your own situation. You claim that you yourself were able to keep it a secret that you had painted this large work, that you had worked on it far into the night, with no one any the wiser.*

"'That was different. If you had met Kenneth you would know that...'

*"But to us it isn't different, is it, Miss Schuyler?*

"'No.' That small round word.

*"In fact, Miss Schuyler, there isn't anyone who knows with any certainty the direction in which Kenneth Paul's painting had been headed towards the end, is there?*

"'No. I suppose not. No.'

*"So it is indeed possible that when others had left the studio Kenneth Paul might have started to paint something quite different. Indeed, it is possible that any artist might have done that, isn't it?*

"'Of course in that sense it is possible. But it couldn't have happened. Kenneth was not the sort to—he was a hard little man. He painted in hard lines, he thought in hard lines. Hard, heavy, straight lines, heavy rectangles. Not clouds, not wavy space, not mist. Not Rising Stories.'

*"He couldn't have painted* Rising Stories? *Are you starting to tell us that again, Miss Schuyler?*

"'No, he could not have painted it. Because he *didn't* paint it. I did. But I see now that you are not ready to accept the truth. That you will never accept that a person such as myself—a woman, I mean—could have painted such a thing.

"*We find it striking, Miss Schuyler, that the name under which the painting was submitted—Pace—bears some similarity to the name of.... Well, I hardly need to spell it out for you, do I?*"

"'*Pace* and *Paul*? They are hardly very similar.' But I could see they were not so very different. Had I somehow been thinking of Kenneth when I had tried to think of names? Suddenly I felt even more fearful. 'I can tell you that when I thought of the name *Pace* I was not...'

*Patterson Kenneth Paul. P.K. Paul, Miss Schuyler. P.K. Paul.*

"'Patterson? He never told me that was his first name. I had no idea that...'

"*We can quite believe you had no idea of that, Miss Schuyler.* It was the third member of the jury, a Mr. Jenkins of the Art Institute, who had been quiet all along. *But you must surely understand that in the circumstances we are not likely formally to associate your name in any way with the prize winning picture.* Jenkins paused for a moment. *There is more, I'm afraid. There is a letter, Miss Schuyler.* He pulled a little sheaf of papers from an accordion file. *I will read it, Miss Schuyler. Listen closely; it seems that part of it is about you.*

> Dear—dear who? Who do I write this to? My father died in the influenza epidemic of '18. My mother understands nothing of me. No doubt that is not her fault; mother, you should not blame yourself when it is discovered what has become of me. There was a moment—only a moment—when I thought something great might be happening. I started painting in a different style; I don't know why, really. I completed only one picture in this style; it was a great struggle for me, and it happened only very slowly. It took weeks, months. But with that one picture I felt I might have found a new way of showing the city. A way of breathing life into its soulless towers, a way of... And perhaps what I was doing was good. Perhaps it was very good. Ha! Perhaps I should have submitted it to the New Horizons competition before doing what I am going to do now.

But is it worth it? Is anything worth it? I tried to paint a few others in the same style; whatever I had done that one time, I found I could not do it again. And then I looked once more at *Rising Stories*. That was what I had called the one picture. I could no longer think it was anything more than very good. I no longer think anything I have done is anything more than very good. My squares of color? Of no more interest than what Ben Nicholson was doing in '24. And with less life. This last stab at giving life to the city? No more lively or soulful than the cities John Marin made, or those of Kokoshka. Look at *Waterloo Bridge 1926*. Or even his bridge paintings of '23. That was the year he wrote to his father, "I believe in all seriousness that now I really am the best painter on earth." He was not yet right, but in a few years it would be true. As close to true as makes no difference. He had that greatness, he had that confidence, he was doing something truly new. Truly different.

For me, what is the point? I do not live for friendship or for love. I have taken pleasure in other humans—but what is pleasure, in the end? I have no friends. That is not to be self pitying or maudlin; it is a simple fact. I have acquaintances, and some of them have been good to me. But no more than that. No more. I have no great cause to fight for, no beliefs that drive me onwards; I despise politics. I have no desire for children and all that comes with them; I am not suited to any of that. And I am not suited for love. Whatever it is that some people find a way to do so as to make something more than friendship, more than pleasure, so that they—whatever it is that they do, I am not able to do that. I might have been able to make myself able to do it, but that was long ago. I was a child. No more. No more. My life is no tragedy and nor will be my death. Life was an emptiness, and now the emptiness will end. There is nothing to be mourned.

I have shown everything to her, of course—to Kip, to Kathleen. The woman who has said she does not love me but that she respects me, respects my work. Ha. Anyone could see what she thought of *Rising Stories*. At best, a novelty. A different style to fiddle with on the side. At worst, a distraction. A blind alley. In the long run, quite worthless. Like the rest of my work. And I could feel in my bones that she was right—she has had such influence over me, and yet even now I can tell she has been right about so many things. Certainly she was right about this. And about me, I suppose. As a painter. As a person.

But I will say it again. This is not her fault; this is not the fault of any woman. It is the fault of no one and it is the fault of everyone. And of course it is my own fault too, my own fault most of all. It was me and me alone who decided what mattered: great art, and to become a great artist. That was the only thing. It has been me and me alone that, instead, has achieved this resounding mediocrity. No more, no more of that. No more. When it ends I shall think of myself as falling from a great height—a height where I have always imagined I would take my place. A height like the heights I gave life to in that one picture I imagined might have achieved greatness. Like those skyscrapers, perhaps like the tower of the Mather Building—yes, like that most of all. Perhaps I shall make that my last place on earth: a height where I have never deserved to be. Farewell, any and all who read this. Fare well.

*That letter was found only last week, Miss Schuyler. But very plainly it was written many weeks before that; very plainly it was Kenneth Paul who met his death on the day submissions closed for this competition, Miss Schuyler. More than two months ago, Miss Schuyler. And you tell us you had no idea he was missing?*

"'No idea. None.' It was a strangled whisper that came out of me.

*"It was Kenneth Paul who jumped from the Mather Building that day, Miss Schuyler. Who took his own life. You knew he was distraught, you knew he was going away. Perhaps you knew he planned to take his own life. You submitted his own work as your own, didn't you, Miss Schuyler?*

"'No! No! Don't you see? This is his revenge. He says he thought he would breathe life into the skyscrapers, make them live. But he could never feel the life that's already *in* them; that's the life you have to feel to paint like that—the life outside yourself. The life that Dinkleberg and Riddle and Hood and all the others put into them, the life that the lives of thousands of people put into them every day, that all the... I cannot say it all. I can only feel it. It was what I felt that went onto that piece of paper. That painting. You have to...'

*"All we have to do, Miss Schuyler, is make a decision as to who is more likely to have painted this watercolor. And there is no actual evidence that you painted this picture. Is there, Miss Schuyler?* A long pause followed. Finally a small light went on.

"'Yes. Yes!' I cried out.

*"Yes, there is no evidence. As we thought, Miss Schuyler. I...*

"'No!'

*"No, there is no evidence. You do not have to repeat the obvious, Miss Schuyler.*

"'Yes. Yes. Yes, there is evidence. Evidence that I painted it.'

*"Evidence that you have just thought of? Or just imagined?*

"'My handwriting. You need to have a record of my handwriting. And you need to...'

*"You should not become too accustomed to telling this board what they need to do, Miss Schuyler. Already we have spent an inordinate amount of time on...*

"'You need to contact my parents. You need to do this right now. While you can see that I have had no chance to contact them, not since I heard this terrible news about Kenneth. And you need to ask them what they have heard from me. Ask them if they have heard anything of what I have been painting. I wrote them! I told them about the painting, about how I had painted the Mather Building and the swirling clouds all wet and...'

"*And what do you expect that we will...?*

"'Ask them. Ask them!'

"It took some time to sort everything out, but over the course of the next hour a trunk call was placed to Mr. and Mrs. Frederick Schuyler in Winnipeg, Manitoba; Mrs. Schuyler said yes, that was right and she knew just where the letter was and she read it out to them, and no, that had been the only thing they had heard from their daughter since she had left and it had been weeks and weeks ago, here is was, she still had the envelope, it was postmarked August 10th, and if they wanted they could speak to her neighbors the Walzers, she had told the Walzers all about it when the letter had arrived and they had read it too, about the painting and all of it, and she agreed to have a photostat made and send it to the judges of this art competition in Chicago, it appeared their daughter was still staying in Chicago, despite what she had written. And the authorities in Chicago had agreed that it wouldn't be necessary to have a handwriting expert compare whatever sample of handwriting Kathleen gave them now with the handwriting on the letter; compensation would need to be offered to anyone of that sort hired for their expert services, and a jury for an art competition didn't have the resources to do anything of that nature. In any case, it seemed almost certain the letter was genuine. The judges had then reconvened to consider the awarding of the prize. I couldn't help but be elated; what more could they possibly want?

"*You realize, don't you, Miss Schuyler, that this is still not proof.* Judge Little was addressing me; it was not a question, and my heart sank.

"*There is no reason you couldn't have been lying to your parents. Pretended to have painted a picture you would have been proud of, if it had in fact been yours. A picture that you had seen, that you knew to have been painted by Kenneth Paul. And we know you lied about...*

"'Nothing in that letter was a lie...'

"*We know already that you were misleading about your where-abouts. It may no longer seem a settled issue that Paul painted the picture, Miss Schuyler, but it can hardly be said to be settled in the other direction. It is your word against his, Miss Schuyler. And he cannot be here to tell us of whatever evidence he might have had, whatever other letters he might have written.*

"But then another judge spoke out. *I believe her.* It was Mrs. Vinall. *Perhaps we cannot be one hundred per cent sure, but I believe her.*

Judge Little gave her a piercing look. *I do not disbelieve her, myself.* The judge chose his words carefully. *But let us look at it objectively. With reason, as well as emotion. We have two passionate statements. They cannot both be true. She stands before us, ready and willing to whip up that passion again. But all her passion must not be allowed to trump this young man having given his life.*

"'Who is saying anything about *trumping* his death, sir? With respect, you are making it sound like a game.'

"*But you are not in fact speaking with respect, Miss Schuyler. You may leave us now to our deliberations.* I was ushered out, and that was that. I thought I could see how it would end; they would decide despite everything that Kenneth had painted *Rising Stories*. He would have something of the fame he craved. I would be a pariah—unwelcome at Higher Ground, unwelcome anywhere except back home in Winnipeg.

"But that was not quite how it worked out, after all. Mrs. Vinall must have been more forceful with Judge Little than I would have thought it possible for a woman to be. More *effectively* forceful. The judges decided that, for reasons they thought it best not to disclose, they had found it impossible to ascertain the painting's provenance with complete certainty. The work would be exhibited with a simple but unhelpful note, *The name of the artist has been withheld.*

"I heard later from someone who was at the awards ceremony that Judge Little delivered a speech both elliptical and amusing. He said little about *Rising Stories* but spoke at some length of other cases in which works had been exhibited anonymously at one institution or another—implying, without saying so directly, that in this case it was being done at the artist's own request. There were one or two questions, no more. And life went on. There was no boom in the reputation of Kenneth Paul after his death, and there were no more buyers for his work after his death than there had been before it. Nor was there much interest in *Rising Stories* when it was exhibited; it did not suit the style of the time. Had any of the personal details been released, that would have piqued interest, of course. But they weren't, and I said little or nothing about the whole thing to anyone—even the others at Higher Ground. It would not have changed things, I decided, except perhaps to make them worse.

"Of course I had to promise to come home and see my parents. I went home to Winnipeg for a week over Christmas. It was colder and smaller than I remembered, but there was still love in my parents' hearts. And in mine, which may have surprised me more. At the end of the week I came back to Chicago. I began painting again, furiously. And I began to think of moving to New York."

# Thirteen

*2011*

"So much happens in all of this, Granny. And there are so many people coming into the story. It's not easy to…"

"Sometimes it is easier to think just of yourself? Of your own story"

"I didn't mean that, Granny. I meant…"

"Does it seem real, any of it? Does it even make sense? It was all so long ago. And now you have the ramblings of an old woman who is barely there—perhaps all the stories she tells are just crazy thoughts that will fly apart, each on its own, spinning away and away. Centripetal force. If you…"

"Centrifugal. Centrifugal is the one that makes all the spinning things want to fly away. And yes. It seems real. Because you seem real, Granny. I think." Robin looked straight at her face. "What happened after it ended? After you didn't get the prize, and whatever it was happened with Kenneth."

"After he died, you mean."

"Yes, Granny. After he died."

"What usually happens after someone dies, I suppose. Life goes on."

"But for you, Granny. For you."

"I like to think of it as mainly being a time when I painted furiously. But if I think hard about it I am sure it was not like that at first. I had seen Kenneth so anguished at not being able to do what I had done. I had.... Well, when he died it was hard at first for me to find the courage again. To be bold again, to be big in what I was trying to do. I would pull out the roll of paper late at night, and I would cut off a large piece. That was how I tried to begin again. Two or three times I cut off large pieces. Very large, even larger than I had used for *Rising Stories*. Then I would lay one of those pieces down in front of me on the table. I would stand and look at the large piece of paper, and try to think of all the ways I might fill it. I would find myself thinking of all the ways a painting could go wrong. Of all the ways I might make it go wrong. And then I would do nothing, and the next day I would fill the large sheet with some flowers in a vase. With rubbish.

"One day I told myself I would not be scared any more. Still, I waited until the others were gone. Usually it would be Giorgio who was the last; *don't forget to turn out the lights*, he would say. As soon as the door closed I pulled out the roll of paper. I didn't try to square it off, to make anything straight; I just hacked off a huge piece. A few quick lines in pencil on the big sheet of watercolor paper. Then a moment standing back, imagining color, imagining it running, spreading, seeping, bleeding. Then pushing the paper under the tap, soaking it, carrying it scrunched and sopping across to the great table, drips spreading on the floor the whole time. A deep breath. And then I was away—the fear was gone and I was flinging color, great wet clumps of it, and pushing and sweeping it with fat, wet brushes, and more color was pouring onto the water, and the water with the color in it kept spreading across the paper and seeping in. Spreading and splashing and seeping, and by midnight I had another. Another great picture—" she caught herself, and blushed. "By *great* I mean very large, large and imposing; I don't mean great like Vermeer was great, like Degas was great, like…"

"But was it great that way too, Granny?"

K.P. looked away. "I don't know, Robin. I don't know." And then she looked down, and it was a moment before she started speaking again. "Whatever it was, I started to do the same thing almost every night. Mostly I would have some sketch ready as a starting point—but that was all, a starting point. Sometimes I'd forget what paint was on what brush and shoot pure Prussian blue into the sky or cerulean into the sea. Sometimes I would squeeze the tube right onto the paper, squeeze the paint in globs across the wet paper and let everything find its own way; when I did that it would leave great lumps, great bright lumps of color that would darken and harden later as they dried. Sometimes I'd use the wrong end of the brush to scrape into the color, sometimes the flat of a thumb to push the color sideways, sometimes a thumbnail to scratch light across the sky in a great wide arc, the lights of a building, the lights of the stars, the light that lived in the…"

"Were you drunk, Granny?"

K.P. smiled, but not too much. "No. Not usually. But often I wanted to be in a state of something like drunkenness. And sometimes I might have used drink to help get me there. Yes, I think I did that. Often I would have a bottle of wine in the cupboard with the paints, often I would pour a glass as I began to paint. And then when the paint began to slow to a dry stop on the paper I would begin to think *Is it there? Is it there? Have I done enough? Will I spoil it if I…?* And then I would sometimes look around me and exclaim to myself 'good heavens, I've drunk almost the whole bottle.'"

"'Good heavens' was what you said?"

"That was what people said in those days. Well, it was one of the things people said."

"What did you do when you had finished them, Granny? Finished all your big paintings. Did you show them to the others? Did you...?"

"No. No, not to any of them. I suppose I started to think I was under some sort of spell. That it might be broken if I.... Ever since the strangeness around the prize and Kenneth's death there had been a distance. People had not been warm. And I was so self-conscious then. Not late at night when I was on my own with the paint flying across the wet paper and the better part of a bottle of wine..."

"The better part?"

"It means *most*." K.P. looked down at Robin with fondness, but a certain sharpness too. "Not late at night with that much wine gone. But in the daytime? I was self-conscious, I was sometimes shy, I was all the things a girl—a young woman of nineteen is likely to.... And I didn't yet understand just how the day slops over into the night, or just how one's life with people sloshes over into one's quiet life, one's private life. When you let the things out that could otherwise never... But you are too young to think of such things," she added absently.

"But I'm not, Granny. Really I'm not." Robin was not sure if she had heard; K.P. had turned away and seemed to be concentrating hard as she poured herself a glass of gin.

"Perhaps I didn't know myself then. But I did know I had to keep those paintings to myself. I had painted the Mather, the Jewelers', the Wrigley, all the skyscrapers by the river, the Reliance, the Board of Trade, then the river again, again, again, until there were more than a dozen great paintings..."

"Large?"

"Exactly, Robin. Large. Large paintings that I could be proud of. With the fog running through them, and the sky and the mist and the river. A dozen, and then there were fourteen, seventeen, eighteen—I stopped at twenty." She stopped now, stopped talking, and looked at the child. "You don't think this is all a tall tale, do you Robin?"

"What's a tall tale, Granny?"

"It's a name we used to give to made-up stories that were larger than life. Larger, and not very believable. Paul Bunyan and the river that would shoot hundreds of feet into the air, Jack and the Beanstalk, ...

"The further from the ground, the less believable?"

"Yes, that is part of it. But it is not a problem unless you try to come back too soon, or in the wrong way. Or in the middle of the story."

"If right in the middle you stop believing, that's when you might fall?"

"Perhaps something like that. Don't fall, child."

"No Granny. I won't fall." Robin smiled as if it were a new way of smiling. "And I won't jump."


# Fourteen

*2011*

By the time Nico Mora met with Harry Phelps it was Tuesday morning. Nico settled into a chair in Harry's office; he liked to take the load off his feet when he could. It wasn't always so easy to do that when you had a job like Nico's, and he wasn't getting any younger. You started to feel it after a few hours; Nico's shins would start to ache, and his back.... It was good to sit down. And if he were sitting with someone rather than standing they'd be less likely to lord it over him, the way some people find themselves starting to do with short people. Nico was very short, but he was stocky too. He had made himself very strong, and not just physically—all of that helped. You could count on Harry Phelps not to try to lord it over anyone; he wasn't that sort. But Harry didn't seem quite himself today.

"What can you tell me, then, Nico?"

"A full written report will take longer. But I can give you the essence now—I know you want it quick."

"You bet I do. I want to be able to tell people *something* at the meeting this Friday. It doesn't have to be conclusive, it doesn't have to be hundred percent definite, I just want to…"

"The first thing to tell them is that nothing is a hundred percent definite with earthquakes. Nothing. At some level it's all guesswork."

"Yeah, yeah. I get that, Nico. I think they all get that."

"And the second thing to tell them is that, on the whole, skyscrapers are safe."

"On the whole?"

"On the whole. Relatively speaking. For the most part they're…"

"Compared to what?"

"Compared to, say, a four-story apartment building. Compared to a townhouse. Compared to a bungalow, even. Steel-frame skyscrapers—and since about 1900 all skyscrapers have been steel-frame skyscrapers—tend to be an awful lot safer than wood-framed structures. Safer than brick, too. Safer than reinforced concrete. Safer than just about anything. And *very* tall structures tend to be among the safest."

"I can imagine they'd be among the safest. It stands to reason you'd put a lot more effort into the engineering side of it; if a building's going to be ninety stories tall you'd want to make extra sure that…"

"You would. You do. More careful planning, stress tests—all of that. But it's not just those things that make skyscrapers, on average, safer than other buildings. It's also the way they shake. The greatest danger to a building in an earthquake is if the natural rhythm at which it shakes—its natural frequency—happens to be in tune with the shaking of the earth. The resonant period of a very tall building tends to be pretty long, and that makes it out of sync with most earthquakes. Most—I should emphasize the word 'most'."

"I didn't know that. Interesting. Now this building is forty-four stories tall; that's tall but it's not *very* tall.

"Exactly. And it's old. Not compared to the Reliance Building or the Wrigley Building, but compared to the Trump Tower, compared to…"

"I hear you, Nico. That's why we…"

"Exactly. Why you called me. The damage would be so catastrophic if…"

"So there is some chance of catastrophe?"

"Here's what I can tell you, Harry. To start with, this building is pre-1994. That was the year of the Northridge quake in California; for tall buildings built after that they put in new requirements for testing steel—testing strength, testing brittleness. New requirements as well for the ways in which pieces of steel can be connected to one another."

"The welding."

"You got it, Harry. Now, I'd need to tear apart quite a few walls if I was going to tell you much about that side of things, and I'm not about to do that unless you tell me to."

"Let's leave the walls for now, Nico."

"Right. I did go into a few crawl spaces, and I've seen a few welds; most likely the rest are pretty similar, though I can't vouch for that."

"And?"

"It's not great, Harry. I can't say definitely that it's dangerous, but it's not great. I've also looked at your walls, and at what your blueprints say is behind the walls, and under the base. In a building this old there's never going to be any roller bearing, there aren't any dampers—you wouldn't expect any of that. Certainly not in Chicago. But there's no X bracing either—that's one way they reduce the risk of damage from lateral forces. And there's not a whole lot of bracing of any sort at ground level, either; obviously that's where the sideways force of an earthquake is going to hit a building hardest. The steel this thing is built with is pretty light. Do you get a lot of sway in high winds?"

"Yeah. A lot. Not like the Sears Tower, I guess. And not like that building off Michigan Carl Smith's grandmother used to live in—that was a new building in '96, but it feels like an adventure any time you're up there in a high wind, you can hear it creak, all those stories, sometimes you can even feel the plates between the floors shifting. That sort of thing can make you seasick a thousand feet above the ground. But this one? Maybe it creaks a little bit, maybe it sways a foot or two back and forth at the top in a high wind. Should that make us..."

"It's not *necessarily* a bad thing. Again, it's going to depend on the frequency—how in sync the swaying and the shaking of the building is with the swaying and shaking of the ground. But more often than not a building that sways a lot in the wind will be more susceptible to damage during an earthquake. Those towers from the 1930s and the 1920s and before, when it was always steel plus concrete, not steel plus glass, they tend to have a lot less sway—and I'd rate them safer in an earthquake than most of the towers thrown up in the '60s and '70s, maybe even than some of the brand new ones. Don't get me wrong: *some* of the tallest and lightest ones are also some of the safest. But without the steel standards we've had since '94, without the bracing? If a real earthquake hit—let's say a 7, not too close to Chicago but not too far away either, and not too far underground..."

"What would happen to this building?"

"In those conditions, I'd say this building is about as dangerous as anything on the North Side. Which is *not* to say—I'll emphasize this again—*not* to say it's unsafe in absolute terms. The chance of that sort of earthquake happening in or near the city any time in the natural life of this building is really, really small. The chance of this building collapsing if one *did* hit is smaller still. But if *any* Chicago skyscraper is a candidate for collapse in an earthquake, I'd say this one just might qualify."

"I hear you, Nico. I do hear you. So what can be done? We can't tear out all the walls and re-do all the welding and put in a ton more steel, can we?"

"No, you can't. You might as well tear the whole thing down and start from scratch. But you might be able to put in some reinforcement at ground level. And you might be able to put in what they call an active control system in the upper stories. It adds weight, helps to stabilize the thing, helps to cut down on sway. In an earthquake it can counteract..."

"What sort of weight? What do they put up there?"

"Liquid: it's a hydraulic system they use, generally. It's got a system of pistons that..."

"And that can be added somewhere in the top floors?"

"It's not easy to do a seismic retrofit, I can tell you. But if you're asking me *Can it be done?*, the answer is *Yes. Absolutely.* You'd lose some space—the equivalent of a couple of units, maybe three. They'd need to be taken out, and then you'd..."

"People would need to move out?"

"Some of them would, for sure. Some of them on the upper floors. At least for a time. And they'd come back to smaller apartments, some of them, if they did come back."

"We're talking tens of millions, I suppose."

"Maybe $10 million, maybe $15. Seven, eight months of work. Maybe a year if things don't go well."

Harry Phelps made a quick calculation. "So that's going to be something close to $50,000 per unit, maybe more. That's a whole lot of money, but it might be... I just don't know if people will want to spend that much for what amounts to a little bit of extra insurance."

"So you ask them, Harry. What else can you do?"

"Right. Sure we ask. But even if they decide they want to go ahead, that won't change anything right now. If there were an earthquake next week..."

"Then you just have to hope that doesn't happen. There's nothing else you can...—well, not quite nothing. I know you used to be a churchgoer, Harry. You can pray. Pray, and hope. But like I say, nothing's likely to happen."

"I'll tell them you said that, Nico. And then they can hope and pray all they want."

Monday night had not been easy for Robin. There had been a little bit of a scene at home. But now it was Tuesday, and it was after school. *Today I will live for today*, Robin thought; *follow the thoughts in my head*, and they took Robin briefly to Oak Beach and then straight for the tall building off Michigan, and the right buttons on the elevator were all there, and Robin went rising higher and higher, and soon was starting to ask Granny some questions. But K.P. would not answer, and would not begin any stories.

"I keep speaking too much about me. Do you have another poem to show me?"

And they had sat down together and read together and talked together about the words. The words were really very good, K.P. had said, the words that Robin had chosen for putting together. And the putting together itself was really very good too, that was what K.P. said, and she meant it, every word. The child was good.

"But these are the only poems that I've done that are any good, Granny. That's what I think, anyway. And I have tried so many words together."

"What have you tried just today or yesterday?"

"A lot of it seems like fun, and then I read it again and it just seems silly. Childish."

"Like what?"

"Like taking the *g* off *gloves*. Like finding the *ache* in *reached*, in *you have reached a wondrous place*. Like *earth* and *heart* being the same but in a different order. Like *earth* being just a letter or two away from *death*. And really silly rhymes. Cantaloupes soften with time, Antelopes come to rhyme."

"Auden sometimes rhymed like that. Even when he was serious. Serious in a lighter-than-air way. He could be serious in many ways. I will read you some Auden. You think you are starting to get too old for such childishness?"

"Yes. Maybe. If I'm trying to understand and argue about factory farming or human rights, shouldn't I stop rhyming antelopes and cantaloupes?"

"I don't think you need to stop. I *hope* you don't stop. You just need to think of them at different times. Build separate selves."

"I am only me, Granny."

"I think already you are many *you*s. You are one *you* when you play with word sounds, and another *you* when you look in the mirror and think how nice you look in your new shirt, and another *you* when you think *I will write poems that will make me famous*, and another *you* when you hear of some disaster and think *how horrible, how can I help?*, and another *you* when you are working with Kathy Snyder on what to say about human rights, and still another *you* when you are alone in your head late at night."

How did she know Robin had sometimes looked in the mirror in that way? And thought that about the poems? But she was still talking. "And I think there are many other *you*s beyond those. Some of them imagined, some of them remembered. All of them real."

"But isn't it better to be only one?"

"Only one *you*? It is not possible. All you can do is try to find good ways for the *you*s to connect. Let the antelopes and the cantaloupes make fun of the *you* that is saying to itself *how nice I look in my new shirt!* And of the *you* that would like to be famous—especially of that *you*. The *you*s cannot all connect all of the time. But most of us do not let them...." She stopped herself. "Most of us? I had better just speak of myself. I too often forget about the antelopes and the cantaloupes; you help me bring back a *me* that for a long while I almost lost, Robin. That is one of the selfish reasons I have for loving you."

"Why don't Mother and Father talk to me like you do, Granny?"

"About some things it is better to talk to people who are not one's parents. Better. And sometimes necessary. But I do not know why that is, Robin."

"Shall we go out on the balcony, Granny?"

"I think we should, child."

ॐ ॐ ॐ

Was this the fourth time in the last three weeks that Robin had missed being home for supper? Carol thought it might have been the fifth time, the sixth, even; Carl just knew it had been too many times. And now twice in a row, without any word beforehand— no explanations, no excuses. And where was Robin's cell phone? A rhetorical question: they could see it right there, sitting on the table in the living room. What was wrong with the child? What was wrong with the lot of them that refused to carry their cell phones? It was one thing to let Robin have some independence; children could never be prisoners, you had to loosen the strings a little as they got towards adolescence. But this was too much; you couldn't just have a child that age carrying on like this. *Is it that girl, Kathy Snyder, do you think?* Carl had thought perhaps it might be, and then they had talked and talked, tramped around and around over the same ground, just as all parents do when they talk of their children—except that Carol and Carl hadn't spent a lot of time being parents in this sort of way.

Kathy Snyder and all the debating—was it any wonder that Robin's marks weren't so great this term? What about tonight? What should they do? When would Robin finally come home? Around and around, back and forth and back and forth. Should they call the police? Should they.... But in the end they had done nothing, they had not known what to do. When Robin finally came home Carl didn't hear anything; he had turned on the White Sox game, and turned it up loud, that was what he always did nowadays, he would need a hearing aid soon, thought Carol. She was in the bathroom but she could hear Robin all right, could hear the sounds of Robin trying to be quiet, Robin getting something quickly from the fridge, Robin going quickly to bed. Carol was blindingly relieved, almost joyful; she was also utterly furious. And Carl would be furious too, would be.... *I won't say anything to Robin tonight,* Carol decided finally. *I will leave it to the morning.*

And she *had* said something to Robin in the morning; by that time she and Carl had talked over what was to be said. She didn't interrogate the child, sometimes it was best not to know the things your children didn't want you to know, but you had to say something, Carol and Carl agreed about that. She kept the focus on the future, not the past—*what matters is not that you be home for supper every night, you're not a little child anymore, your father and I understand that. But you're part of this family, you have to let us know where you'll be, let us know what's happening, let us know when you'll be home, it's just common courtesy. And you have to keep your cell phone with you,* she had added. *And turned on. Have to!*

It was a question of safety, too, Carl had felt obliged to point out, and he had pointed out quite a few other things too. They had both made it clear to Robin in no uncertain terms that all this had to stop, that Robin had to be part of the family, and had to keep up with school work too. Being able to give a good speech in a debate wasn't what really mattered, it was algebra and history that mattered. And the periodic table, too. And Robin had said that yes, all that was understood. Sometimes you couldn't say everything about where you had to go or what you had to do but yes, this sort of thing would stop.

"Is it Kathy Snyder?" Carl had interjected; "is it her you're spending all this time with, her and with the debating?" But Robin had said no, there didn't need to be much time spent on debating now. There was only the "friendly" debate at the end of the term and you couldn't prep for that, it was just between teams in the same form, it wasn't part of the schedule with the other schools. Hadn't they realized that?

Carl was a little taken aback and said that of course he had known all that, but that he had somehow thought there would be more debates, that there might be... He had let it trail off. But in any case he wanted to make it clear that Robin's debating wasn't the point, the point was that Robin had to be home at a reasonable hour and had to let them know what was happening in Robin's life.

And now it had happened again. Less than a week later, here it was almost 8:00 and they had no idea where Robin had gone, no idea where Robin was right now. Kathy Snyder's number was on the list of phone numbers on the side of the fridge;

Carol thought she would phone it now and speak to her. No. She would speak to the parents, not to the girl.

ক ক ক

"Why twenty, Granny?"

"To this day I have no idea. Perhaps I needed a round number. More likely I needed a rest. By that time I was working two jobs, you see."

"In a shop? Was that when you worked at Macy's?"

"Marshall Fields it was then. The same place, the same place. The vast atrium, the high ceilings, the grandeur. I was in socks. In the *Socks and Undergarment Department*, to give it its full name. *Socks and Underwear*, they would say today. No they wouldn't; *Intimate Apparel* is what they would say today. We will change the subject now."

"And you will tell me what happened to the twenty paintings?"

"I bundled them all up in a great roll, and shipped them off to the Art Institute."

"I don't understand, Granny. Why would you send them there?"

"I asked myself the same question. But it didn't stop me. I kept telling myself I couldn't face having everything re-opened, being interrogated a second time. And yet I suppose a part of me must have wished for exactly that to happen—if not for an interrogation, at least for a fuss to be raised. For the whole thing to be reopened. And then splashily given a very different ending. For anyone who had said it was hardly likely that a young woman could have painted *Rising Stories* to say *Good heavens! What a remarkable talent. How could we have been so wrong?* I thought if they could see all these other paintings they would realize that the same person who had painted them must have painted *Rising Stories*. And that it couldn't have been Kenneth Paul."

"Not when he was dead."

"Exactly, Robin—not when he was dead. *That young woman must have been telling the truth after all*; I must at some level have been hoping Judge Little and the others would say that. I thought it would be obvious. Is anything in life ever obvious?"

"Ms. McLenithan says the obvious is difficult to prove, and often wrong. She says somebody famous said that, and that it's true."

"Your Ms. McLenithan is wise about some things."

ॐ ॐ ॐ

There was no answer. Carol hesitated and then decided she would try again in a little while rather than leaving a message. But Kathy Snyder had phoned back a minute later; she had seen the number displayed and thought it must have been Robin calling. No, she didn't know, she didn't know where Robin was tonight, and yes it had been busy all those weeks with the debating, and no, they weren't so busy with the debating just now.

Where had Robin gone? Where was Robin going on all these evenings? Carol and Carl started at the same time to worry, and then took turns telling each other that there was no need to worry, that there must be some perfectly ordinary explanation, that Robin was at an age when you had to expect the unexpected, that the city was a lot safer than it had been when they were that age. But still.

After some time they found themselves also agreeing that maybe if they walked to some of the places where Robin walked every day they might have some new ideas about what could have happened, about where Robin could...—well, you never knew. And out they went, following the route they thought their child walked every morning, along Erie to LaSalle, north on LaSalle past the other Lakes, Huron and Superior. Then east on Chicago and north on Clark and cut across Washington Square. From there you could see the fine old lines of the William B. Ogden School. After this year Robin would be gone and the building itself would go; the odd but lovable 'Art Nouveau meets Prairie School' was to be torn down, with a new Ogden of bulky brown rectangles taking its place. Everyone had always said you couldn't do better than Ogden for a public school. Of course it was deserted at this hour. It was hard to think where the child might have gone; Robin had sometimes said that a group of them would go to Oak Street after school, would go to the beach—Carol remembered Robin mentioning that. How often had Robin gone there? You never knew, you never knew. And on they went. Hadn't Robin said it might even be good just to come by yourself to the lake, sit and watch the water and let your thoughts be like waves on the beach? Yes, those were almost exactly the words, Carol was sure; she remembered saying *go with your friends, Robin—not on your own*.

The lake stretched out wide, and the dark water shimmered under the glitter from the lights of the Oak Street Bistro. People drifted by on the lakeside trail and you could make out couples on the sand. Of course there was no Robin; they kept hoping that at any moment..., but of course that was all you could do— hope, not expect.

Did Robin often walk down Michigan on the way home? Take the long way? Robin always said that didn't happen, but how could you be sure? No doubt it was pointless, trying to follow everywhere Robin might have walked. But maybe the child had made a habit of going where they had said *don't go*, maybe Robin had made a habit of walking home along Michigan. And maybe if they walked that route they would think of something, maybe they would see someplace where you might stop if you were Robin. Where you might forget things so much that you wouldn't think *I should have called my parents, this time I should have brought my phone, I'll have to find a pay phone or borrow a phone*, where you might forget all of that. Where you might still be at 9:15 in the evening—at 9:30.

It was almost 9:45 when they walked past the great flat black of the Hancock Building, tapering on and on up into air. Carol looked up at the other towers, and then pointed on ahead and to her left, *do you remember how we all used to go up and see your grandmother there every week? Up to the—what floor was it? It's starting to seem like a long time ago now.* And Carl agreed that it was sort of a long time, but not really. And then the same vague thought came into his head that was in Carol's. You could never know. It couldn't hurt; what were the chances? You never knew. And then they were climbing the few steps outside the front of the building, *would it be open at this hour? If you weren't a resident?* Yes, yes, the revolving doors still turned, they could ask the concierge if he…, if there had been any…. You never knew; you could never know.

# Fifteen

*2011*

"They didn't believe you the second time, either? What happened, Granny?"

"It may have been partly the pictures, Robin. Maybe the twenty just weren't as good, weren't anything like as good as the first one. *I* was sure they were just as good, maybe better. But artists always think their latest work is their best, and ninety-eight per cent of the time they're wrong. Why should I have been any different?"

"But even if those judges and whoever else didn't think the other twenty were as good, they would have to see that everything was painted in the same style, wouldn't they?"

"So you might think."

"And you sent some sort of note with the pictures? Pointing out that these paintings were like *Rising Stories*? Saying they were by you? That they were not by Kenneth Paul, who was dead. You let them know, didn't you, Granny?"

"I was so arrogant. And so foolish. One sentence, that was all I wrote to them: 'For your collection—twenty more works by the painter of *Rising Stories.*' I thought they should bloody well be able to put two and two together without more help than that. Should be able to figure it out."

"You signed the paintings, though. Didn't you, Granny?"

"I have never signed my pictures. Why do people think they have to spoil the front of a picture by displaying their me-ness? What I put on each one of the twenty was a small mark. On the back—in the top left corner on the back of each painting. Very faintly I wrote my initials—my real initials. Just *K.P.*, that was all. Why I had not thought to do something like that with *Rising Stories* I do not know. At any rate, that was all there was on any of the twenty to say that they were mine.

"Later, of course, I could think of one reason after another why I should have done things differently. I could see that they might think these were just-discovered pieces that Kenneth Paul had painted before he died. Pieces that I had found somewhere stashed away at Higher Ground. After all, he had written of having tried 'a few others in the same style.' What was there to prove that these were new? Nothing. What was there to prove, even if it were accepted that I had painted these twenty, that I hadn't just copied the style he had pioneered? Nothing. I could have taken over his style and made it mine, the perfect mimic. They might have thought that. Or—and the more I thought it through, the more I thought this was the most likely of all—they might not have thought anything at all. Why should they have paid any attention?" Her voice grew suddenly fainter. "Twenty paintings arriving out of the blue. Perhaps by a dead person who might have painted a picture that had won a minor prize, perhaps by someone who had done nothing at all except create trouble by pretending to win that same minor prize. Perhaps by anyone— who knew? Was there any reason to think any of this was of any importance? Was there any reason to keep the paintings at all? Certainly there was no obligation to do so. No institution has any obligation to do anything at all with a package sent to them unsolicited. They can just throw it out. Into the bin. That's likely where they went—into the bin. I can see it now, some young boy in the mailroom, *not long now, two more hours and I'll be out of here for the week, just get through this last pile and tidy up like Gerry said I should, they might even let me go early on a Friday like this, with the nice weather and all, anyways I know I can see Jennifer tonight, she'll finish early for sure, we can see that Ida Lupino picture everyone's going on about, she'll like that and what with her folks going away, maybe this is the night, you never know, maybe this will be the night. What's this big roll? Not addressed to anyone. Another 'unsolicited'; they hate getting these. And half the time they glare at me as if it were my fault that somebody... Can't even see any return address on the thing. Well, if nobody's expecting it, nobody's going to miss it.* Yes, right into the bin. Barely looked at, perhaps not even opened." She looked out at nothing for a moment. "That's what happened, Robin, that or something very like it. I feel it in my bones." Her voice had gone low and started to shake.

"But maybe your bones aren't reliable, Granny." K.P.'s face was in shadow. "Sometimes we don't know, Granny, that's the thing. Sometimes we don't know." K.P. lifted her head a little, and Robin could see tears on her cheeks. An old person should never have to be this way, that was what Robin thought. Should never have to cry. Robin reached out towards her. "We'll go together. We'll find your paintings—and we'll bring them back."

"I will be all right, Robin. It was all of it so long ago. Yes, we can ask, we can look. But they won't be there anymore. Nothing will be there, child. Nothing lasts."

"But they must have kept the one that won."

"Why *must* they have?"

"Because it was good, Granny. Because the pictures were good. I think they must have kept them all." Robin stopped for a moment. "They must have been good if you did them. They were good, weren't they?"

"Yes, Robin, they were good—I knew that. *Knew*, not thought; I knew they were very, very good. But what is there that we do when we are still young that we don't *know* is good. Brilliant, ... superb, magnificent And then we look at it ten years later—sometimes even ten days later—and we see emptiness, we see a veneer of ego and nothing beneath. We see just how much everything that we thought was blindingly original is derivative, is..."

"I don't think I'm like that, Granny. Often I think right away the things I've made aren't very good. Often."

"I shouldn't have said *we*, then, should I? It's so easy to forget that everyone else's past isn't like our own past. That everyone else's world isn't our world. I have too much ego. I have always had too much ego. And you, Robin? Perhaps too little. Shall we look at one more poem of yours?"

"I think we should do that later, Granny. Now we should make a plan for finding out about your pictures."

"You are a remarkable child. And you should see the Caillebotte; that is important. Let us go tomorrow and be done with it, and then…"

"Ben Kwan and me are supposed to stay after school tomorrow to work on a project with Ms. McLenithan." That was not exactly the truth. The truth was that Robin thought maybe there would be too much trouble the next day, and that it might not be possible to avoid all the trouble and come to see K.P. But you didn't have to say all of that.

"Yes," said K.P. "Well, the day after tomorrow, then."

"Thursday," said Robin.

"Thursday," repeated K.P. "It is supposed to be misty and overcast the next few days; that will be good. I do not like to go out when it is too hot, too bright. Not at my age. Let us go the day after tomorrow, and that will be that."

"I would like that, Granny." Robin paused. "But I don't want to go home yet tonight. Can you keep talking? Talking about you, not about me."

৯ ৯ ৯

Abe Ereshefsky liked to say that he didn't know much about art; what he knew about was paint. In fact he knew more about the painting styles of just about any artist you could name than did just about anyone. What he lacked were preferences. He appreciated everything, while almost never losing his heart to a particular artist, or a particular theory, or a particular style. Perhaps the only exception was Grant Wood's landscape style of the 1930s—a strange choice for a love, perhaps, but when is love not strange? In the 1970s he had been one of the first to suggest that *Young Woman by the Casement* was in all probability an early twentieth-century forgery, not a Vermeer. In the early '80s his article on the first stages of the restoration of the frescos in the Sistine Chapel led to a new appreciation of Michaelangelo's use of brilliant hues as underpainting—and led Colalucci's team to modify their techniques. Now he was no longer at the top of his game, but of all the people on the Art Institute's staff he was still the best person to ask if you had questions about how to rebalance color tones during a painting's restoration, or about why Sir Joshua Reynolds' carmine reds had faded so badly.

Abe shuffled about the place without saying much, and he worked only part-time now; when you were getting on in years, what sense was there in pretending otherwise? The place was filled with up-and-comers, and he was a down-and-goer. But he had found a way of heading out that led down a long and pleasant corridor. And he had kept up with the times; he knew almost as much about visible reflectance spectrophotometry, and multi-spectral imaging, and probability analysis of the intensity distribution of pigments as did any of the young ones.

It was Abe himself who had stumbled upon the long-forgotten question of who had painted *Rising Stories*. He'd been asked to help out a little team that was researching the history of the New Horizons Prize. There would have to be something of a fuss made on the 75th anniversary; it would be coming up in 2013, and for that they'd have to know something of the history. Of course the controversy of '38 had caught his attention, and of course he had followed up in the files, had read the accounts in the press, had ploughed through the transcripts of the prize jury's interview with Kathleen Schuyler. But he had had less interest than you might expect in the sensational aspects. What caught his eye was the difference in styles between *Rising Stories* and the two or three verified examples the Institute had been able to obtain of Kenneth Paul's other work. Of course painters can paint in a variety of styles—everyone knows that. But usually there is some similarity in the brushstrokes, and usually too there is some similarity in the use of color. With some painters one gentle color fades into another gentle color; with others brightness comes constantly up against brightness; with still others everything seems defined by shadow. Whatever tendencies of that sort a painter might have, he or she usually carries them over from one style to another. The squares of color that were the essence of the only works the Institute owned that were universally accepted as having been painted by Kenneth Paul were saturated in the same way. Up and down, left to right, the same intensity of color. The yellow might come forward and the blues recede, but that had nothing to do with any variation in the intensity of the paint.

*Rising Stories* wasn't like that. The intensity varied in every direction and in every way; a washed-out cerulean would fade into a blaze of Prussian so intensely saturated that it jumped out at you hard and bright from the paper. Conventional color theory told you that any deep blue should have depth, should recede into the canvas or paper. The reds should come forward, the yellows and the cool colors should recede. But if you put enough intensity into any color it could defy that. Saturation. That was how the splashes of color in *Rising Stories* operated—and it was the same with the other twenty-odd paintings said to have been painted by the same hand. Had Kenneth Paul changed everything just before he died? Or had he lied?

ৰ ৰ ৰ

No, the concierge had not seen any child who looked anywhere in the range of eleven to thirteen, certainly not tonight. And no, he could not confirm who was living now in the apartment formerly occupied by K.P. Sandwell; all information as to present, past, or future occupancy of any of the residences was strictly confidential. If someone was expecting the two of them this evening, they could phone up and speak with the party concerned, and the concierge could assist them in any way they might require. Otherwise, he regretted that he would be unable to be of assistance.

Should they call the police? *Our child hasn't come home for supper tonight and we're worried.* It was easy to imagine the response. *Is this the first time this has happened? The fourth or fifth time, you say? And each time before the child has come home safe and sound later the same evening?* There would be endless questioning, endless forms to fill out, and by the time all that was done Robin would be home again, tired but safe, and saying sorry, sorry, it had all been a misunderstanding. No, they would not make that call yet; *it will all be fine,* they took turns saying to each other, *it will all be fine.*

At the next corner they turned and looked back and looked up, at that one apartment very high up with all the lights on and none of the curtains drawn; you could make out two tiny figures silhouetted on the balcony. Was that where she had lived? Had it been quite so high? But there would have been no reason for Robin to have gone up there, to have…. Would there? They should move on. Sometimes Robin had talked of how pleasant it could be to walk beside the river. And Millennium Park and Grant Park, and the mirrored glass on the Bean—Robin loved those as much as anyone did. Should they go there too before they gave up and went home? Yes, that was what they should do—unless it was worth trying Granny's building one more time, just quickly. Perhaps if they explained things a little more to the man. Of course it would all sound odd but almost anything that was true had some part of it that sounded odd; people understood that. Why did Carol have a hunch that Robin might have gone in there, might have gone unnoticed past everyone and up the elevator? She looked back again. *Carl, don't you think we could…?*

צ  צ  צ

"I won't talk about me anymore," said K.P. "I will talk about me-ness. Me-ness in art. Where does the urge to write your name on something come from? Has it always been there? No. Nothing has always been there. But by the nineteenth century almost everyone was signing their paintings, but a lot of people made their names very small, very faint. They didn't want their *me* to come into the picture; they just wanted to be sure they could be identified, to be sure they were remembered. I suppose too that people were already thinking of protecting a brand, of..."

"They didn't have brands in the olden days, Granny."

"I think they were beginning to have them, Robin. But not like today, you are certainly right about that. And some people had no sense at all of the commercial—there was so much inconsistency. Some men signed their pictures on the back; some changed what they did over the course of their working lives; some acted without any rhyme or reason."

"What about women, Granny? What about you?"

"In the middle ages, in the Renaissance, even in the eighteenth century, the few women who did art seem to have been scared of signing it. Women dabbled and women copied—so few had a chance to truly paint. Here is sadness: a young woman named Sarah Cole wrote nine words on the back of a painting called *A View of the Catskill Mountains House*: 'Copied from a picture by T. Cole by S. Cole, 1848.' Not much *me* in that!"

"What about women and buildings, Granny?"

"Even less me. A woman architect? For the longest time such a thing was almost unimaginable." She shook her head, and then a smile started to come. "Now it is starting to be different; now it has begun to change." Her smile deepened and broadened as she led Robin back out to the balcony and pointed out towards the south, towards a building of curves, a building of strange balconies, all blue. Twisting and bending and curling, undulating up into sky. "It is as if there is a pulse inside it, as if it were always moving. When they designed it they made a model and measured with string where the views were, and where the light would go. The balconies surge and shift and shiver with purpose; it is all planned so everyone will have the light of the sun. Each balcony different."

"It changes in the light, Granny. I see it when I walk back from school. When I walk home, I go in different ways. Sometimes I walk to where that building is. Or further." They looked out together at the building—Aqua, it is called—in the light of the night. "It's always a different blue, Granny."

"Like air. Like water."

"Like your paintings from long ago?"

"I would like to think they are like that. When I saw that building I felt as if I were somehow alive again in a different way."

"And is it somehow about change for women?"

"A woman made it. A team headed by a woman, I should say. Jeanne Gang. She makes shapes. Before Aqua she made only low shapes. Now she makes curves that climb into the sky. A man named Gehry did something similar a little after Aqua was built, on the East River in New York. It is almost as beautiful as this. It may be the Bjarke Ingels Group tower at Beach and Howe in Vancouver will be as beautiful as this—they have not built it yet. To me this is as beautiful as the Wrigley, as the Mather, as the Chrysler."

"We must find your old paintings, Granny."

"Yes, Robin. We will find them together when it is light. When it is light, on the day after tomorrow."

ॐ ॐ ॐ

Of course Robin was there by the time Carl and Carol finally got home themselves. *I know, I know, I'm sorry, I'm sorry, like, I really am sorry* was what they heard before they could say anything themselves; Robin was learning to do *sorry*. But it wasn't good enough, it wasn't anything like good enough. Carl made that clear and then Carol made it clear, and then Carl made it clear again. It had to stop, it had to stop right now. Did Robin have any idea what Carol and Carl went through every time this happened? They had been walking the streets, they had been worried sick. This would have to be the last time, this would have to be the *very* last time. Straight home after school every day or Robin could...

"No, Carl, we've never threatened, and we're not going to start now. There will be no threats, Robin. You simply have to learn how not to be a child; you have to learn that other people matter." Robin sensed there was something true in what they said, and something missing. But it would all be over soon, and then something would be changed.

The next day was Wednesday, and on that day Robin did exactly as Carl and Carol said. On Thursday there would be field day again in the afternoon; you could slip away. While it was still daylight Robin would go with K.P. for the pictures. And then it would be over, it would be another time.

# Sixteen

*2011*

The day after tomorrow was Thursday, just as Robin had said, and it was gray and misty, just as K.P. had said.

"Let us take an umbrella. We mustn't catch our death."

"How can you catch your death, Granny?"

"It's an expression, child, an expression. *You'll catch your death of cold.* Now hold the umbrella."

There seemed to be almost no one about as they came out of the elevator—no concierge, no one. Not another soul as they made their way across the vast, shining lobby. It was the middle of the morning: where was everyone?

But on the street it was Chicago again—the pavement full, motion, motion, motion. Robin started to worry that K.P. might be jostled, might fall. A high-heeled young woman clutched a tiny handbag fiercely as she brushed past them, and they were nearly bumped by a gray-haired man with a briefcase, and a belly straining against his jacket. A delivery man in brown shorts carried three large packages. There was a group of Japanese tourists. A distracted father pushed his small children forward in a double stroller. They were all moving at such different speeds. K.P. shuffled sideways a little.

"Take my arm, there's a good child." She was so thin that it felt almost like nothing as she leant against Robin. And then once more she put one foot in front of the other. She looked back towards where the stroller had been. "They didn't use to do that in my day," she murmured. "Fathers." She paused for a moment with her feet and with her words. "But no doubt it is for the best. I wonder if Arthur.... Well, we'll never know, will we?" Her voice faded into the other sounds, the wind and the traffic and all the people. Robin heard almost like a whisper: "I do miss him." Would she cry again?

"Shall we stop for a moment, Granny?" But her ears were not as good as Robin's. One foot kept moving ahead of the other, and the whisper went on in the wind. "I almost forget him sometimes. But then I remember how.... That night on the beach in Rio comes back to me. We held each other close for a long time. As if we were still very young. And talked to the stars and to the sea as if they were real. As if they could hear. Robin, do you mind if an old woman rattles on?" But she did not wait for an answer. "We walked along the sand by the water, holding hands. We walked very close to the water; the sand was hard and wet. The sea was rolling gently in, and the moonlight kept quivering on the waves. We stopped again and held each other. Time disappeared. And then we both looked up behind us. Sugarloaf Mountain was clear and vast in the moonlight. But just at its peak a line of cloud pressed in softly and you couldn't see the statue, that famous statue. Anyone would have thought there was nothing. Just air, clouds, sky."

"What is it a statue of, Granny?"

"Of God, Robin. Of God. The child of God, but if you are a Christian you think that the child of God is also God. It is a strange thing to be a Christian. I did that for many years when I was young. All that seems so far away now. Farther away even than my earliest memory." She had stopped now and was paying no attention to all the people going by. Robin stopped too, and waited. Maybe Granny's first memory would not take a very long time to tell. "The earliest thing I can remember is the light on the trees and how they jumped about when my father lifted me up. That must have been in the garden in Winnipeg. Perhaps in 1918? The year the war ended." And she looked up, and Robin looked up. There were no trees and there was no god along this stretch of Michigan. The tops of the skyscrapers were missing, lost in mist, just as they had been the day before, and the day before that. The mist lay stalled, soft wisps. Above it there were clouds, clouds moving very fast.

"We'll be at the park in a moment, Granny. And then we're almost there."

"Almost there," K.P. repeated it as they crossed Lake Street. "Almost there." She was panting a little. She leaned into Robin even more as they crossed Randall Street, and then the park was beside them. To the east a space came open in the clouds and the sun filled it with blue. Brightness gleamed on the mirrored sculpture, the Kapoor, *Cloud Gate*, the Bean. "Mirrors never show things as they are," said K.P.

There were fewer people on the sidewalk beside the park, far fewer. The two of them were not being jostled now. But suddenly Robin's great grandmother looked more tired than before, more old. "Granny, if we walk into the park just a little... there is a bench you could rest on. We could both rest. You see, just over there."

"No, Robin, we have decided to do this thing. You must see the Caillebotte. I am only..." As she tried to finish the sentence she stumbled a little bit. Robin held her up and a long moment later could hear her say, "perhaps." And then a moment later, "perhaps I should rest for a little time. For just a little time." She turned and Robin began to steer her towards the bench. "But you are too young to rest. You would fidget, and that would make me nervous."

"I have to stay with you, Granny."

"You have to do no such thing. You have to lead your own life is what you have to do. After you have seen the Caillebotte," she added.

"Then we wouldn't see your pictures until another day, Granny. That's why we have come. To find your pictures."

"Another day will do as well for that. If they have waited more than seventy years, they can wait another few days. Now you must listen. The Caillebotte is at the top of the great staircase. You will see it in front of you when you go up the stairs from the lobby. You don't need to pay…"

"Everyone has to pay, Granny."

"You must read the fine print, child. Everyone most certainly does *not* have to pay. There will be little letters at the bottom of the sign; look for them. It will say *suggested admission price* or *payment voluntary*. When people used to give things to galleries and museums, they would insist on that sort of thing. *I will donate my Raphael and my Leonardo and a great deal else to the city's grand new gallery, on condition that the public be allowed to see these wonderful works at no charge, for all time.* That was what used to happen—this was long before my time, before my parents' time too, for that matter. So the great museums and galleries were not able to charge mandatory fees for admission; they could only ask for donations. When you go to New York, to St. Louis, you will see the same thing. Nowadays, of course, they would not let people give things with those restrictions; it is a different world." The breath came more and more slowly out of her. "Go, Robin. I will wait for you. When we see each other again, you will tell me what you think of it—of the Caillebotte. Of the two people, of those French streets, of that one great line that breaks the picture in two. Things keep getting broken in two. It is all different. You will tell me, won't you?"

She was drifting, she was not herself; Robin could not leave her here like this. But K.P. saw the thought in Robin's face. "Yes, child. I am an old woman. I know that. But now I want only to sit on this bench in this strange light, alone, and to know that you are doing something new, and something good. Go, child. And be in no hurry; I am in no hurry."

"I love you, Granny." Robin had not meant to say that, they had been words that had come on their own from somewhere inside. Somewhere near where the knot that was near your heart was, but now it was as if the knot had been untied, and something else was pulling from the same place.

"I know you do, Robin. I love you too. I loved Arthur. And you are just a child."

"I will be 13 next week, Granny."

"Of course. I had forgotten. Not a child for so very much longer. Sometimes you have been such an old child. I shall miss that, Robin. I shall miss you."

"It's just a birthday, Granny. I won't be any different, really."

"But you will, Robin. We all grow different. We keep growing different, until sometimes there is nothing left of what once was us. You must always keep inside something of the you that was once a child, of the you that was here at this moment, at this park, in this sun, with your strange...." She had lost the thread. "Hold on to it, hold it tight. It will be so hard sometimes, but you must never let it go."

"I will try, Granny. Let me hold you now." Awkwardly Robin held out both arms to hold her, and for a moment it was as if they had embraced, Robin's thin little arms around a wisp of an old woman, and then she felt for a handkerchief. "You must go, child. And I will..."

"You *will* stay here, won't you? You must stay just here, Granny, and then we can walk all the way back together when I come for you."

"I would like that, Robin." And she smiled, and now she did not need the handkerchief, and the child started to walk away. Only once did Robin look back and wave uncertainly; it was into the sun, and it was as if there were nothing there.

ৱ ৱ ৱ

Thursday was a school day for LeShonna, and she had no plans to skip school or to leave school early or do nothing like that. But when she woke up she felt cloudy and aching on the inside, in her head and in her stomach too. It looked gray and cloudy and aching out the window too, and her mama had said she should stay home and that was exactly what LeShonna had done. But it was so quiet and so boring. When your mama is at work and your daddy is at work and everyone else is at school and you're all alone it's always too quiet, even when the TV is on, and LeShonna didn't like to have the TV on all the time anyways.

Plus there was your whole life to think of. If you had your whole life to lead you didn't want to waste it lying around; maybe you had to lie around a little bit if you were sick but now LeShonna was awake and some of the cloudiness and the aching had gone. Could it hurt to go out for a walk? The gray and the ache were still a little bit in the air but there was no rain. Sometimes LeShonna liked to try to paint the air when there was that aching in it, do a painting of air and houses and warehouses and rusted cranes against the sky, and she would always put people in it too, LeShonna thought any world should have people in it, so if she couldn't see any people as she was painting the air and the houses and the warehouses she would make them up: little kids in yellow raincoats or a little old man shuffling along carrying a big paper bag, or a whiteman on a bicycle, riding fiercely. The paints and the brushes and LeShonna's pad of paper were always on the same shelf on the bookcase; LeShonna got into her outside clothes and put everything in a shoulder bag and as she started down the stairs her heart began to lift, you can make your heart lift if you go out into the world and try to make something beautiful and LeShonna skipped down the stairs to the third floor, taking them two by two by two.

ॡ   ॡ   ॡ

In a moment Robin was climbing the steps by the lions and was through the doors and taking in the height of the lobby above, and the people all around. Where were you supposed to go? It was hard to be sure, especially when all the people milling around were taller than you were. It was not like going with your parents, being on your own like this. Robin was told to check the umbrella; it would have been better to have left it outside with

Granny in case it started to rain. But it didn't seem right to go back outside now. Finally Robin found the right place to line up; you had to wait your turn and then pass your umbrella over the counter to a young woman who gave you a little disc with a number on it. And then, before Robin could figure out where the grand staircase that went up to where the Caillebotte was, a security guard tapped Robin on the shoulder.

"Y'all missing somebody, kid?"

"My grandmother is just outside on a bench. She is resting. She wanted me to come inside and see the Caillebotte." Robin could see the guard hesitating. "Could you tell me please how to get to the Caillebotte?" Robin asked. Perhaps the guard did not know what a Caillebotte was.

"You gots me, kid. Is that some type of vase? Pottery and textiles is straight to the back, lower level, y'all can just…"

"It's a painting. A painting by someone called Caillebotte. *Kai-bot*, that's how it's pronounced. I don't know his first name."

"Him and me were never on a first name basis neither."

"It's a rainy day. In Paris. In France."

"I never been there, kid; I'm from New Orleans. But I can try and…"

"My granny says it's near the top of the grand staircase, right near the top of the grand staircase."

"Now you're talking my language. Right over that way—you see, you got to go…"

"Granny said I wouldn't have to pay."

"Your Granny knows a lot about how things used to be, kid. Used to be you didn't have to pay a nickel if you didn't want to. The signs made it seem like you had to, but you didn't. These days, even students is $12. Not childrens—childrens is still free." The guard peered a little closer. "You under 12? We're gonna say y'all is under 12. Then all y'all needs is a tag, you don't need to pay nothin'. You gets in this line right here." One of the women by the cash registers had seen, had overheard, and was coming out from behind the counter. She said something about how children were always welcome, and a moment later she was pinning a green metal tag onto Robin's sweater and pointing towards the grand staircase, and then Robin was through the check point, and the vast stairs stretched wide, straight ahead. To one side was a group chatting loudly about what one of them had said concerning a certain type of person, and what they had said had been funny, *impressionista*, they were laughing and laughing and on the other side were signs giving directions for *Photography* and for *Prints and Drawings*, and for *Textiles and Ceramics*. And for *Washrooms* and for *Archives and Storage* too; you had to go down the staircase to the left for those.

The woman was gone, the security guard was gone. Robin was alone in the crowd as group after group headed up the grand staircase. *Archives and Storage*—that was where Granny's paintings would be. If they were here. But they *must* be here. Robin looked round once more, all around, and then started down the staircase. It was just as wide as the grand staircase that led upwards but it was empty. There must be some people that come down here, Robin thought, people who work here and people who have to pee. There was an old man coming out of the Men's just as Robin reached the bottom of the stairs. *Archives and Storage* was to the other side—there was a small sign beside a set of double doors, and there was no one about.

Should you just walk in? How could you ask what you wanted to ask if you were Robin? Robin stood and thought and made words move about in different arrangements. *My grandmother was called Pace, and also Schuyler, and also Sandwell, but that was later. And long ago she painted some pictures that we think you may still have here, she sent them to you long ago and she won a competition. One of the judges of the competition thought someone else might have been the painter of the painting that won the competition, but really it wasn't, it was my granny.* None of it sounded quite right; how did you learn to make the things you said sound right? If adults were doing things that were strange they found words that made it sound if they were doing something normal. And if they were doing something nasty they found words to make it seem as if they were doing something nice. Maybe if you started with one of the names it would be best. Pace—was that the name K.P. had said?

There was suddenly a noise; Robin stopped thinking and started to hear and to see. Another door had opened further down the hall; Robin could see two people and between them a huge canvas. They carried it awkwardly, holding out arms at odd angles to make sure the door would not close against the painting, make sure that nothing would hurt it. One of them grunted as she reached back behind her and then they were both free of the door and walking away from Robin down the hallway, and the door was closing slowly, slowly, ever so slowly, it must have one of those pneumatic door closers to make it go so slow, Robin had learned about those last term, Kathy Snyder had said it was boring but Robin thought it wasn't, the air was slowing the door as it closed, slow, slow, there was no handle on the outside so once it closed you would never be able to get in through that door, you would have to go through the double doors, the main entrance to *Archives and Storage*, and then you would need to choose words to use. Did this door lead to the same place? Maybe it was a door to some completely other place, some place that didn't connect to *Archives and Storage*. But now the tips of Robin's fingers were pressed against the edge of the door as it started to settle into the jamb. It had almost settled in but there had been no click, the lock had not quite clicked into place and Robin's finger tips pressed harder, now with both hands, harder, harder and now the door was no longer moving, and then slowly, slowly, it started to pull back, ever so slowly and then in another few moments Robin could get two, three fingers inside the door and then it was easy, it pulled back softly and slowly, and slowly and softly it closed behind Robin, and made that little click.

At first there was nothing except dark. Then Robin started to be able to make out great tall rows of shelving, vertical shelving, this must be where they kept the paintings, the ones that weren't on the walls. Each row rose up to a high ceiling, and the rows went on and on till you couldn't be sure where they ended.

There was a tiny bit of light from somewhere high, somewhere far away. Robin began to feel a way forward into an aisle between two of the rows. On each side huge paintings were stored upright, sometimes two or three to a compartment, sometimes one having a compartment all to itself. And above the first set of upright shelves was another, and then another after that; they must have huge ladders to reach the highest ones.

As the end of the aisle came closer it became a little brighter and Robin could see that this wasn't the end at all; there was a wide open space and then the same pattern carried on again on the other side, aisle after aisle of vertical storage, row after row of paintings. Robin pulled one out a little way from its compartment; it was a picture of sailing ships. Then another; this was of sheep in a field. Where would you begin to look? These were all big paintings in frames. Granny's watercolors weren't like that, they were on paper and no one would have framed them. Robin moved on through the second series of aisles. At the end of that there was another wide space with another faint light somewhere at the end of it. This time there were different sorts of rows on the other side; there were cabinets and drawers instead of vertical compartments—row after row of wide cabinets with shallow drawers. In the dimness Robin could just make out the letters on the sides of the cabinets. One row was *Bonington, Richard* to *BOT*, the next *BOT* to *Bourgeois, Louise*. Look for *PAC*— would that be right? Yes, Robin was sure, Granny had said she had sent her pictures in as P.K. Pace. Robin would have to find *PAC*.

Now there were voices again. Was it the two people who had been carrying that picture, coming back again? Robin tiptoed along one of the aisles between the cabinets and crouched down low. The voices were nowhere close—it sounded as if they were in the open area where the first faint light had come from. Robin looked at the names on the drawers to one side. *COU—Cox, David. DAW—DAY.* Keep going, keep going.

For a moment the voices seemed to be getting a little closer. But no, now they had stopped, and there were no footsteps. Robin would have to try; this was the time to try. If you stayed low as you crept along the aisle maybe no one would see you that way. Along to the end, then dart across another wide space. And then row by row, ever so quietly, check the letters, *Grosz, George—Hamilton, Richard*; *Haring, Keith—Hartman, John*, and on to *KAL* and *KIM*, *Klee* and *Kline*, *Parker* and *Parrish* and—no, that was too far. There—there it was, up high, *PAC—PAL*. It was right at the top of a cabinet; could you reach it if you stretched high as could be, on tiptoe? No, no, Robin was not quite tall enough. What if you jumped? But that would make too much noise and...—there was a noise again now. Were the two of them coming? Had they heard anything? Robin crouched low again, right by the floor. Even if they passed close by they would have to look long and hard to see the little lump on the floor pressed into the shadows at the side of the aisle.

You could hear the footsteps now, a little closer, a little closer—no, now they were moving further away again. They must be somewhere in among the stacks of framed paintings. Now it sounded again as if they were coming closer. Robin crouched down lower—and then saw the letters on the lowest drawer: *OXL—PAC*. Of course! Why should there be any reason to think *PAC* would have to be all in one drawer? Granny's paintings might be right here, in this drawer at floor level.

Now the little clicks of heel on floor were moving farther away again, farther still. Slowly, ever so slowly, Robin started to ease the drawer open. It was almost a yard wide but it slid smoothly, quickly; there must be rollers, ball bearings. The drawer was filled with paintings laid flat. Were they watercolors? It was hard for Robin to tell. Some of them were printed, not paintings at all. Between each piece there was a thin sheet of something like tissue paper, and over the lower left corner of each piece had been slipped a little cardboard triangle, and to each cardboard triangle had been stapled a sheet of paper. Robin looked closer and could see that the sheets of paper named the work and also the artist, and that sometimes they gave other information too: *Included in the Montreal Retrospective of the Artist's Work 1945, Study for* Dimanche Du Mer *84 inches x 96 inches, 1908* (*also in the permanent collection*). Was it all alphabetical? *Oxley, Cynthia* and *Paber, Charles* on down to *Pack, Robert,* and then *Packer, James.* That was all. No *Pace. K* came after *c*; the letters had passed where she would be. She was not there; nothing of hers was there. Robin felt a wave of loss, felt it everywhere you could feel. It was like the time they had moved when Robin had been little and when they had arrived at their new home they had opened all the boxes and somehow the box that had Robin's favorite things, the floppy stuffed leopard and the Lincoln logs and the Mexican puppet—that box was nowhere to be found, it was lost. They had asked and asked and checked again and again, it was gone forever.

That was how Granny would feel if she found out her pictures were gone forever. Maybe she didn't need to know. Maybe it would be for the best if Robin said nothing to her about any of this, just told her about seeing the Caillebotte. Robin could go up the staircase now and see the Caillebotte; maybe this had all been a mistake, a sad thing. Slowly Robin eased the great wide drawer back again, and slowly straightened, and slowly began to step away.

No. Wait. The other drawer. The drawer at the top, it had said *PAC-PAL*. Maybe *Pack* had been put in the wrong drawer, maybe *Packer* had been put in the wrong drawer, maybe they had put *Pace* after *Packer* by mistake, put it in the other *PAC* drawer, the top drawer. You never knew; you could never be sure without checking. But how could you check when it was so high? And then Robin thought of a way: the other drawers could be steps. In a quiet rush Robin pulled out the *Orkin, Ruth—Osler, William* drawer a few inches, and then went a bit higher and pulled out the *Omer, Frederick—Onley, Toni* drawer a few inches, and then on beyond that *Oakley, Samuel—OLA* came out a little bit too, and then one more, two more, until there were steps. And then nimbly, nimbly Robin scrambled up. There had been hardly a sound and it was done. Up here you could spread yourself out on top of the vast cabinets. The ceiling was still far above you; if you were not full grown there was plenty of room to turn around, even to stand. Robin knelt and looked back down at the cabinet, at the top drawer, *PAC-PAL*, and started to pull it out from above, pull it out far enough that you could see what was in it. *Paciet, Karen*. Robin's heart fluttered a little; *Paciet* came before *Pack* and *Packer*—the pieces had *not* been put properly in alphabetical order, not all of them, anyway. Here was *Pact, Nathaniel*. And then *Pace*—yes, here was *Pace*! But it was *Pace, Frederick*. It was a painting in watercolor and there were buildings but they were low white buildings on hills. And here was another *Pace*, there were naked people and columns of stone, and then one more, just fields and sea. And then that was all, all the Paces were over and there had been no P.K.

Robin felt suddenly tired. The pictures went back in their places and the drawer was slowly closed, but when it was done it hardly felt as if it had been done by Robin.

It really was over now; it was time to climb down.

No. You should never give up until—when should you give up? Perhaps Granny could be under *Anonymous*, would they have a separate section? Or maybe there were separate places where they stored contest winners. But how would Robin find them? It was too difficult. It was too much. Robin looked down at the other drawers. *Palmer, Samuel—PAV. PAV—PAY.* For a second Robin's mind drifted.

Wait. *PAV*. The other name. Maybe the pictures would have been filed under the other name, the name of the one who had died, the one who they thought had painted them when they hadn't believed Granny. What had been his last name? Kenneth, Kenneth,... Kenneth Paul! That was it. Kenneth Paul. *Paul* would be just one drawer below where *Pace* had been, where there had been the wrong *Pace*s. Robin's eyes went quickly back to the letters on the drawers. Yes, *Palmer, Samuel—PAV*. Robin eased the drawer out and began to finger through one more pile, fingers moving picture to picture, name to name, *Patrick, James*; *Patrick, Jennifer*; *Patz, Gerald*. And then suddenly there it was.

*Paul, Kenneth (attributed)* was what it said, but of course it was not a painting by Kenneth Paul. Robin started to pull it gently from the drawer, and even in the low light could see at once that it was by K.P., could see the swirls, the curves of light and of water and of cloud and of concrete, story after story draining up into sky, the skyscrapers and the mist and the curls of deep blue and of black, river, bridges, wet lights of cars running into the mist, flashes of people in motion on the streets, light sifting through as if from somewhere above the sky. Robin's hands shook a little as the last of the painting came free from the drawer, and still the small hands were shaking as they held the great piece of paper ever so carefully and then gently set it down in the fine dust on top of the vast cabinet. This was it, it had been here all along. *Rising Stories*.

And all the others were here too. Now Robin forgot about footsteps or about anything except the paintings. One by one Robin pulled them gently from the drawer, and looked with wide eyes in the dim light, and then reached with small arms for another, and until all been gently piled one on top of the other. The Board of Trade was here, the lights of Wacker Drive were here, the L was here, the Mather Building, the Wrigley, the Jewelers', everything that K.P. had described. They were all here. Robin counted them twice—eighteen, nineteen, twenty, twenty-one with *Rising Stories*. Then Robin turned each one over and looked on the back, in the top left-hand corner. There it was, on every painting except *Rising Stories*, a tiny "K.P." painted ever so lightly in the top left hand corner. Not in handwriting, just printed in the same way that anyone might print the two letters. Robin started to put all twenty-one back in the drawer and began to think. Anyone could paint those letters. Anyone. *I could paint those letters*, Robin began to think. *I could do it ever so lightly, so lightly that when a person looked they could say "look! Look here! Here is something that must have been missed, way back then. It's the same mark that's on the other paintings! They must all be by the same artist. K.P."*

Robin looked again at the front of the painting, and at the sheet of paper stapled to the cardboard triangle.

> Attributed to Patterson Kenneth Paul (1916-1939). This painting was awarded first prize in the Art Institute's New Horizons competition for works on paper, 1939. The work was submitted under the name of P.K. Pace, a pseudonym for one of the artists working out of the Higher Ground studio (located on the fourth floor of a warehouse at 620 Hubbard Street). A certain Kathleen Schuyler came forward, asserting that she was the artist, but her claims were disputed. The jury for the prize concluded that the work should be classed as unattributed; it appears that for a time they received sympathetically the suggestion that the then-recently-deceased Patterson Kenneth Paul (an artist working out of the same studio as Schuyler) may have painted *Rising Stories*. The issue of attribution remains unresolved.

Each of the other twenty bore an identical message on the sheet of paper attached to the cardboard triangle: "one of a series of twenty paintings in a style reminiscent of *Rising Stories*, tentatively attributed to Patterson Kenneth Paul. Received anonymously, January, 1940."

Robin thought once more of *Rising Stories*. No, it wouldn't be wrong. It wouldn't be forging if there was truth underneath. This wouldn't be hiding the truth or trying to change the truth; it would be making the truth more clear.

Now Robin did think of footsteps. Sometimes your body could be moving as you were thinking, Robin realized. Your feet could be making a little tapping sound as they moved with your thoughts. Robin fell perfectly still all over. Nothing. No sound except low voices far away, back beyond the first light.

There was this one more thing to do, perhaps it was the most important thing. But how would Robin make the right mark on the back of *Rising Stories*? You needed a pencil or a pen—no, it would have to look like the "K.P." on all the other paintings.

Paint was what Robin needed, not a pencil, not a pen. And there was nowhere you could find paint—no, that was dead wrong. Paint was all around. Every one of these drawers was filled with it. Robin could almost hear her now, "great bright lumps of color that would darken and harden later as they dried." All Robin had to do was find one of those lumps of paint, and break part of it off. Robin lifted two, three, four paintings, and then the next one was just right; this was just what was needed. A great lump of blue-gray rising up off the paper. Rising up high, and not too thick—it was easy to grip a hard little nugget between your fingers. A little pressure—very little—then a little more, then off it snapped.

Rising Stories came out from the high drawer in the cabinet once again, and Robin laid it face down on top of the cabinet. You had to have another to compare; the Wrigley Building came out again too, and Robin turned it face down and then looked more closely at the top corner where "K.P." had been written. And looked one more time, and pressed the lump of paint tighter between thumb and forefinger. And listened: you couldn't hear any footsteps, you could hear only the faint humming of fans from the heating system. I have to try, I have to try. Ever so carefully Robin started to mark the top left corner of the back of Rising Stories. "K." It was ever so faint, you could almost imagine it had never been there. And then the "P." Did they look right together? Yes, they were perfect. Robin looked at the marks again and again. You could see clearly that they were exactly like the marks on the top corner of the Wrigley Building painting, except maybe a little fainter. You would have to look and to look and to look to know that the marks were there on either painting—but no one would ever think that the marks were different, that they could have been made by anyone different.

Robin put the little lump of blue-gray into a pocket. It was dry already, the paint had been dry; you didn't have to wait. Robin lifted the Wrigley Building picture by the corners, turned it over, and then eased it back into the drawer. Then, ever so slowly, Rising Stories went back into the drawer as well. And ever so slowly Robin eased the great wide drawer on its rollers back, until there was a soft click and it was closed. It was as if nothing and no one had been there.

Now, down again. Using the same drawers as steps until you could feel your feet touch the floor. Closing the drawers, one by one, until everything looked the same. Robin glanced around; everything was quiet. It was done, the first part. Now that they knew the pictures were there, Granny could make a fuss and get them noticed—get them noticed as hers. And the fact that all of them now had her initials on the back—that would have to convince any doubters.

How long had it been since Robin had left her outside? Too long. Far too long—it was time to go to Granny now. Would it be better to pretend to have seen the Caillebotte? You could see that any time—but then Robin thought of how much the Caillebotte meant to Granny. It would not take too long to have a quick look; Robin would dart up that staircase and it would take no more than a minute or two. "You'll see it as soon as you get to the top of the staircase," the lady had said.

Robin started back along the aisle, between the cabinets, across the wide space and into the second set of aisles, between the long rows of paintings and across the other wide space and into the first set of aisles. It didn't really matter which aisle you chose. You would need to go sideways when you reached the end—whichever aisle you had chosen. The door would be to the left; Robin was pretty sure you would have to go to the left to reach it. Almost completely sure.

Would Robin tell her about the initials? Tell her that now *Rising Stories* had "K.P." written on the back, just like her other paintings? How should you tell a person if you have done something to help them? Should you tell them at all? For a second Robin thought of how different a thing this was. When you were little you did the things you were told to do, and then you looked for praise for doing those things, and that was how you were good. Or if you didn't do them—the thought of Hope flashed for a second through Robin's mind, every day there would be something to bring back the thought of Hope—if you didn't do them, that was how you were bad, that was evil or sin or whatever different people called it. But what Robin had just done was going beyond what Granny or anyone else had expected; it was a different sort of good. Were other people the same way? Was there another type of good that you discovered when you became a grown-up, where you tried to do good things that went beyond what would be expected? And where you didn't look for praise for doing them, not even from yourself? Maybe you wouldn't even want the good you had done to be found out.

Would Granny think Robin had done the right thing? Suddenly that was a terrible thought inside. Granny talked a lot about doing good, but maybe for her this wouldn't be that. Maybe she would think this was something you shouldn't meddle in, that it was none of your business. She might think that what Robin had done had been just plain wrong, that no one should... Robin forced the thought to go away. Maybe you could never know what was right to do or to say until you had said it or done it, and sometimes not even then. But you had to try, you had to keep trying.

Now there was a sound—was it the same sound again? Was it the same two people? They had been quiet for so long. No, the sound was not a sound of people. Robin could feel it as well as hear it. It was a sort of vibrating, a light shaking. A steady shaking, then stronger, shimmering, shivering right through you. And then suddenly it was everywhere, shaking and shaking, shaking hard through everything inside you, hard through everything, everywhere and all around. Everything was jarred and it was deafening, the paintings rattling in their compartments, the shelves stretching and shrieking, a voice screaming, a voice coming from where the light had come from but not very far away. It was in the aisles, it was a human scream, the two people must still be nearby.

Now Robin was on hands and knees, you could try to stand but it was no use, it was as if a giant had lifted the whole building out by its roots and was shaking it, would keep shaking it until it fell apart, this was the basement, everything was below ground but it felt as if there was no ground, the tiles were buckling off the concrete and everything rolled and pitched, rolled and pitched and shook, Robin thought of that time on Joel's parents' sailing boat, when it was far out on Lake Michigan, far out where there was nothing but blue, only a thin green line far away that was the land and tiny little black and white and gray sticks that were the skyscrapers of the city. Robin had kept looking at those sticks far away, looking at them and trying hard to think only of Kathy Snyder, trying hard not to think at all of the rolling, of the rolling and surging and shifting, and everything was shifting now but it wasn't like water it was like air, it was like what they called turbulence when you were in a plane but more violent, a hundred times more violent.

It didn't matter what noise you made, you had to get out, anyone would have to get out, get out and find Granny, find Granny. Robin tried again to stand, hand grabbing something and pulling upwards, it felt like there was no upwards but yes, now Robin was almost standing, shaking, trying to dart to the end of the aisle but you couldn't, something would make your body pitch from side to side. Robin's shoulder banged hard into one of the storage shelves, really hard, and a voice called out with pain. Was it Robin's? Why wasn't it clear? why couldn't you hear? why couldn't you tell what anything was or what was going where or what was happening? you couldn't do anything, could you hear the voice again?, if you knew it was your own voice you knew you were there, you were alive, you were you, but now Robin could hear only everything and nothing, all at the same time.

৯ ৯ ৯

She skipped down the next flight too, LeShonna did, and started to skip down the last—but something was happening, it was as if the second stair had gone missing, LeShonna missed it completely and then felt a foot glancing off the end of the next step, it was as if the step were moving and not her foot, and then suddenly there was a crash and something had twisted. It was LeShonna's leg, the left one, and the bag had flown off LeShonna's shoulder and clattered on down the stairs and then the light was gone, there had been a crack and there was glass and then there was no light, gone, it was all shadows in the dark, there were no windows in the stairwell, not well not well not well o god o god o god went looping through LeShonna's head and the shaking was all around something horrible was happening and LeShonna could hear a scream and somewhere a dog barked and to the other side or was it behind there was a slamming door and then something crashed past on the dark stairs *you're in the way! you're in the way!* the voice was shaking to and fro in the darkness, *everyone's gotta get out* and the stairs were shaking and then the darkness shook with its aching and its fear, and the fear became louder and louder and then you couldn't hear the other things but you could move, you could move, there were people moving all through the dark. LeShonna couldn't move, *why couldn't you move a leg that was only twisted?* but the twisted foot hurt so much so much so much and then it didn't, it had stopped hurting, it was only that someone else could feel it hurting, far away. It was so dark. Just here on the stairs it was so dark and they shook and they shook and they shook and now it was only the stairs and the dark, the people had stopped their crashing and their shaking as they passed by, had stopped passing by, and the dust began to come out from the walls that rose up shivering above the stairs, more and more dust, dirt and plaster dust, was it from the wall or from far above? And then LeShonna began to hear sounds like she had never heard, the sounds of wood being wrenched *was it wood?* and splintered, yes she could feel something sharp press into her somewhere down below, her other leg, and the weight of everything, great shards of it shivering into slabs, falling, LeShonna reached out to the wall *steady, steady, balance,* but it rippled and quivered and quivered and quavered and then it was gone, the wall had gone, falling away, crumbling and falling away and the whole staircase was falling away and was it someone else who was far away?, there was a sound, had they felt the hurt? *was it screaming?* was screaming was screaming was screaming until all the noise and the dust and all the dark that was everywhere was over, until everything was over.

ও ও ও

Robin forced a way forward, rolling, shivering, gripping the shelves and pulling, but sometimes you couldn't pull there was just rolling air. And there was wall; Robin stumbled forward and was thrown forward, and the shrieking grew louder and a ripping sound tore through everything, and the paintings clattered louder and louder, and then a terrible crash of something falling, and then the floor began to heave more than ever and Robin could hear something else, a stretched shriek of wood giving way and then another and another and another, the aisles were falling in on each other. Robin pressed in against the shaking wall, if you put your head down maybe it would be all right but if you looked just a little to one side with one eye only you could see it wasn't all right, you could see wood and metal coming at you and then you knew that the scream was in your own mouth, Robin suddenly knew that. A section of shelving screamed past and a long shard of wood trailing bits of canvas speared into the wall overhead for a moment and rolled on. Row after row of shelving was tipping, rolling, falling, *dominoes* was the word people used but dominoes were harmless, everything here was sharp and shrieking and there was no end to it, sharp and shrieking and shaking, on and on and on and on and on and on, and Robin rocked back and forth and back and back and forth and on and on, *how long could it go on?*

ও ও ও

Nico Mora had been in his car when the shaking started, the old Volvo as sturdy as anything on the road, for years he had been telling anyone who would listen they should buy such a car, but suddenly it was shaking and shimmying and almost jumping, and then Nico saw a huge pothole open up just ahead in the center of the road; was it safer to stop or to try to keep on going? Some part of his brain kept saying *what's happening? what's happening?* but of course he knew. This was it, it must be, this was the once-every-200-years or once-every-500-years, and Nico thought not of what he should do now but of what he would have done just a few years ago, how he would have rushed home to Rhonda and little Jessica, pedal to the metal no matter what, but now he and Rhonda had gone their separate ways. How long was it now she had been in Boston—eight years? No, it was closer to nine, and little Jessica wasn't little anymore and not with her mother either, she'd gone way up near Duluth with her Kevin, everything would be all right, he was a good man Kevin, had a steady job, a good man. And then Nico thought of 300 Erie and how nothing had been done and how there were probably a hundred buildings with similar issues in the city, a hundred buildings where there could be similar levels of catastrophe. Maybe a thousand. He could not have done something about all of them, but 300 Erie? If only he had had more time. He was not so far away; he would... Now the shaking was so strong he could hardly think of anything, the doors of the Volvo were rattling, you could hear metal scratching against metal but somehow the car was still bouncing forward, no, no, no it was stopped *had he stopped it?, how could you drive through something like this?*

ℵ   ℵ   ℵ

Rolling, surging, shaking, and then a crash again as the shaking rippled within itself and then another blinding crash in the dark, rolling and grinding, rolling and crunching, and somewhere screams but finally there was a sort of easing, the floor was rolling more gently underfoot, a little more gently, more softly, and then there was no roll at all, just a quivering that felt like it would go on and on but it didn't; very soon it stopped going on and on, and everything was still. More than a minute had gone by since the old stillness had ended, and now it was a different place. The dust floated everywhere in the dim light and a woman was screaming, it had to be a woman's voice, Robin thought. It was only one voice; where had the other voice gone? Robin would have to find Granny, would she be all right out in the open? *The child has been gone too long*, she would be thinking, *the child is in danger*, but something kept Robin's body moving towards the scream. There were no words, it was just a scream, on and on and on. Was it under the rubble? Was it...? Now there was more light, how could the shaking not have taken away all the light? The glow was from above, there was light from above coming through all the dust, and for a moment Robin couldn't stop coughing, but then it was all right to breathe, to see, to clamber across the huge chunks of broken shelving and of paintings and of—you couldn't tell what most of it had been. Then there was a space where you could get under and the screams were coming from under there. And there she was, you could see a figure twisted awkwardly, it must be her leg that had been pinned, *oh my god, who are you? Where have you come from? Please god please help me.*

They had done levers in science just a month before, levers and pulleys, so anyone could tell what you should do. Just to the right of Robin there was a long metal bar that had broken free of something. Words started to come from Robin's mouth, *I'm going to try to move that shelving unit, you have to keep still.*

*No, no*, the woman was saying. *It won't work, you'll make it worse. You have to go and get help, don't try it yourself....*

But Robin lifted the pole and found a place where you could stick one end of it in between two sections of the shelving that was pinning her down, and you could wiggle it in further and then wiggle it in a little further still. And then lean on it, lean on it, press down on the end. *Try now*, Robin grunted and coughed, *try now, pull your leg, pull it, harder!* and she screamed again, for a moment she screamed even louder, and then it came free. Robin could see her pulling herself free, was she clear, was she clear? Robin kept holding the bar, pushing down, pushing—yes, yes, she had to be clear by now. Robin eased up and the shelving eased back down into the rubble and Robin began to cough and cough, the sort of coughing that bends you over and shakes you, and it won't stop.

"He's dead!" a voice was saying, it was the woman's voice. "I'm sure he's dead. But he can't be dead, he can't be."

"There were two of you, I could hear. Is he…?"

"Yes. He's under there. I can't, I can't…"

"We'll go and get help. Come on, we have to get help, we can both—"

"No. I have to stay. I have to stay with him, he was…"

"I have to find my granny. I left my granny outside. I'll send help, people will come as soon as…"

"Who are you? Where did you come from?" But already Robin was leaving her. When would they come? Robin had no idea, there might be places like this all over, places with people under them, whole buildings that had collapsed, even skyscrapers—no, Carl had said skyscrapers wouldn't collapse, almost certainly whole skyscrapers wouldn't collapse. Robin was clambering over the rubble towards the wall, along the wall. Would the door still be to the left? There was no way to know, but perhaps you could see. Robin stepped up on a little mound of rubble and peered through the shards and the spears of wood and the clouds of dust. Yes, there it was. Robin started towards the door and then everything went dark; the light had gone. Robin stumbled trying to scramble over the rubble towards the wall. But if you knew where you had to go it was not too bad. If your shin was scraped or you stepped on a nail or you fell and a nail made a hole in your hand, you knew none of that mattered really. Some strange thing had happened, but Robin was still here, and maybe almost everyone was still here except that the woman had thought the man she'd been with was dead, maybe there were a lot of others like that, you couldn't know unless you could get outside, unless you—first the door, first the door.

Robin felt along the wall, there were wires and boards askew and broken pillars *I can do it, I can do it*, Robin's fingers followed along the wall, *I will find it, it was just here*, a little further and then, *yes, yes*, there was the door and the bar that you could push, just as Robin remembered it. The heavy door pushed outwards and Robin was out in the great wide hallway again. There was darkness, and dust swirled in the dark air, and a thick piece of ceiling hung down like someone's arm, dangling strangely, and Robin could sense someone rushing, was it one person or two or three—no, there were more than that, cluttered voices of people stumbling in darkness for the stairs. Now there were more of them, *I don't know if we can get through* a voice was saying ahead in the darkness, *is it blocked? Are the stairs blocked?*

ৡ ৡ ৡ

As soon as the shaking stopped Nico Mora put the old Volvo back into gear and felt it move. There was a grinding sound from something under the hood but he was moving, he could drive forward. He picked his way through the branches and the rubble, making his way past Superior, past Huron, heading towards Erie and he started to think when he was still a block away that it was all right, *was it?, was it?*, sometimes a building might look all right from a hundred yards away when really it was ready to fall, the slightest little thing might bring it down, an aftershock, a gust of wind, even. But as Nico got closer to 300 Erie he thought it looked good, it looked good. He pulled over and went in and walked up one floor, two floors, three. No, there was no structural damage or almost none, they were lucky, these people, and he was lucky; not having been able to do anything would not be hanging on his conscience. Nico went back down to the street and now there were a few people shouting they kept saying *it's all right, it's all right, we're OK, everyone's OK,* it looked as if one of them might be Harry Phelps and Nico could hear the word *lucky* that had just gone through his own head, but he didn't need to talk to Harry Phelps now, *enough, enough thinking of the lucky.*

Nico pulled the front door to the Volvo open; it didn't want to open now, it scraped and squealed, but still you could open it, and he got in and turned on the radio and sat and listened, *reports of damage to buildings are just starting to come in,* they were saying, and Nico heard *Aon Center* and he heard *Art Institute,* and he heard them say *no reports at this time of fatalities at those locations*, but then the newscast turned to the rest of the city, *according to reports just in, at least three apartment blocks on the South Side have collapsed.* Nico heard *Ellis Avenue, Marquette and Ellis,* and he started to wonder if he could do anything, if he could help, *could they use an engineer?*, he thought, *maybe if there are people trapped they could use someone who can tell them what's safe and what isn't, or at least what's least unsafe; maybe I could help if they have to try to dig their way through.*

ৰ ৰ ৰ

When something happened people always looked for the way they had come in, they thought of getting out the same way, it was only natural, Robin's father had said that last year when they had read a report of a terrible fire in Cincinnati. But sometimes you couldn't get out the way you had come in, sometimes no one could get out that way. Sometimes no one could get out at all and that was the way it would end, but you should look for the signs, the red signs, there were always signs. *Exit, Exit, Exit.* Robin thought and turned and twisted, looking through the dark and the dust, and then you could see it, yes, *Exit,* all in red, there must be some extra power somewhere that had kept those lights shining. The other people must have kept on going, must be trying to struggle up through whatever was blocking the stairs, Robin could hear voices round a corner. *This way, this way!* Robin called, *you can get out this way!* But it was a little voice and perhaps no one could hear. *Exit, Exit,* the sign seemed to be flashing faster now as Robin moved towards it in the darkness of the wide hallway. There was no rubble here, it was all open. Even the ceiling had not been damaged; nothing was falling, almost nothing was torn. The light kept blinking, *Exit, Exit.* And then Robin had pushed the bar on another door and suddenly everything was light, it was all open air, there were shafts of sunlight, the dust was gone.

Which way? Which way? Would she have stayed on the bench? Where was she? Robin began to run, turned a corner, turned another corner, following the lines of the building—yes,

yes, this was the way, if you followed this path you would come to the front, to where Granny was, it would be all right.

There were screams here too, but they seemed far away, everything seemed far away, Robin had to find her, she would be there, Robin knew she would. If you turned to the right just ahead, would that take you to those benches? That was where Robin would find her—but had the terrible shaking been here too? It must have been; why was the earth not torn open?

Here. Was this the bench? That one? That one there? There was no one on any of the benches. They were empty. The earth had not been torn or torn open, the benches were not broken. But everyone had gone. There was no one. Robin felt a moment returning from long ago, felt it clenching a wall of tight muscle circling heart, lungs, everything. In the moment from long ago Robin and Granny had been together but it had not been just the two of them; Carl and Carol had been there too. Carl and Carol had been in the kitchen and Robin had been on Granny's balcony with Granny, they must have been visiting Granny, all of them together. And there on the balcony Granny had asked Robin how Robin's music had been going, Robin's mumbley songs, and Robin had turned to her and looked up and said with a hard little voice *No, Granny. I'm too old for that. You don't need to use that word anymore.* And Robin had seen tears forming in Granny's eyes and Granny had turned away, and when Robin and Carl and Carol had said goodbye a little later, Robin's eyes and Granny's eyes had not met.

Had that been the last time they had seen each other, the very last time? Now Robin could not tell. No, she had been here, she had been real. Was that the bench? Was anything where it had been? Had everything been turned around in Robin's head? No, no, it had to have been, she had to be here, Robin had left her just here. But there was no one, no one. She must have gone home when she had felt the shaking, of course she would have gone home, would have tried to go home but there would have been no one to help her. Robin should have come sooner, should have—it was so hard, so hard, to do the right thing in life. *Now turn, go, run. To the sidewalk, quickly, to the street. On up Michigan, run.*

Hardly anything was moving on the streets. There was a car with its front stuck inside another car, horns honking. Cars and trucks were pointed in different directions, none of them moving. People walked about in among the cars, some of them dazed, some of them hurt, Robin's granny might have been hurt, Robin had to find her. There was a little crowd of police officers at the corner as Robin crossed Lake, almost jostling one of them, *look in the Art Institute, in the basement,* Robin panted. *There's a man who needs help, he might be dead but the woman isn't, there's a woman there too…. The basement—the basement of the Art Institute.*

Had they heard? Had they understood? Robin thought so but it was hard to be sure when you had to keep running, keep running. What were the chances that anything could be done for the man? What were the chances that Granny had made it back to her apartment, that she would be…? How could you know anything like that? There were tears in Robin's clothing, and it felt as if there might be a cut somewhere. Robin didn't think of any tears or any cut, but somehow thought of the green tag from the Institute that had come off, who knew where, it was the sort of thing you'd never need again. At Grand a water main had burst and the pavement had heaved up into a great pyramid. There were sirens and a man was moaning. Just beyond, Robin could see where huge holes had opened up, like potholes; someone had taken a garbage pail and put it over one of the holes, a warning. You could see only the top few inches of the pail, that was how deep the hole was. Robin kept running, running, if you kept running you would not feel the tightening round your heart, you would feel other things but not that.

And then Robin was there, this was her building. Another door to open; there was no one. The lobby was empty again, no, no, not quite empty, the concierge who worked the afternoon shift was there as usual and he had someone else with him, someone in uniform, Robin could ask if they had…

"Where are you going, kid?"

"I have to go up and see if my granny is safe."

"No one's going up just now, kid. Din' you know? There's been an earthquake. Everybody's got to stay where they are till things have been checked out. We got to check everything out, we got to take precautions. For now, nobody gets to use the elevators. You better just go back to…"

"What's your grandmother's name?" the other one asked.

"Sandwell. K.P. Sandwell. She lives on the…"

Suddenly Robin paused, looked down.

"Yes, child. Which floor?"

"*Child.* That's what my granny always calls me. She always calls me *child* or *my child*. Don't tell me she's gone, please don't tell me she's gone. She was just here and then we went to the Art Institute, I left her there, left her sitting outside, she wouldn't come in with me, she was tired from the walk and she said I had to go in without her, she said that she would sit and wait for me, that it would only be for no time at all. And then I never went to see the Caillebotte and I went the other way and through the door and I can't tell you everything that happened but you have to let me through, let me find her, let me go up. I can walk, it doesn't matter about the elevators, I can…"

"Listen, we can help you. Just tell us what floor your granny lives on."

But then when Robin gave him the number and said how high it was and how you could look over everything from Granny's balcony, how you could see almost the whole city from there, there was no sound. And then the arm of the one who was not the regular concierge but the other one, then her arm was around Robin's shoulders and she told Robin that there was no such number. The woman in uniform told Robin there was no such floor. But there had to be, Robin said, and Robin had to see her, had to find her, they had to understand that. *There's a special way, I can show you at the elevator*, and they decided to humor Robin, and in a moment they were standing beside the bank of elevators with this strange, distraught young person—no more than a child, really, and Robin tried to press the elevator panel in strange ways, the strange ways that were familiar, but nothing happened. Robin pressed and pushed and pressed again, there were no higher numbers, there were no extra floors, *Granny, Granny*, Robin was sobbing now, Granny had to be there, had to be there, *she has to be here*, but there was nothing, nothing, nothing.

א א א

How long had it taken Nico to get from 300 Erie to Ellis and Marquette? Ten minutes? Fifteen? It couldn't have been more than that; despite all the debris, despite all the stoplights not working, despite all the confusion he found his way to within a block and then he walked, scrambling over the slabs of skewed pavement, there were no firefighters there, no police even, they must feel they were supposed to be everywhere and who could be everywhere?, so no one in a uniform was here but ten or twelve people were trying to shift some of the rubble, *try lifting this slab*, Nico said, *no, not that way, to the left, that's it*, yes, yes, he could help, but as he looked at the heap of bricks and beams and plaster he thought *we can only find bodies here, no one under there is alive*, and a minute later they pulled out one body, then two, a man and a woman whose faces—no, there is no need to speak of how they had been mangled, and then there was a child, was it a little boy?, and he was another that nothing could be done for, and his parents were there, they had been pulling away the bricks until their little one had come loose, and Nico had to turn away. And then to the other side there was a shout, they had found a young woman, no more than a girl, really, her leg was all twisted and it looked as if her chest had been crushed, you could see how sweet she must have been, Nico thought, there was fear in her face but there was sweetness too, and there were no parents to pass the child to, a young man held her body uncertainly, *is there anything…?*, and Nico knew that no, there was nothing, but he said *lay her over here* and he found himself bent over beside the girl and bending her head back and trying to resuscitate her as if there were something you could do, as if there were some hope, and he breathed into her carefully, carefully, his face was getting wet and he could feel something in his eyes, *an act of god*, that was what people said when something like this happened, you heard the phrase again and again, *an act of god*, and you could read the words in insurance policies too, they would never cover acts of god, but surely no god would do this, no god that was a god of goodness, He could not let this happen, Nico went to church every Sunday and he would keep going to church every Sunday because that was what he had always done, and those were his people, and you had to respect what you were, but first that other little boy and now this girl, and those other two as well, their heads torn and faces mangled, *what god? what god? what god?*, for Nico it would never be the same.

Her name was LeShonna Jones, someone said, *had been*, had been LeShonna Jones. Nico kept on slowly breathing, slowly breathing but it would be no use, they said you should keep at it but you could tell it was no use, no use.

And then it was as if Nico had felt something, it was as if there had been some tiny movement. Had her chest moved? Nico's hand held still, you could not dare to hope, everything held still except for turning his head and his own breathing, the slow breathing. Yes, yes, there it was again, a tiny movement, again, a tiny movement, you had to dare to hope, how could you not? you had to think that maybe even when there was no chance there could be some hope, and then she was breathing, Nico could tell it was the child's breathing, ever so faint but not his own breathing it was the breathing of this child—Shawna, was that her name?—she would live, she would live, she was living she was living she was living.

੨ ੨ ੨

Four days later Nico went to the funeral of the young boy— Rayshaud he had been, Rayshaud Evers. No one had used the word *died* in the service, and people didn't use it after the service, either, as they spoke in low voices, *he is gone* was what people said, or *he has passed away* or simply *he has passed*, as if he might have passed by for a moment on his bicycle, his life a passing moment, and they said he had gone to a better place, another place where he would live forever, and they said that here on earth he would live forever in their hearts, but what sort of forever is that?, Nico thought.

Nico passed near the parents as everyone came out of the church. He wasn't going to say anything to them at first but then he found himself speaking to them, the mother and the father, *I was there*, he said; *I'm an engineer, I tried to help, I'm so sorry*, and he started to reach out to shake the hand of Mr. Evers but then he found himself hugging him, his arms wrapped right round the other man. Nico Mora never really hugged people, but sometimes there was nothing else you could say and you did what you never did.

# Seventeen

*2011*

"You are safe—thank god you are safe!" Carol hugged Robin hard, harder than she had done in a long time, and Carl hugged Robin too; they all hugged each other again and again.

"Your mother's been so worried, Robin. I told her you'd be fine, *just wait and see*, I said, *Robin will be here any moment now, if only the child would carry that cell phone*, I said, *though it may be you can't get a signal in a lot of places*. I was sure the land lines were down, we both knew that you would be trying to call."

But of course Robin hadn't tried to call, hadn't begun to think of looking for a pay phone or of asking to borrow someone else's cell. What was wrong with a person's heart if you didn't think of your parents, if you didn't think of calling them when something like this happened? Robin thought of them now with a feeling strong and pure as grief. Suddenly they were not the ones who were hounding Robin about the work Robin couldn't do, wouldn't do. They were the ones who had cared for Robin and loved Robin before Robin could remember being Robin. Your parents would always be sort of wooden sometimes, but you had to try to think of them as people just like anyone else. Robin asked them now what anyone would ask when such a thing had happened.

"Are you all right? Is everything all right?"

"We're fine. I think everybody's all right pretty much everywhere. A few things fallen down, but only a few, and nothing big. All the tall buildings have held, they're saying just about everything has held. Chaos on the streets, of course—things fallen, pavement buckled, a lot of debris. But it could have been so much worse. Here, listen." Carl turned towards the television where the lips on a face were moving; there was a jumble of cars in the background and a fire truck. "They're saying it was a 7.0." Now a woman's face was on the screen. Behind her you could see a tangle of branches and broken glass. "That's what the one in Haiti was, isn't it? And how many died there? 2,000? 3,000? Engineering. That's the difference—engineering."

Carol thought all the engineering a rich country could buy might not help. She thought it was luck, just luck. But tonight she kept her thoughts to herself.

There were several items on the news about the people who had died; in the first hour or two they had counted fifteen dead, another twenty-four missing, but of course in the end it was thirty-seven or thirty-eight dead. At first individuals weren't singled out, but in the days that followed there was a lot about the young archivist who had died on the lower floor of the Art Institute. All the reports mentioned too the damage to thousands of works of art—perhaps tens of thousands. There were appeals for funds to help repair the Institute, and of course it was just the sort of thing to attract the generosity of the well-heeled. Some of the reports also told the story of the woman who had been rescued at the Art Institute, and of how a young person, "almost a child" had "come from nowhere" to pull her out. The woman had had no idea of the young person's identity, was not even sure if it had been a young man or a young woman, and whoever it was had never come forward.

The other fatalities had been largely in tenement buildings on the South Side; several young children were among the dead, and their stories were on the news as well. In the case of several of the buildings that had collapsed, it came out that the landlords had not been keeping their properties in anything close to a state of good repair, and at once there were calls for stricter enforcement of the relevant provisions of the landlord/tenant act.

ॐ ॐ ॐ

Always there are aftershocks. For days they went on—for almost two weeks. The worst measured 4.6, and brought down two more buildings—two more old tenement buildings on the South Side, and two more people were left dead, two old women who had lived together for forty years. Both must have been weakened by the initial quake, everyone agreed—both buildings, they meant, but perhaps the same had been true of the old couple, you could never tell. You could see a pattern in it all, though; anyone could. And there were loud calls for something more like justice across the whole city, the whole region. For people to be treated more fairly. Poor people, brown or black or white. People without enough learning, people without enough work. People missing arms or legs, people missing a father or mother, people who needed help for any reason. All over the country more and more people said something had to be done. And this time the calls were not ignored; slowly, slowly, over ten years, over twenty years, in Chicago, in Cleveland, in New Orleans, everywhere. Even in the smaller centers, Morgantown and Muniz and Money. Even in Detroit. Things began to be a little less unequal; things began to get better for the people who most needed things to get better.

ॐ ॐ ॐ

With everything that had happened and with Granny suddenly gone, it did not seem right to Robin to ask anyone about her pictures. Perhaps in a year, perhaps in two or three years it would be the right time—that was what Robin thought.

But by then other things had happened. Even before the earthquake the Art Institute had been planning a retrospective on "Art in the Age of the Skyscraper." It had originally been a concept thrown together rather hastily to fill an opening created by the unexpected refusal of the Louvre and the Rijksmuseum to allow a major exhibition on "Art at the Birth of Capitalism" to travel across the Atlantic; the Institute staff were asked to put together something that could serve as a replacement, and someone came up with the skyscraper idea—no doubt aware that a number of the key works people might expect to see in any such show were already in the permanent collection of the Institute. The quake set everything back, of course, and the Institute staff ended up having a good deal more time to research and assemble a show that would be truly first-rate—that would break some new ground. One of the researchers happened to be chatting one day with Abe Ereshefsky and the little group that had been spending a bit of time researching the history of the New Horizons Prize, and had thought to ask Abe about the winners of the now-long-defunct prize, on the off chance that there might be some hidden gems relevant to the skyscraper theme. And of course Abe had told her all about *Rising Stories*, so far as he knew the story.

Had it survived? Had it been damaged? He hadn't had a chance yet to check—there had been so much for everyone to do. But the aisles of cabinets with drawers had suffered far less damage than the rows of stored canvasses, and he thought there was a good chance that it would have survived—that all of those paintings would have survived, the twenty as well as the one. Sure enough, it turned out that *Palmer, Samuel—PAV* had been completely unharmed. Nothing more than a film of dust, that was all the damage. The researcher was extraordinarily impressed with *Rising Stories*, and with the other twenty paintings they unearthed, and so too were most of the rest of the team at work on "Art in the Age of the Skyscraper." They listened eagerly to everything Abe could tell them about saturation and the style of these skyscraper watercolors, and the style of the three paintings known to be by Kenneth Paul, and became thoroughly taken up with the long ago controversy. More tests were carried out with all the latest technology. More experts on pigments and on brush strokes and on handwriting were called in to work with Abe—and eventually the descendants of K.P. Sandwell were called in as well. It was not difficult to locate some of the relatives, and they were able to confirm that the watercolorist who had later made a minor name for herself as a painter of angled windows and glowing sunshine in little scenes in Brazil—*diplomat's wife, and an artist too!*, as one article had put it—had had a "false start" painting skyscrapers, but that there had been "some sort of controversy" over the awarding of a prize—a controversy which had ended in her never getting the recognition she had thought she deserved. That was more or less how her step-grandson Carl had put it, but he was "bound to say" it was "not something that had ever seemed to gnaw away at her." Sandwell had only ever mentioned the controversy two or three times, so far as her step-grandson could recall.

In due course Abe and the experts were able to confirm to their complete satisfaction that the hand which had created *Rising Stories* was also the hand of the painter of the further twenty works in the same style that had been sent anonymously to the Institute—and the hand as well of the writer of two handwritten notes that had been sent by Kathleen Schuyler to the prize committee at the time they had been deliberating. The controversy, such as it had been, was finally laid to rest—and K.P. Sandwell was suddenly established as an artist of real stature. The curator of the exhibition asked to interview her descendants, and of course they were invited to the gala opening of "Art in the Age of the Skyscraper."

There was only one more thing left unexplained in the whole matter. It appeared that Sandwell (or Schuyler, as she had been then, and as many argued she should still be referred to, given that her most important work had been done when Schuyler was her name) had painted her initials on the back of each of the twenty works that had been added to the collection later. There were similar marks on *Rising Stories*—but the experts were unanimous in their view that these were not in Schuyler's own hand. Assurances were given that this discrepancy was in no way material to the issue of the provenance of *Rising Stories*; it was entirely clear from the unusual palette, the patterning of the brush strokes, the distinctive treatment of the paint that the same hand had painted both *Rising Stories* and the other twenty. It was merely an oddity, that was all. One or two had wondered if somewhere along the way a curator might have decided to his or her satisfaction that the same artist was responsible, and had thought to add the initials to make that plain. But surely any trained curator or archivist would choose some other way of recording their conclusions; even in the 1940s or 1950s, people were trained not to scribble on the back of a work of art. It *was* odd—one of those little footnotes to a moment in art history that would remain forever unexplained.

ৰ  ৰ  ৰ

Some part of Nico had wanted to be in touch with LeShonna and with Mr. and Mrs. Jones as well, but he never did that—what would you say, *I was the engineer who showed up and breathed life into your little girl*, it wouldn't sound right. Nothing would sound right. And then there was the whole thing about privacy, the girl wasn't even identified by name on the news, that was how the mother and father wanted it, apparently. But Nico heard about her recovery, they didn't give her name but of course if you had been there you could tell, it was on the news for quite a while about the little girl who had been pulled from the rubble and been resuscitated and how her chest healed and her leg healed and it had almost seemed miraculous that she had survived, everyone said she was a symbol of hope but what did that mean, really? LeShonna herself often thought of how lucky she had been, though it sometimes seemed funny to think of her being lucky when there were all the millions of people who hadn't even been injured at all, they were really the lucky ones, weren't they? Of course it was the people who had died who were the most unlucky, what were they symbols of? Did it make any sense for anyone to be a symbol of anything? And deep down LeShonna knew that, when it came to the living, the most unlucky were the people who were far away and were far poorer than anything any of us could imagine, and wasn't it just as important for us to think of them and hope for them and help them as it was to help anyone close to home? It was those people her pastor spoke of most of all when she said that we should be tithing, that we should always give at least a tenth of what we earn to people who need it more than we do, and try to give some of our time too, and LeShonna started to do that and kept doing it almost always, even when she didn't have much time or much money, if you wanted to be a good person and act as God wanted, you had to try to help people you would never know and never meet, just as much as you had to try and help people right in your home town. Except of course you would always want to help your mother or your father or your brother or sister or your special friend, first and most, that was only natural.

Of course the Joneses had had to move again, they had nothing from the rubble, almost nothing, but people were generous. Years went by. LeShonna grew up and everything was sort-of all right again. But LeShonna ended up leaving Chicago; sometimes years later when she was in New Orleans she would think—but no, the rest of LeShonna's story is one for another day. She never tried again to go back to see the others at Ogden, Naomi and Torii and Robin and them, she sort of meant to but then she didn't, sometimes when time has gone by you just end up not staying in touch, there are different people and you *feel* different and it's a different time, and that's just the way life happens.

# Eighteen

Once everything had died down Robin grew up more or less in the normal way. That year at school turned out to be a matter of scraping through, and the next year was difficult too. But you could get better at working on things you didn't like or that didn't interest you. You could do them well enough, and that would sometimes help you do the things you really liked really well, and that's how it was for Robin. The resolve not to use a cell phone did not last, of course, but the resolve not to eat non-human animals did. Robin stopped complaining and started to cook—sometimes just a meal for one, but then more often than not it was for the whole family.

Of course there were things that changed after the earthquake. *We should help*, Robin had said, *we should do something to help*, and Carol and Carl had said that there wasn't much a few individuals could do to help after an earthquake. They could make a donation, of course, but the government was providing help, the government would help rebuild whatever needed to be rebuilt. Robin had said *no, I mean help for people who have been needing it for a long time. Like half the people on the South Side, for instance. Help for people in Haiti who have nothing. And in Bangladesh. Help for whales who are going to be extinct if we don't do anything. Help for the whole planet, help for...*

"And what can you or Carol or I do to help all those people? To help the whole planet?"

"Maybe not a lot. But something. We can all do a little. And a little is better than nothing."

"All right. Anyone can do the math: is that it?"

"Yes. Anyone can do the math. Even me." They were looking at one another a little guardedly but they were smiling, sort of, and a couple of months later Carl decided to volunteer Saturday mornings at a food bank, it made you feel a little strange and a little insignificant to be told to sort bread and decide what could be eaten and what was too old, and bag what was edible, but Carl found he felt oddly happy after a couple of hours of sorting and bagging; he decided that he would stick with it, that there were worse ways to spend a Saturday morning. And by then Carol had read a book by some philosopher who said we should all be giving ten per cent of our income to charities; Carol wasn't sure, she thought ten per cent might be too much but she would do something, definitely she would do something was what she had decided, so she was helping out Thursday evenings at a women's shelter and Robin was working twice a week for a few hours at the animal shelter, and the SPCA didn't seem very interested in anything except cats and dogs and maybe animals in zoos, they didn't seem to care about pigs and cows and chickens and lambs, and Robin was trying to change that.

Eventually the family moved out to Lisle, Illinois—that was just after little Danielle was born. By then both Carol and Carl had given up on nine-to-five; Carol was freelancing as a book designer, and Carl had gone out on his own as a technical writer—both of them able to work from anywhere. Could they have afforded a nice big apartment in an old graystone house like once they had dreamed of? Just maybe they could have, but you could get so much more space for the same dollars if you went farther out. And of course everything seemed safer there, and who doesn't want that? Everything was quieter, too, and moved a lot more slowly; as they got older Carl and Carol discovered that these were things that made a difference to them. And really you could find just about everything you needed in Lisle. But they didn't stop their volunteering; Carol still went into the city for that on Thursdays and Robin switched to working at the Humane Society in Lisle and Carl even found a food bank right in Lisle where he could help out, it was surprising all the places people were going hungry. And it was surprising how much good giving could do, even when you weren't on the receiving end; in their fifties Carol and Carl thought again about that book Carol had read years before and thought maybe it made sense, maybe they *could* begin to give ten per cent of what they earned to people who needed it more than they did, and they were surprised at how much better that made them sleep, how much happier that made them feel.

By that time Robin had grown up—really grown up—and was ready to move on. What followed? A degree at a small college in Milwaukee, broken up in the first year with a lot of time writing poetry and a lot of time spent at poetry readings, and then, as time went on by, more and more time spent at the baseball park. And then a career in insurance—it was the sort of career Robin found you could sort of drift into—at a firm based in London, Ontario. You always had to correct people, this was the London that had only a couple of hundred years of history, not a couple of thousand. But it was quite a little center for insurance. Robin's outfit wasn't one of the larger ones, it was just scraping by, really, the sort of business where you might plausibly be thought to be telling the truth if you said you felt it wasn't anything special to have been promoted to Regional Manager. As Robin had been, and as Robin did say. Still, it was a life you needn't be ashamed of. By the time another Regional Manager's job came up with a small firm in Providence Robin had taken out dual citizenship and bought a house, nothing grand, you really didn't need anything grand in life, it was surprising how many people didn't understand that. And it wasn't for the grandeur that Robin moved to Providence, just a feeling that—sometimes it was hard to know why you did things in life. But it wasn't hard to re-settle in Rhode Island. Providence wasn't the happiest place economically, hadn't been for a long, long time; maybe not since the eighteenth century when it had been the most prosperous slave port in America. Now it was—what? A mid-sized town, a town like any other. But poorer, perhaps. Yes, poorer. Once or twice a fleeting idea went through Robin's head that the town's poverty now could be some sort of punishment for the slave-trade riches of yesteryear. If there were a god, might he think that way? But you could think too much about those sorts of things. Mostly Robin just somehow felt comfortable here, more comfortable than in London, where most everyone had been comfortable.

Not all of Providence was depressed or run-down, of course, and Robin loved the charm of the old buildings that had been restored, of the murals behind Bliss Parking on Orange Street, of the lighthouse and the little park out at Conimicut Point, and of course you could see the minor league Red Sox play at Pawtucket, and that had its own beauty. But there could be beauty in the run-down too, in the parts of town that were down and pretty close to out. Beauty in some of the people who were that way too, and maybe if you saw a lot of people who were worse off than you were, you might think a little more often about trying to help the people in the world who needed help, Robin had done a bit of volunteering in Milwaukee, then nothing in London, really, but in Providence you really wanted to help, anyone would, and before long Robin was volunteering at the New Hope Shelter out in Pawtucket, it was a place that catered to families, you didn't think of mothers and children being homeless people but a lot of them were, it was amazing how many. Robin liked helping out there, liked being there, liked hearing the stories, liked playing with the children. Of course there was the name, too, at first it had just been a name that had just popped out from the list of shelters, Robin hadn't thought anything of it, had just liked it that the New Hope was for anyone, Jews or Muslims or atheists or anyone, not just Catholics like the shelter had been reserved for long ago. It hadn't been until months later that Robin had thought about the name and then about names and lives, and after that there were sometimes moments when Robin was playing with a child at the shelter that there would be a warm feeling that was mostly the warmth of the new moment and the living child but that was also a little bit memory. A little flicker of Hope running, or of Hope laughing, of Hope smiling into the sun and the wind.

ॐ ॐ ॐ

For a long time after the earthquake Robin had become one of those people who don't really think very much about whether there's a god. They don't really believe but they don't really disbelieve either; if they do start to think about any of it, they think they don't know if there's a god or not—how could you know a thing like that? But after a few years in Providence Robin started to think a bit more about it for the first time in years, and to think that you should face something like that squarely; if you always ended up thinking it was really, really unlikely that there could be a god, or anything like a god, then maybe it was better not to be saying *I don't know* and calling yourself an agnostic. Of course you couldn't know, not for sure. No one could. But what were the odds? Robin had learned so much about probabilities. You needn't use the word "atheist" if you didn't want to. You could just say *I don't believe in a god* or *I don't believe there is any god*. And that was what Robin always did after that.

ৰ ৰ ৰ

It was a small city, Providence, and sometimes Robin would think it might be nice to be able to spend more time in Chicago, and then as the years went by Robin would think that it might *have been* nice to have been able to spend more time in Chicago, sometimes in the evening you might sit and wonder about that, wonder what life might be like if life were different.

And sometimes when Robin was on the road, in a hotel or a motor inn of some sort—the job required a certain amount of travel—a poem would start to appear and Robin would write it down, a poem about skyscrapers or about the nothingness of money, or the sounds of the air, or the light as it flattened out on Lake Michigan in the evening. Or about certain people and how they cared for each other.

ৰ ৰ ৰ

Carol and Carl managed all right in the end. They spoke on the phone with Robin every so often—the real phone, as Robin always called it—and as the years went by they found more and more warmth to send over the line. And they found it became easier and easier to be truly interested in what Robin was, in what Robin was doing. Insurance was one thing, but they were thrilled when their child was short listed for a poetry prize; it was something obscure in Canada named after some general, and Robin was a finalist, not the actual winner. But still.

When Danielle had arrived that had meant a big change for them all, of course. Some couples who lose a child want to start in right away at a new one. That hadn't been Carol and Carl, of course; they had had to get through the hate, they had had to feel sure of each other before they started to think of anything like that. But after a few more years had gone by—by the time it got to be eight or nine years since Hope had died—well, they weren't getting any younger, and you never knew. What if something were to happen to Robin as well? It wasn't that you could ever write over the memory. And it wasn't that they would ever want to forget what they had lost. But you had to look forward too, and a new child was a new future.

Sometimes they were bothered by the thought that they might not have done enough for Robin, that they could have found ways to—well, just that it might have been better if it could have been different. It had taken Carol a long time to come to terms with the truth and what she had done with the truth—the truth about Robin and Hope all those years ago. Shaping it. Twisting it a little bit, truth to tell. How many years had it taken after Hope was gone before Carol had been able to face it squarely, what she had seen on the balcony? Maybe it had not been until Danielle arrived. At first Carol had always said that none of it had been Robin's fault—especially to Robin she had said that. Told the child that there was nothing else that could have been done, that no one would have been able to hold on to little Hope. Not when she had started to lose her balance. That had been what one had to say, but deep within her Carol knew it had not been true. Knew that Robin had not done everything possible for Hope, had failed to grab her, failed to hold her. Carol had seen their fingers touching, clutching, and then seen something pushing forward, pushing for only a split second but it was enough—that was all it took, a split second. She could never tell Robin, she would never tell Robin. After a certain point you were your own person. And there comes a point with any child when you have to let go.

She did not try to twist the truth inside herself any longer. But nor, as she got older, did Carol ask as often what the point of it all was, what point there could be in any of it. More and more she felt proud of what Robin had become. More and more she found that little things pleased her. It pleased her when she saw someone, anyone, do some little thing to help someone else, when she saw someone trying, even in some tiny way, to make the world a better place.

Robin did not tell everything, either. Carol and Carl never heard what had happened those afternoons and evenings in the months before the earthquake. Even Kathy Snyder did not hear everything. The story of what happened to Robin and to Kathy Snyder, and the story of what love Robin found in the end when Robin was no longer a child, and the story of Robin and of Robin's own children—like LeShonna's, those are stories for another time.

Robin's mind was never troubled much by what had happened that one strange year. If your life moved on and you managed all right you never needed to ask what had "really happened," you never needed to revisit the past. It was enough to keep heading forward, and to try to do something here and there to make the world a better place. Of course you were bound to sometimes feel old aches and pains flare up again. Once, a couple of years after the earthquake, Robin found a seashell under the bed, an oyster shell. It must have fallen and skittered under there, and Robin had never noticed that it was gone. Was it the shell that Robin had pulled from a pocket one day in that strange year, and put somewhere, and then hadn't been able to find? You could never know something like that. But where else could it have come from? Robin had never been to the sea.

Robin kept the shell, and sometimes it would bring thoughts of an old woman who was gone. The same thing sometimes happened when Robin saw a painting where the colors had been given water and a space to run free, or when the fog rolled in to whatever city Robin might be in, and the tops of the towers began to be lost.

From Providence Robin began to travel often to New York, and would sometimes stay in Brooklyn, in Red Hook, at a squared off motel where the bright red *Motor Inn* light flashed on and flashed off through the night, and where a stairway no one ever seemed to use led up beyond the third story. There was only a simple bolt on the door leading out to the roof, and for many years you could pull it back and step out and take everything in as the sun was going down and almost the whole of the world would be laid out before you, the inner harbor, the statue with the poem you knew was at the base of it, and all the lights of the city and the Brooklyn Bridge, the Manhattan Bridge, the lights of all the ships and all the small boats bobbing on the water, and if you looked the other way you could see past the dark warehouses and the great orange cranes to the far harbor and beyond, the lights of the cars on the Verrazano twinkling high above the narrows, always moving, on their way to Brooklyn, on their way to Jersey, on their way to beyond. The company could afford better for a Regional Manager, better than the Brooklyn Motor Inn, but Robin never cared about that. After a few years, though, they put in closed circuit cameras at the front desk and then they would know if you were up there, and they said they didn't want that, not unless you had a special reason, and wanting the beauty of it to swirl through your head and scraps of words to lean together towards rhyme in the setting sun were not special reasons, and after that Robin stayed more often in Manhattan, or in a little place over towards Park Slope.

When the children were old enough Robin took them to see the great cities, to see New York and to see Chicago, once even to see Chongqing and Hong Kong. They had gone up the Hancock and the Sears and they had gone as high as they could go in the Wrigley and the Mather, and they had found the little round elevator in the Jewelers' Building too, it was still there after all these years, it was good that people cared about that sort of thing nowadays; you would never see the Wrigley or the Mather or the Jewelers' Building pulled down like they had torn down the Singer Building in New York all those years ago, like they had torn down the Schiller Building in Chicago. The Wrigley and the Sears and the Hancock would always be there, would be there forever, but Robin knew that this was the *always* and the *forever* that we use when our friends and our relatives die, or sometimes when someone famous dies too, we say to one another and to ourselves *her memory will live on forever* or *he will always be remembered*, and yet we know what is coming, how soon they will be ashes, letters on a tomb, names and dates we can barely make out, *is that Kitty or Katy?*, *no it's not a six it must be an eight*, *you can just see where…*, *she must have been over 90 when she died*, and then nothing, old papers in a box for a while and then the children or the children's children have to move, *you'd like to but how can you keep all this forever?*, *there isn't space, there isn't time*, and then the papers gone, the stories gone, new life piled upon new life upon life that once was new.

All of it will end, we know that, and the sun will burn out. But it is too far to see or to think, we bury the thought that soon we will be as nothing, a wisp in some old person's memory of a memory of something they heard as a child. We say of a poem, of a painting, of a sculpture, of the colors, the shapes, the words, *it will stand the test of time*; what do we mean? Decades? Centuries? We turn in the night—is it three o'clock? Four? How long till the light?—and we know for a moment how all the colors and all the words and all the millennia end, and we turn again, again, until finally we wake, or turn until we find a different sleep. Robin knew how that sort of knowing could be more than a moment in the night, could be held in the dark colors that the sun carries, could be held in the hopes and dreams of the bright day, could be in everything. Knew how we can feel it deep within the heart of love, and in our children's hearts as they begin to learn to love; how we can feel it in our longing as our eyes and the light take us on beyond Aqua and the Jewelers' and the Mather and all the tall towers, on beyond Red Hook and across the harbor, on beyond all the lights of the city, how we can feel it in our longing as we age and age, and still have love living on within us.

Knew that it is the one true always, that none of these things will be without end, that there is no forever in this, that all of us will die, that everything will die, that nothing will be remembered, that the earth will end, that the sun will go dark, that the stars will burn out, all of them, that the universe itself will be nothing but cinders, that we must make our own sky and our own heaven, always.

# Twelve Stories, as told by
# K.P. Sandwell to Robin Smith

## The Childs Building

"Have I told you about the skyscrapers in Winnipeg?" K.P. enthused to Robin as they looked out from the balcony. "The Childs Building was all of twelve stories; the McArthur Block was its real name but everyone called it the Childs. Nothing to do with children; it was where the Childs restaurant was. You wouldn't know about that, Robin, but long before there was a McDonalds or a KFC there was a chain of great restaurants that had been started by a couple of men called Childs. They were brothers, I believe, was there a William? Healthy meals at fair prices for working people, that was what they did. When I was little, Childs went vegetarian and became famous for the Childs' Unique Dairy Lunch; one of the brothers thought it would be healthier than meat, and I'm sure it was but it damn near drove them out of business and they had to bring back beef and chicken and pork; they'd been too far ahead of their time. They had started in New York in the old Singer Building, and then they were everywhere, I believe the Winnipeg location was their largest in Canada. The most beautiful building in Winnipeg, with a great cornice curling out above its vast top story, one of the most impressive skyscrapers in the city. You'd hardly call it a skyscraper now, so much has changed…"

"The sky has moved. It's higher."

She chose to ignore the child. "They tore it down, the Childs. In the 1980s. Tore it down and built a bank tower made of glass that was no different from a thousand other bank towers made of glass. Did they think we'd think of them as transparent? Banks!" She huffed a little before she went on. "It was so lovely, the Childs. Chicago School, that's what they called it, the style of those buildings. Everyone in Winnipeg used to call those buildings 'the very finest examples of Chicago School architecture.' But then they would always add, 'outside of Chicago.'"

# The Wrigley Building

"If you're going to learn about the Wrigley Building," K.P. began, "there are two people you should know about first. The strange and rather sad thing is that I can only tell you about one of them."

"One of them was called Wrigley. Did I guess it?"

K.P. smiled. "Yes. One of them was called Wrigley. William Wrigley Jr., he was. He grew up in Philadelphia, where William Wrigley Sr. made soap. No, that's putting it wrongly. Where William Sr. owned a soap company—I very much doubt he did any of the actual making of the stuff. Little William was evidently something of a trouble maker; he kept getting expelled from school—he once threw a pie at the principal, I believe. When he was ten he ran away from home. He made his way from Philadelphia to New York and stayed there for a whole summer; he worked as a newsboy and he slept on the street, or so the story goes. He did go to work in the soap business by and by, but a sort of restlessness must have always stayed inside him. He ran away again when he was nineteen, but lost his railway ticket in Kansas City and came back to Philadelphia, broke. By the time he moved to Chicago he was not yet 30, but he had worked on and off in the soap business for almost 20 years. His big idea in business was to give people something for free—'for nothing' was what he called it. 'Everybody likes something extra, something for nothing,' that was Wrigley's motto.

"Little William wasn't a rich man. He had almost nothing himself; William Sr. thought a man should have to earn his way. The boy—the man, I suppose we must start to call him at this point in the story—had gotten married when he was twenty, and was earning $10 a week. He had gotten himself a wife, and soon he had a daughter too. That's when he came to Chicago. It was 1890. There were a million people here but there were still no skyscrapers."

"Was it in Chicago that he started making gum, then?" Robin paused. "I mean, started a company that made gum?"

"Not at first. At first he was selling soap and he offered baking powder as a premium. There seemed to be more interest in the baking powder than the soap, so he started selling baking powder—offering chewing gum as a premium."

"That was like a prize?"

"I suppose you could call it that. Only it turned out that people wanted the gum more than they wanted the baking powder. I find that impossible to imagine. Do you like to chew gum, Robin?"

"I do, Granny."

"You and a billion other children. Unfathomable. But yes, evidently people wanted the gum more than the baking powder. And so he borrowed $5,000 from his uncle. Not from his father, the soap maker—that's an interesting detail. And with the $5,000 little William started his gum company."

"And made Juicy Fruit, and made Doublemint, and made the Wrigley Building?"

"One step at a time, Robin, one step at a time. There was no Doublemint at first; what Wrigley's made at first was called *Lotta Gum*. That was for children…"

"Makes a lotta sense, Granny."

"I'm sure it does, child, I'm sure it does. It was also for grownups, apparently—grownup men, supposedly grownup men."

"Not for women?"

"No, the women were evidently thought not to care so much as the men did about quantity. William wanted *classy* for the women, and that meant a different name for their gum. 'Vassar Gum.' I will tell you another time about Vassar."

"All right, Granny." But there was a pause. K.P. had suddenly lost the thread. There was a strange light in the sky. You often got that light over Lake Michigan at this hour, this time of year. Dusk. She could remember…

"The building, Granny. You're telling me about the Wrigley Building now."

"So I am, child. So I am. The building, and who made it. A lot of people have written about how wonderful Wrigley was. *Larger than life*, they say. How he gave his workers Saturdays off when everywhere else people had to work a half day Saturday, a full day sometimes. How he put baseball games on the radio when everyone else thought that would just encourage all the fans to stay home. And he… —no, I am just going to tell you about the building."

"Yes, Granny. The building, Granny."

"Wrigley wanted height, wanted graceful height for his gum temple. But with the Wrigley Building, the height is just a small part of it. Sometimes people make it sound as if the design was ersatz—more or less copied from some Spanish cathedral, or from the Woolworth Building in New York. But it isn't like either of those. Even the tower is only a little bit like that silly Spanish cathedral. And there's so much more to the whole thing than the tower."

"The angles are all set at an angle—I remember you said that when I was here before, Granny."

"And the proportions, child. I trust I told you about the proportions."

"You told only me a little," Robin lied. "Who made the angles and the proportions Granny?"

"That's just what I was getting to, child. No one has ever heard of him. It's the most famous building in Chicago, and no one has ever heard of the person who made it."

"Made it, Granny?"

"Who designed it, Robin. Who made the designs. Sometimes people mention the firm—Graham, something, something and something. One of those firms where a lot of people have jostled to have their own name be part of the company name, where everyone wants to be known and remembered. And of course the more names there are, the more forgettable it all is."

"So Graham and the Somethings had nothing to do with the Wrigley Building?"

"Graham may have done. But none of the Somethings, so far as I know. Mainly it seems to have been a young man named Charles Beersman. And we know almost nothing about him. Oh, there are some basic facts. I said 'young'—he was just over thirty when he came to Chicago and joined Graham and all those Somethings in 1919. The Wrigley Building must have been just about the first thing he worked on—they broke ground for it in 1920. Beersman came from New York but he went to college in Philadelphia. We know that he won a fellowship there and we have a list of some of the other buildings he designed later. The Federal Reserve Bank of Chicago may be the best known of them. It's a design in a certain sort of classical style, Greek pillars slapped onto a very ordinary skyscraper. Nothing hideous about it but nothing very remarkable either. Copying Greeks badly: it's been done a million times before, and a million times since. And maybe the Wrigley Building *began* with copying. Copying that cathedral, copying those towers in New York—the Woolworth Building, the Municipal Building, the Metropolitan Life Building. But something magical happened. Maybe Beersman was pushed into genius by the lines of the street and the river. By the way they push together, those strange angles. Whatever it was, it was genius. And then nothing, nothing that he is remembered for. No one remembers what he was like, no one remembers his name. I tried once to look up something about him—there is almost nothing. When I was a toddler he was getting married; that much there is a record of, I can read you the few lines from *The New York Times*:

> Mrs. Sarah L. Broffe of 149 Lexington Avenue announces the engagement of her daughter, Miss Beatrice Livingston to Charles G. Beersman, of this city. Mr. Beersman is an architect at 18 West Thirty-fourth Street. He was graduated from the University of Pennsylvania and is a member of the Acacia Fraternity.

Who were these people? Were they happy? How did Beatrice take to Chicago? Did they grow rich? Did they...? There are so many questions, and none of them can be answered. Beersman died July 29, 1946, aged 58. A more or less forgotten life, a more or less forgotten man."

"But you remember things about him, Granny."

"This evening perhaps. As a shadow, as a name, a name to give to something that was human and that gave shape to the finest of all the buildings in this city. But a name and a shadow only. And only now: there is no forever to it. Tomorrow morning there may be nothing there."

"The building will be there, Granny."

"Yes, child. The building will be there. There will be no earthquakes, and the building will be there in the morning."


# The Mather Building

"I suppose the story of Alonzo Mather and of all the Mathers is a lot like the story of America. But with most of the selfishness and cruelty left out. It has religion in it, and kindness to animals. To non-human animals. And moneymaking, but not just for the sake of moneymaking. And skyscrapers, of course."

"You'll tell me the story, won't you, Granny."

"I would love to, Robin. It begins a very long time ago, with one Richard Mather of Liverpool, in England, being suspended from a church where he was the minister. This was the Church of England, in the early 1630s. Suspended twice for what they called nonconformity. Mather's particular way of not conforming had to do largely with baptism. You know what baptism is, don't you, Robin?"

"It's when you are put under water to show that later you can be put into heaven."

"That is, I suppose, the gist of it. And in Richard Mather's England the established church was reluctant to let children be baptized—to admit them to the church, essentially—if their parents were thought to have strayed from the path of righteousness. Mather wasn't a total free thinker on the matter, but he did feel that such children should be admitted to the community of the faithful if they were prepared to declare their own faith and confess their own sins—never mind the sins of their parents, was Mather's view. By the 1650s, when England had had its revolution, such views had become the norm. But in England in the 1630s, if you were a clergyman, they could lose you your job. So it was that Richard Mather and his wife and their three sons left England for New England. It was 1635, and they became five of the Massachusetts Puritans. Mather became a clergyman near Boston. He helped to write the first book printed in America—wrote all of the preface to it and a lot of the…"

"What was the book, Granny?"

"No one can remember the title. If you give me a moment to look it up you will see why. Ah! Here it is." She had pulled a book from the shelf, and held it open. *The Whole Booke of Psalmes Faithfully Translated into English Metre. Whereunto is prefixed a discourse declaring not only the lawfullness, but also the necessity of the heavenly Ordinance of singing Scripture Psalmes in the Churches of God.* "That was another thing about the Puritans; they wanted the old psalms heard by everyone, sung by everyone. Here you are—'O thou that sittest in the heav'ns, I lift up mine eyes to thee.' That sort of thing. Translations from the Hebrew, all of it in rhyme. He made rhymes. And he and his wife kept making sons too—the last of whom, oddly enough, was called Increase."

"Increase was the end of increase."

"He was, for that generation. But Increase Mather became a clergyman too—and president of a new place of learning they called Harvard

College. Increase found himself a wife and they begat Cotton Mather, who was—well, Cotton Mather is a whole story unto himself."

"What about the animals, Granny? That aren't us."

"I am coming to that, child. I am coming to that directly. There were a lot of begats between Cotton and Alonzo; we will skip over those. Alonzo was born in New York; his father was head of a college, just as Increase had been. But Alonzo was restless and he left home when he was young."

"Like Wilbur."

"Exactly. Like Wilbur Foshay. He never went to college. He went to Utica. He went to Utica and started to sell men's clothes. And then he thought there would be more opportunity where things were growing fastest. He moved to Quincy, on the Mississippi. But that wasn't getting big enough fast enough for him, so he moved to Chicago. And instead of a store selling clothing he started a wholesale business, selling clothing to people who sold clothing. He was 27. Four years later is when the non-human animals come in. Here, I will find it in a book. I will let Alonzo speak for himself."

"The Internet, Granny, You could find it there."

K.P. hid any trace of irritation. "Not anything like so quickly, I'm sure. Here, you see?" Her hands rippled at the pages, and soon enough she had found it. "Alonzo is travelling by rail to New York on a buying trip when he writes this:

> In March 1879, on account of a wreck ahead of our train, we were delayed over 10 hours. During the night, I was kept awake on account of a stock train on the siding directly opposite my section in the sleeper. As dawn approached and there was sufficient light to see, I raised my curtain and saw the most shocking sight: In the car opposite my berth were five dead and bleeding animals and a furious bull working his way from one end of the car to the other, horning the weaker animals that got in his way.

I should explain. On railway cars at that time they would put the animals on every which way, not thinking of who should go together with who."

"Who?"

"Should it be *whom*? Grammar has never been my strongest suit."

"I mean why *who*? Why not *which*?"

"We can say *the cat who* and *the dog who*. And people don't just talk about dogs who follow us around and love us; they also talk about dogs who bite. Surely a cow or a pig or a dolphin is more like a dog than it is like a stone."

"Or a bird. An owl. *Who* is good for owls too. *Who*."

K.P. thought that was best ignored. "Or a bird, certainly. A duck, a turkey, a chicken. An owl. We should extend the same courtesy to them that we do to dogs and cats. They are not senseless things."

"So what happened, Granny? With the animals in the railway cars?"

"By the time Alonzo got to New York he had sketched out a design for a new type of railway car—one with barriers to keep the bulls away from the cows and the calves, the strong away from the weak. Of course it did nothing to keep the human killers away from all of them. But it was something. And he started a company—the Mather Car Company—to make those cars. The Mather Car Company went from strength to strength, and Alonzo became very rich."

"And the skyscraper, Granny?"

"The Mather Building was completed in 1928. Alonzo was 80. He hadn't gone to one of the big established firms; he'd asked an independent architect to build him a tower. Herbert Hugh Riddle. And Herbert High Riddle did just that. He would have built a second one beside it if the Depression hadn't come."

"Why is it so narrow, Granny?"

"The law. The Zoning Ordinance of 1923. The law that let Wrigley build high, that let everyone build high. It stipulated that a building could be as tall as you wanted, so long as the highest story did not cover more than a quarter of the building's footprint—the space the lowest story took up. So long as you had enough setbacks on the way up, the sky was the limit."

"Setbacks?"

"Places where the higher stories are set back from the lower ones. New York had the same sorts of laws. They were for light. They were to make sure that light could make it down to the street level from more than one angle. That the places between skyscrapers wouldn't all become dark caverns as the buildings went higher and higher."

"The Mather Building isn't very high, Granny."

"When they finished it, it was the highest in Chicago."

"And the thinnest."

"And the thinnest. Not just for the top stories, either. Even the base is thin—then and now, the thinnest skyscraper in the city."

"What happened to Alonzo, Granny?"

"He lived to be 93. When he died he was trying to design a plane for anyone, a plane you could buy for less than $1,000."

"So the sky could be the limit for everyone."

"Exactly, child."

"But he died before that could happen."

## Dinkelberg, the Flatiron, and the Jewelers'

"Frederick Dinkelberg had worked for Daniel Burnham, you see."

"Who was…"

"Burnham and Root was the top architectural firm in Chicago. They made their money making grand houses for wealthy meat makers, businesssmen who had grown rich by being cruel to cows and to pigs. But then Burnham and Root turned to skyscrapers. Root died young, but Burnham went on to greater and greater things. So it was that Dinkelberg became involved in some of the greatest skyscraper projects of the time. He was the main architect for what some still say is the finest of them all, the Flatiron in New York—a building credited not to him but to 'D. H. Burnham & Co.' Burnham himself was too senior, too busy—how often that happens in life! That was—" What year had it been? K.P. could not come up with a number. "It was early in the century. The century that's over now," she added. "Like Burnham, Dinkelberg never believed in architecture that would break new ground. He…"

"You always have to break the ground to build a building, Granny. You…"

"It's a metaphor, Robin. A figure of speech. They never believed in architecture that would do anything radically new or different. Burnham and Dinkelberg always wanted a bit of ancient Greece and Rome on the outside, even if the skeleton was modern steel. Nothing revolutionary, they insisted—and yet what an extraordinarily bold thing the Flatiron was! The Fuller Building, I should say. That's what they called it originally, for the company that had commissioned it. But even before it was finished people called it the Flatiron, for the shape of the space it occupied. Not everybody was happy. Let me read you what *Life* magazine said." K.P. fumbled for a few moments amongst all the books until she found the one she wanted, a whole book about the Flatiron. "Here it is—I'll read it to you:

> In this partly civilized age and city, it is proposed to erect on the flatiron at Twenty-third Street an office building more than twenty stories high. New York has no law that restricts the height of buildings, and there is nothing to hinder the consummation of this appalling purpose. Madison Square ought to be one of the beauty spots of the city. It is grievous to think that its fair proportions are to be marred by this outlandish structure.

Of course all that conservative huffing and puffing was soon forgotten. Within a few years everyone loved the Flatiron—the outlandish had become the iconic."

"Translation?"

"The thing that had been mocked had become revered." Would the child understand *revered* any better than *iconic*? One couldn't explain everything. "That was the Flatiron. But then Burnham died, and the firm went into decline. Dinkelberg struck out on his own with a colleague, Joachim Gaiver, an engineer. The company they started took on all sorts of work, but they only received one commission to build a skyscraper—that was the Jewelers' Building. Commissioned in 1924, constructed 1925-27, and for a brief time 'the tallest building in the world outside New York City.' The style was old fashioned—Dinkelberg never gave up the fondness for Greek and Roman classicism he had shared with Burnham. But it was very modern in its way; instead of having an airshaft in the middle of the building, Gaiver and Dinkelberg used that space for cars. It was the 1920s, and most everyone wanted an automobile. Mothers especially wanted to have a secure place to park their car so that they could take their valuables straight from the safe in their office to their vehicle and then drive to—well, to wherever they needed to go. That was the idea, anyway, and a clever idea it was. Gaiver and Dinkelberg built 23 floors of garage in the middle of the Jewelers' Building."

"But you can't park there now."

"When does anything turn out exactly as it has been planned? The Jewelers' Building had been commissioned on the assumption that jewelers would love to have one building where they could carry out all their transactions—everyone in one convenient place instead of strung out along Wabash Avenue. But for whatever reason the jewelers decided they preferred life on Wabash; almost none of them moved into the new building that had their name on it. And the garage? Well, it wasn't used by people visiting their jewelers. Pure Oil took over most of the building, and had it renamed, and the executives loved having such a convenient place to park their cars. But their cars quickly got larger, and the tight turns on the ramps of the garage in what was now the Pure Oil building didn't change their size or their shape at all. By the 1940s Gaiver and Dinkelberg's wonderful idea wasn't working anymore. They made all that garage space into storage space and dingy cut-rate office space with no light. Only now, in the twenty-first century, has the Jewelers' been made elegant and beautiful again."

## Schuylers and Smiths

"Why am I a Smith, Granny? What's a Smith?"

"A smith is a maker, Robin. And that is what you are. A maker with words, for now. A maker of—well, time will tell."

"Why are there so many of us? So many Smiths, I mean?"

"History. All of it is history. Every little village would have its smith. They might not have a carpenter, because people would do their own work with wood. And they didn't need plumbers or electricians; there was no plumbing or electricity. But they needed one person in every village to make things with metal. That took a forge, and it wouldn't make sense for every household to have a forge. One per village is what made sense. An ironsmith would make iron shoes for the horses; those were the smiths you would find in every village. A goldsmith would make the finest, most valuable jewelry; there was one of those in every great city, sometimes many more. A silversmith would make jewelry too, but also bowls and cups and goodness knows what all. There were blacksmiths and whitesmiths, there were…"

"But Hope wasn't a Smith, Granny."

"Hope was a Leslie. Hope Leslie. Your mother is a Leslie, and when she and your father were naming your sister she thought of a character in a book, a famous book from long ago. A book about the Massachusetts Bay colony, the place where…"

"Mather. The first Mather."

"Just so. A book about the Puritans. And about the native people too, the people the Puritans started to push out. The Pequot. Your mother thought of Hope Leslie as a strong young woman, a woman of principle who…"

"And Mother is a Leslie but Father is a Smith."

"Why more parents don't do as yours did I cannot fathom. Your mother no more wanted to give up her name than your father wanted to give up his. And why should she? Surely it's enough to give your love to someone. Why the name too?"

"The me-ness."

"Exactly. The me-ness. Your mother didn't want to lose that, and he didn't want her to lose it. So they took turns giving their children their names. You came first and they flipped a coin, and you were given your father's name. And then Hope, and she was given your mother's name. But you know all this, I'm sure, I was only…"

"What's a Schuyler, Granny?"

"A schuyler is a scholar. That's what the word means in Dutch. It used to be only a last name, just as Smith is only a last name. Or Carpenter, or Shepherd. A way of identifying who people were by what they did. *Which John do you mean? John the smith? Or John the cooper?*"

"Cooper?"

"It meant barrel-maker. I suppose it still means that, if anyone makes barrels with their hands anymore."

"And what's a Snyder, Granny?"

K.P. looked down at Robin, and a smile played at the corners of her mouth. "A Snyder is a sort of a maker too. A tailor. Snyder, Snider, Schneider, there are many variations. All from an old German word for cloth cutter."

Robin looked at the floor for a moment and then looked out over Grant Park to Lake Michigan. Kathy Snyder's father worked for a drug company, and her mother was a banker. Kathy Snyder wouldn't do either of those; sometimes you could tell things like that. Or you thought you could.

"Not everybody gets a do-er name."

"No. When there started to be enough people in an area that you needed last names to know who was who, some took their father's first name as their last name. *Which Will do you mean? Will the son of Ben? Or Will the son of John?* And some people took the names of places, and some people took the names of colors, and…"

"Why didn't you get a color name, Granny?"

"Color names seem to come from hair color more often than skin color. And the Schuylers already had that name before color became an issue. When the Schuylers who became famous Americans came to New York—except it wasn't New York then, it was New Amsterdam—I'm sure they were all a good deal whiter than I am. Philip Schuyler, who was a general in the Revolutionary War, and planned the invasion of Canada—he was as white as they come. Other Schuylers stayed loyal to Britain and moved from New York to Canada, to Kingston or to farms north of Lake Ontario. But the Schuylers I come from didn't come to Canada that way. That set of Schuylers had gone from Holland to the Caribbean. This was in the seventeenth century, and Holland was the most powerful nation in the world. Like the British, they were great colonizers. Great producers of sugar. And great slave owners—slave owners on a vast scale. Of course it was the slaves who were forced to produce the sugar."

"Are you getting to the color part, Granny?"

"I am getting to the color part, child. The branch of the Schuylers that leads to us came to Canada from Curaçao in the 1880s. They had fallen on hard times in the 1860s, after slavery had been abolished. That happened in 1863 in the Dutch Caribbean colonies—the same year Lincoln signed the Emancipation Proclamation here in America. It felt like hard times then for the Dutchmen who before that had used slaves to get the job done. And it felt like hard times for a lot of them on through the 1870s. I don't know quite what sort of farming Augustus Schuyler was doing on Curaçao, but by the 1870s he was apparently doing it mostly with his own hands, and it wasn't going well. In the early 1880s he and his wife and children moved to Winnipeg. The railroad had just arrived on the Canadian prairie, and Winnipeg was starting to boom. Good-sized lots were almost free, and no one had been told much before they came about how cold it could get in January or how many mosquitoes there would certainly be in July. Back then it wasn't so easy to emigrate if you weren't of good British stock—the days when Canada courted immigrants from Latvia and the Ukraine were still twenty years on. But Augustus had found himself a British wife—Mary Schuyler had grown up in St. Lucia. She was the family's ticket to the young province of Manitoba."

"And she was black, Granny?"

"No, Robin. In those days British citizens weren't black. The one who was black was Janna."

"Their cousin? Their aunt?"

"Their slave, she had been. And then she had become the family's domestic servant. Free in law to go anywhere, do anything. In practice, bound almost as surely as before to the Schuyler household. In 1863 she had been only thirteen. She had no education, she had no money. She had no idea who her mother or father or brother or sisters were. The Schuylers had acquired her when she was eight. That was the way it often happened then.

"When the law said she had been freed the Schuylers were the closest thing to family Janna had. They said she could have her room and board for free and maybe they could pay her a little beyond that sometimes. She stayed through the 1860s, her teens. And she stayed through the 1870s, her twenties. By the end of that decade she was their only servant. When the 1880s came, she moved with them to Canada."

"And what happened then, Granny?"

"Mrs. Schuyler died is what happened then. Four times she had been pregnant and four times something had gone wrong. She and Augustus tried one more time, and this time she died in childbirth. But the child survived—you can find him on the family tree, Walter he was." K.P. rustled amongst some papers and then drew out a large, folded sheet that had yellowed badly. When she opened it there indeed was Walter, and Janna, and Mary, and Augustus, and on down to Hope and Robin—all of the names, some of them going back centuries. "He was a sickly child, Walter was, and without Janna's care and Janna's love he would have died too. At least that's what he told me when he was old."

"You knew him, Granny?"

"Walter was my uncle. I surely did know him. He lived into the 1950s. And I knew Janna, too; she was my grandmother."

"I'm confused, Granny."

"Most anything that happened long ago is confusing, child. But let me finish and it may be more clear."

"Did Augustus Schuyler and Janna…?"

"Yes. Four years after Mary died Janna became pregnant. By Augustus. That was perhaps not so surprising; she had stayed on in the household after Mrs. Schuyler had died. The shock was that they married. That Augustus was willing to marry her. And that they stayed on the same street, amongst the same neighbors, right there in Winnipeg. Those were the days when even people who believed in what they thought of as complete equality felt there was something not quite right about a black person marrying a white person. And that was just as much the case in Canada, where they hadn't had much by way of slavery. But Augustus and Janna Schuyler stayed. Augustus saw business drop off for a time at his dry goods store, but he had been through hard times before, and he survived. Janna raised the two Schuyler boys—and as they learned to read and write, so did she. Friedrich was her own child. And then, much later, he became my father. Janna was…"

"Could you have chosen to be either white or black, Granny?"

"I suppose so. Yes, I think I could. As it was, I tried not to call myself anything. I had heard too many stories from Janna of how people used to be named by fractions, *half-caste, quadroon, octoroon*. I let it go—and hoped, I suppose, that I would be thought of as a dark-skinned white person. It was so much less trouble that way. So you see, I was not as courageous as I might have been, child. As I should have been."

But Robin was looking at the yellowed chart again, and only half listening. "What does it mean, *Friedrich*?"

"Peaceful ruler. As the story goes, he was anything but a peaceful two-year-old, but he did his best to rule the household."

"And Friedrich was your father?" K.P. nodded, and a smile came to her face.

"Father led a more simple life than Augustus had done. He stayed on the Canadian prairie, in Winnipeg, in Calgary, then in Winnipeg again. He married in Winnipeg, he died in Winnipeg. Another time I will tell you about Friedrich, and about my mother."

"Emily," Robin read off the large, yellowed chart. "Why do they call it a family tree, Granny? It grows *down* from the top of the page."

"And the branches of trees grow the other way. You are right, Robin. Long ago they would always picture family trees *as* trees, with the earliest ancestor you knew anything about at the base and then the tree and all its branches growing up from that. You still see that sometimes, but not often. This one was made by my father, I believe. It sat in a closet for years, and then Arthur and I found it and added two more generations to it, one day long ago. Yet people have kept that name, *family tree*, not *family chart* or *family diagram*. It is better to see it as a tree, I think. Growing upward, endlessly growing upwards, more and more branches forming with the generations. And each generation with its stories."

"Rising stories. But the stories are never on the tree, Granny."

"No, child. They have to be remembered, or guessed at."

"Or made up."

K.P. looked down sharply at Robin, and at Robin's lively eyes. "You are quite right. Or made up."

# Grant Park and the Chicago Convention, 1968

She began with 1954. With Dien Bien Phu, with a story of how the French had colonized a far-off country and had stayed too long. She told how, against all the odds, they had been defeated by a ragtag rebel army that had ended up with half the country. She told how America had told itself it would try to help the ragtag country's other half after the French had given up. But that other half hadn't been sure it wanted to be helped; it had been a corrupt place, and a place divided. She told how a strange American President, a great President in his way, had become lost. A rough, crude Texan, wily as any snake. But a man who held, somewhere strong and deep within himself, a true need to help the people who most needed help. Poor white people who had been denied jobs and a fair chance; poor black people who had been denied just about everything. And K.P. told Robin how he had done that, how he had helped those people. But at the same time how he couldn't understand what was happening in the far off country, couldn't think of those rag-tag people in the same way as he thought of his own people in the Texas hill country or the Louisiana bayou or the blue collar streets of St. Louis, could only think of the ragtag people as part of a great struggle of ideas. And K.P. told how, because of all that, America had somehow found itself dropping chemicals on the people in that far off country, chemicals that burned their flesh off so that they could be brought democracy. So that they could all be free.

"I don't understand about the chemicals, Granny. Please tell me about Chicago, please."

"Chicago was where the strange, great President would have been nominated for a second term, where his party—the Democratic Party—would have chosen him as its candidate in the election. But the strange, great President was not chosen to be the candidate. The war in that far-off country had become so unpopular that he said he would not run again. The man who had done the most to push him aside was a stubborn Senator with a mind of poetry, and a reedy voice. He was not very good at politics; after he had said that he was against the President and against the war, he had run out of things to say. The convention was not about to choose him, and they probably would not have chosen a Kennedy, either, though that is something that can never be known for sure."

"They teach us in school all about the assassinations, Granny."

"I had thought that, child." She looked down for a moment and then found the thread of her story again, of America's story. "Instead, they chose the great President's deputy, his Vice President, a man who had a lot to say about everything but a man who may by that time have forgotten how to stand for anything—anything except election to public office."

"And when they chose the Vice President to try to be President for their party—that happened in Grant Park?"

"The choosing happened in the old Convention Center. But what happened at the same time in Grant Park became the main story. Thousands and thousands of people gathered to say no to the President, and to his party, and to the war in the far-away land. They called themselves revolutionaries, many of them, but this would not be a revolution with guns. They would walk along the street with the signs they had made and they would shout out again and again. *What do we want?* one would say; *Peace* would say all the others. *When do we want it?* would say the one; *Now!* would say all the others. *When do we want it?* would say the one; *Now!* would say all the others. *When do we want it? Now!* And most of them were scruffy and ragtag but not in the way that the people in the far away country were ragtag. Some called themselves hippies and some called themselves yippies, and they bothered a lot of people. Especially they bothered the fat man who was the mayor of Chicago."

"I know who you mean, I think, Granny. The fat man who was mayor had a son who was another fat man who was mayor until just a little while ago."

"That is it, Robin. Precisely. Well, when the first fat mayor saw all the ragtag hippies and yippies shouting and carrying on, he put an army on the street. There were officers with billyclubs and helmets and National Guardsmen, and they all had to wear masks to protect themselves against the teargas they were going to use against the yippies and the hippies and the—whatever else there were. Scruffy, they were certainly that, most of them."

Tell me what happened, granny. Did you see it?"

"I saw a good part of it. And a lot more of it afterwards, on the television. The real trouble started when a few young men climbed the statue—can you see it out there? Ulysses S. Grant on a horse. They climbed up his horse and they climbed up him. They shouted, they waved banners, they were doing no real harm. There was a flagpole there; another young man climbed that, and managed to lower the flag to half mast; they said it was in honor of all those who had been killed in the war in the far-away place. Then the policemen in their masks grabbed him and clubbed him and kicked him, and grabbed the ones who had climbed the statue of Grant and began to do the same to them. People tried to pull the police away from the protesters, and soon there was teargas everywhere. By that night...—but perhaps I have talked enough. Let me find something that will show you that night, and we can watch it together."

"I would like that, Granny." Robin paused. "But why do you make it sound like a fairy tale, Granny? It's as if I were little again."

"A folk tale, child. It is from a long time ago, and I suppose that is how I remember it."

"Do folk tales have happy endings?"

"Even fairy tales don't always end happily. Come, and I will show you what happened."

ও ও ও

It took a good deal of rummaging, but in the end K.P. found what she had wanted to find and they sat together and watched grainy video footage of the clubbing and the kicking and the clouds of smoke.

"It was foggy on that night too, Granny."

"I don't think so, child. I think what we are seeing is the teargas." She paused. "It could have been worse: no one was killed. Some of the most important things happen without anybody dying, anyone being killed. That's something you'd never guess from the news, but it's true. Death isn't everything—how people live their lives is so much..." she broke off. "But some people will tell you something died that day in the park in Chicago. And that what died was not reborn for 40 years."

"I don't understand, Granny."

"Something died in people's minds, in minds across America. People refused to see what they had seen. They had seen peaceful people being beaten up for no reason. But they thought about it and they thought they had seen punks who deserved it, punks who must have done something vicious to provoke the authorities, punks who had whatever they got coming to them, and probably a lot more. That was the word they used—*punks*. And the people who thought that and said that, the people who refused to see what they had seen, they all voted for the party that would give the troublemakers what they deserved, the punks and the agitators. A lot of people in Evanston and in Lisle and on beyond those places, in South Bend and in Fort Wayne, and in Des Moines and in Cedar Rapids, and further still, in Spokane and in Fresno, in Tulsa and in Little Rock, in Birmingham and in Tuscaloosa. A lot of people in the great cities did that too. And in all the outskirts, the places you could only drive to. They were people who knew that the police were the nice men who would give you directions, who would apologize if they had to give you a speeding ticket. It was only if you lived in a different place, or if you were black or Latino, or poor or homeless, or gay or lesbian, or political in the wrong way—then you knew that a policeman could be someone who would rough people up from time to time for no reason, or shoot first and ask questions later, that a policeman..."

"Officer, Granny. Police officer."

"Ah yes. I am showing my age again. Even back then, some of them were women."

"Were you an activist, Granny?"

"Not enough of one, Robin. Never enough of one. I think I was always too much the diplomat, even before I married one. Someone has to do that side of things, I would tell myself, someone has to be boring and polite..."

"And kind, Granny."

"Oh, but I wasn't always very kind, Robin. A lot of the time I'm afraid I was thinking only of myself." She paused and looked out once more at the darkened park. "We should go in, my child." She paused again, for longer this time. "Don't let me lead you into thinking it's all been downhill. Perhaps it's wrong, what I said about America and those forty years. It's an old person's habit to be always thinking things have been getting worse. There has been good too. Even over all the years when we were carpet bombing the far-away lands, when we were teaching torturers their trade, when we stood idly by as a holocaust happened. Even in the early years of this century, when we became war mongers and decided it was better to help the rich help themselves than to help the people who most needed help. Even through all that, some good was happening. Maybe not here, but in Asia, in Africa, in South America—what Americans call *America* is so little. And even here, even in America there were some things that got better over those years. This much at least is true: even in the 1960s no one of my color would have even dreamt of living in this part of town. And anyone who was openly homosexual…"

"Gay or lesbian, Granny."

"…Exactly. Who was openly attracted to their own sex wouldn't have dreamt of living in almost *any* part of town. Wouldn't have been allowed to."

"It was illegal?" Robin almost whispered the words.

"It might as well have been. You could always refuse to rent or to sell to someone if you didn't like their color. Or if you thought they were queer." She looked at the child, but this time Robin let her use her old word. "In this part of town you didn't have to be black or even darkish brown to be something a lot of people didn't like. Anyone who wasn't pinky-yellow belonged on the South Side, that's what people thought, though you wouldn't hear them say it to your face. And even on the South Side there were a lot of neighborhoods where you couldn't get housing, where you couldn't get so many things. But if you were a homo—if you were gay or lesbian, even if you never admitted it openly, even if it was more of a nudge nudge, wink wink thing—right around here was about the only place you could feel even halfway comfortable. Towertown, they called it. After the Water Tower; there weren't many skyscrapers north of the river back then. If you tried to live that sort of life in most parts of town—well, good luck to you. It wasn't easy. But people had determination and they had hope—to have had hope may have been the most important thing."

# Spires and Aspirations

"What about the church that's a skyscraper, Granny? Will you tell me the story of that?"

"The Tribune Tower? It's a story most everybody…"

"No, I mean the real church, Granny. You know. The one on Washington. Is it Washington and State? Washington and Clark?"

"Ah, the Chicago Temple. The United Methodists. Shall I tell you a little about all that, and then tell you about the Chicago Tribune?"

"I think so, Granny."

"The Chicago Temple was the tallest building in the city when it was finished. Like the building it replaced, it is a church. But not a church."

"How do you mean, Granny?"

"Back in the 1850s someone among the United Methodists had the idea of a multi-use building that would have stores and offices on the bottom floors, and a church on the top floors."

"Closer to God."

"I would like to know if that was their reasoning—or if it was simply a case of hard-headed Methodists thinking that they could pay for the church with the rent from the stores and offices below. At any rate, that's what they built, and ever since then they've stuck with the idea. The skyscraper that's there now went up in the early twenties; it's the third building on the site. I went up to the top once—that was back in '38, when everything was still more or less new. I gather it's a lot now as it was then. There are some church offices on the lower floors, and at the top of the skyscraper is a good-sized church. But most of the space in the middle is filled with the offices of lawyers and accountants and what-not. People sometimes bandy about the phrase 'cathedrals of commerce' when they talk about skyscrapers—I know that was how they used to speak of the Woolworth Building in New York when it became the world's tallest—and it was a minister who first used that phrase. With the Woolworth Building it's a metaphor. With the Chicago Temple? That's quite literally what it is. If anyone thinks that steeples and skyscrapers have nothing to do with each other, all they have to do is…"

"But what about tall churches, Granny? Churches that are *just* churches?"

"What about them? In 1890, do you know what the tallest building in the world was?"

"Was it one of those insurance buildings?"

"Very good! And almost right. An insurance building here in Chicago was the tallest *skyscraper*—it's long gone now, it was gone even before I first came here. But it was no more than 150 feet tall. In Germany there was a church in Cologne and one they had just finished in the town of Ulm that were both more than three times as high. And they weren't alone. Of the ten tallest buildings in the world in 1890, I think there was only one that was not a church. And that was the Great Pyramid at Giza—hardly a skyscraper. It was the tallest from thousands of years ago until—was it 1130? 1131?—the spire at Lincoln topped it, and Lincoln Cathedral remained the tallest building all through the rest of the Middle Ages and the Renaissance. But then it fell down, the spire I mean, it collapsed, and…. But I mustn't go off on too many tangents. 1890, we are in 1890. That was just before everything changed again. 1890—still not a single skyscraper among the tallest buildings in the world. But twenty years later? There was not one church left in the list of the world's ten tallest buildings. And all of them—every one of these great new skyscrapers—had risen in America."

"But not now."

"No, Robin. For a long time, but not now. In 1990 almost all the world's tallest buildings were still American skyscrapers. Twenty years later? The Sears Tower is the only American skyscraper to make the list. All the rest are in China, Saudi Arabia, Malaysia,…"

"And Dubai, Granny. The Burj Dubai."

"It's the most extraordinary thing, isn't it? I wish I were younger; I would love to…"

"But the churches, Granny. You were going to…"

"Are they any different? Were they any different? People nowadays insist on believing that medieval people did everything for the sake of God when they built cathedrals, that they had some sort of pure desire to be close to God. But do we know that? And did that same pure desire drive the good people of Ulm to go just a little bit higher for the spire of Ulm Minster in 1890 than the good people of Cologne had gone with their spire a few years before? Had that same pure desire driven the good people of Cologne to go just a little bit higher with their spire than the good people of Rouen and of Hamburg had gone with their spires just a few years before that? Do you think all they aimed at was to be closer to god?

"It is the same in America. When the Catholics completed St. Patrick's on Fifth Avenue in New York in the 1880s it was the largest cathedral in the country. The Episcopalians saw how large and how impressive it was, and they vowed they would go one better; they decided to build the largest cathedral in the world. St. John the Divine was started early in the 1890s—and it's still not done. Larger than the others, higher than the others—it amounts to much the same thing."

"But maybe they wanted both things. Maybe they thought that being higher and bigger than the next church would give them bragging rights *and* bring them closer to God. Plus it would make more space."

"More space for God?"

"And for themselves too."

"Robin, you are learning of how motives get mixed up in the heart. And that is a good thing."

"That they get mixed up?"

"That you are learning about it." Her eyes sharpened as she glanced at the child. "Beauty is mixed up in it too, of course. Some builders don't care about being highest; they want only to build the most beautiful—or to be known for having built the most beautiful…"

"Which are different things."

"Which are different things, child."

"And who gets to decide what's beautiful? Do they decide for themselves or leave it for God?"

"That's done on a case-by-case basis, I believe."

"Aren't you going to tell me about another skyscraper today, Granny? One that isn't a church?"

"I will tell you a little about the skyscraper that looks so much like a church, but isn't."

"The Tribune Tower? With its flying things? Ms. McLenithan told us that…"

"Buttresses, Robin. Flying buttresses. Which of course there is no need for. When you build a cathedral in the true Gothic style you really *do* need buttresses to support all that arching, all that God-seeking height. And people must have believed that..., some people must have believed...." K.P. looked up for a moment. She had lost the thread.

"But for the Tribune Tower?" prompted Robin.

"The Tribune. Yes. No. None of it is needed. It is the purest decoration. Decorative reaching not towards any god but towards, but towards..."

"Towards sky, Granny?"

"Yes, child. Towards money, and towards empty sky. It was the winning entry in a competition. Everyone knows the story."

"I don't, Granny."

"Of course, Robin; you are not everyone. It is a good little story. It starts in 1922; they announced a competition to build 'the most beautiful and distinctive office building in the world' as the new headquarters of the Chicago Tribune."

"Who were 'they,' Granny?"

"Well, I suppose mainly 'they' was a 'he.' Robert McCormick, the publisher of the paper. He was about as conservative as they come, and a little bit crazy too. He was what they used to call an 'America-Firster'; a lot of America-Firsters were a little bit crazy. McCormick called his radio station WGN for 'World's Greatest Newspaper'; for all I know he believed that the Chicago Tribune *was* the world's greatest newspaper. And he used to tell people how he helped to keep America safe after the First World War—safe against the threat of invasion from Canada."

"Did Canada plan to..."

"No, Robin. No. But let me get back to '22. McCormick wanted something special for the new headquarters of the paper. So he announced a worldwide competition with a $50,000 first prize. These days that would be like..."

"A million dollars?"

"Just about exactly. A million dollars. And the entries came in from everywhere."

"But the buttresses were best? They thought the buttresses were best."

"They did, and that is what you see now on Michigan. A man called Hood was the winner. One or two people made jokes about having been hoodwinked—" K.P waited for a smile that did not come—"but overall it was a very popular choice. A lot of people in the 1920s still thought well of the idea of cathedrals of commerce. But of course the tower soon began to look old-fashioned, to look like it was..."

"Too much?"

"Exactly. And people began to think that the essence of fine building was not decoration but purity—*integrity,* they called it; *clean lines,* they called it; *form following function*—they called it that too. (Once again, 'they' were almost all male, of course.) And then they started to look again at the designs that could have won, but didn't. There had been one by Eliel Saarinen with much cleaner lines; it looked a lot like what most skyscrapers would look like ten years later. And there had been one by Walter Gropius with lines that were cleaner still; it looked a lot like what most skyscrapers would look like thirty years later. A lot of architects and architectural historians spent a lot of time regretting that the judges hadn't chosen differently. That they hadn't been more forward-looking. Here, I can show you." After a little groping about, K.P. found on one of the bottom shelves a book of architectural history that showed both the winning design and the ones that had been rejected.

"There!" she pronounced, once she had located the page (having insisted there was no need for the child to help, as Robin had offered to do).

"It doesn't look very special, Granny," said Robin of the Gropius.

"It surely doesn't. It would have been absolutely ordinary in the 1950s or 1960s. The only thing special about it is that it was ahead of its time. Oddly, that is often counted as a good."

"What happened to Hood, Granny? The one who won?"

"Raymond Hood. It's an odd thing. An interesting thing. His design won the battle but lost the war, of course. Never since then has there been a skyscraper as busy in that churchy way as Hood's was. But Hood himself changed sides. By the early thirties he was designing modernist towers himself—and highly admired ones at that..."

"Highly admired. I get it, Granny."

K.P. chose to ignore the child. "The Daily News Building in New York, the McGraw Hill Building too. A little later, the Rockefeller Center. Did he fall into line with what he had realized was a new orthodoxy, a new future? Or did he have a genuine change of heart?"

"Or both, Granny. People can change. But maybe they can also sort of stay the same as they are changing."

"Yes, child. People can change in many ways, and can stay the same in many ways. Most of them we do not understand."

"Most of the people?"

"And most of the ways."

"All these things you tell me about. They really happened, didn't they, Granny?"

"Yes, child. They really happened."

"If a person started to believe in God, would they have to believe that all sorts of things that couldn't have happened actually did happen? I mean *really* happened—not just happened like things happen in a story."

"Yes, Robin. A person would have to believe just that sort of thing. And to believe that people who couldn't be real are really real."

"Could you believe that *some* of that could happen without believing there was a god?"

"I think you could, Robin. I think you could. But of course I'm the worst sort of person to ask; I don't believe in any of it."

# The Smith Tower

"The name Smith Corona means nothing to you, does it child?"

"No, Granny."

"And soon the word 'typewriter' itself will mean little or nothing to anyone your age. But it was a big thing when the Smith brothers' company created a machine that could efficiently type either capital letters or lower case. No, that's not right—the *company* didn't create such a machine. They had hired one Alexander T. Brown to improve on some gun designs, and along the way he thought of a new typewriter design; it was Brown who did the creating, not any of the Smiths."

"From working on a gun?"

"I guess the way a shooter's finger activates a striker to fire a gun is not that different from the way a typist's finger activates a key to type a letter of the alphabet. This was before everything was digital; people actually used their fingers to do things." K.P. allowed herself a slight smile. No, she would not explain the roots of the word *digital* to the child. One need not always digress. "*A key for every character*, that was what they called the invention, and it made the Smiths into major players in the new industry. This was in the mid 1880s. Lyman Cornelius Smith was only 35 but already he was on his fourth business—there had been livestock in New York and lumber in Syracuse, and then—very successfully—the gun business. But the typewriter offshoot would be far more successful. He and his three brothers, Wilbert and Hurlburt and..."

"Were those their real names, Granny?"

"Those were indeed their real names, Robin. People will find the sounds of Ayden and Brayden and Jayden just as odd a hundred years from now, I imagine. Perhaps you will also be amused at the name of the other Smith who figures in this story: Lyman Cornelius's son, Burns Lyman Smith."

"Burns? That was his real name? His first name?"

"His father wanted to call him that in honor of his wife, the boy's mother, Flora Elizabeth Burns. She and her dressmaker figure prominently in this too. As the story goes, her dressmaker had moved to San Francisco, and the Smiths took a trip to the west coast in part to try to lure her back. That, plus the enthusiasm of Burns Lyman Smith for the west coast in general and Seattle in particular helped encourage Lyman Cornelius Smith to think of investing there. He was persuaded by J.W. Clise, a Seattle real estate agent who visited him in Syracuse, to buy several parcels of land around Pioneer Square in central Seattle. Sight unseen. And he eventually came round to the view that a highrise tower in the downtown of this fast-growing timber town might 'produce a satisfactory return.' He engaged a Syracuse firm that had never built anything taller than five stories. A firm once again of brothers: Edwin and Thomas Gaggin."

"Gaggin? That was their real name?"

"You are like a broken record today, Robin. Certainly that was their real name. Everyone nowadays knows the name of Bilbo Baggins; if there can be Baggins, why should there not be Gaggins?

"Bilbo Baggins isn't real." Robin paused for a moment. "Are you real, Granny?"

She chose to ignore the child. "One of the Gaggins had studied in Paris at the École des Beaux Arts, and there is a little of Paris in the decorative tone of some of their buildings—including what became the Smith Tower. But there is something of Syracuse in them too; the proportions often seem a little odd, a little awkward. Often the proportions just don't work. With the L.C. Smith Building, though, they made it all work to perfection; it is still one of the most beautiful skyscrapers in the world. Perhaps that is a little because of its setting; it is on a hill and it stands a little taller, becomes a little more impressive as the land slopes away from it, down to the sea. But the son must also get credit—as he often reminded people himself. Instead of fourteen stories, Burns Smith suggested that his father add a tower, a tower he said would place the Smith *in a class with the best of New York*. They weren't thinking *best* only in terms of what was beautiful or impressive; they thought too of the money side of things—of the company's reputation, I mean. This was the age of the Singer Building and the Metropolitan Life Building in New York—and the Woolworth Building, which had just been completed. Skyscrapers that had become famous and that had helped their companies to become famous. Skyscrapers that had held the title of world's tallest. Skyscrapers that featured tall thin towers rising from a wide base. The Smiths would tell the Gaggins to add a thin tower to the wide base of the Smith Bulding, and the name would help their company grow, just as Singer and Metropolitan Life and Woolworths had grown. That was the idea."

"Branding, Granny."

"Yes, I am aware that is what they call it nowadays. Remember our discussion of painters signing pictures? But I will own I do not like either the word or the practice. In my day branding was what people did to cattle. Nasty and unnecessary, in my view."

"Did it work, Granny? Did Smith typewriters become famous?"

"They did, but it seems to have had little or nothing to do with the building. It is a building that has almost always lost money, that has been sold and re-sold many times over. And a building Lyman Cornelius Smith did not live to see completed. Nothing worked out, really, except the beauty of it, and you could argue even that was partly an accident. Beauty often is. But there was a great celebration when it opened, and people gawked and gasped as the great 8-foot ball at the top of the tower was illuminated. Tallest building west of the Mississippi, they said. And for quite some time it was."

# Creators' Marks

"Where does it begin, this signing your name to a work of art?" K.P. was in an expansive mood. "I suppose you might say there's an equivalent in prehistoric times; what may be the earliest known artworks of any sort are stencil images of hands in caves in Spain. Thirty thousand years ago? Forty? I don't know if anyone is sure. But someone wanted to leave their distinctive mark, even before there was anything like what we call art."

"A hand print isn't really a signature, Granny."

"No, Robin, it isn't. And quite possibly those people weren't really humans, either, though certainly there still seems today to be a human urge to leave handprints, in paint, in..."

"Concrete. I've seen that lots of times on the sidewalk."

"And like every other child you've probably left your mark." Robin colored slightly, and said nothing. "But when something more like what we *do* call art appears, there's nothing of that me-ness to it. No one signed their work in the Lascaux caves, or the caves in Murewa. No one signed their work in ancient Egypt. Did they sign their work in ancient Greece? In ancient Rome? Those were places where people loved to puff out their chests and display their me-ness. But no one signed the pictures they had made. No one. And not for something like eight centuries after the fall of Rome, either. Around 1240 a William de Braile—we know almost nothing about him—wrote W. de Braile in an illuminated Book of Hours, and in a Psalter too. He had made them, and he had made them beautiful. No. God had made them beautiful. If you were alive then you had to believe it was God's work. But somehow William had had a hand in it too. By the early 1300s there seem to have been more and more people wondering *who made this?*. Giotto—do you know of Giotto, child? Here, I will show you some things he did." She pulled a fat book from the shelf. "He began to sign a good deal of his work. And also some work that the experts now think had been mostly painted by his assistants. Everything that came out of his workshop was by Giotto; what God had done was no longer entirely clear.

"Before too long an even greater genius—and greater ego—began to sign his work Io, Leonardo—I, Leonardo. And the egos grow and grow from there. Look at the brazen display that you find on a

Monet—" K.P. pulled another book from the shelf and flipped it open; her mouth wrinkled with displeasure at the huge letters of the name. "You will hear people say that the swirl of color of the Monet signature is part of the appeal of the thing—well, it takes all sorts to make a world."

"Why don't they put the names on buildings, Granny? The names of…"

"Of the architects. I don't think anyone knows why they don't. Perhaps there is no reason. Perhaps there are just too many people involved. You know, the firms like Smith, Graham, Something and…"

"All the somethings."

"Yes, all the somethings. Yet nobody says there were too many people involved in making *Citizen Kane* to put Orson Welles' name on that." Robin looked blank. K.P. tried again. "A poor example. No one says there were too many people involved in making *Avatar* or *Titanic* to put James Cameron's name on those. No doubt my own views are a little out of step; I have a strange history when it comes to putting names on works of art."

"A strange history?"

"You are learning the echo technique of conversation."

"But I really like to listen to you, Granny."

"I believe you do, Robin, I believe you do. And yes, it is a strange history. Will you come all the way up here again? If you do, I shall finish the story of the picture with no name on it, the picture they did not believe I had painted."

"I would like that, Granny."

"But another day, child. Another day."

## Happy Accidents

K.P. stood alone now, on the balcony in the air of early evening. Was it only with the crash of '29 that people had begun to jump from high buildings? Businessmen, ruined, jumping from windows high above Wall Street—that was what everyone thought of. K.P. had looked up "Suicide" when she had begun to be fascinated by tall buildings. "There were no more than 100 such cases between the crash in October of 1929 and the end of that year...." No more than? She had worked it out; roughly two a day. And that was only in New York; people were ruined and jumped to their deaths in Chicago, too. And in Detroit, and in Philadelphia, even in California, in Los Angeles and San Francisco.

Had Kenneth known anything about history? Had he known that in the early years of the Chicago skyscraper the favored jumping-off point was not a skyscraper at all but the "suicide bridge" in Lincoln Park? Just 52 feet high, but high enough. There were so many suicides that they shut the bridge down. Then the skyscrapers started to be used more often. This was in 1919, 1920—long before the Great Crash. At first it was the hotels more than anywhere else, the Drake and the Palmer House especially. But office towers had had their small share as well, the Mather and the Tribune Building among them.

K.P. knew too much of that history, almost all of it sad—pathetically sad or tragically sad. But in amongst it were buried a few happy accidents. Stories such as that of Elvie Adams. A twenty-nine-year-old woman from the Bronx: poor, depressed, facing eviction from her small apartment. One evening in 1979 Elvie had climbed the tall, spiked fence on the 86th floor Observation Deck of the Empire State Building, and she had jumped. But just as she jumped an extraordinarily powerful gust of wind came up; she was slammed back into the building, and her hip was broken, and she did not find herself tumbling down, down, and on down to her death; somehow she found herself caught on a ledge on the 85th floor. A security guard quickly rescued her. Did her landlord relent over the eviction notice? Did she live a long and happy life? She was sent immediately after the incident to an institution for those suffering mentally as well as physically, but beyond that we do not know.

And stories such as that of Libertad Lamarque—a story K.P. had heard during her years in Rio. A singing sensation and movie star: she had starred in the first talkie made in Argentina. But her marriage had been desperately unhappy, and in Argentina in those days divorce was not an option for a woman. Her estranged husband moved in 1935 to Uruguay, taking their daughter with him. We do not know all the details. But we do know that when she was on a concert tour in Chile that same year, at the age of twenty-seven, Libertad Lamarque jumped from a tall building. And we know that an awning above the sidewalk broke her fall, and that she did not break anything. She went on to regain custody of her daughter, to star in Luis Buñuel's first film, to be a leading light of Mexican film in the 1940s, to become established in Miami as well as in Latin America. She lived for 65 years after the awning had saved her, dying at the age of 92 in the year 2000.

## A Human Scale

"Do you think there should be skyscrapers?" Robin asked K.P. "Do you think they are a good thing?" Robin told K.P. what Carl had said about wanting buildings to be on a human scale..

"Of course it is important to have human life lived on a human scale—to have humans connect with one another. But do people in tall buildings have to be less a part of a community, and people in short buildings more a part of a community? Look at what happened in so many suburbs when they made everything one story and took away the front porches, and took away the sidewalks, and made it so that everyone had to drive everywhere. What matters is not how many stories there are, but what we do with them. I've been in four-story apartment buildings where people never catch a glimpse of their neighbors, year after year, and I've been in four-story apartment buildings in Montreal where everyone has a balcony out the back and the balconies wrap around a courtyard so everyone sees everyone else all the time. And they say hello, they chat. Maybe that's too much community for some.

"But if you *do* want a real community, you can make one in a skyscraper if you want; a lot of people are starting to realize that." Robin nodded seriously. "A tall building doesn't need to make a statement about how powerful and important people think they are, or their gods are, or their corporations are. A tall building can mix up offices and apartments, it can have communal areas with little parks and balconies every ten floors or so. It can have shops every ten floors or so as well. You can have retractable dividers between neighbors' balconies so if they want to be open to each other and have a conversation every once in a while, they can do just that. You can have grass and gardens and park benches on the roof. You can have…"

"But *you* don't have any of these things, Granny. Why don't you…"

"These things are just beginning, Robin. They are not for my lifetime. For me, what I have is enough. To look out, to see all the buildings and the sky, to look up—for me, that is enough. I said that, didn't I? I am at the point of leaving the 'human scale' behind, I suppose."

"I want you to stay human, Granny."

"I know you do, Robin. I know you do."

# The Sears Tower

The two of them were standing together as the sun went down, looking at all the skyscrapers from the '70s, the '80s, the '90s, and from the beginning of the new century.

"For a long time, you know," K.P. advised the child, "the Chicago skyline stayed still."

"It didn't move to Milwaukee?"

"Cheeky. I mean it didn't go up. Nothing new was built that was big and tall."

"Nothing?"

"Of course I exaggerate, Robin. You know I must always exaggerate. But it's more or less true. From 1930 or so, for almost 40 years. After the Board of Trade went up there was almost nothing really high until suddenly in the late '60s people were building skyscrapers so high they broke records. The Hancock, the AON, the Sears Tower. Of course the Sears was the grandest of them all."

"Will you tell me the story?"

"I was beginning to think you would never ask. When they started to think of building a new headquarters, Sears Roebuck was the world's biggest seller of things. One of the most profitable too."

"And they wanted to be the tallest?"

"More or less, yes. They had begun by selling watches and jewelery; Richard Sears had started doing that way back at the beginning of the last century. Then hardware, appliances, clothing. They had the catalogue business, they started their own insurance company, they started to do just about anything and everything they could think of. They were outgrowing their headquarters—and I guess they wanted something to show how impressive they had become. So they hired Skidmore, Owens and Merrill to make some plans. The tower was still in the design process when someone noticed that it was going to end up about ten stories shorter than the World Trade Center in New York—those twin towers were already under construction. Just ten stories shorter. And they began to think maybe they could add a few floors onto the Sears, and become the tallest. 'Take it as high as the aviation authority will let you,' —that's what the powers at Sears said. And that's exactly what happened.

"I will not tell you much about the two people whose names should be on the Sears Tower; I do not know enough about them (though I don't think any of it is hard to discover). They were both from outside America, interestingly enough. Fazhur Khan configured the steel in a way that was stronger than the old steel frame construction, the method they had used since the 1890s. Stronger, and cheaper too. So that was Khan's contribution. And then one of Khan's colleagues, Bruce Graham—another foreigner, at least originally, half Peruvian and half Canadian—made the nine columns that made the tower." She saw Robin looking at her in that way the child sometimes did. "Made the *design* for the nine columns that made the tower." She saw Robin's little smile, and gave a little smile in return. "And brought beauty to a building that would be the tallest in the world for a quarter of a century. The same two, Khan and Graham, designed the Hancock Building too. Perhaps even more striking, but less beautiful." She looked down, and then her face started to look a little different. "Two buildings that helped to mark the beginning of a new age of inequality in America."

"The Sears Tower made America less equal?"

"Perhaps better just to say that it happened at the same time as America started to become less equal, less fair. And maybe with that company, with that building, it was just coincidence. But most things connect in the end. You know how I love skyscrapers. I can't help it. But there is a horror to them too. It seems that a great age of skyscrapers must also be a great age of inequality. Of the rich getting richer..."

"You have to have rich people to build a skyscraper, Granny."

"You are a child of your times, Robin. Though I think you are also learning to outgrow them."

"Do you have to have poor people too? Is that what you mean? You have to have poor people in order to have skyscrapers?"

"Do you have to have people who are very, very, poor, and getting poorer as the rich get richer? Do you have to have everyone except the rich getting poorer as the rich get richer? Those are the questions."

"Couldn't you have a great age of skyscrapers where a few people were rich but not so very rich, and most people were doing all right, and a few people were doing not quite so well?"

"I'm sure that would be a better world than the world we have now. Far better. But great skyscrapers, it seems, are not likely to rise in such a world. I don't know exactly why, but I assure you I didn't make this up. I heard the idea first as not-so-idle speculation from an old friend. She said she thought the societies where the tallest buildings have flourished are places where a great space has opened up between rich and poor. And then I looked it up. I checked. It's all true. The economists have an index of inequality, I do not know how they calculate it, I cannot tell you the first thing about it except that it tells you if the rich are getting richer and the poor poorer, or the other way around. And that the economists say it is dangerous for any society if this index goes to 40 and above; at that point, they say, societies start to become far too unequal. Below 40 things are likely to hold together well enough: poor people are not living in utter despair, the wealth of the wealthy is not so very obscene. At 40 and above? The economists say that's when it all starts to unravel. The poor become desperate, the middle class begins to feel horribly stretched, and people start to seethe with resentment. Not at the rich, usually. Resentment at each other, at spouses, at people of a different color, at immigrants: the poor are tricked into thinking the rich are not to blame. Even for the rich it becomes bad, no matter how much money they have. They live behind walls and iron bars and barbed wire, and they start to live in fear. And fear and guilt breed in them a rich person's anger.

"Look for scores of 40 and above on the index of inequality—presto, you have found every golden age of the skyscraper. America in the 1890s, the 1920s, and then again beginning in the 1970s. Hong Kong since 1970. Dubai since the 1990s, China since the late 1990s."

"What about Europe, Granny? Europe is rich."

"Europe *is* rich, on the whole. But the difference between rich and poor in Europe is nothing compared to the difference between rich and poor in Shanghai, or in Chicago. Just as the skyscrapers in Europe are nothing compared to the skyscrapers of Shanghai or of Chicago. Canada is rich too. But its inequality index is down around 30, and has stayed there a long, long time. And the skyscrapers of Toronto? Just as in Europe: they are nothing compared to those in Shanghai or in Chicago."

"There's the CN Tower, Granny. We went to Toronto and saw it. You can see right across that big lake to Niagara Falls. It's lovely."

"It *is* lovely. A little bulbous, perhaps, but lovely. There is always an exception to test the rule. But then again, they call it a 'free-standing structure,' not a building. Perhaps there is a different set of economic principles for free-standing structures. Perhaps they can rise up from something else besides excessive wealth. And excessive expectations—there seem almost always to be those too with the great skyscrapers. Look at the Jewelers' Building, the Empire State, Burj Dubai—in every case there were excessive expectations, in every case they had trouble filling the building once they had built it. The Sears Tower was the same way. When it was conceived in '68, '69, everyone knew that Sears Roebuck would just keep getting bigger and bigger. Everyone. Not just the managers and executives at Sears—a lot of investment people too. Bankers and brokers. I knew one of them slightly back then. I remember one night at a cocktail party he couldn't stop talking about how much room for growth the company had. And the tower had to have that same room for growth, had to be able to hold all the additional offices the company would need for more accountants, more buyers, more secretaries, more managers, more everything. Sears Roebuck would keep growing and growing and growing. That was another reason why they built 108 floors when fifty or so were all that Sears needed in 1970. Fifty vast floors—so vast that an office worker with a cubicle near the center of one of them would be hundreds of feet from the nearest window. But that would be only to start with. Everyone knew that by 1980, 1990, the company would be far larger. Thirty percent larger? Forty percent larger? Maybe more. You had to leave room for that! In the meantime they would rent out the space Sears didn't need yet. But vast floors where workers were buried so far from a window might not be the most attractive arrangement for prospective tenants. Other companies were smaller than Sears; they would want less space, and they would want their own windows.

"It was Bruce Graham who worked out the brilliant solution. The whole thing would be built not as one tower but as nine—nine tubes, they are often called, even though they are all square. I think they should be called columns, and that is what I shall call them. Up to the 50th floor the columns would rise together as one, and Sears would spread the Sears workers over each of those 50 vast floor plates. Two of the columns would stop there. Above that the different columns would rise to different levels: two to the 66th floor, three more to the 90th floor, and then the final two would just keep going up, on up to the 108th. The plans had to be revised more than once; Sears' expectations of how much space it would need in 1985, 1995, 2005, continued to grow and grow and grow. They knew that gradually the renters would all be replaced; every bit of space on the upper floors would one day all be used by Sears workers. The top Sears buyers, the top Sears managers—they would keep going higher and higher and higher.

"But none of it turned out that way. All those projections of more and more growth for Sears Roebuck turned out to be nothing but blue sky. The company had almost reached its peak even as the Sears Tower topped out. For years sales grew only marginally, or not at all; some years there were declines. They couldn't fill the building with Sears workers—and for many years they couldn't rent out the space they didn't need, either. In 1994 Sears sold the building; by 2010 it had been swallowed up by Kmart and the two combined were less than one quarter the size of Walmart, the company that holds bragging rights today as the world's biggest seller of things. In an age of great inequality, it was Walmart—and, at the other end, Neiman Marcus and Saks—that could thrive. Not Sears. Sears was one of those companies for which profits come naturally only when the world as a whole is becoming fairer, when things are flattening out."

"So they made the tallest building out of the profits they had made when things flattened out?"

"It's an odd sort of thing, isn't it? And they made one of the loveliest buildings in the inner city, the skyscraper that defined the center of the city, with the money they had made by trying to kill the inner city."

"To kill it, Granny?"

"Am I exaggerating? Again? They did not kill it. Perhaps they did not even try to kill it. What they were doing was betting on the suburbs over the inner city. They were the first department store chain to put in free parking beside their stores. They looked at the map and they saw where the next suburb would be. And the next, and the next, through the '40s and the '50s and the '60s. And each time they would see a suburb being planned, *there* they would put a store. Montgomery Ward was their rival then, their much larger rival, another company of the middle. But Montgomery Ward was from a more careful and conservative part of the middle. Montgomery Ward thought that because people had always gone downtown to shop, people would always go downtown to shop. It was only natural. Sears and the car and the freeway changed all that, and Montgomery Ward couldn't keep up. Neither could Sears, in the end. Neither can any of us, in the end."

"Shall we go inside again, Granny?"

"Yes, Robin, let us do that. There is starting to be a chill. But the light is still lovely, isn't it, child?"

# Acknowledgments

In many ways this book has been a collaborative effort. Along the way I have received gentle criticism and helpful advice from a considerable number of people, and as a result of their comments this book is in a great many ways better than it would have been had I worked in isolation. My greatest debt is to Maureen Okun, who carefully reviewed the full manuscript at two different stages, and who has offered invaluable advice at many more. I am indebted as well to many others; I would like to thank in particular Tom Hurka, Joseph Dimuro, Eileen Eckert, Marc Ereshefsky, Melissa Free, Rebekka Gondosch, Beth Humphries, Sean Kane, Naomi LePan, Brett McLenithan, Bryanne Miller, Daniel F. Vickers, Elizabeth Brake, John Casey, Jackie Kaiser, Ann Levey, and Mimi Rosenbush.

"*Animals* ... has the moral clarity and narrative drive of the best of the [dystopian] genre. ... Even those who might disagree with LePan's thesis will be compelled by the implications of this well-plotted and formally audacious tale."
  – *Publishers'Weekly*

"When Margaret Atwood wrote *The Handmaid's Tale*, she didn't take kindly to the label of science fiction, eventually telling the *Guardian*, 'Science fiction has monsters and spaceships; speculative fiction could really happen.' Apply her definitions to fellow Canadian Don LePan's first novel, and it becomes clear why *Animals* is so disturbing: the monsters are all-too-recognizably human. *Animals* depicts a terrifying future not too many generations down the road. ... *Animals* ... is an enchantingly horrifying orphan's tale. Its message [is] that our choices at the grocery store can relieve or engender unconscionable suffering."
  – *The Montreal Gazette*

"Provocative, original, beautifully crafted and achingly human, this is a novel that illuminates what we so called 'higher beings' strive to keep darkly hidden from our consciousness. No more, no more. *Animals* is destined to become a classic."
  – Catherine Banks, twice winner of the Governor General's Award for Drama

"A deeply moving narrative that can change your life—it did mine."
  – Thomas Hurka, Professor of Philosophy, University of Toronto

"An engaging story that asks deep and challenging questions."
  – Peter Singer, Ira W. DeCamp Professor of Bioethics at Princeton University

"*Animals* is a rare work of imagination that addresses a very real issue — it might remind you of *Animal Farm*, *1984* or *The Jungle*. The story is brief and compelling, and LePan's prose is, at times, lovely and lyrical."
  – *Sante Fe New Mexican*

"*Animals* is an impressive book that makes a powerful statement—I think it is the *Animal Farm* of these times."
  – Victor Ramraj, Professor of English Literature, University of Calgary, editor of *Concert of Voices: An Anthology of World Writing in English*

"...devastating. *Animals* is a powerful novel, and a fully convincing one. ..."
  – P.K. Page

"... a chillingly plausible tale which confronts us with the wilful *aporias* in our cultural approach to meat production and with the ease by which, it seems, any exploitation can be normalised by categorising those exploited via the discourse of animality. ... LePan's *Animals* compels us to feel with the suffering of animals in the factory farm system and provides intellectual tools to undermine the cultural logic that has enabled us to rationalise this exploitation until now."
  – *Australian Literary Studies*

"One of the biggest strengths of the book is the way LePan uses the figure of a child to question these arbitrary lines separating pets from farm animals, humans from non-humans, and consumers from those consumed.... *Animals* is an original attempt to restructure the relationship between animals and fiction and put together instead a narrative that blends the fictional worlds we crave with the stark realities we prefer to stay in the dark about."
– *The Brock Review*

"*Animals* is fearless and ... makes a compelling case. ... Sam is the emotional heart of the story.... [His] life as Naomi's pet, and the divisions his presence exposes in the attitudes of her parents, carry manifest social implications. Here, LePan's storytelling skills are on full display and the narrative brims with tension.... *Animals* is a brave and frequently fascinating debut novel, wrought with painful choices, harrowing journeys, and a deep passion for its subject matter."
– *Montreal Review of Books*

"*Animals* is the most important new book I have read in a long, long time. I'd class it with Atwood's *The Handmaid's Tale*, Saramago's *Blindness*, and Coetzee's *Disgrace* as a novel that has relentlessly gripped my conscience."
– Melissa Free, English Department, Arizona State University

*Animals: A Novel* is available in the United States
through Soft Skull/Counterpoint
(distributed by Publishers Group West/Perseus Books)
and in Canada through Press Forward Publishing
(distributed by Broadview Press Inc.).


For more on *Animals: A Novel* and on *Rising Stories: A Novel*,
see the author's website, <www.donlepan.com>.

# Index

This index is of the names of buildings, free-standing structures, architects, engineers, building owners, politicians, and cities (other than Chicago).